VERTICAL
HOLD

VERTICAL
HOLD

LAUREL BAUER

St. Martin's Press
New York

Library of Congress Cataloging in Publication Data

Bauer, Laurel.
Vertical hold.

I. Title.
PS3552.A8362V4   1986   813'.54   86-13799
ISBN 0-312-83879-4

First Edition

10 9 8 7 6 5 4 3 2 1

For my mother and father
Stella and Herbert Levy Werner

Thanks to my husband, William G. Bauer—a man of many parts—and to my editor Michael Denneny—yes, the sine qua non.

1

THURSDAY

On the Alert for Something of Value

I t was the first day of the new year according to the Jewish calendar, an ordinary Thursday for all the world. The weather was exemplary: explicitly ecumenical and decidedly seasonal. On such a fine autumn day, the village of Lynford, for that is the name of the world in question, was shown off to great advantage. Well-proportioned and prosperous, with the lush look of suburban maturity, it could yet boast the natural shoreline and noble shadows that had marked its infancy as a summer resort. Wealth and pride had given nature and artifice both a tranquil turn, as if getting and spending could just as well prove a comfort to the soul. And it did seem to some, perhaps on looking down a vast expanse of dusk-blue lawn, that the spirit, if it did not actually increase its substance, grew very calm indeed.

In the great metropolitan area nearby, where the commuter trains came and went, in the news department of a great television affiliate, the decision had lately been made to feature this same Lynford in "a-series-of-live-remotes-from-the-scene-upcoming-this-Monday." The news-gatherers, globe-shrinkers, and on-the-air tom-toms were alive with the possibilities: Lynford, the very reality of the place would be up for grabs once the Minicams began to roll. Hoopla followed. Fate, however, being the fickle thing it is, and channel loyalty her youngest daughter, many citizens—or viewers as we may with equal justice call them—had remained ignorant of the prospect.

On this first day of the Jewish year, one such man now stood, hatless, lost in thought, on an outcropping of rock along the Lynford shore of Long Island Sound. He was a man of forty whose clear eye and cheerful aspect bespoke his reaching the middle of his life moderate in all things except the habits of his mind. In appearance he was unremarkable in the most pleasant way imaginable; for such were the times that this very lack of emphasis on all but God's own sense of proportion was perceived with satisfaction, even downright relief, by the eye of the beholder. A breeze blew across the water. It riffled the pages of the open book in which the man was finding his place. Jacob Geller was perplexed. It is customary, that much he had discovered. On the first day of the New Year, in the afternoon, it is customary to go to the banks of a river, or of any other water. And to pray there.

He had made this discovery several weeks earlier while inspecting a new art book in his brother's living room. The painting, its somber colors expensively reproduced, had caused his normally red cheeks to redden with its appeal. There, on the muddy bank of a Polish river, a dozen Jews prayed. Each black-daubed figure stood apart, the prayer book in his hands appearing to draw the late afternoon light. Several rafts were tied up along the shore. Perhaps later in the week these same Jews would embark and travel the river on certain of their commercial errands. A Polish river—Jake couldn't name one. Were there, then, rivers in Poland? It had never occurred to him.

Later, at home, Jake had lost no time in tracing the courses of the Warta and the Oder, the Narew and the Niemen, the Vistula and the Bug. He had stayed up late with his books that

2

night. It is customary, he had learned, to go to the banks of a river.

So Jacob Geller was perplexed. How does one engage in customary behavior for the first time? In this suburb, renowned for its yacht club and summer regattas, he had decided on Long Island Sound. In one medieval city, barred from the banks of a great German river, the Jews made do with a ditch of stagnant water. There was, however, a falling away from the custom in that community.

Jake planted his feet firmly and began to read the verses from the prophet Micah. He read the Hebrew with many hesitations, translating the words one by one.

> Who is a God like unto thee, that pardoneth
> the iniquity
> And passeth by the transgression of the remnant
> of His heritage.

"Remnant." He read the word over again. It burst in the speaking, releasing, it seemed to him, a sacramental essence which at once made the customary familiar. "Remnant." He preferred its shimmering modesty to the unthinkable infinitude of the failed prophecies: Grains of sand. Stars in the heavens.

The wind began to gust. The day became at once less fine; the air was losing daylight quickly. Whitecaps appeared and the boats in the yacht-club marina rocked at their moorings. Water splashed against the breakwater, spraying the trousers of Jake's navy-blue suit. Even here, however, in a setting so suggestive, the suit smacked more of the synagogue than of the sea. And yet Jake, like many a mariner, hankered for a life of freedom and discipline. On the village beach behind him a man was raking the autumnal debris into damp piles. His tool marked the sand. He worked slowly, and in a young man such deliberate movement might suggest a daydreamer, a lollygagger, a contemplative mind; but no, Vincent DiMaria worked slowly, his back to the water, on the alert for something of value, anything inorganic.

Jake read on.

> And Thou wilt cast all their sins into
> the depths of the sea.

A sudden flash of color distracted him. A dinghy had appeared among the cabin cruisers. It was tough going for the yellow-slickered oarsman rowing toward the dock at the yacht club. Jake followed his progress intermittently, reading now with less attention until he stuck at

> More eagerly than watchmen for the dawn
> Than watchmen for the dawn.

He repeated it yet a third time and he felt his heart expand.

He read to the end and then turned the pockets of his blue suit trousers inside out, pulling free from the lining the crumbs he had dropped in that morning. Then he threw the crumbs into the water. This was customary. Jake Geller was not a self-conscious man. Standing thus with his pockets turned out, his sins, for all he knew, cast into the deep, he felt a kind of dignity. For underlying this homely, perhaps even foolish, pose was the reality of an idea.

Of course, it was equally likely, Jake acknowledged, that his sins had not been cast out. Still, hope for the best. He scanned the shoreline to the north and to the south. In his mind's eye it continued to stretch up and down the coast with its familiar turnings until the entire continent was revealed breasting the Atlantic. He alone stood and fed his sins to the fishes. The harbor in Charleston, the boardwalk at Atlantic City, the docks of Gloucester—all empty. And what were these sins? He picked them over. Gluttony and pride came to mind.

It began to rain. Jake looked for the dinghy just in time to see it slip out of sight behind a larger craft. He wrapped the prayer book in his suit jacket and held the bundle clamped under his arm, protected as he made his way carefully off the breakwater. No frigate like a book, he noted fondly. The young man on the beach was shoveling the last heap of blackened leaves into a plastic bag. Jake stopped in spite of the rain, convinced of the efficacy of a cheerful greeting. It was written, "Receive all men with a cheerful countenance," and he took these words to heart. There were some who begrudged Jake his measure of good cheer, who took a more sanguine view than he did of their life and times. Yet were these not the very ones—grim-faced, stress-ridden, infected by herpes—who appeared to bear up only with great difficulty under the technology and titillation which were the hallmarks of the age? Some took drugs; all lived their lives with a deadly seriousness under the mistaken impression that this was the way to go.

Jake spoke. "You don't hear a thing with these on," Vinny DiMaria replied, pointing to the earphones bulging under the hood of his rain cape. He looked half loony, his dark face framed completely by the crimped orange hood.

"Careful you don't get electrocuted." Jake's advice was well-meant but without foundation in the natural sciences. In the instant before the man turned away, Jake entertained the notion that another more acceptable physiognomy would be revealed, Janus-like, on the back of the orange hood. Here his imagination had brought him very near a genetic reality, for Vincent DiMaria was a twin in a large family of brothers. Helpful by nature as well as policy, Jake shouldered the rake and shovel and, keeping his left arm folded to his chest like a chicken wing, followed the other as he dragged the heavy bag toward his truck. Placing the tools in under the canvas roof, Jake took his little bundle from under his arm and set it down just inside the door flap.

"Can he hear me now?" Jake wondered aloud, half a vaudeville team. His white shirt was soaked through and the dye from his maroon bow tie had begun to transfer. The man nodded several times, smiling. "Did you see that dinghy?" Jake

5

asked. Again his companion nodded, pointing a dirty finger at his head for a second time. "'If thou canst nod, speak too,'" Jake muttered.

Still smiling, Vinny DiMaria climbed into his truck and, ever ready for conversation, rolled the window down. He threw back his orange hood and tossed the headset onto the seat. His black hair was matted and hung to his shoulders. In his left ear there was a small gold earring. Jake approached then, a sucker for good talk; but the man drove off with a friendly salute, taking with him Jake's blue suit coat and a damp copy of the Daily Prayer book, New York City, 1912. Did he have a gold tooth as well? Jake was fancying him a gypsy just an instant before he realized his loss.

He shouted after the truck. Hapless, he thought; bootless cries. But then it occurred to him that the day's mail had comprised but two pieces and he had simply packed it into his breast pocket upon leaving home; the gypsy would discover his address and make restitution by dinnertime. So likely did this seem, based as it was on groundless optimism, that he quickly put the loss from his mind. Vinny DiMaria, however, had his dinner that evening on the road, eating his chicken from a cardboard bucket. And the following day this gypsy escorted his mother to a warehouse sale in a nearby city. Saturday and Sunday Vinny did not work.

Jake began to walk before he had his destination clearly in mind. He walked bouncing on the balls of his feet as men who are less than tall often do; but for Jake it was the spring in his step. He knew these streets well. He had grown up here and his attachment was deep; perhaps not quite the mystical feeling for the land, but nonetheless a genuine emotion of the same order. The crisp classic lawns, the strong trees, the bright substantial houses had a claim on him, pleased him, provided him a cool comfort. And this oasis effect was in no way diminished by his living now in an apartment above the toy store. In fact, it was this small, successful business, owned and operated by his wife Mitzi which allowed Jake to take his pleasure and his comfort where he found it. His own contribution to their enterprise, for in this as in all things they were partners, was largely physical, that is to say, janitorial in nature. While his line of work was acknowledged if at all with an embarrassed smile, Jake was satisfied to be doing something useful. And what could be more useful, more plainly conducive to a civilized existence than the simple chores designed to keep things clean?

Here, I'm getting my exercise already, he thought, slightly short of breath. Would not rowing do for him as well, he wondered, recalling the figure in the dinghy. "I must go down to the seas again." He would ask his brother Bruce if there were rowboats at the club. Yes, that would suit him, Jake decided, apparently unaware that people no longer went rowing. Put a man behind a plate-glass window at a shopping mall, however, and he would row his heart out. Canoeing, meanwhile, had gained in popularity, especially among liberal politicians. For the conservatives, of course, the fact that such exercise might involve a portage tended to weaken its credibility as a genuine water sport. Sailing was their pleasure. Spinnaker, winch, luff, and boom: a sport on which to build a country club or a reputation or even an eponymous law firm. Sailing, that was the thing in Lynford.

Jake's skin felt cool and clammy where the wet clothing clung to it and warm from his walk where it did not. The rain had stopped, yet, characteristically, Jake still stood under a dripping maple trying to decide if he should seek refuge at his brother's home; for he had now reached the foot of its driveway. The gray frame house, like its neighbors on Shore Lane, stood on high ground overlooking the Sound. It was larger than it needed to be; Bruce had had the third story sealed off and he stocked barely half of the climate-controlled wine cellar in the basement. Nonetheless, the children had a children's room and the family had a family room. Jake looked up the drive and the house looked back, welcoming. An old-fashioned porch was its false face to the world, for within it was all cool modernity.

The door opened smoothly and Bruce Geller looked out,

shirttails hanging, his moccasins in his hand, at forty-three an
Ivy Leaguer on vacation. Jake bent to pull off his own shoes.
His socks were soaked through, so he took them off too. There
was a strong family resemblance between the brothers, yet it
was the difference which was striking. Bruce, the elder, was
taller, with hair and eyes as light as Jake's were dark. In a gesture bespeaking welcome and putative ease he pushed his reading glasses up onto his head, from which position they
immediately slipped back down again, landing askew on his
nose. Bruce winced. "Why do I bother?" he asked under his
breath as he removed the glasses and led the way into his den.

"It's Jake," he called out, the tone of announcement just
sufficiently grim to convey a warning to his wife, as he intended, and to his brother, as it happened.

The skins of several wild animals covered portions of the
den's cork-tile floor. Marilyn rose from the plump armchair
done in a polished, flamboyant material, which marked her spot
amid the leather and the chrome.

"You're wet," she said by way of greeting her brother-in-law;
and she shivered pointedly as she kissed him on the cheek.

"What the hell were you doing out in the rain over here in
our neck of the woods?" Bruce poured a brandy from the decanter on a little rolling cart, his glasses falling from the pocket
of his shirt as he bent forward. "Why do I bother," he said
aloud, passing his brother the drink. Jake took a sip and recalled for him the Discovery of a River in Poland. "Countries
usually have rivers, don't they?" Bruce was icy in reply.

"But a person has ideas about countries. For instance, Bolivian tin. You get that idea in your mind and then one day, let's
say you grab a handful of travel brochures and one says 'Ski
Bolivia.' Well, it would shock you: the snow, the fashionable
resorts, even the colors. Switzerland, you say, sure. But
Bolivia! No. That's tin."

At this point Marilyn left the room. She still wore her short
white tennis dress and now, with Jake about to dissertate,
she was acutely aware of the need to change her clothes.

8

"Honestly," she often told her husband, "my time is just too valuable."

Bruce was relieved; her presence often constrained him with his brother. "I don't have *ideas* about *countries*." He italicized the nouns as if to show them up for the poor things they were. "I may know a thing or two about them, facts and so forth, but I do not have ideas about them."

While the truth of the latter clause was in no way a guarantee for the truth of the former, Jake gave his brother the benefit of the doubt. "But I'm not talking about facts," he nevertheless felt compelled to point out. "Let's say in the case of Bolivian tin, you never gave a thought to the production of tin, to tonnage and purity and other matters of fact. Just Bolivian tin, Bolivian tin rattling around in your head all those years since grammar school."

"Cut, Jake!" Bruce drew his hand swiftly across his collar with the enthusiasm he reserved for the purely visual. "Wind it up." He left Jake to sip the brandy while he walked through the house to the new addition at the rear and turned on the sauna. Soon the two brothers sat sweating and silent in the extreme heat. It is good for brothers to sit together, Jake improvised.

"This would've made Dad happy." Bruce said it one way or another every time they were alone together. As this was not frequently, the thought appeared to him fresher than it might otherwise have.

Jake smiled uneasily. The hot air entering his mouth seemed unsuitable for normal breathing. He began to gulp at it with a growing sense of urgency. Was he breathing at all, he wondered. Panic rose from his stomach to confront the hot fog. He pushed himself up from the slatted bench, weak in the knees, and looked for the door, lunged for the door. Out in the dressing area he was light-headed, his stomach queasy.

"Take a cold shower," Bruce shouted from inside, "you're supposed to take a cold shower." Jake squatted just where he was and let his head hang down over his belly. He reached up

9

blindly to pull a large terrycloth robe from its peg, letting it fall where it would around him. Motionless, half-covered, he waited for his strength to return. Bruce was right, he thought, it would have made Sam Geller happy. Start with the idea that he had been mentioned at all.

A father like Sam had worked hard to be remembered. In fact he had spent much of his free time presenting himself to his family, seeding their memories, and Bruce, his firstborn, had bought the act lock, stock, and barrel. Sam would have been happy on another count. From their earliest days, he had attempted to cultivate in his sons an inclination for each other's company. His own brother Nathan had chosen as a young man to live on the other side of the country, thereby leaving Sam free to re-create their relationship as an exemplar for his sons. The truth of the matter was that Nathan's name stuck in Sam's craw. Nathan was a homosexual. Nathan spent his days at Santa Anita. Nathan was "a commercial voice." Not that Sam had always known the specifics. He had only sensed, while they were still boys together, that there was something in Nathan that would not go along with his, Sam's, rage for public relations.

Bruce's acceptance of Sam and Nathan Geller as model brothers was not eroded by the puzzling fact that years went by without either brother making any effort to see the other. Bruce's head was filled with a great many such incompatibles, but they troubled him only when he was brought face to face with the rude reality. The day after Sam's funeral, for example, as the family sat about the house making small talk with visiting neighbors, Bruce took Uncle Nathan aside. "I wish Jake and I could have the kind of relationship you and Dad did." Nathan had given him a stunned but not unfriendly look. A short man, he nevertheless reached up to put his arm around Bruce's shoulder. Bruce felt the soft cashmere sleeve brush against the back of his neck as Nathan cackled in one of his cartoon voices, "Go west, young man, go west." Bruce gave ground immediately and went to pour himself a drink. Later he told Jake, "Uncle Nathan is a weird bastard. I don't know what Dad saw in him." At moments like that Jake felt a surge of love for his brother.

Bruce came out of the sauna, his light complexion flushed, his eyes bloodshot. "You've got to build up your tolerance, Jake. It's just like anything else." As the current century had progressed and occasions for astonishment had multiplied, it had perversely become common for people to suggest that any given thing was somehow just like any number of other things. In the face of constant change, this made for a more comfortable, if hardly a more nuanced, life.

Jake rubbed his curly hair this way and that with the skirt of the robe. Dressed in white wool socks and the sweatsuit Bruce had laid out, he felt fit again. "Dad would have hated it. He hated the heat."

This was not altogether true. The sauna, too, would have made Sam Geller happy. Though he would never have set foot in it, he would yet have understood it exactly as Bruce wished it to be understood, for he and Bruce had seen things the same way. There had been no uneasiness between them when it came to interpretation.

"So, what did your research turn up?" Bruce stood at the mirror combing the wave out of his hair.

Jake aimed an inquiring look at the back of his head. It was not like Bruce to return to a subject for its own sake. "Geography as revelation," he said casually, throwing a roadblock. "Mainly, it's the custom to go to a river and read certain verses and . . ." Bruce shrugged his shoulders dismissively, already sated, or perhaps it was his way of relaxing. "The point is this," Jake went on, following his brother out the door. "Suddenly a new reality is revealed. A peak in Darien."

"By the way," Bruce interrupted without breaking stride.

"Let me put it this way then." Jake glanced into the so-called sewing room, and through its window he saw his nephew Sandy get into a green sedan.

"By the way," Bruce said again.

11

But Jake would brook no interruption. "The Warta and the Oder," he continued, "the Narew and the Niemen. . . ."

"I meant to ask," Bruce began once more as they entered his large country-style kitchen, "what are you up to these days—aside from goddamn Polish rivers?"

Instantly Jake was on his guard. He knew that it was at those moments when Bruce employed an innocuous transitional phrase like "by the way" or a falsely motivated "I meant to ask," that he was in fact seeking to introduce a potentially dangerous topic of conversation. "Did you ever find your atlas?" he parried, looking on as Bruce chose among the brands of beer with which his outsized refrigerator was stocked.

It had been the same evening Jake discovered a river in Poland that Bruce discovered he did not own an atlas. He had gone into his den and looked on the lowest shelf where all the large books were stacked, pulling them off one by one because he was certain that he owned an atlas. And yet he did not own one, it seemed, and this embarrassed him before his brother. And he was embarrassed by his embarrassment, for he thought of himself as a man difficult to embarrass. His eyes narrowed now at the recollection, but as far as Bruce was concerned, it was simply the effort of pouring a perfect head of foam into the thick glass steins.

"There's an atlas in the newsroom," Bruce informed his brother, allowing a bit of the romance of the set to rub off on his own corporate office at the great television affiliate.

They drank their imported beer sitting at the island counter. Above them a display of copper cookware hung from a wrought-iron rack. Jake finished his beer quickly, then stood up on the rungs of the stool and tapped one of the highly polished bowls. "It's not the rivers, Brucie, it's the Jews." This was the sort of remark that gave Bruce very little to work with. He did not like to go below the surface with Jake.

◆

In another part of Lynford, while the rain hesitated, Gena Stern stepped out onto the walk from her carpeted, glass-enclosed breezeway. In the street's silence and the heavy air alike there reigned something that seemed very much like peace but was, when you came to live with it, more open to interpretation. At thirty-four, with her slim figure and agreeable features, Gena Stern would have made a wholly favorable impression had she not so completely lacked the glow of health on the one hand and, on the other, the animation of cosmetic artifice. She took in the neighboring properties with a practiced glance, automatically noting the deficiencies that marked her own. As the first drops of rain fell, she bent to pick up the local newspaper and threw it toward the metal garbage can at the corner of the garage; but a gust of wind intervened and blew the sheets across the lawn. She sucked in her breath at the affront. Would nothing go right anymore? She was dizzy with the prospect.

Her skirt hadn't been pressed correctly. That morning when she pulled it from the cleaner's clear wrapper, she saw immediately that the pleat had been mispressed. There was a crease where none should be. She had looked at the skirt for a long time and then, throwing it to the floor, began to cry bitter tears. This had surprised her. She sent Douglas to Temple with his grandmother. As it turned out, she did not dress at all, and she stood now in her front yard on a holy day with her old blue bathrobe pulled tightly about her. She stooped to gather up the newspaper sheets and dropped them into the can. But then her fingers were blackened from the newsprint; this too she took personally. She rubbed her hands through the ragged grass. Since the divorce she could no longer afford a full-time gardener.

On the kitchen counter the television set presented concurrent state-of-the-art reality; and though the picture was temporarily soundless, it struck Gena as a welcome and compelling alternative. Passive, innocent, seeking pleasure and modest edification, company and surcease from pain, Gena yielded herself up on a daily basis to the brute force of babble, the sex appeal of unreason. A big fly, staying on beyond the season, entered the kitchen with her. She waved her hand at it and it made for the television screen, camouflaged there in the blur of motion. That was no ordinary flying insect; it was a prosperous fly, bloated, self-confident, high-tech. Gena frowned. She heard it buzzing against the warm screen, contented.

The kitchen was filled with a purple light and outside the rain fell heavily now, spilling from the leaf-filled gutters. The gutters needed cleaning. Who would clean the gutters? She heard the television go on in the next room. Automatically she tried to fit its sound with the picture she was watching. A door upstairs opened and her mother came down into the kitchen quickly, snapping both light switches as she entered. But Gena's gloom did not disperse.

"Douglas should not watch television today," Helga Grossman said.

"What should he do then?"

"Read a book. Go for a walk. Think about what it means to be a Jew."

"It's raining, Mother."

"A Jew knows worse." Helga pulled at her gray blouse which, though guaranteed as wrinkle-free, nonetheless looked a great deal worse for her recent nap.

"He's a boy, Mother. What do you want from him?"

"From him I want nothing," Helga made herself known instantly, "but from you and Stanley . . ."

"Don't start with Stanley." Gena sat down at the Formica table and rested her head on her forearm, for the mere mention of her ex-husband's name induced in her an infinite and painful weariness.

"At thirteen you are more than a boy in any case." Helga threatened to reopen a delicate subject bearing on her grandson's religious education.

"Give me a break, Mother, please?"

"Ah yes," Helga said, her disappointment undisguised under the sarcasm, "I almost forgot. You deserve a break today." Her heavily accented English made much of the sinister psychic implications of this all-American jingle. "Some tea?" she asked abruptly, filling the kettle and setting it on the stove.

The doorbell rang and Gena, expecting she knew not what, jumped from her chair and left the room. Mrs. Grossman sighed. She was losing respect for her daughter. This made her more than ever grateful that she was only a guest in her daughter's home. She opened the door and looked through the window of the storm door at a narrow-eyed, neatly dressed man of about Gena's age who was struggling to fit his dripping umbrella somewhere amid the clutter of the breezeway. He looked up and smiled at her, speaking loudly through the glass.

"Are you the mistress of the house? My name is John White and I'm a Soldier for Christ." Although holding her gaze, he tapped the lapel pin he wore. "I've come here today with a very important message, a message that could change your life. May I come in?"

Helga looked over her shoulder at the teakettle. What did he want? A Soldier for Christ—on Rosh Hashanah, no less. She called her grandson. Let him hear this at least. But Douglas did not answer.

John White was determined. "All I'm selling, ma'am, is right here in this book." He held the Bible up for her to see. "Jesus loves you."

The kettle began its piercing whistle and Helga half turned toward it. She wanted her afternoon tea.

"That's all right," he said, "you go ahead and have your cup of tea." There was genuine accommodation in his tone. He tried the handle of the storm door and then entered while she poured the water into her teacup. When she turned around John White was already sitting at the table, his Bible open before him. "As I was saying," he smiled reassuringly, "Jesus really does love you."

Helga pulled her lips to one side but her face did not relax. She set her teacup on the counter. "Perhaps he does. I really couldn't say." She was very formal, correct.

15

"You can count on it, ma'am. It's the one thing in this world you can count on."

"Ah-ha," she said with grim enjoyment, "something to count on. Yes," she pretended to consider, "this idea interests me." She felt it was strange that he should be sitting so familiarly at the white Formica table while she stood apart like a distant relation, but still she did not want to join him.

"Let me stop you right there then." He placed both hands palms down on the table and leaned slightly in her direction. "I'm not talking about an idea. Get that right out of your head. We can't expect you to develop a personal relationship with an idea." He chuckled. "Jesus is not an idea. An *idea* does not answer your prayers." He gave the word a distinct edge of contempt. "An *idea* does not love you. *Jesus* loves you." Suddenly his voice turned ripe. "He really does." He ended with especial emphasis, as if bringing forward in triumphant conclusion a new thought.

He has a face like a sponge, Helga was thinking. I could squeeze it in one hand and cause that little nose to disappear entirely.

"See," he continued in a heightened boyish cadence, "I have a special relationship with my Savior. That's why I'm here to witness to you. I'm saved. I'm going to heaven. And how was I saved? An idea didn't save me." He picked up his Bible and caressed it with a knowing smile, bringing it all home now. "No. Jesus saved me."

"To tell you the truth, I don't even know what it means. Why should Jesus love me? I don't love him."

John White gave her a sharp look.

"Oh no, not again. Wait a second, you're not even a Christian either, are you?" He stood up, abashed.

Helga looked over the rim of her cup with tired eyes.

"No, I'm not a Christian. Where I came from, there were no Christians." She smiled for the first time.

He looked at her strangely, the unspoken challenge doing much to quell his embarrassment.

16

"I can hardly credit that, ma'am—there's Christians all over, even in Communist countries. What are you? A Jew? We support Israel, you know."

"I came from Czechoslovakia."

"Czechlosovakia." He stumbled over the word, relegating one more ethnic minority to oblivion. "Czechlosovakia is a captive nation. We support the struggle of the captive nations." Helga held the door open for him and they both looked out at the heavy rain. John White fumbled with the boxy black case he had with him. "I'd like for you to have these folders, ma'am."

But Helga was not listening. "The weather is always good for our holidays," she said blandly, the perversity of the assertion seeming to lend it very nearly the force of theology.

Nor, in his turn, was John White listening. "This material has brought untold people to the Lord." He pushed his large umbrella out into the rain ahead of him. "'Except ye be converted,' it says. That is not John White, ma'am; that is Scripture."

Helga watched him go down the walk. She sensed Gena behind her. "That's some way to start the new year. An invitation from the goyim. Doesn't he see the mezuzah on the door?"

"How's he supposed to know what's in that little thing even if he does see it? Don't be ridiculous." Gena herself did not know.

"'Thou shalt love the Lord thy God,'" her mother informed her, "so what makes more sense—that we love Him or that He loves us? Jesus loves you. Jesus loves you. O.K. So then what?"

"Stop going on, Mother." Gena closed the door firmly.

"We must love God. This is clear." Helga Grossman began her answer slowly, thinking it over.

"Why, pray tell?" Gena took several plates from the dishwasher and carried them to the cupboard before realizing that they were dirty. This she experienced as a blow.

"Because we need to, we want to do it, and we are able to do it. So if we didn't love Him, what would we do instead?"

17

Gena said nothing, returning the dishes to the washer. She had noticed a change in her mother and she did not like it. Above all she did not like the faraway speculative look that often came to her mother's eye.

"We would love an idol. It happened." There was nothing ponderous about Helga now. "Or a politician. Or the television. We would love the television. This is what would happen."

"Mother, we love the television now." Hadn't she heard all this from Helga before? Yes, she knew what to expect next. "We also love pizza and Chinese. As a matter of fact . . ." Gena opened a drawer and shuffled papers, her eyes on her mother.

Helga had awaked from her nap with a start, the familiar fear hammering from within. She had hurried downstairs, waiving her customary toilette; her wiry gray hair was matted on one side and standing in a tuft on the other. What a pair, Gena thought, considering her own coiffure, too long unwashed, dreary and out of shape.

Helga was nodding slowly and with satisfaction. "It is not a proper conclusion that He loves us. This much is clear. It is a matter of history, and I lived in history." She brought her eyes back to focus on Gena. "I lived."

As to where the Lord her God might have been during the time to which she referred so delicately as "history," she left such speculation to those who had some idea of where He was, as she put it, the day before yesterday. Helga had simply offered up her appeal on a daily basis without the slightest hope or expectation that His help would come.

"I lived," she repeated, always coming back to what she knew best.

Gena studied the take-out menu from the Chinese restaurant. "What is it with you? Can't you stop?"

But Helga could not stop.

2

MONGAY
MONDAY

The Excess of Things

It was just past seven o'clock on Monday morning when Jake's gypsy returned the prayer book and the blue suit coat, still damp in the wrinkles. But Vinny himself did not appear; the delivery was made by a boy of about thirteen, a younger brother paying his dues, who rode by on a bicycle and tossed the balled-up jacket against the door of the toy shop. Jake observed this from the vending machine across the street where he had just purchased the morning paper. Instinctively he waited until the bicyclist was out of sight before approaching the store. Through the plate-glass window he admired the merchandise in all its healthy well-regulated profusion. Toward the back, where on this overcast morning the sunlight could bring no cheer, the handlebars on a row of bicycles gleamed nevertheless, and, high on a shelf, the abundant hair of an expensive doll shone like a golden nimbus. Picking up the bundle from the tiled floor of the entry, he let himself into the store.

To the right of the counter, bent over a wire barrel containing rubber balls of different sizes and colors, Jake could see a man from another time. He was dressed as usual in the white tunic of an ancient, but today for the first time Jake saw that he wore as well white socks and cheap black oxfords. The sage did not look up but continued to rummage among the rubber balls with his long hyper-articulated fingers. The scalp he presented was absolutely smooth and pink. As he sought to pull first one ball and then another loose, the remaining balls tumbled about the barrel. Jake turned absently to remove the key from the lock. And the man was gone. As always, Jake felt his absence more keenly than his presence; and such an apparition lends itself to no other form of verification.

He walked back to the little windowless office between the store and the stockroom. Here was Mitzi Geller's desk of varnished wood, her invoices, her filing cabinet, her typewriter, and, under a tablecloth, her old-fashioned floor safe. The faded pink cloth was coffee-stained and smudged with cigarette ashes. Mitzi did not permit smoking in the shop proper; in the office, however, her assistant, Mrs. Helga Grossman, smoked rather too much and in a careless fashion. Positioned by this semblance of a table was the upholstered chair in which Helga sat to rest her feet and drink her tea. With all this furniture there was barely room to turn around, but it suited Mitzi well.

The stockroom itself, smelling of cardboard cartons and more cardboard, was crowded with merchandise. Here Jake had an old card table set up in a small island of space behind the door. He placed the returned prayer book on top of a stack of books which served as a bookend for yet more books. It was none the worse for wear; nor could it have been, as its spine was already cracked and the corners worn to board when Jake bought it for seventy-five cents at a flea market in the country. He shook out the suit jacket and two pieces of mail fell to the floor. Immediately he conjured up the gypsy squinting over the advertising circular, flashing his supposititious gold tooth. Did Jake have an anti-gypsy animus or was this imagining simply the product of baleful literary influences? Contrite, he resolved to learn the gypsy's rightful name and call him by it should they ever meet again. He hung the jacket on the back of the metal folding chair, turned over the flat plaid cushion which his brother Bruce had brought him for a stadium seat, and sat down to the *New York Times*.

He read the paper slowly and with a sense of duty which was at odds with his need not to know much of what he read. It was once possible for a man to spend a lifetime free from the hollow-eyed women who, demented by war and grief, materialized from worlds away to confront him daily; it was once enough to look into the mirror each morning, Jake thought obscurely. He liked to imagine a time when men were starved for news; he liked to think of Henele who wrote from Prague to her sister in Vienna during the Thirty Years War: "I have been told that the Duke of Bavaria has captured Nördlingen. I should like to know whether this is true." Today, Alvin Quint would be dispatched from the bureau in Bonn to tape twenty seconds in front of the St. Georgskirche. Jake could hear him now: "It appears that the Duke of Bavaria has captured Nördlingen. . . ." Henele would be advised early that evening.

In another time, when a courier arrived in Paris, say, with a choice bit of news, parched and grimy as he was from days on horseback, his thick fingers tugging impatiently at the leather straps of his saddlebag, the French had an adage to put him in his place: "Do not look for truth in a man who comes from a distance," they cautioned each other. But what could one say about this man, this Quint, who managed to be in Nördlingen and at the same time in one's den, bedroom, or kitchen? What warning now?

Alvin Quint, tall and gangling, his smooth high forehead dry in the light from the fire, had been the center of attention at Bruce Geller's big party the previous winter. "Germany's my beat," he'd said with his familiar twisted smile, "it's my turf, my terrain, my bailiwick, my baby."

Jake, shorter by nearly a foot, spoke up. "How's the food?"

But at that point Marilyn had given him her pursed-lips-eyes-right look, so suggestive of suppressed hostility, and taken the

21

newsman by the arm. "I want you to meet Fred King." She had walked Quint toward the lavish buffet. "Do you remember what happened at those Munich Olympics? Fred was on our team."

Later, Quint held forth on the proper function of the television newsman. Bruce had plied him with Glühwein and Quint had become, as Jake had it, quintessentially himself. His voice grew to assume a quality of stentorian certainty, and Bruce's young daughter Sara, troubled by wakefulness, was drawn downstairs to the sound of its security.

"It is our responsibility to report the news," he said as Sara settled herself on the sofa next to Jake. "The news is our responsibility. We're responsible for it; and I believe that by-and-large-for-the-most-part we handle that responsibility responsibly."

Jake pulled Sara to her feet with a whispered promise of hot chocolate and moved her toward the door. So firm a grip did Quint have on his audience that no one except Marilyn was aware of the presence of a little girl in pink pajamas; and Marilyn watched their progress across the living room with a fixed smile, giving away nothing.

"Sometimes I'm overwhelmed myself at what a big responsibility rests . . ."—Quint shrugged comically, a kind of Ichabod Crane with a press pass—". . . on these narrow shoulders. I was talking to Fred here about Munich." The name drained the humor from his face telegenically. "Of course, that was early in my career."

Jake and Mitzi had been among the last to leave. Alvin's voice was booming now. Larger than life, it filled the baronial living room, threatening to burst through the walls on the strength of its urgency. It drove them out the front door where they were met by a winter wind of nearly equal force.

"'Blow wind, crack your cheeks,'" Jake had quoted, his belly full of cognac.

Where was Alvin Quint these days? Jake wondered. He had been replaced in Bonn without fanfare. Perhaps his voice had

atrophied and his knuckles, resting on a paper-free desk somewhere, had grown large from cracking. He would ask Bruce.
Bruce was in television news too. There was a knocking at the
rear door; Jerome had arrived to wash and wax the store's
linoleum floor. Behind him stood a tall, good-looking boy with
aggressive eyes and a practiced smile. His skin was a medium
shade of brown and marred by tiny eruptions under its surface.

"Car's broke again," Jerome said by way of introducing his
driver. "M. L. is over in college." He looked from one to the
other. "This is Mr. Geller. His wife's the one to run the store;
but you could get you some good sense from him, always reading like he is." All three of them smiled, each for a reason of
his own.

"Nice to meet you," M. L. said politely and Jake extended
his hand. The boy shook it with appropriate pressure and
backed off, still smiling, toward his car.

"That boy has got things on his mind," Jerome remarked as
M. L. Johnson drove off so slowly and so quietly that Jake had
to listen twice for the sound of the motor running.

"You're only young once," Jake said, relocking the door.

"No sir, it ain't that." Jerome's cockeye held him as the suspense built. Jerome folded his light jacket neatly and exchanged his shoes for a pair of old slippers before finally
concluding. "I hope he ain't involved in none of that . . ."—
here he glanced uneasily around the tiny room—". . . other
business."

"I doubt it, Jerome." Jake began his reply without any idea
of what his reassurance might apply to.

"Looks like I got a big job here today," the other said, with
the phrase he ritually used to close their chats.

"I'll get out of your way then," was always Jake's response.
Jerome turned on his portable radio and began to wheel the
bicycles into one corner of the store.

Now Jake set the newspaper aside reluctantly; forty-five minutes in the morning, forty-five minutes in the evening, that was

23

the regimen he had prescribed for himself, employing the suburban-commuter analogy.

"Dear Uncle Nathan," he wrote neatly on a sheet of Mitzi's blue deckle-edge stationery. "Happy New Year. May you be inscribed in the Book of Life. For Good—and for good, too. It was very thoughtful of you to send Mrs. Oliphant's book. I hope you didn't go through a lot of trouble to find it—but I'm sure you did. I've put up some shelves in the garage. But this one I'll keep by the side of my bed—just to feast my eyes on it. We hope you'll come east soon to visit. The time is ripe; they're running at . . ."—Jake leafed through the paper quickly—". . . Aqueduct." He read the letter over. "Best from Jacob," he signed off, observing Uncle Nathan's ancient dictum: "No Nate, no Jake."

Jerusalem: Its History and Hope by Mrs. Oliphant, author of *Makers of Florence, Makers of Venice*, etc., London, 1891. Nathan had bought it for its title and its binding, which was olive-green leather with jazzy marbled boards and endpapers. The gift had touched Jake. Nathan was no habitué of the secondhand book scene, where the dust, the chaos, and the cramp would all discomfort a man used to the fresh-aired splendor of Santa Anita. "I like to make book," Nathan always said with jocular emphasis when the conversation turned literary. In fact Jake did not intend to keep the book by the side of his bed. He would have Mitzi read the note over later for sincerity.

He opened a thick black loose-leaf notebook and copied in an entry: "Researchers at Bell Laboratories estimate that there is more information in one weekday edition of the *New York Times* than a person in the sixteenth century processed in an entire lifetime." "The nub of it," Jake muttered.

Information, everybody's darling! And this must be considered too: the *Times* had provided no information at all on the levitation of Wisconsin housewives or the interior decoration of alien spacecraft. What's more, there was nothing that day on the artistry of rock singers, the vices of tennis stars, the recipes of operatic tenors, the fears of best-selling authors, the insecuri-

24

ties of female jockeys, the childhood traumas of talk-show hosts, the crotchets of ambitious lawyers, the struggles of working mothers, the experiments of unknown biochemists, or the paralysis of promising young dancers. Much of this information was common knowledge in any case.

The buffer, a comfortable noise, stopped without ceremony. "I'm finishing up, Mr. Geller," Jerome called from the shop. Jake went forward, money in his fist. The back door was open and Jerome was propped against the jamb putting on his street shoes, long, narrow, brown-and-white wing-tips. "Oh what a day," he half sang under his breath, "Oh what a day." Jake knew without asking that this was an allusion to the weather having been permanently and fundamentally altered by the advent of manned space flights. "Messing," Jerome termed it.

It was odd, perhaps, that while Jerome was so profoundly convinced of the result, he wrote off as "the television" all proof of the cause. The moon landings in particular he rejected out of hand, and yet any unexpected darkening of the sky, any unseasonable heat or cold, was charged off without a qualm to that giant leap. How capacious was his mind can be seen in this ability to embrace the contradiction and live at peace in the universe.

"I don't think you need to worry about M. L.," Jake counselled and put the money into Jerome's calloused grayish palm.

"I ain't worrying. I learned better than that." He adjusted his plaid cloth cap and hitched up his trousers, a man who knew life.

Soon Jake heard his wife Mitzi enter the shop, her fashionable shoes tapping across the linoleum with a lopsided gait that meant she was carrying him a cup of coffee. He knew the brightness which came to her eyes and the energy which shadowed her movements like static as soon as she entered her shop. For Mitzi Geller, though not much taller than a large child, was as regal as a queen in her own domain. She was descended from a family of shopkeepers and had understood very young the respect due a shop, that unity which provided

25

so faithfully, if modestly, for all their needs. She seemed to have been born with this affinity for the life and struggle of the small-town merchant, for her parents were of one mind in keeping her from it. They worked the long hours themselves, seven days a week, and set her out to play as an equal among the children of doctors and lawyers. Mitzi grew up independent and proud and ambitious. When her mother died an early death, embittered, and her father took up chess, she made of it an opportunity. From the beginning she had an instinct for success and the new shop thrived. She started to diversify, became a member of the local business community, made trouble at the Merchants' Association. With her stylish hairdo, her vividly made-up eyes, her fashionably colored fingernails, Mitzi was clearly a woman intent on making the most of things.

She brought Jake a piece of raisin toast with his coffee.

"Do you know the big house on the corner by the Temple—the Pelt house?"

"Pelt house?" The coffee lapped the rim of the cup as Jake took it from her hand.

"The Pelts live there." She motioned him away, putting down the toast herself. "Gwen Pelt is a friend of Marilyn's. Your sister-in-law Marilyn?"

"Let's say I do."

"Well, you do. It was burglarized. Apparently it's the fourth house." Mitzi was characteristically brisk. "They don't think it's professionals."

"What do they think?"

Mitzi took a bite of his toast. "They've seen a lot of those clean-cut Jesus Loves You people around lately."

"Helga mentioned it; she got one at Gena's." Jake blew on his coffee.

"Oh poor guy! Helga."

"It doesn't seem likely, does it?"

"A religion can be a cover-up, you know."

"And the disciples are second-story men."

Mitzi gave him a look and turned to leave. "I'm only saying it's not an unheard-of idea."

26

"The Old Testament was the first story; and the New Testament was the second story; and it came to pass that at that time the houses of the Jews in Palestine were single-story dwellings and . . ." Jake swore at his coffee cup.

"Drink your coffee before you spill it," Mitzi called from her desk.

"She knows me too well," Jake said with love in his voice. This was not absolutely true, but it was true enough.

"Today is my lunch with the Merchants' Association, remember; Helga will be here. Maybe she'll give you a piece of sour rye."

"The heel, I hope."

"Please don't get her talking. Just let her watch the store."

———◆———

Gena Stern stretched her arms and legs under the covers and yawned a chain of wide-mouthed yawns. True, hers had been a tiring marriage; but it struck her as unfair that dreaming of Stanley should leave her exhausted as well. A dream, she believed, should spare the dreamer. She had gotten up in the middle of the night and tried to put some order into the room but, as she saw now, to no purpose. Then she discovered a purpose: the television set, having been left on, did not need to be turned on. I'm an invalid, Gena said to herself. She glanced at the spot where Stanley's lounger had been and wished for a lounger. She wanted to lounge. The deep pink color there was just beginning to catch up with the rest of the rug. It was taking too long. And there was no one to take care of her.

I'll go to a coffee shop, she decided suddenly. And so she got up, tied a scarf around her matted hair, stepped into her espadrilles and put on her robe. I'll have a sweet roll and a cup of coffee. She sat down on the edge of the bed to wait for the weather report.

It was a measure of her condition that she was oblivious to the fact that young suburban mothers did not go to coffee shops in the morning. They had better things to do. And they drank their coffee at home. She reached for the furry spoon and

27

saucer on top of the television set and as she leaned forward her attention was arrested by the sight of Alvin Quint standing in the rain at the Lynford railroad station. The commuters carried umbrellas but Quint wore a green loden hat with a little feather in its band. Several umbrellas bore the channel number of the local public television station and Alvin joked about this with Mary Alice Mustard, his anchorwoman. Gena envied them their relationship which, as she could not know, was characterized by suspicion and dislike.

I'll sit at the counter and someone will bring me a cup of coffee and a sweet roll, she fantasized, her eyes on Quint. Quint tried to raise the issue of guilt with a female commuter but this went nowhere as the woman kept her lips clamped around the straw in her can of nutrition substitute. He turned immediately then to crime in the suburbs. One man, hugging a walnut briefcase, mentioned the recent rash of burglaries, and another, grinning like mad, claimed to be involved in the manufacture of alarm devices. The train arrived and, to Gena's chagrin, Quint climbed aboard with the others. Without waiting for the weather report, up next, she pulled her raincoat on over her robe and left the house, pressed by her need.

The place she found was more a delicatessen than a coffee shop. Indeed, the Gold Cup Deli had no counter. But it was cozy and comfortable and she enjoyed the sweet familiar music. She drank her coffee slowly. I'm feeling better and better, she noted, and ordered some white toast, slipping the partially eaten sweet roll into her pocket. She chewed the insubstantial bread purposefully, opening herself up to her new environment, watching the two waitresses, soothed by their small talk and competence. Eventually she even wished to become a part of their small society. She wondered where they bought their pink uniforms, wondered if the plastic name tags were for any Ruta, any Dolores, or had been made up especially for this Ruta, this Dolores.

Alvin Quint had come to Lynford for a story. This meant, it was Gena's sudden intuition, that there was a story in Lynford;

that Quint would put the Lynford story together for her bit by bit, day by day, that he would help her to feel at home in her world once again. In the face of this promise Ruta and Dolores lost a lot of status. Perhaps, Gena thought, she might actually meet Quint. There was something vaguely alien in his long narrow face which encouraged her speculation; she, on the other hand, had been described as pretty-in-a-way and that would help too. She must find out more about him. Had she not perhaps already met him? It seemed to her that she had seen him once, seen him standing by a fireplace, very pre-possessing. Drunk, too, she thought. Her eyes lost some of their dull opacity just considering the possibilities.

Life was so simple at the Gold Cup Deli. Unseeing and be-lieving herself unseen, Gena had grown comfortable in her booth at the rear, had found it such a pleasant way to spend the morning, that she determined suddenly to have lunch there as well. Then two carefully groomed women, dressed for exercise under see-through rain capes, disturbed the dazed late-morning calm. They conversed in loud energetic voices, as if accus-tomed to talking over the wind. Gena recognized Marilyn Geller and Gwen Pelt and quickly turned her face to the wall. Flinching from its mirrored surface, she noted that with her pale face, lowered eyelids, and vulgar kerchief, she had an in-timidated, dim-witted look. Her own mother might not know her. Nevertheless, she pressed herself into the corner of the booth and shielded her face with a cupped palm.

Marilyn Geller had a grievance that was forever dancing at-tendance on her self-esteem. She was too busy, she never had a minute, she was always on the go, she didn't know what to tackle first! Now she tapped her long red fingernails impa-tiently on the glass case.

"Watch out you wake the fish," the beetle-browed counter-man joked. "They only smoked, they ain't dead."

Marilyn gave him a perfunctory smile. "So Bruce said we should have him over." The resignation in her voice was so deeply felt as to suggest that their guest must surely travel with a large retinue.

"Did you see him this morning?" Gwen Pelt watched the man lift the pink squares of lox from the tin. "I almost died when he said about the burglaries. I thought, oh my God they're going to show our house; but they didn't." And here she sounded as if the medium had missed a sure bet. "He looked cute in that sort of German hat though."

Marilyn grimaced disparagingly, her face vivid with makeup. "Actually I was there at the station. The weather being what it was, I thought I'd take Bruce to the train."

"Well, you're nice. Putrid weather." Gwen took the paper bag and Marilyn took the check.

"He was at our big party last winter." Marilyn paid quickly, following at Gwen's very heels lest her companion shut the door on this further evidence of the burden which was her crowded social calendar.

This is fate, Gena mused. So she had seen Alvin Quint before. Bruce and Marilyn had invited her at the very last minute; she recalled the slight at once. She hadn't known then who he was; she watched another channel. "Don't tell him," Marilyn had warned. "He's so sensitive." But just to make sure, she never introduced them. Her vigilance as a hostess was well known.

The departure of the women sealed the change their entrance had signalled. Gena's lunch arrived too quickly and although she dawdled and fussed, rearranging her sandwich quarter by quarter, Dolores did not refill her coffee cup. The tables were all occupied now, a line of customers formed beside the cigarette machine, and conversation covered the sweet lush music threatening Gena's hard-won sense of well-being. Hurrying by, her slip hanging slightly below the shiny pink uniform, Ruta was quite another woman as she slid the check across the Formica. Gena looked around the room surprised. She had come away without her money. But everything had gone along so smoothly, everyone had been so nice, she felt as secure as if she had been an old and valued customer, perhaps even their first. Nevertheless, A. Poulos, manager, became impatient. Gena was at a loss.

"Excuse me, miss." She heard a smooth yet boyish voice. "I can loan you the money."

A clean-cut, snub-nosed man not much younger than herself left the line and approached the cash register.

"This is fate," John White said complacently as he sat once again at the round table in Gena's kitchen.

Gena sat across from him, fists massaging her pale cheeks, trying to think. "I was thinking about fate before, as a matter of fact. What is it really?" She held up her hand as if to forestall the rotation of fortune's wheel until a satisfactory answer could be found.

John White was only half listening. In his haste to come to her assistance he had left his Bible and furled umbrella lying atop the cigarette machine. Well, he would do the best he could. He did not even want to risk fumbling with his bulky case, so certain was he that she was one of the easily distracted.

"Fate is when God makes the connections." He listened to himself: like seeds onto the turned earth, he thought in the words of his mentor. "We call it fate because we can't see those connections. Like they say, the Lord works in mysterious ways." He took a satisfied breath: so far, so good.

"No, it's not God." She seemed disgusted with him suddenly. "God is something else. I'm thinking of something like luck. Some people have all the luck, if you know what I mean." In spite of the hopeful thrust of these final words, Gena was quite certain that there would be no meeting of minds here.

"Well, really, luck is God too." John White was smug.

"You've got God on the brain," Gena said, suddenly fearing the worst. She looked at the kitchen clock and then got up to turn on the television. "Do you mind? You know the doctor, the younger one? He goes to Spain today." There was a new assurance in her voice. "That means they're taking him off the show." When she turned back John White had the black case open.

"It sounds to me . . ."—his voice had turned avuncular as if he would pull her onto his knee—". . . like you would like to learn more about God and how you can develop a personal relationship with Jesus Christ." He wondered whether he had picked the right moment.

"Oh no, you're that guy." Gena sent him back to the Gold Cup Deli in a taxi.

———————◆———————

Eckhart's restaurant, well-located across the street from the Lynford High School complex, lacked the validation of a nationwide chain, yet it served food of the same kind and quality. It was not heavily patronized. M. L. Johnson entered, placed his order, and made his way to the room at the back where five white boys worked the video games on their lunch hour. As he passed through the nearly empty restaurant, it was enough for him that he himself was intensely conscious of his presence, of the impression he made.

"Hey my man," Douglas Stern greeted him. He was the youngest of the group. Gena, who for reasons of her own often told her son that she admired his maturity, would have nonetheless been stunned to discover him thus out with the boys.

There was something about M. L. that drew them away from the games. His was a polished, compelling presence set amid these petals of raw and aimless youth and they clung to him. M. L. sat, stretched his long chino-clad legs onto the chair opposite, and crossed his ankles. He wore bright yellow socks and polished loafers. M. L. Johnson was comfortable with these Jewish boys. He was used to them. His family had worked for families like theirs. Before he started school he used to be brought for the day, set out in the yard or down in the playroom with a white boy about his age, and be expected to play without a fuss. It was easy once he understood that he was to be treated as a guest—a guest, while his aunt Marva worked in the kitchen.

"Dougie, you want to pick up my burger and fries, Babe."
Douglas, caressed, moved fast. He wore chinos, too. The others pulled up chairs.

"Listen to this, man. I got a ticket coming over here." M. L. tapped his well-shaped fingers on the aqua-blue plastic. "I got a ticket coming over here for driving too slow. They do not give the white man a ticket for driving too slow. No way." He turned his hand palm up and continued tapping with the turquoise of his silver Indian-styled ring. "They do not give the white man a ticket for driving too slow."

"You pay it off?" Douglas put the food down carefully; watching M. L. encouraged precision. "That's what my Dad does." He looked at the others, suddenly embarrassed. "I mean, I don't know about now, but I mean before they, you know, he used to."

M. L. covered the boy's discomfort, looking around to include all of them.

"Pay it off! Hey, am I Mr. Stanley Stern? I mean think about it. 'Your Daddy's rich and your Momma's good-lookin'.' They's rich folks." The boys loved to hear him do that. Squinting, he extended his lean brown arm, thumb up, as if taking their measure. "And so are you. You guys, you guys is rich." He cackled. "What are you going to do about it?"

They all laughed at this; but after a moment Jason Herz, a purist at heart, said, "Hey wait; I don't think my Mom and Dad are rich. We're just regular, you know what I mean."

M. L. fixed him with a stare, brought both feet suddenly to the floor, and leaned across the table with mock menace. "To my certain knowledge, you got a person of color, a Third World lady, working for you once a week. She pick up after you. You all make the mess and she pick up."

Jason Herz turned to the others. "Hey, my cousin Louis is rich. You know Louis, right? I mean we're not the same as him, right."

"Who gives a shit." This from David Pelt, the only true believer. "We're going on the general idea. Rich is rich and poor is poor."

"Hey that's brilliant." Ben Finkle, elegant in a black cowboy shirt, was scornful, impatient with theory. "We know what we're doing, right, Geller?"

"We're doing it, aren't we?" was Sandy Geller's curt reply.

Sandy's beardless cheeks were rosy, but there was a manly rasp in his voice, perhaps because he had grown up without using it very much. Naturally, Marilyn and Bruce Geller expected nothing less than conversational ease from their children, but as the risk of exposure was high, Alexander, called Sandy, had often chosen silence. In all, he was a shy, cynical, unsmiling youth; but this look, as luck would have it, was currently the fashion.

"I've been thinking more and more about Haiti, man." David Pelt, hard-eyed, his long dark hair combed back behind his ears, rubbed an acned cheek. "You talk about poor. Shit."

"They talk French there," Douglas put in automatically.

"Leave that to me." M. L. was mild.

"You mean being poor is not enough." Ben Finkle smiled at M. L. "We'll have to discriminate." Sandy Geller slapped his palm.

M. L. pretended hurt. "I'll tell you one thing, Cowboy, they wake up in the morning and they don't smell no lazy maple bacon smell floating up the stairs. In fact, there's no stairs there. Mud—that's what they got—mud." He finished the last of his hamburger.

"You ever heard of kosher, man? Pelt don't smell no bacon at his house either."

"He got stairs though, don't he now? We know that little thing for sure." They all laughed; but Douglas felt he was missing something.

———◆———

Mitzi Geller gave the impulse items near the cash register a sharp admonitory glance before departing for lunch with the Merchants' Association. The stumpy rubber figurines grew clammy then and the bits of pastel fluff appeared to shiver and quake until the door closed behind her. In the office at the rear Helga Grossman lit a cigarette and squinted at it through the smoke, as if appraising a piece of paste jewelry. In fact, her family had through three or four generations been associated with jewelry—the making, selling, buying, wearing, and, finally, by necessity, the smuggling of it. *Schmuck* was the German word; whenever she used it, Douglas would laugh. She loved to hear her grandson laugh. Helga was a tall woman, angular and stiff-limbed, and she held herself a little aloof from the people she knew. But she made an exception for Douglas; and for Jake.

From where she sat in the office the shop door was in view. She was glad to work at the store for the independence it gave her, but she did not like to be in the store. It was the simple abundance of merchandise, the excess of things, which oppressed her. Helga shunned excess. But she made an exception here too because she loved the rich chocolate and marzipan cakes Jake brought her from the European bakery in the city. She craved them with an appetite which inevitably led to excess.

And, while she longed for her little cakes and therefore an occasion for one of Jake's infrequent trips into New York, she especially liked sitting in the office knowing he was at his table just inside the stockroom door. Though he was young enough to be her son, she thought of him more as a brother, for she had had a brother like him: Franz, who was killed very young but already was known for his brains. It was not only the capacity that reminded her, the minds *felt* alike. Often, as she sat reading or knitting for Douglas, it seemed to her that she could almost feel the power of thought infuse the silence between them. It was a power she had learned to recognize at an early age. At first she had even imagined it as a kind of beam which seemed to emanate from Franz's intense black eyes when he was explaining something to her. The last time she saw Franz, it was on the railroad platform. He could explain nothing, but

35

only looked at her and looked at her; and now she felt he had passed on the only thing he had to leave—a vivid impression of his mind. Of course, it wasn't quite the same, that she saw clearly. Jake had lived to trade the glitter of youth for a static urgency, to laugh at himself.

"What's for lunch?" he called just as the shop door opened. Helga enjoyed his familiarity. She rose at once and walked into the store.

A young man had entered and was making a note on his clipboard. He held his body ready for action. It was evident that he had come on business.

"Mrs. Geller?" He looked up, sharp-featured, a whippet. Helga thought he seemed disappointed.

"I'm Jake Geller," Jake said stepping forward.

Again the man seemed disappointed. Jake looked odd to him; so resolutely out of fashion, so unimposing. He checked his notes. "I have Mrs. Mitzi Geller down here." His eyes avoided Helga. "Is she . . ." He stopped uncertainly when Jake, thinking about lunch, let the question hang. "At any rate, I'm Mark Cone." He held the clipboard with both hands and the opportunity for a handshake did not present itself. "As you might know, we've started our series on Lynford and we thought a merchant, a lady merchant . . . Did you happen to catch Alvin Quint this morning?"

Mitzi Geller, lady merchant, Jake thought. Many a time and oft in the Rialto. Most likely, Bruce had set it up, taking advantage of his position to put a relative on the TV news, to provide a little free advertising, to pay a compliment. Jake was amused. "Alvin Quint? He recently came to mind."

"Life's like that." Cone was supremely unimpressed. "You know what I'd like to do? I'd like to move this barrel out of the way." He nudged it with his sneaker. "Are they still selling these pink rubber balls?" He picked one from the barrel and bounced it several times. "Do kids want them anymore?"

"Why not? A ball is a ball." Helga selected a large striped one and shifted it from hand to hand like an apprentice juggler.

36

Cone looked at her apprehensively. He didn't like the sound of her.

"There's no story in that, Helga." Jake took a small dense ball out and let it drop to the floor. It bounced twice his height. "This is new." His voice rose and he drew the word out. "It has improved bounce capacity and increased height potential. It's a ball for the eighties!" He displayed the multicolored ball in his palm. "Please give one to Mr. Quint with our compliments."

To Helga this was nonsense. She walked back to the office. The television cameras were coming into the shop; Douglas would want to know.

"Sorry, verboten." The whippet was matter-of-fact, his glance wandering, boylike, to the merchandise-covered walls. "No telling where it would stop." He took the ball from Jake and dropped it back into the barrel. "No offense; credibility of a news organization b.s., etc. When can I catch up with . . ."— he looked at his clipboard—" . . . Mrs. Mitzi Geller?"

When he left, Helga sent Jake upstairs to bring the lunch. She lived in one of the apartments above the store; Jake and Mitzi lived in the other. Above them, on the top floor, lived Mrs. Sloane, a wealthy and eccentric old woman who rented both apartments and lived in one or the other as the spirit or the season moved her. It seemed from the sand on the doormat and the potted palm that she considered one of them a summer home. Someday Jake and Mitzi intended to convert the two apartments into one large apartment and move up. It was part of Mitzi's plan. They already owned the building.

Helga's living room, dim and stuffy, furnished with too many miscellaneous pieces, had a censorious air, which capacity for comment resided not in any component but in the overall effect. There was no pretense that this particular arrangement of furniture was preferable to any other, or that these colors had been chosen with any regard for their impact. Yet, seen in their proper context, the elements did combine to convey an attitude, to render a kind of judgment. There was once a room in

37

an apartment in Prague which was not at all like this room, but was nonetheless its progenitor. The bourgeois furniture of genuine design and material, the rich colors of velvet drapes and opulent carpets—this was all nearly regal. But it had spawned this grand indifference, this jumble of plastic and cheap, scarred wood.

One might be tempted, then, to conjure up that time and place, where sofas were built by stiff-tongued craftsmen fed on principles of design, where tables were polished by young girls from the country who admired fashion and curtsied to wealth. But, no! This was not the point. Rather it was as if Helga were saying, there is so much that is nonsense to me, that does not pertain, does not stand up, is of no use. I don't play that game, she often said, proud of the tough American sound. See! This is how I live.

On the other side of the maroon drape, a tiny cactus in a green plastic pot, a gift from Douglas, was dying on the window sill. Jake pulled aside a corner of the drape. Yes, dying. If Helga was not a gardener, neither was she a cook. The spice rack Mitzi had given her remained empty. In the refrigerator Jake found liverwurst, a container of potato salad, some sliced tongue, and a piece of elderly cheese. He prepared two plates.

Putting the silverware and paper napkins into the back pocket of his corduroy trousers, he balanced the plates atop two glasses of iced tea and carefully threaded a path out between the fringed hassock and the low glass coffee table. Just at the door, which he had had the foresight to leave open, he saw the picture of Kafka in its blue-gray cardboard frame. Helga had said, "If not one Franz from Prague, why not another? It serves the purpose."

The staircase was well-lit and brightly painted, their first improvement as landlords. At its bottom Jake faced a challenge. He must negotiate two doors to reach the street and yet another to enter the shop. His luck held, the vestibule door had not clicked shut. In the entry, setting one lunch down, he pulled the street door open, braced it with his foot, retrieved the burdened glass, and finally backed out onto the sidewalk just as an unmanned shopping cart clattered by, missing him by inches before it glanced off the plate glass and came to rest against the grill of Marilyn's Buick.

It was a close call, and Jake, hampered though he was, gestured as much. His sister-in-law got out of the car looking angry. She glared in the direction of the supermarket up the street.

"What are you wearing?" she demanded of Jake.

He opened his arms, taking care with the lunch, and looked down at himself.

"Is that your idea of something to wear? In public? Please Jake!" Marilyn pushed into the store without a backward glance. Jake's arms were tiring. He called to her with unusual sharpness and she caught the door and let him enter.

"Have I ever mentioned the fact that your nephew Sandy is a very bright boy?" Marilyn put the question while Jake had a mouthful of liverwurst. "You've never made a comment on it but I suppose you do realize it. He has a high I.Q. It's higher than Bruce's."

"What kind of a comment would a person make in that connection?" Jake was genuinely curious. It was not unusual for Marilyn to feel he was remiss. Now he meant to learn.

"If you don't know, I can't tell you. At least my friends know."

"Just give me one example."

Marilyn was losing patience and she had not yet come to the point of her visit. She forced herself to humor him. "Well, for example, this morning at tennis Gwen Pelt said, 'It's always the bright ones, isn't it.'"

Jake felt cheated. He inquired after Sara.

"Jake, will you listen to me!" Marilyn narrowed her eyes angrily. "I am talking about Sandy! I am trying to have a conversation with you; please pay attention."

Helga picked up the empty plates and the silverware and left the office. She had not enjoyed her lunch. She had eaten quickly, silently, and there was little satisfaction in that. Beyond a perfunctory greeting, Marilyn Geller had not addressed her, leaving the older woman to feel a poor relation at her own board. Seated at a dining table Marilyn would as a matter of course follow the dictates of etiquette if not actual courtesy, but there in the cramped office, sharing Mitzi's cluttered desk with them, she had felt adrift, had resorted perforce to a kind of protective rudeness.

It was difficult for Marilyn. After all, she thought Jake was a buffoon, a dreamer, a fool. You live in your own little world, she would accuse him, what do you know? And yet she could not escape the feeling that he did know. What, she sometimes wondered, did she think he knew?

"Why is he supposed to be such a genius?" she had asked Bruce more than once, thinking what a fool Jake seemed.

"No one ever said he was a genius." Bruce bristled.

"Your father did." Marilyn thought Sam Geller had.

"Luftmensch is not genius. Luftmensch is something else."

"I thought it was," Marilyn had complained. "Your father made it sound like genius."

The misunderstanding calmed Bruce. "It's just that Jake's interested," he had suggested. And it is possible that his father did have this far-reaching context in mind when he called Jake a luftmensch, for it had been Sam's way to want to encompass everything. What he did not understand was that Jake too wanted to encompass. But where Sam would possess, ingest, encircle, it was Jake's way to be interested. However, to the same end, to make the thing his own.

Marilyn reapplied her lipstick. She had nibbled at the cheese.

"Is Helga offended?" She never knew how to start with Jake.

"She understands. Does Sandy have a problem?" He gave her the opening.

"No. I'm not saying that." There was annoyance in her quick reply. "It's just a feeling. I've seen him twice now."

40

"Seen him where?"

"With a black man. I've seen him with a black man."

"What do you mean, 'a black man'? Where did you see him?"

"Walking." Marilyn, seated in Helga's chair, adjusted the footstool to suit her short, athletic legs.

"Have you asked him?"

"He was strange about it. I think maybe he sells Sandy grass. What else could it be?"

"What did he say?"

"He said he was a great guy and all the guys liked him."

"What's strange about that?"

"He seemed awkward."

"Maybe because the guy is black."

"Does it sound like a connection to you, Jake?" She spoke the word trippingly, making of it an everyday thing.

"I don't think so. He told me he's not doing that anymore."

"Who told you what?" Marilyn was disbelieving, her tone instant hauteur.

Embarrassed, Jake tried to minimize. "Just in passing."

"I wish you wouldn't talk to the children that way, Jake. You mix and meddle. You pump. And I don't like it." Marilyn stood up quickly. "You always have to be involved somehow, don't you? I know you."

"Marilyn, stop it." Jake focused his voice around the command and she looked at him strangely. "I'm sure your feeling is right. Sandy wants something. But it isn't dope."

Marilyn struck a pose in the doorway, fashionably sporty in her hot-pink jogging suit. "Oh, you just think you know everything. I have news for you. Sandy wants for nothing. So try another theory, Doctor Geller." This was Marilyn at her most cutting. Jake was neither an M.D. nor a Ph.D.; he wasn't a psychologist, a podiatrist, a chiropractor, or a dentist. For years Marilyn had assumed that Jake had received his degree. When she discovered this lack, it became, she believed, her most potent weapon.

Jake felt she relied on it too heavily. "Give it some thought, Marilyn." He gave her an encouraging smile.

3

WEDNESDAY

Lost at the Point of Embarkation

Several days later Gena Stern faced the morning with a degree of anticipation she had not known for some months. Not that she had slept well; she had been up again in the middle of the night to confront the lacks of the day. The spoon and saucer still sat atop the television. Yet, Alvin Quint coming to her live from Lynford had made all the difference. Gena began to dress; she had not truly dressed for a week. On the screen Mary Alice Mustard read the news: An English soldier blown to bits in Northern Ireland. This morning Mary Alice wore a white blouse with a tiny plaid bow at the throat; she was a career woman.

Gena opened the door to her walk-in closet. The floor was strewn with the shoes and boots of several seasons. She was ignorant of the claims of Protestants and Catholics, but she had heard that the children of Northern Ireland were no longer sleeping well, and she could sympathize. Mary Alice moved on, her tone hypnotic, an odd combination of deadly calm and clarion call: Two Armenian terrorists gun down a Turkish diplomat. Gena examined her skirts one by one; she had a large collection. She was not informed on the national identity of the Armenians. Even Turkey, illusionally familiar, she could not place for certain, nor could she conceive the existence of a single city there.

Gena pulled on a denim skirt and faced the mirror. The skirt hung loosely on her. She tried on another; it was tight. Gena felt herself flagging; Mary Alice Mustard set a terrific pace. The bright bright voice continued with no diminution of vigor: Basque separatists kidnap local mayor. In a hurry now, Gena put on a black velour jogging suit. With her uncared-for hair and the circles under her eyes, the outfit gave her the look of an immigrant lost at the point of embarkation. Mary Alice was wrapping it up, smiling now, unfazed; not yet aware that the Moluccans, the Walloons, the Croats, and the Huks had grievances too.

Gena sat down and searched the closet floor for suitable shoes. There was no one who could exhaust her, deflate her, like Mary Alice Mustard, the spirit of Vulcan. It was the voice as weapon, forged to cut cleanly, to hack away, to lop off, to run through. I've had it this morning, Gena thought, defeated. Bits of gray fluff had transferred themselves from the floor to her black velour. She looked into the mirror and over her shoulder, saw Mary Alice Mustard, head and shoulders, who even at this remove had an unearthly vibrance, as if colored by the heat of the forge. Gena shuddered. I've had it; I give up.

But then Mary Alice swiveled in her chair and, preparing to listen intently, allowed a slight frown to form. Gena approached the set on her knees. Quint was already standing outside Mitzi Geller's toy store. In spite of the early sun, he too appeared disgruntled. The camera moved up the street and then down the street and Quint's commentary followed along: Small Business Administration loans, bankruptcy court, women in the Chamber of Commerce. Quint's tone turned sepulchral: an underground parking garage. At the corner, a bus sighed and two black women stepped down. The jeweler cranked his green-striped awning. Douglas's bicycle rested against a parking meter. Quint, with his twisted smile, turned and walked into the store.

Mitzi Geller stood, stage center, dressed to kill. She dressed just as her customers did, made a point of it, and they always took silent stock, as if they were dressing as she did instead of vice versa. Her well-ordered, well-stocked store, like a mob under control, set her off. Mitzi's composure was absolute, her instincts impeccable, and her buoyancy apparent. Grumpy Alvin turned sweet. Gena began to revive. To finish on a lighter note, Mitzi displayed several Halloween masks and Quint put one on, an ugly little monster, elite of some unknown galaxy. Intuitive, Mitzi had ordered in quantity. Quint spoke with difficulty from within the rubber, Mitzi acknowledged his thanks; then there was a loud snort and a suppressed childish giggle as a great cascade of rubber balls came bouncing and rolling from the rear of the store.

Mary Alice Mustard, eyes sliding left and right, thanked the now unseen Quint, promising to check in again tomorrow. Gena identified the cozy superiority in that cooly amused voice. I'll show her, she thought angrily, and turned once again to the closet. She was looking for something in a pastel shade.

—————◆—————

Mitzi informed Jake and Helga that their bit of guerrilla theater—she called it "mishegaas"—had not been televised. The thought of their conspiring in this childish prank displeased her. But not on her own account. Her magnificent serenity of position was unassailable. She would not be knocked off her pins. Shenanigans, she called it, and left for the dentist's office. Douglas left with Quint's autograph, unprized, secured by Helga. Jake began collecting the rubber balls and reestablished the wire barrel at the corner of the counter. He tried to conjure up the image of the bent ancient, the sage rummaging among the rubber balls. He went so far as to turn his back on the barrel, then to approach it as if anew, hoping to fool the sight into sight. But will they come when you do call for them? This spirit from the vasty deep—the Talmud was likened to the sea, after all—Jake wished to see it again, for encouragement, for comfort, for the plain thrill of seeing something that wasn't there. Helga finished wheeling the tricycles back into place, testing their bells, feeling strangely satisfied.

And Jake felt inspired. Rabbi Judah, he recalled, who himself was called The Prince, once likened Rabbi Tarphon to "a heap of stones" or "a heap of nuts." An awkward but telling compliment. Remove one stone from the pile, or one nut from the heap, and they all go tumbling over each other. When a man came to Rabbi Tarphon and said "Teach me," the sage would cite not simply Scripture but the panoply of Jewish law, commentary, and lore. It was with respect to this quality of mind that he was called "a heap of stones": the clear clicking sound as the stones went tumbling—precise, playful, sensuous to Jake's ear.

Mitzi had given Jake a bicycle for his birthday. She had his health in mind, his blood pressure, cholesterol level, sodium intake, muscle tone, joint articulation, overall flexibility, and his paunch. Now, with time to spare, Jake rolled his trousers, took the bicycle from the garage in the rear, and headed toward the water. The morning was bright, the air clear and crackling. Jake, in the heavy wool sweater Helga had knitted, rode at a measured pace, sitting straight and proud, all attention. The last of the commuters passed him headed for the station. As he pedaled he sang a bathetic, many-stanzaed folk ballad of the sort with which he had become familiar at an impressionable age. In fact, nothing evoked his younger self so quickly now as a recording of a cracked Appalachian voice singing a capella. The ugly dry purity of the sound, its insistence—Mitzi ran from the room at the first raw note.

It was a short ride. He walked the bicycle down onto the beach and looked out across the Sound toward Long Island. The number of cabin cruisers and sailboats bobbing in the cove at the yacht club had decreased during the week. Jake breathed deeply but he did not smell the ocean. Nevertheless, it left him feeling fit, even adventuresome. Settling the bike, he bent at the waist to touch his toes.

"Excuse me, sir."

Jake saw the black trouser legs from between his own knees. He could make nothing of them except to note that they were only intermittently creased. He righted himself and turned to face a man with close-set blue eyes who was extracting a cigarette from a half-crumpled package. He smoothed the cigarette and held it out between them, asking for a light. Jake didn't have one.

"It's fate, I guess. Serves me right." John White indicated his lapel pin. "We're not supposed to smoke or drink." He smiled as temptation receded. "I found these in a phone booth," he lied glibly. "I was going to take a chance."

The desire for a cigarette grew in Jake.

"I don't smoke either." He glanced over toward the green bathhouse. "Let's see."

John White followed him. Several beer bottles stood beside the door, and the drain of the outdoor shower was filled with cigarette stubs. Rolled into the neck of one of the bottles was a matchbook, a single match remaining. John White lit up and Jake, stretching his neck, inhaled noisily. A moment later he was accepting a cigarette from the proferred packet. They sat down in the sun with their backs against the rough wood, smoking in a spirit of comradeship.

"How's your campaign going?" Jake asked, to get the other side of the story.

"Campaign?" His frown was fierce. "Oh. We don't call it that. We call it 'outreach.'"

"Outreach," Jake repeated.

"Well it's not going that great. It seems like there's a lot of Jewish people in this town. I've never had this many."

"There are quite a few, you're right."

"They don't know what they're missing." He sighed.

"What's your tack?"

"Tack?"

47

"What do you say to them?"

"The whole thing is based on the idea of Jesus is Your Friend." He hummed a few bars of "What a Friend We Have in Jesus." "That's the theme. Jesus is your friend. He loves you."

"Well, keep at it." Jake was jovial. And you should, if you please, refuse till the conversion of the Jews.

"Why are Jewish people like that?"

Jake took it as rhetoric and remained silent.

"They always think they're so . . ." John White was genuinely puzzled. "Well, for instance, they don't need a friend; they don't care if Jesus loves them. Et cetera. My Dad doesn't like them." He stood up and brushed the seat of his chinos.

"Lots of people don't." Jake threw the beer bottles into the empty trash barrel. "Stiff-necked."

John White gave him a close look. "For sure."

They parted company at the roadside. John White, with his brush-cut hair and squint-eyes, looking more like a Seabee than a fisher of souls, had been spared Jake's vinegar. Grouse and grumble, that was Jake's weakness, and the degree to which grandeur absented itself from such a dreary pitch as he had just heard drove him to silent fulmination on the ride back. Friendship, ripped from its human context, put in an impossible position. Here was an American theology for the desperate, the unloved, the friendless, the ones who pray for a miracle. God as friend. But can a friend perform miracles? The Leader of the Free World is not looking for a friend; he has a valet, he has a barber, he has a kitchenful of entrepreneurs.

Jake peddled hard up a slight incline and stopped at the top, opposite the brick-colonial Temple, to catch his breath. Something gold twinkled amid the dry leaves the wind had swept to the curbstone. He bent to pick up a gold cuff link. Behind him a car pulled to the curb abruptly, as if the driver had missed his mark. Jake turned just in time to see a woman sprint across the sidewalk and into the shelter of some greenery. In that instant he realized that here was the private entrance to Dr. Pelt's of-

48

fice. He studied the Pelt house; beyond its color, which was a salmon pink, he saw nothing there to attract a burglar. He looked at the cuff link with renewed interest; it was, no doubt, part of the loot. On the back he found a date engraved: April 31, 1978. April 31st! Thirty days hath September, he said under his breath, April . . . Now did all consideration for the cuff link's sentimental value, or indeed its status as a clue, evaporate; for Jake felt in that moment that he held in his hand the key to a reality beyond time. April 31st! This cuff link was a certain sign sent into the world (the unwitting work, as it appeared, of a carefree relative and a careless jeweler) to represent by its engraved implication another reality, a universe of thought which had existed forever. Jake was elated, electric with the romance of the thing.

He scuffed the dull leaves this way and that but the other cuff link did not show itself. Pocketing the mysterious token, he resumed his ride, his mind now on strictly calendrical matters: In the days of the Jewish Temple, calculation played its part in fixing the New Moon but actual observation was required as well. Two witnesses had to appear before the Sanhedrin to give evidence that they had seen the new moon. On the other hand, if by the thirtieth day no observers had appeared with such evidence, the New Moon was declared anyway. Messengers were sent to the Jewries in the Diaspora to inform them of the fixing of the calendar, of New Moons, leap years, and related calendrical concerns. Ha! Jake thought suddenly, the Jew takes hold.

He was coasting now. Rabban Gamaliel I, teacher of Saul of Tarsus, had communicated such a decision of the Sanhedrin: "We let you know hereby that sheep are still small, the doves not yet full grown, and the time of the first harvest has not yet come. It pleased, therefore, me and my colleagues to declare this year as a leap year."

Now here he was, Jake, bearing a calendrical message, bringing news of the 31st of April to an increasingly cufflinkless world.

On an average day Bruce Geller arrived at his office on time, thereby creating each day anew in his own image: an average day for an average guy. Greeting his associates, a hand on the arm here, a nod there, friendly and casual, a wink to his secretary, this was clearly an average guy. A study in image-building, so Bruce thought. But he was wrong. He thought he was a whiz kid. Jake's the quiz kid, he told his father once, but I'm the whiz kid. I'm running the big race. And he gave Sam Geller a big wink. Nevertheless, the key to Bruce's success was simply his own brand of mediocrity; it was the useful kind, the good kind, top-flight, the kind of mediocrity that sparked the system.

Today Bruce would be late for work. Agitprop from Sandy for breakfast. Civil conversation was no longer possible. Marilyn stayed in bed, Sara practiced the cello in the basement, and he and his only son stood in angry silence waiting for the frozen waffles to pop from the toaster. A college campus in the sixties, a tour of duty in Viet Nam, a career in television news—none of this had made politics interesting or important to Bruce. Nevertheless, politics had recently made him late for work more than once.

"Shit." Sandy was scornful. "If you only knew what was going on."

Bruce was watching the coffee drip into the glass flask of the automatic coffee maker.

"Let me tell you something, smartass, it's my business to know what's going on."

This bit of dialogue, this exchange excerpted at random, would have stunned Sam Geller. It was not the way a father and son talked.

Bruce would have found these arguments tedious had they not filled him with rage. That the son he loved held him in contempt as a shill for the government, an oppressor, a racist, a hostage to capitalism and even imperialism—none of this did he take seriously. The charges had no power to move him, were in fact unreal to him, because they existed in a universe which at no point intersected his own. But the attitude, the attitude, he could not tolerate. This morning his carefully crafted invitation to accompany them to Temple on Yom Kippur eve had evoked something beyond the predictable response.

". . . Nazis now," Sandy mumbled so that Bruce, at the sink with the water running, was unable to catch the beginning.

"What did you say?" He spun around, flushing.

"Never mind." Sandy kept his eyes on his plate.

"What did you say?" Bruce repeated; but checking his watch was almost ready to let it go. He had a train to catch.

"They're the Nazis now." Sandy looked his father in the eye, as much as to say, I'm my own man.

"Oh, don't start with that Third World crap. Your grandfather would have had a heart attack."

"I've got news for you. Everybody thinks that. They're terrorists, fascists, Nazis. They're putting the Palestinians in concentration camps. It's a fact." He ran a finger through the syrup remaining on his plate and sucked it like a lollipop.

"Where do you pick up this stuff?"

"I just do. I'm informed."

"Informed, my ass. You don't have the remotest goddam idea what you're talking about. You've got no sense of history."

"Don't bullshit me." Guessing at Bruce's own lack, Sandy, at the door, thrust home.

Alone, clearing his mind, Bruce poured a glass of tomato juice, added a squirt from the plastic lemon, and went into his den. He mounted the stationary bicycle and began to pedal very slowly against the heavy tension, glass in hand, eyes fixed on the blank television screen. Gulping the juice, he bent, let the glass drop onto the thick rubber pad, loosened his paisley tie and pedaled as hard as he could for three minutes. Then he went upstairs to change his shirt. He had had his ride earlier, his daily half-hour while watching the morning show, and seen

51

Quint interview his sister-in-law. It had come off well, he thought; Mitzi was a good interview, a smart cookie.

In the bedroom Marilyn was stepping into her tennis dress. She was in a rush and, while surprised to find him still at home and puzzled to see him remove his shirt, her time, she felt, was too valuable to investigate the circumstance. They spoke in short sentences to arrange a date for the Quint dinner. Their calendar did not lend itself.

"That leaves Saturday." Marilyn put in the small gold earrings she wore for tennis. "What about Saturday, then?"

"It's Yom Kippur, isn't it?" Bruce had a great many shirts and was fond of shuffling through them in their clear laundry wrapping while the plastic still camouflaged the manifold imperfections left by the ironing machine.

"Just until evening; so we could easily have dinner."

"O.K. I'll see if he's free. Will you be fasting?" Bruce chose a shirt with narrow blue stripes but found, too late, the button at the cuff was gone. He threw it toward the bed where it lay sprawled, sleeve dangling, as much in disfavor as only moments before it had been valued.

"No. It means nothing to me." She posed in the doorway, hands pulling her short white skirt at the hem as if to curtsey. "I'm off, sweetie. Have a good day."

Bruce half turned from the bureau, another blue-striped shirt in hand. "Dad always fasted. You can do what you want."

"Bruce, I'm late."

"Let's just have something ready early then." He matched her tone of warning. "I'll be hungry."

Glancing at the digital clock display in the television control panel, Bruce saw that he would miss the next train too. He wondered what he should do with this odd little scrap of time, unencountered since he had been laid up with the flu in the early spring. He sat down on the bed, activated the remote-control command, and began to button his shirt; the television screen developed its picture as ordered, but Bruce walked out on it. Down at the end of the hall he pushed open the door of

Sandy's room. He was struck and reassured by the similarity it bore to other rooms he had entered, mistakenly, perhaps in search of a bathroom at a party in a strange home. The corners of the rock posters unstuck from the walls, the video games, the dirty socks: he enjoyed seeing his son through the prism of other men's sons. He took solace in the conformity. These rooms fitted up with every comfort and device for distraction did not seem a likely breeding ground for revolution.

Sandy's shades were drawn, the air dim and slightly dank, the bed unmade, a small tape player lying on the pillow, earphones trailing. The empty turntable on the stereo was turning and Bruce flipped the power switch. Amid the record albums on the floor a page of newsprint was visible. Sandy was not a newspaper reader. Bruce squatted for a closer look: an article on the Students for Third-World People Conference in the Croton Community College *Clarion*. Why not People for Third-World Students while you're at it for Christ's sake, Bruce said aloud. Instead of reading the article, he walked over to the built-in desk, sat down gingerly, trying to spare his knife-crease trousers, and opened the deep bottom drawer. Although designed to hold file folders, it contained instead a ramshackle ensemble of books. Bruce pulled them out one by one: a dictionary, an almanac, a thesaurus, a Bartlett's, and, at the bottom, wedged at an angle to force the fit, Bruce's atlas.

"Ah ha, ah ha, ah ha," he said as he worked the atlas free. He smoothed the torn corners of the dust jacket, reverent in a moment of triumph. Suddenly, however, it occurred to him to wonder why a boy of Sandy's known proclivities and determined parochialism should have removed this large unwieldy book from its shelf in the den and hidden it here among these other little-used volumes. And well he might. The Global Village—by implication it rendered the atlas obsolete, obviated the appeal of a map. A steamer capsized on the Nile, a train that jumps the track in central India, a jet struck by lightning over Helsinki—these were all neighborhood catastrophes, their

53

sites familiar without implying familiarity. Just as one referred to the cleaner on the corner as the cleaner on the corner.

———◆———

Though Gena could not know it, the mood at the Gold Cup Deli had started to turn dark and oppressive; the Greek had grown increasingly capricious and overbearing. He monitored the news for dispatches from his homeland, but received small satisfaction; as far as the media knows, he once complained to his wife, only Jackie O is a Greek. Poulos had always felt that his own fortunes rose and fell with those of Greece; how young and proud he had been in the halcyon days when Melina Mercouri was a movie star and big in America. Now, as the Turks and even the Armenians were gaining media attention, it would take a hell of a lot more than screwing good old NATO to bring some kind of prosperity to his poor deli, he thought sourly. Ruta and Dolores, for their part, chalked up his ill humor and stepped-up surveillance to the temperament of his people. No day went by without the one or the other waitress adding a new chapter to the folklore of ethnicity. "Look at him, will ya!" Dolores would demand, stopping dead in her tracks. "The Greeks'll do that," Ruta would reply casually, her field work the more extensive.

Ruta and Dolores had from the first taken an interest in Gena. Now, after a mere four days, they thought of her as a regular and were pleased with her development. Never had they witnessed such a rapid transformation. In fact, they had not had much hope for Gena that first day, vague, disheveled, broke as she seemed. They guessed she must be a loony, recently released. A loony always threw the uncompromising sameness of their own lives into pleasant relief. As Gena took her accustomed place in the rear booth, Dolores, getting the coffee, passed Ruta with a whisper, "Look, she's getting her act together."

"That's a cute outfit," Dolores said sincerely, putting down the coffee.

"Oh, my closet's such a mess," Gena revealed, and Dolores

54

moved off, concerned again. "She's still got a ways to go," she told Ruta. "Her closet's her own business."

Later, Ruta stopped to chat, addressing her customer on a topic which had previously promoted a feeling of sisterhood: the younger doctor, the one who had gone to Spain.

"Stanley called out of the blue," Gena replied with unusual alacrity, primed for reality. "He says he wants to talk about the *Shooting Star*. He never asks for Douglas."

Ruta gave her a blank look, chagrined to confess, "Actually, I haven't been watching lately."

"Stanley, my ex-husband." Gena identified him for Ruta with no reproof in her voice. "The *Shooting Star*, our boat. Douglas, my son."

Ruta broke it off then, saddened.

"I see what you mean," she told Dolores at the first opportunity. "But still," she added, the softer heart, "she's come a ways."

Gena, mesmerized even at this remove by the energy of Stanley's pitch, sat with her second cup of coffee unaware that she was the object of such concern. Stanley has the will of any ten men, she thought, the persuasive power of a strong arm. Just thinking about him always made her tired, and for several instants she actually teetered at the edge of sleep. Then, at this delicate juncture, as the stream of hope ran backward to its source in dreams, Gena heard a voice which made her sit up and take notice. There was no mistaking the voice of Alvin Quint. Then she saw his back, recognizable though rarely televised. Quint slammed the telephone receiver onto its hook. A. Poulos, frisky in his presence, set a complimentary cup of coffee on a nearby table. Quint, however, resisted the hospitality with downcast eyes, apparently at a loss. Then he walked rapidly to the restroom at the back. Gena smiled, unnoticed, as he passed. She saw that he was wearing makeup. Minutes later he emerged, hands and face dripping, and grabbed the napkins from the nearest table. The Greek rushed toward him, ripping open the wrapper on a package of paper towels. But Quint ignored him deliberately, using up the table napkins and disrupting the silverware. Gena offered him a fresh napkin from her table to finish the job. She hadn't realized his skin would be so white, nearly as pale as her own.

"You don't remember me," she began once their eyes had met.

"No, I do; I think I do." He deposited the soggy napkins in the Greek's outstretched palm.

"You couldn't! How could you?"

"You look familiar. We've met before, haven't we."

"Not really met, but—" She averted her eyes to watch him in the mirror.

"But we've seen each other. That's it." Satisfied, he paused naturally, holding her gaze. His eyes were slightly bloodshot from the water.

"I didn't think you'd still be here. I watched you this morning." It was easier for her this way, more natural with the mirror between them.

"It's an unbelievable story really." Quint pulled at his shirt cuffs. They were damp.

"You got left behind?"

Quint was incredulous. In the mirror he checked the length and breadth of the room; he knew no one.

"Somehow or other they left without you?" Gena persisted. "You know, by mistake."

"You must be psychic." Was this Mark Cone's idea of a joke, Quint wondered. He studied Gena's little face but found there only mute absorption. "How did you know?"

"Well, I just always thought there'd be people all around you all the time." She gave him a small smile to show she hadn't meant to spoil his story; he answered with his patented grimace, as much to thrill her as to confirm the gulf between them. Her look made clear his success and suddenly he felt more comfortable with that pinched intensity than with Ilse's broad blond ease. Nevertheless, he hoped it was only skin deep.

"If you're in a hurry to get back, I could drive you."

Quint was touched. However, he was in no hurry to return to the station. Mark Cone would claim it was a misunderstanding, driving away while Quint was in the florist's shop, confusion over which car he was in. Cone would pretend he was sorry, Mary Alice would pretend she hadn't heard, and Ilse would pretend indifference to the flowers he had sent. A far cry, he thought sourly, from the Ilse he had once known; the Bonn Bombshell (appearing nightly), she had set her cap for him. He called for a cup of coffee and sat down opposite Gena. "Oh no, I wouldn't want you to do that."

"But I could." Gena was determined to be positive. "I would take you right to your, to where you work. I like to drive." Driving was in fact one of Gena's strong points. She enjoyed the company of her car, its comfort and response. They were the perfect suburban couple, Gena and her car.

"Well, we'll see," he soothed her. Was the look he found so appealing a variety of desperation?

There was a pause and Gena looked first at the photograph of the perfect fried egg above the rear counter and then down at her wristwatch, wishing she had an appointment or a lunch or anything that would keep her in the booth at the Gold Cup Deli. But just because she had no reason to leave, she felt compelled to go. Vanity demanded it.

Ever alert, Quint rose to the bait. "I'm keeping you."

"Well . . ." Gena played for time, studying the contents of her change purse. A strategy suggested itself. "Not if I drive you into the city."

"It's a tempting offer," Quint said, flaunting his urbanity, "but why should you bother?" He waited, truly interested, for her reply.

Quint had got ahead of her and she scrambled for specifics. "It's no bother really." A simple untruth, vanity's erstwhile companion, sprang to mind. "I have an appointment in midtown."

At this moment Quint first became aware that she had a potential for radiance. Basking, he was inclined to suspect himself as its cause, when in fact that flush and sparkle signified nothing less than the rebirth of the will.

Ruta was in the restroom applying a poultice to her bunion, but Dolores saw them leave and was proud. Giddy with romance, she approached the Greek and directed his attention to the closing door. But Poulos was cranky now, believing that a commercial opportunity had slipped through his fingers once again. "Whadafuh," he muttered, "whadafuh."

◆

This is perfect, Bruce thought, spotting his brother bicycling a block ahead. With time to spare before the next train, he lowered the window electrically, hailed Jake with a shout, and pulled into the curb up ahead, waiting, legs stretched out the open door. Watching Jake pedal toward him, he was surprised to find himself admiring the sweater his brother wore. Closer inspection, however, caused him to reverse his judgment as he noted that in several spots the sweater's pattern was incomplete and there was even an area on the sleeve where it ceased to exist altogether.

"Is that a homemade sweater or what?" He looked down at Jake's rolled trousers and short green socks. "I don't think people roll their pants anymore, Jake."

"Rubber bands? Bicycle clips? Either would go well with a homemade sweater." Jake borrowed Uncle Nathan's announcer voice. "Argyle pullovers and rolled trouser legs; the year is 1942 and America is at war."

"Hey, guess what?" Bruce had no intention of letting the conversation go Jake's way. "I found my atlas."

Jake reached into his pocket for the cuff link. "Look what I found."

Bruce, never secure in the allusive power of simple assertion, persisted, "Remember? I said I had one. Remember! When I came out of the den I knew I did. And I did." Bruce snapped his fingers twice as if he intended to materialize the atlas out of thin air right there and then. At a loss for a response of equal intensity, Jake put his right hand on the top of his head and let it rest there. This always brought a momentary solace, as if it had been another's hand.

Bruce, not one to linger consciously in an area of his own need, even a need now met, pressed on. "Of course, now that I've got it back, there's no way anybody's going to ask to see it again, Polish rivers or whatever." He laughed dryly, oblivious of the newly self-advertised need. Bruce had a way of digging himself in deeper at the very moment he finally got a foot planted on firm ground again. Jake managed a feeble smile.

"You know who had it? My son the anti-Semite. So now I'm late. The kid can barely read and he's lecturing me on the news." This was Bruce's way of advancing information; his was the style of a hummingbird. He wished to tell it but not to know it.

Again, responding was difficult. Unconvinced of his nephew's literacy, Jake nonetheless rose to his defense. But he had addressed the wrong issue.

"Can you picture Dad? I mean the kid has got so much contempt; calls me a Zionist. What is that crap? Send him to a damn kibbutz for a summer." Bruce's face was flushed.

"He'll be all right," Jake said uneasily. Bruce calmed himself at once; another man's judgment always struck him more forcefully than his own. And yet, Jake had once again missed the mark.

"I don't like his attitude, that's all." Attitude went a long way with Bruce.

Jake was uncomfortable with the comfort he had provided. His nephew put him off: the way he cultivated his limitations, circumscribed his intentions, codified his ignorance, and gave his father a hard time.

"He's deprived," Jake said solemnly.

Bruce gave him a big, knowing wink and brought his legs back in under the steering wheel. "Oh right! Sure he is. I'll tell you one thing—I'm the one who's going to deprive him if he doesn't come with us Yom Kippur." He started the car. Suddenly he seemed in better spirits. "You and Mitzi are coming Saturday." He hurried on, aware the invitation had not been extended. "We'll break the fast together. Alvin Quint, too." He winked again. "For him it's only dinner." He drove off with a wave, his gold watch winking now, leaving Jake to review the conversation. Often it was the only way to understand what Bruce was getting at.

Atlas, Anti-Semitism, Attitude, Atonement, Day of, Jake outlined. This was Bruce's way: to operate with a highly developed sense of urgency, oblivious to the havoc he played with the sensitive machinery of dialogue.

Alexander, called Sandy, what did he want with the Atlas? As far as Jake knew the boy did not share the Macedonian's curiosity about lands not his own. Then, Anti-Semitism. Here too, Jake thought, Sandy did not appear anxious to emulate that other Alexander, who upon conquering Judea showed kindness to his Jewish subjects. In fact, Jake recalled, in order to commemorate his benevolence every Jewish boy born in that year was named Alexander after him. As to Attitude, Jake merely wondered in passing why it was that Bruce, with whom attitude counted for so much, did not take a more objective interest in its variform expression. He moved on to Atonement, Day of. What it came to, he decided, returning his bicycle to the garage, was something more than the boy's unwillingness to attend the Temple service. Bruce had a deeper worry—the sum of the parts. Jake determined to observe his nephew closely on Saturday to see what he could learn. In any case, he must remember to call Marilyn and encourage her to serve a coffee cake and herring in sour cream that evening. It was a good way to break the fast.

Jake reached into his pocket for the cuff link, but it was gone. He searched all his pockets. The cuff link had already become a talisman for him. He rode back to the spot where he and Bruce had stopped to talk. Beneath the cover of autumn leaves he saw the grid of a storm drain. He took the loss hard.

"It escapes me," said Helga when he returned thus unhap-

60

pily. She put her bookmark, a present from Douglas, into her novel. "It's a cuff link, Jake."

"Yes and no." He thought a minute, debating whether to let Helga in on the significance of that engraved reference to a reality as playful as it was profound. If Helga Grossman was a woman of many moods, and she was, it will not be counted so very much against her to admit that playfulness was not among them. "Let me put it this way, Helga," Jake was intrepid, "if today is Wednesday, the . . ."

"Wait!" Helga put her hand on his arm. "Don't tell me today is Wednesday!" She was already reaching for the telephone. "My class meets on Wednesday. The semester has begun." Gena was not at home to answer the phone, but even the prospect of making the trip to Croton by bus could not dampen Helga's enthusiasm for learning.

4

FRIDAY

The Junk and the Horror

To see and be seen, it was the last thing Gena wanted. Yet here she was, husbandless, lackluster, marched past a cross section of Lynford Jewry, and for protection only a young son and a foreign-born mother on stork legs. A sharp-eyed multitude looked her way with that mixture of curiosity and déjà vu which marks an ancient people; and she looked back to forestall, she thought without much hope, further speculation.

The sanctuary was jammed, it was packed with the overflow crowd in whom only the very holiest day of the Jewish calendar could induce attendance. The three had just time to struggle along a ragged aisle into the folding chairs at the rear before the rabbi and cantor, robed and capped in white for Yom Kippur, strode modestly, but without a trace of humility, to their walnut lecterns. Behind them rose the bronze latticed facade of the ark, a work in which the absence of inspiration and the absence of artistry combined to cooly secular effect. On either side the luminaries sat, their somber finery and pious faces not quite transforming the weary Friday commuters they were.

The enormous, high-ceilinged room was as brightly lit and feverish as a movie set. The heightened intensity of people coming together for a common purpose, gaining and affirming a
common identity, so palapable in the pockets of air which
formed and reformed as the crowd settled itself, dissipated in
the forlorn airy wastes above their heads. The orotund praying
of the rabbi, the congregation's tentative response, the anxious
modern sounds of the choir, struggled alike to escape this in-
hospitable republican environment and lodge in the ear of God.

Opening her prayer book, Gena set herself the task of eval-
uating her chances with Alvin Quint. She stood with the others
to recite and from time to time she glanced at the book in
Douglas's lap and turned it ahead to the correct page, but her
thoughts were elsewhere. Leaving Quint in midtown, she had
without compunction broken faith with her fabrication and
headed straight back to Lynford and the beauty parlor, surprised at how easy it was to take up old ways.

"A person's gotta live for themself." Her beautician spoke of
her own tangled affairs, but, Gena sensed, the statement did
have a universal application. At any rate, the sentiment was in
the air and ripe for plucking. Gena, of course, had always lived
for herself, but the justification lurking behind that imperative
had never been sounded in quite this way. A sudden epiphany
led her to conclude that the problems she was having all
stemmed from this lack—she had never lived for herself. How
satisfying it was to gain such an insight. Well, she would start
right now.

That evening she had informed Douglas over pizza that she
intended to start living for herself; she had to, she told him,
and here she was more naive than disingenuous, "for both our
sakes." Nonetheless, the evening had progressed just as it always did and Douglas was left at bedtime to puzzle over the
implications of this announced policy change.

Gena reached up and patted her hair in several places, wondering whether she ought not to try something new with it:
highlights, a cut, a perm. After all, Quint had been around the

world. Yesterday she had taken her usual place at the Gold Cup Deli, but Quint did not oblige her by showing. With her new-found interest in the news, however, she passed the time pleasantly enough leafing through a day-old paper. On page five Poulos had drawn a mustache on the photo of Andreas Papandreou and this helped too to lift her spirits; her mood held up. At home, however, as the afternoon had stretched out, a crack appeared; an emptiness, so immense that it could not be measured except from within, threatened her, tempted her with its paralyzing infinitude. But for the first time since the very first time Gena was genuinely surprised to find such a crack; and so the crack did not grow. She had turned her thoughts to Quint; then Douglas had come home from school, stood by her, mothered her. She had forgotten how deep he was.

So Gena had been able to sustain and nurture her hope. The following morning it had seemed that Mary Alice Mustard could do little beside babble impotently in the background. Curious, Gena took a closer look at her rival; a little green around the gills, she was pleased to note, and that fuzzy yellow sweater, that sweater did nothing for her. She had watched Quint's concluding segment on Lynford and then rushed off to the Gold Cup Deli, hope and its opposite struggling in her breast.

Perspiring in her impatience to get the car parked, she had just turned off the ignition when someone opened the door on the passenger side and climbed in. It was Quint with his twisted smile. He had suggested they drive over to The Pancake House; he had suggested something he called, with his inbred dependence on hype, "a real breakfast." Gena had agreed with alacrity; it seemed to her he gave the world such substance.

One may imagine Ruta and Dolores as that morning dragged on and no Gena; they simply did not know what hit them. Speculation was rife. Poulos, however, had seen it all through the front window. He cursed the Fates. "Whadafuh," he said to his beetle-browed counterman, "whadafuh," but to the girls he revealed nothing.

Hearing an appreciative murmur among her coreligionists, Gena looked up at Rabbi Loren Brody bobbing and weaving behind his lectern. The rabbi was delivering his sermon. In the praying mode, he remained immobile, a dignified, devoted stone; but when he sermonized, when he really got going, his arms thrust out in fervent gesture, his body canted this way and that, his tallith slid repeatedly from his shoulders, and his eyebrows worked overtime. Rabbi Brody had a message. Gena, however, bypassed the substance for a formal consideration. She leafed through the prayer book, making sure she remembered correctly. Yes, after the sermon it was one-two-three and out.

What was a rabbi good for, she wondered. When it had come to light that Douglas was not being prepared for his Bar Mitzvah, Helga insisted that Gena go in to speak to Rabbi Brody. But the rabbi was not at all sympathetic, although Gena, cutting a pathetic figure, poured out her heart to him.

"I'm under a lot of stress," she told him. "I just haven't gotten around to doing anything about it; I couldn't manage it."

"Gena," Rabbi Brody had replied, his voice steely, "that way lies the demise . . ."—he paused to allow the full weight of the burden to transfer itself to Gena's shoulders—". . . of the Jewish people."

On a good day Gena would likely be no match for the mix of professional fulmination and P.R. flackery with which Loren Brody assaulted her, but the day in question saw Gena at her lowest ebb, red-eyed, lethargic, and whispery. He made mincemeat of her, and in the end she agreed to see to it that Douglas was prepared for his Bar Mitzvah. But, whipped as she was, Gena had a glimmering that before long she would not be fit to "see to" anything.

Gena remembered that day now with a wave of revulsion. What in the world had been wrong with her? She was not at all sure she was the same person she had been even a week ago. Whatever had possessed her had vanished into thin air. She considered the possibility that she had been the unwitting object of a Jewish exorcism. Did Jews do that? Exorcism was one among a myriad of ill-defined notions in perpetual free-fall in that part of her brain the media had appropriated, a place in the mind beyond knowledge, outside experience, crammed full yet barren, unfettered yet unfree.

There was something of Quint, it occurred to her then, in the dark shadowy figure of the Exorcist. She narrowed her eyes in sudden concern: or was it Extortionist? Exhibitionist? Abortionist? No, she shook her head in irritation, it was Exorcist after all. It was this uncertainty, this undignified going round in circles which often brought Gena to the verge of shame. The world was awhirl about her. She tried her son with a gentle nudge to the ribs, wondering whether Alvin Quint liked children.

Douglas shrugged her off without irritation; he was always very matter-of-fact with her. Now, as the rabbi droned on, he was leafing back and forth through the prayer book in search of the two or three phrases that had caught his fancy. Finding one, he said it over and over to himself. These phrases, the ones that made him feel a peculiar noble kind of exhilaration, these, he thought, must be the religious ones. And the few scraps of Hebrew the reformers had seen fit to retain were for Douglas the very mystery of religion. Incomprehensible, bursting from time to time through the familiar waves of sound, they carried the glint of a magic efficacy.

As Gena had foreseen, Douglas received no preparation for his Bar Mitzvah. During the grim time after Stanley left them he had not been very inclined to spend his Wednesday afternoons in a dun-colored classroom, nor to choose between his mother and grandmother as they argued over it endlessly. As it turned out, it would have provided some relief. At home Gena grew increasingly and carelessly garrulous, forcing him to pretend to nonchalant inattention. But his apparent preoccupation

67

only emboldened her and she became reckless with her revelations and bitter self-pity. She said many things which had been better left unsaid; and of course Douglas heard it all. He began to dread the time he must spend with her, to flinch from the feverish imagining and then later from the wantonness of her resignation. He sought refuge with Jimmy DiMaria, the youngest in a large family of brothers. At this time too he discovered certain books of high adventure, stories about valiant boys—often they were Danish or Norwegian—who risked their lives in the dead of winter to carry a crucial coded message to the Allies. In these books, he had noted, a family did not count for much. He glanced over at his mother. Today she looked quite a bit like other mothers. She might make a comeback after all. The guarded observation was very much Douglas's way.

On the other side of Gena, Helga sat, uncomfortable on the metal seat, discomforted by her thoughts. Rabbi Brody had been of no help; certainly he ought to have been capable of prevailing with Gena in the matter of the Bar Mitzvah. Helga had been to his study herself, to see for herself, and she came away affronted by the intimacy, the heartfelt platitudes. For his part, the rabbi felt himself shrink before her stern intensity. Helga Grossman was the type of woman who put him off—ruined his timing, diminished the vigor of his performance. He heard himself tinny, unpersuasive, out of his depth.

Helga had expected the book-lined study of a scholar and found instead a scattering of self-help books, a shelf devoted to Israel, several books on nuclear disarmament, and an array of magazines. Without much hope she summarized her position. "I am concerned that my grandson is not being prepared for his Bar Mitzvah." She glared at the No Smoking sign on the rabbi's desk. "I do not want him to be like the little Jewish boy who boarded the transport for Auschwitz asking his father, 'Vatti, what's Jewish?'" The rabbi nodded sympathetically. In the end he had offered to lend her his copy of *Parents, Children and Divorce*. Now, from the very rear of the Temple, she shot the rabbi a sour look. He had been good for nothing.

Marilyn and Bruce stood with their daughter between them while the rabbi recited the benediction. Marilyn studied her beringed fingers splayed on the blond wood of the pew. It was the fashion to wear more than one ring on a finger and she was well able to comply. This was the part of the service to which Marilyn could relate; she liked the feeling of being blessed by someone in authority, by an official representative. When she was a child and her father had blessed her on a Friday evening, she had dismissed it as a futile gesture; of what use could the blessing of a handkerchief salesman possibly be to her, a modern girl in a Kleenex world? Her father had been full of futile gestures, a good man but not a successful one. Bruce put his arm around Sara's shoulder and she smiled up at him, baring her braces. The service was over and the congregation turned as one toward the doors. Bruce was ready for them. He always arrived early enough to assure himself the seats he wanted—front and center, but within striking distance of the exit. Driving Marilyn and Sara before him, he made his move.

Meanwhile, Sandy Geller stood looking out the window of David Pelt's darkened, throbbing bedroom; head bobbing to the beat, lids lowered, he was nevertheless keeping a keen eye on the Temple doors across the street. As the first worshippers emerged onto the broad steps, he rushed from the Pelts' back door and pedaled his bike in open-mouthed haste the several blocks to his own home. It was he who called the police. Several minutes later, Bruce and Marilyn, hearts pounding, drove up behind the police cars obstructing the garage. Lights were on in every room. Marilyn grasped what seemed to have happened almost from the first. She put her arm around Sara as they approached the house, half hoping the burglars had stolen Sara's cello. She worried about Sara, an intense child who resisted all her mother's molding with a friendly passivity. Hurrying ahead, Bruce found Sandy telling his story to the police. It was a simple story. Forbidden to leave the house that evening by his father, he had nonetheless gone out to visit a friend. Yes, he was sure he had activated the alarm system, but . . .

and here he shrugged as if to say, ultimately who knew? In any case, the police noted, the alarm had not gone off. Caught between relief and anger, Bruce maintained a stunned silence.

A cellist was unlikely to be well-rounded, Marilyn felt. The cello, perhaps for this very reason, had been left behind, while three television sets, two stereos, a tape deck, a video recorder, a home computer, and an undetermined number of portable radios and tape players were all gone. The police went from room to room looking for clues. In the den Bruce was slumped in his leather swivel chair, jacket off, sleeves rolled to the elbow. He foresaw a great deal of paperwork, and then, too, it was Yom Kippur. Sam Geller would have been outraged.

"Ha! Ha!" Marilyn said, returning from the bedroom triumphant. The recent rash of burglaries in Lynford had convinced her to put her best jewelry into their safe-deposit box at the bank. "Ha! Ha!" she repeated, eyes sparkling, "and I'm wearing everything else I really like." This was Marilyn's attitude toward the burglary; she took it as a challenge. It was crucial that she be in no way diminished by the losses; and if she could deny the burglars, discomfit them in any way, so much the better. "That one TV was barely working . . ."—she perched on Bruce's exercycle—". . . and Sandy's stereo has definitely seen better days."

But Bruce would not be cheered up. "What about tomorrow?" he asked gloomily.

"The silver!" Marilyn gave him a piercing look. "With my luck, they probably didn't bother with the silver." She headed for the dining room. "That would have been too perfect." But, to her satisfaction, the silver was gone. "That old silverware had had it," she told Bruce. "We'll use the stainless tomorrow; no problem. I know just the kind I want to buy this time."

"I liked that silver," Sara said softly, scared out of her wits.

"I did too." Bruce had not known she was in the room. "So, tomorrow is on?" he asked again to reassure Sara.

"No reason why not." But Marilyn's geniality moderated just a bit as she considered whether Marva would be willing to

70

cook, once she knew of the break-in. "They're so superstitious you never know. In a way it's funny," she continued, half to herself, associating in a manner common to her set, "they think they can hurt us; but we fake them out. We buy new things. What's the point?"

"It's a simple point, Marilyn." Bruce felt exhausted and in need of a stiff drink. But it was Yom Kippur. He looked at his watch and sighed. "Those were our things; they were in our house; they belong to us. Someone took them from us, broke into our house and stole them from us. That isn't right!" Bruce couldn't figure out whom to get on the telephone. It was Yom Kippur and his insurance man was a Jew. So were his lawyer and accountant; not to mention his doctor, his dentist, his favorite waiter, and the salesman he knew at Brooks Brothers. "I think I should call Jake."

"Why?" Marilyn asked as he left the room.

Because we're brothers, he said to himself. To Marilyn he called over his shoulder, "You know Jake; he'll be interested."

———◆———

Jake was in his pajamas when the telephone rang. He lifted the receiver and listened for several instants before dropping onto the bed like a dead weight. The tiny light clipped to Mitzi's crossword-puzzle board drooped and she gave him a dark look. "I'll be right over." Jake fished for his socks. But Bruce didn't want that. He was sure. They were all going to bed. No sooner did Jake, still on his hands and knees searching amid the ruffles of the bedskirt, hand the receiver to Mitzi to replace, than the buzzer at the downstairs door sounded. Jake was bewildered.

"Was Bruce burglarized?" Mitzi asked, pencil poised.

"On Yom Kippur." The buzzer sounded again. "Who?" Jake put on his maroon paisley robe and responded with a buzz of his own. Minutes passed.

"Poor Marilyn. I'll call in the morning." Mitzi watched Jake pace back and forth along the foot of the bed. "I like you in that robe," she told him, her eyes filled with love. "I'm going to get you an ascot." In truth Jake did look dignified, though far too rumpled for Hollywood.

"How long does it take to walk a flight of stairs?" Jake sat down on Mitzi's side of the bed looking worried.

"Burglars do not buzz up first," Mitzi said as the knock finally came. "Maybe it's a telegram."

"I don't think they have telegrams anymore." Jake went to the door and looked through the peephole, another landlord improvement. "It's the police," he called to Mitzi, opening the door.

Officer DiMaria identified himself. "Do you know her?" he asked, pointing out to the landing at a shrunken, stick-like figure wearing a cloche hat. "Does she live here?"

Mitzi came in from the bedroom in high-heeled, fluff-trimmed slippers and a stylish peignoir, composed, exactly as if she were expecting the unexpected.

"It's Mrs. Sloane," Jake told her, adding for the policeman's benefit, "she lives upstairs."

"The problem is, she doesn't know that; I checked her pocketbook." Officer DiMaria fingered his dark mustache, giving the living-dining room a quick once-over. Later, as he walked the quiet streets of the business district, trying locks and keeping a weather-eye out, he would test himself trying to remember what he had seen: the brown corduroy couch, a flame burning in a wax-filled glass on the bookcase, an etching of an old-fashioned street. Officer DiMaria was training himself up. His rapid advancement had been alluded to in his hearing. "I found her wandering; she didn't seem to know how to get home."

Mitzi stepped out onto the landing. "I'll help you take her up," she said, holding Mrs. Sloane by the elbow where the old fur coat was worn smooth.

"Ah, Mitzi," Mrs. Sloane said distinctly. But that was all she said.

"Which door is it?" Officer DiMaria asked after the slow climb up.

"I'm not really sure," Mitzi answered to his surprise. "Mrs. Sloane, let me help you with your key." The old woman opened her capacious pocketbook and handed Mitzi a single key on a yellow metal twist.

"Autumn is an awkward season, isn't it." Mrs. Sloane hit a note of cool empathy. She had a thin, cultivated voice.

While Officer DiMaria pondered his response, Mitzi tried the lock on the winter apartment and the key fit. "This hasn't happened before," she told the policeman in a low voice as Mrs. Sloane entered her apartment. "She's eccentric, but she's always taken care of herself."

"How do you mean eccentric?" Officer DiMaria was anxious for exposure. He had seen the sand on the mat outside the other door. "Is she—?" He broke off in mid-sentence as Mrs. Sloane, clearing her throat with astonishing vigor, thanked them and shut the door firmly in their faces.

"In that way," Mitzi said. "Also, she might be a miser; and I don't think she eats very well."

"Micer?" The policeman wasn't sure what she meant. He had recently watched Alvin Quint's startling piece of investigative journalism, "Dogfood Diet unto Death." But mice had not been mentioned. Stunned, Officer DiMaria settled for a heartfelt exclamation, awful to hear, but presumably designed to encourage elaboration.

Mitzi was quite unused to being misunderstood. In fact, being understood was one of her strong points; she had an easy time of it with all kinds of different people, as she spoke simply, saying exactly what she meant. Nevertheless, she had lately begun to sense that a new variety of bare-bones communicator was rising up to give her a run for her money.

"I don't really know very much about her," Mitzi half-apologized, thinking perhaps the policeman was holding her to some higher evidentiary standard. "Maybe I'm just being romantic."

This was of no help to Officer DiMaria, who was nothing if not a romantic himself. "Well, I'll try and keep a lookout for her." He reached down for a handful of sand and let it run

73

through his fingers. It was very clean. "Does she have any family, do you know?" Johnny DiMaria was himself one of the middle brothers in a large family of brothers.

Mitzi led the way down. "Somehow I don't think so." She paused in her own doorway. "She does have a lawyer, though."

Jake joined them. "Her son Geoff, believe it or not, lives in China. He prefers it that way, she says. He's a scholar and a true believer."

Mitzi stared at him. "Don't tell me you know her life story."

"She's told me all sorts of stories from time to time. She always has one ready. We meet on the stairs and she might say something like 'Iris was a very flighty girl, no interest in religion whatsoever.' Just like that—she starts a story."

"What would you say?" Mitzi tried to picture it. "She's never said more than two words to me."

A certain delicacy caused Jake to step back into the apartment and the others followed. "Something like 'Religious feeling can develop beneath an unlikely exterior'; then she smiles and puts her hand on my arm and says 'I know just exactly what you mean, exactly.' She's very warm to me."

"Who's Iris?" Officer DiMaria jumped in, fearing another bafflement.

"Her daughter by a second marriage, to an American. It seems that one day without warning Iris turned Catholic."

Officer DiMaria, a casual but contented Catholic, accepted the conversion without comment. "Maybe Iris comes over to visit and check on her. Does she live around here?"

"Caribbean," Jake answered, his eyes on Mitzi. "Eventually she became a nun." Mitzi jerked at Jake's elbow as if to call him to order. Instead, the elderly material tore away in her hand.

Embarrassed, the policeman stared down at his sturdy black shoes. His brother George, an Assistant District Attorney and a fancy dresser, always joked about the shoes of the lawman. But from Johnny's point of view, they were both lawmen. Finally, recalling that his official duties lay on the mean streets below,

Officer DiMaria took his leave. He came away invigorated by the conversation and impressed by the appeal of his Faith.

On the one hand, Mitzi had awaited his departure eagerly; to reveal the extent of her curiosity, her suspicion of Jake's embellishments, she required a greater intimacy. On the other hand, she had been responsible for keeping the policeman there at the end, using the opportunity to urge his zealous application to the especial safeguarding of her property. She was good at that, a friendly egalitarian in the face of her clear demand for special service.

Jake marvelled at her, the way she rose up dripping out of the bath of her self-esteem to make herself known. As many times as he had witnessed and pondered it, this Botticelli effect, he still wondered at the source of the source. Who had drawn her bath? Even Bruce, confronting her security, dropped back a bit out of range. Beyond allowing her to deal and handle, to motivate, to get things done, it also, Jake sensed, allowed her to love him.

"What now?" Mitzi called from the bed. Jake had remained behind, undecided, fingering a stack of books in a corner of the couch. "I have questions, Jake." But Jake had questions too.

"On Yom Kippur . . ." He had a thick volume open as he crossed the threshold, weaving, bumping his shoulder hard against the door frame.

"Jake!"

"Listen." He found the place. "'Before going to sleep, one should recite the first four Psalms, which recital serves as a prevention against nocturnal pollution.'"

"Jake! Nocturnal pollution! If that's what I think it is, they are pathetic. I only hope that no one in the world knows about this. It's repulsive, and what it is to you I cannot imagine." Her disgust was great.

"You're being too specific. The idea is that everything in the world is attached somehow to something higher, something noble." His cheeks reddened. "Or do you prefer the world de-

75

graded and base, reduced, diminished, everything so determinately only what it is?"

Mitzi did not care to address this question head-on. "Jake! Nocturnal pollution! You've got to be kidding!"

"O.K. But where do you draw the line?" Jake felt he was making a point here.

Mitzi looked up at the ceiling. "Are you going to be a religious fanatic or what?" Nevertheless, she tried to offer him the comfort of her own experience. "Besides, the world isn't really, what did you say, debase, is it?"

"But sometimes doesn't it take the heart out of you? The junk and the horror." Strangely, he smiled then, and Mitzi marveled at him as he went on, extending his fingers to keep count. "The Insulted and the Injured, The Sorrow and the Pity, The Hedgehog and the Fox, The Naked and the Dead."

"The Young and the Restless." Mitzi usually found a way to stay in touch. She yawned and stretched with satisfaction. "You have a long hard day ahead of you tomorrow."

"Some people stay in the synagogue all night reciting hymns," Jake read from the Code, pacing.

Mitzi turned out the lavender-shaded lamp on her lavender-skirted night table. "What does she do up there alone all day?" But Jake was in the other room already. "Jake!"

He actually came running, the loose material at his elbow flapped, his slippers slapped, and one finger held the place in yet another book. "Just one more. Listen, because this will make it clear. Question: Why is it customary on the eve of Yom Kippur to eat kreplach? Answer: 'Meat symbolizes stern judgment, while the dough in which it is wrapped symbolizes the mercy with which we hope God's justice will be "coated."'" His eyes shone with delight.

"To show you the kind of wife I am, I will buy you some kreplach for next year. All right, now, what does she do up there alone all day?"

Jake took off his robe and lay down beside her, letting the luxury of a bed, the comfort of a wife strike him anew. "She gives her money away."

"No. Really, Jake, tell me." She turned on her side to face him.

"Really." He took the Bible from the pile of books on his night table and opened it to the first Psalm, just to see what was there. " 'Happy is the man that hath not walked in the counsel of the wicked,' " he recited aloud, taking a chance.

Mitzi turned away from him and yanked the covers hard so that she had all the blankets and he had none. And even as they debated the point, above their heads Mrs. Sloane, far from sleep, poured herself a shot of port and went to work. Mrs. Sloane was a charitable foundation.

───────◆───────

Victor DiMaria, a young Queens homeowner and part-time chauffeur, was burping the baby. His twin brother Vincent loomed over the electric-blue easy chair making faces.

"Vinny, get a haircut; you're scaring the baby." Candy DiMaria tried to tempt her brother-in-law away by putting a bottle of beer on top of the television console. "Or wash it, or do something," she continued without rancor as Vincent shook the lank black strands out of his face. As he brought his head close again, the baby reached up to grab the tiny gold earring he wore.

"She's strong, Vinny, look out," Victor joked.

"Men do not wear earrings, Vinny." Candy put another bottle of beer down on the crowded coffee table in front of her husband. "It looks stupid."

"Queers do," Victor said matter-of-factly, bringing to the provinces news of a larger world. He handed his wife the baby. "She's getting distracted by Vinny."

Vincent straightened up and scratched his nose. "Can't I try?" He wiped his hands on his dungarees in anticipation.

"Once you get a haircut. You could look like Vic, you know, if you wanted to." She took the baby into the kitchen.

"With a nose like that," Vinny called after her, "no way." With blow-dried hair and the advantage of regular meals, Victor was definitely the mainstream twin. Nevertheless, it was true that his nose, broken playing high-school football, had never regained its former aquilinity.

"I got to check out in back." Victor got up stretching and they went outside together, Vincent carrying the beers. Behind the house, according to a hand-lettered sign on the garage, stood Vic's Appliance Repairs—Large and Small Fixed. The windows of the garage had been bricked in. "Put your car out on the street, Vinny. I told you that."

Victor watched Candy's silhouette with the baby on the kitchen shade. "Why," Candy often asked her husband, "doesn't Vinny ever spend time at Johnny's; he's married and he lives right there. What's so great about us that he's here all the time?" Unmarried, living at home, Vincent often spent the night at Victor's, sleeping on the convertible sofa without ever bothering to convert it, a final bottle of beer open but untouched on the floor beside him. Twins, Victor thought, but he paid his wife a compliment instead, "Vinny likes your cooking, you know that."

Now he looked up at the sky. The moon was nearly full. "You can see everything tonight. Dumb jerks," he commented as Vinny drew the chain-link gate closed across the driveway.

"Maybe it's darker where they are," his twin replied, lighting a marijuana cigarette. He had from the first preferred marijuana to football; it was safer, he thought.

The brothers sipped their beers in silence. Under the circumstances Victor appreciated Vinny's presence. These guys were amateurs, he estimated; they used a sedan for Christ's sake, a real pain to unload. Just then a green Oldsmobile rolled up to the gate as silent as could be and with its lights out. The driver, a young black man, swung out of the car complaining.

"I can't believe you got me driving all over hell . . ."—he reached back for his cap—". . . with all this shit under a couple of raggedy blankets."

"Hey look," Victor whispered, hoping the other would follow his example, "I got a reason for asking you to come past twelve and if you don't like it . . ." He motioned to Vincent to open the gate. The gate and the brick wall had been Candy's idea. "For privacy," she said because they never talked business. "Pull it up; let's go." The light went out in the kitchen window. Victor was anxious to be inside. He and the black man emptied the trunk without further conversation while Vincent struggled with the items in the back seat, pulling and pushing, head-first, feet-first, whatever worked. When they were finished, Vic's Appliance Repairs—Large and Small Fixed— housed three television sets, two stereos, a tape deck, a video recorder, a home computer, and an undetermined number of portable radios and tape players.

5

SATURDAY

Breaking the Fast

The salubrious effects of prayer, repentance, and benediction were lamentably short-lived. At the conclusion of Yom Kippur services the following evening Marilyn and Bruce drove home from Temple with a gripe. Sam Geller's name had not been read. The rabbi had gone straight through the list of "dear departed" during the Memorial Service but, unaccountably, Sam Geller's name had been omitted.

"I couldn't believe it. The guy donates the whole goddam Yahrzeit board and they don't even read his goddam name." Bruce took it to heart. He was always comforted hearing his father mentioned in the company of other souls: safety in numbers, Sam Geller had not been singled out.

Marilyn heard him out sympathetically. But she had a more worldly concern; she had guests coming. A motley crew, she thought, what a mix. And as if things were not bad enough to begin with, that morning the telephone rang just as they were leaving, already late, for the morning service. Uncle Nathan was in town. Marilyn assumed a gracious pose. What better day for the family to be together. Nathan was hesitant; he was with a friend. Hearing this, Bruce was displeased. He kicked Sandy's basketball across the lawn.

"Look at it this way," Marilyn had soothed him on the way to the Temple, "With this group, Nathan might actually help."

Now the event was nearly upon them. In the driveway, Sandy was shooting baskets in the dusk.

"I hope you'll change for dinner." Marilyn spoke through the open window before the car came to a full stop.

"Guess who's in the living room already," her son retaliated.

They entered the house reluctantly. Bruce went directly down to his wine cellar, taking his time, secure in the belief that the size of his house, the carpeting throughout, would keep Uncle Nathan in the dark. Marilyn, too, tried to busy herself. In the kitchen she supervised the slicing of the turkey, admired Marva's standing rib roast, and sampled the herring. The sound of the doorbell finally flushed them out. But they were too late; Nathan was at the open door receiving their guests, Gwen and Leonard Pelt. Outside, young Dave Pelt, one hand clawing at the knot in his tie, took a bounce pass from Sandy and went in for a basket.

"Uncle Nathan, Uncle Nathan," Bruce strode into their midst. "Nobody told us . . ."

"We didn't realize . . ." Marilyn gave Nathan a kiss. "It's wonderful to see you."

"So it's Uncle Nathan, is it?" Leonard Pelt, who listened to people talk for a living, had developed an undiscriminating taste for irony. Leonard was a tall rangy man, cadaverous, with dark, craggy features; Lincolnesque, he liked to think.

"It's a real family party," Gwen Pelt said joyously. "We're family; that's just how Marilyn and I feel about it!"

Leonard Pelt, Ph.D., whose thriving practice was built largely on the disintegration of families, looked at his wife curiously as the group started down a hall lined with silver-framed photographs. This was Bruce's collection of famous news photos, put together for him by an ambitious young gallery owner.

"Uncle Nathan is in town from the Coast." Bruce dared to hope for just an instant that Nathan had come without his friend after all. A spat, he thought with an inward smile, they were known for their spats.

"Bi-coastal, eh, Uncle Nathan?" Leonard gave the shorter man an ironic smile.

"This is a friend of mine," Nathan said, leading them all into the living room. He was using his I'm-as-straight-as-you-are voice and Bruce loved him for it. "Billy Blanc," he said without a touch of pride, frenchifying the name. A pale, blond man, who looked to be under forty but was in fact at least five years over, rose from a terribly long white sofa and came forward smiling easily. He was dressed in a pleasing variety of brown shades, achieving a degree of understatement that no one could accuse Nathan, in his baby-blue turtleneck and green-plaid sport jacket, of having taught him. All the men shook hands. Billy Blanc had the stubby, slightly reddened hands of a cook.

"There's nothing like a little cognac on an empty stomach," Bruce said, indicating the cut-glass decanter he was holding. "What can I get you?" Marilyn moved about the large blue-walled room turning on a series of elegant Italian lamps, and suddenly Bruce saw their ill-assorted little group reflected in the wide expanse of picture window. Catching his glance Marilyn went to draw the stainless-steel mesh drapes.

"We're all taken care of, Bruce." Nathan pointed to a bottle of white wine and two glasses on one of the several small tables stationed along the length of the sofa.

So, Bruce thought with satisfaction, the kid comes through in a pinch. "I hope Sandy got you something nice and California." Suave, a host's host, Bruce walked over for a look.

"If the shoe fits, wear it," Leonard joked, being pleasant.

Mystified, Gwen engineered a diversion. "What have you two been doing in New York? Have you seen anything good?"

"We've done an awful lot of eating." Billy laughed; his voice

83

was light and energetic. "There're all sorts of places I'd heard of that I wanted to try. We've had a wonderful time."

"Billy's a chef." Nathan seemed a bit shy about this.

"Thank God I didn't do the cooking tonight," Marilyn joked.

"A chef," Gwen gushed, "how marvelous." Leonard sighed; Gwen was no cook herself.

The doorbell rang and Bruce returned with Helga Grossman, her daughter Gena Stern, and her grandson Douglas. Gena hung back until Marilyn came to her and welcomed her formally face to face. She had not wanted to come, knowing they had been included only because Jake had insisted. Was this how she was to be taken care of from now on, tolerated through her connections? Was she to be a charity case? "Get a grip on yourself," her mother had advised earlier. "You don't know what trouble is." This, of course, was not true.

"By some miracle they did leave us with one TV." Marilyn, who entertained no great expectations of children other than her own, chose to welcome Douglas with this bit of comfort. The boy glanced politely at the front-projection giant-screen television at the far end of the room but he was not enthusiastic. He continued to look around the large room, sensing its cool formality. At home they had no living room; they had a family room instead. But they had no family to go in it. Douglas could be sardonic.

"I can't imagine why Jake has to go to Bet-Shar-Whatever for services. We're not good enough for him?" Marilyn handed Douglas a glass of Coca-Cola, addressing Helga over his head. "Has he suddenly turned religious?"

"Frankly I envy him." Helga was flattered to be asked. "At least he didn't sit through another one of these fascinating sermons. How did Rabbi Brody call it?"

"Computers: How We as Jews Can Plug In," Leonard Pelt said with ironic emphasis.

Marilyn turned to other duties and Douglas set his drink down untouched. He put his icy hands into the pockets of his gray flannel trousers.

"I don't know, Helga . . ."—Bruce handed Leonard a glass of tomato juice—". . . at least it was relevant, at least we could relate to it. I thought it was pretty meaty myself."

"Leonard!" Gwen gave a little shriek, bobbing over to stay his arm. "You're fasting."

"Not anymore." Leonard drank off the glass and handed it to her. Gwen giggled; she liked that in him—he was a law unto himself. "I don't agree, Bruce," Leonard said, turning back. "I like my religion straight."

Bruce looked around the room guiltily, but Nathan and Billy were off on Marilyn's art tour. "I think you'll find, Leonard," Bruce took refuge, "the majority of the congregation goes for it. We like something timely, something to relate to. As I said. Besides . . ."—eyes glinting, he appealed to Helga—". . . you have to give Brody one thing—he gets us out of there on time."

Helga refused the gambit. "To my taste, I think he talks down. We should be lifted up!"

Bruce saw that he was outnumbered. "Helga, what about something for you? A sherry?" When Helga declined, he departed on another pretext.

"I think this is also part of what Jake is seeking," Helga went on to Leonard Pelt. "Something that is not so everyday."

Something that is not so everyday, Douglas repeated to himself, automatically, silently.

"Well my only problem is when do we eat." It was as if Marilyn had never left the conversation. "They read every single word of every single prayer at Shalom-Bet-Whatever, and Jake will stay 'til the bitter end. I know him." She found Bruce at the wet bar getting out the cork coasters; it was like him to take up the slack. "Marva has got to get home sometime too, and I'd like her to do the dishes at least; otherwise what do I have her here for?" Marilyn clenched her teeth. "And to top it off, I'm hungry." To cheer her up, Bruce admitted to breaking the fast by pinching a petit four from one of the white bakery boxes. "Honestly, you and your brother, if it's not one thing, it's another." But she walked away smiling, heartened by his transgression.

Douglas watched Bruce give his mother a coaster, then discover that she was without a drink. But Gena did not know what she wanted to drink and, at Bruce's persistence, repeatedly shrugged her shoulders, smiling weakly. To her son she appeared undignified, helpless. Douglas thought of the half-eaten sweet roll he had found, fetching the car keys from her raincoat pocket. It had disturbed him, like touching a cobweb or tasting an oyster. He moved closer to his grandmother, who had remained in conversation with Dr. Pelt.

"I think what contributes to the feeling you're getting is that the man is a master of banality." Leonard tapped his breast pocket. "Clichés are a hobby of mine. Do you by any chance remember the sermon he gave his first year?" He accepted a glass of tomato juice from his wife, but returned it this time after a single tiny sip. "Lightning never strikes in the same spot twice, Gwen."

She peered up at him, her blue eyes narrowed and glittery under the blondish bangs. Leonard's idiosyncratic use of the proverbial, a source of pride to him, always threw Gwen off. "A simple 'no thanks' will do," she said, dignified, taking the tomato juice away with her.

Leonard could hold a thought. "'The Turned-On Generation: Should We as Jews Tune Out?' Perhaps he could go to the Bible for his text; but no, that would be too easy. He prefers to get his ideas from *Time* magazine and *Popular Psychology*."

"Perhaps there's nothing relevant in the Bible." Helga could be ironical too.

"Leave that aside for a minute." Leonard spoke with a hint of impatience and Douglas flushed on his grandmother's account.

The doorbell rang and this time Marilyn responded, bringing back Alvin Quint. Catching sight of him out of the corner of her eye, Gena moved quickly to the opposite side of the room.

Staring unseeing at a large work of modern art, her back to the others, she began to compose herself. She tried to remember how she looked, to picture how she would look from a little distance. The suit was right at least; Marilyn's was very similar. As the introductory small talk faded, Gena gave her cheeks a pinch and turned to greet him. Bruce, ever mindful, took her by the hand and drew her forward.

Quint, who had seen her when he first came in, was prepared for the supposition of his host. "Doesn't happen often, Bruce," he smiled his twisted smile, "but this time you're wrong. This is the one who rescued me the other day when Cone left me high and dry up here in Lynford." He gave Gena a wink.

"Speaking of dry . . ." Bruce exchanged one duty for another. "What can I get you?"

Gena waited attentively for Quint's reply and then she asked for one of the same. Bruce was pleased; he went off to make the preparations. But Gena did not like the harsh, straightforward taste of alcohol; Quint manfully declared himself willing to drink her martini as well as his own. "It's not the first time," he said to reassure her, and to boast too. He looked deep into her eyes. "Let me think a minute." He handed her the two glasses. "I may have just the thing for you." Never had a simple sentence sounded so full of hope. The pang of jealousy she had felt at the allusion to his past subsided in an instant.

Gena watched Quint lay a casual hand on Bruce's shoulder; the two approached the wet bar together. She felt strangely detached from her own hands, holding the smooth-stemmed glasses at arm's length; she did not want to part with this trust of his, and even the conviction that she must look foolish did not persuade her to set the glasses down.

Douglas suddenly became aware of David Pelt lounging in the arched doorway. He seemed to be staring at Gena who Douglas now saw was standing alone in the center of the room, dazed, a statue holding two long-stemmed glasses. Just as Douglas was about to go to her, to wake her up, Sandy Geller appeared behind his friend and the two left the room without a glance at Douglas. Douglas didn't mind. The older boys, he understood, only tolerated him for M. L.'s sake. What they didn't realize was that he tolerated them: Jason Herz was too soft, Sandy Geller too hard, David Pelt too rough, and Ben Finkle too smooth. Douglas, as he was beginning to know, was too drawn to the schematic. He watched the newsman approach his mother with a drink the color of creamed coffee. A collar of icy froth stood above the rim. Now a coy comedy ensued, a piece for three glasses and four hands, but this was resolved when Quint held the glass to Gena's lips. Douglas could see that it pleased her. So did the drink. But he had watched too long, for Gena caught his eye and waved him over to be introduced. He went reluctantly, remembering Quint at the toy store; but Quint did not remember him.

Just when Bruce least expected it, the doorbell rang again. He was positively jubilant, the brandy at work. He jerked the door open. "Guess who's in town," he shouted, presuming on kinship.

"Good afternoon, sir. I'm glad to find you in. I've come here today with a very important message, a message that could change your life. May I come in?" The stocky blond stranger fingered his "Soldier for Christ" lapel pin, waiting.

While Bruce stared in disbelief, behind him in the dim light a ghostly figure crossed the spacious foyer, beige on beige.

"Bill!" John White was startled yet not unused to the twists of fate. "Bill," he called out again boldly and Bruce jumped aside, breathing fast.

"Oh goodness!" Billy Blanc called in his light, pleasant voice, coming forward, wine glass in hand. "Is it you? What in the world are you doing so far away from home?" He accepted the hand John proffered. "It's nice to see you, Brother John."

Bruce pushed the door shut. What now? He walked to the corner and looked down the hall to the living room. There was Nathan, one arm on a metal sculpture the other around Sandy's shoulder. The boy was laughing so hard he doubled over suddenly and the arm fell away. I'm broadminded, Bruce thought, compared to Dad. He called out to Nathan in such a loud anxious voice that his uncle approached at a trot.

"Nathan," Billy Blanc said, "you'll love this. Guess who he is. It's little brother John." He paused significantly, "The one you've heard so much about?"

"Hi ya, son." Nathan shook John White's hand. "No doubt about it," he drawled, "there's a family resemblance, wouldn't you say, Bruce?"

Bruce didn't know what to say so he turned up the dimmer on the stainless-steel wagon wheel which hung overhead until the neon spokes glowed white. Yes, he noted with relief, this was no perverted joke; these two men were clearly related. The older was simply a slighter, softer version of his brother; all in all, Bruce thought, the older looked to be the younger. No harm in that. The observation made him jolly again; he was an older brother himself.

"What about a drink, John? This calls for a drink. Come on in." Bruce was expansive.

"It's not necessary, Bruce, really." Billy Blanc was gracious.

"Of course it is," Nathan said, putting an arm around Bruce's shoulder. "This is a family reunion anyway. What's one family more or less?"

"What're you drinking, son?" Billy did his Nathan imitation. John looked at him suspiciously. "Coke or something. Thanks."

"Years go by and nothing changes." Billy was sentimental.

"Some things do change." His brother was earnest, even fervent, outreach ever on his mind.

"Hey, hey." Billy laughed a warning and nudged John's bulky black case out of the way.

Bruce switched off the light. As they passed under the domed skylight, he looked up and saw the moon in a pale sky. "Where the hell is Jake? I'm starving," he said to Nathan in an undertone.

In the hall Billy and John paused in brotherly fashion to look at some of the photographs. One showed bearded men in frock coats and big fur hats throwing stones at an orange car. The sun was bright and there seemed to be a great quantity of dust in the air.

"We support the State of Israel," John White mentioned in passing as they moved on to General DeGaulle entering a liberated Paris.

"So do we." Billy's eyes were friendly behind his tinted steel-rimmed glasses. John stopped and looked him full in the face. He never knew when Bill was joking. "Nathan and me."

"Look, I didn't ask you," John said, bristling. "Remember you said the only way I'd ever know was to ask. Well I didn't ask." He started to move away from his brother before realizing that he was a stranger in a strange house and he might need the support of kin.

Bruce entered the living room forgotten by all but Marilyn. "Is anything wrong?" she said, "I couldn't believe how long you were out there. What is it?"

"I'll get that Coke," Bruce said half over his shoulder, uncertain how she would take the news.

Marilyn was impatient. "Was it Jake at the door, Nathan? We're all starving."

Nathan stepped forward and took her hand. "Marilyn, my dear," it was the voice of a rich old duke, "is there room for one more? This is John White. God knows what brought him here, but he turns out to be Billy's long-lost brother." Marilyn stared at the brothers, momentarily expressionless, calculating; then, with a little yelp, she returned to herself.

"This is a scream," she said loudly, turning to the room, "an absolute scream. Come here everyone. This is Billy's brother." John White shrank from the barker in her voice; what kind of a place was this that brotherhood should be put on show?

Gwen Pelt came over right away, as did Alvin Quint, a good guest and a newshound. Bruce returned with the Coca-Cola. Passing through the dining room he had eaten a spoonful of potato salad. The spoon, licked clean, rested in his breast pocket. Gena drifted over slowly, eyes on Quint. She called to her mother across the room. Helga, however, had just challenged Leonard Pelt on a minor point and could not afford to leave it.

"I know him," Gena said under her breath, pulling Marilyn aside. Realizing an explanation was required she added, "He seemed very nice." She saw that Marilyn was surprised. "I mean, helpful," she gave a worried laugh as she saw that Marilyn's curiosity did not abate, "but it turned out he had a one-track mind." She felt she owed Marilyn the warning.

To her amazement, Marilyn gave her a roguish look. "He's not my type," she whispered. "Too goyish."

"But that's exactly it!" Now she would not have to explain after all. "He's just totally Christian."

For his part John White could not place Gena. He had been in so many kitchens, bared his soul to so many women, that in spite of the uniqueness he knew God had implanted in each one of them, they had begun to blur; still, some were easier to remember than others, the devil in him mused, waiting for an introduction. His brother had remained loyally at his side, supporting him with his social fluency, making things easier. John took a good look at him. The sleek hair combed slick, straight across, seemed a bit blonder than he remembered. Nevertheless—John couldn't account for it—after all these years of being one, he still didn't look like one. "Fate," he said then to Gena, remembering suddenly. "We were talking about fate."

She seemed pleased to be remembered. He must work to sharpen his memory; you needed that—especially in mission work. Gena answered him with some animation: "This is a good example of it. Finding your brother here."

In his element, he began to relax slightly. "Look at it this way . . ." He took a few steps away from his brother. "We support the nuclear family. I believe the Lord brought me to this house for Bill and me to have the example of a family reunion." He pointed to Nathan. "Like he said." As she seemed to be waiting for some further revelation he added for good measure, "As a Christian, you hate the sin but you love

91

the sinner." Among the several members of his audience glances were exchanged. In addition there was evidence of less than rapt attention.

"What *is* with Jake?" Marilyn queried the room at large in time to forestall a reply from Gena. John White thought at first that Marilyn was joining their colloquy and struggled to discover her meaning. "Did he go to Williamsburgh, or what?"

"Williamsburgh," John White muttered, frowning.

But Marilyn's question was revealed to be rhetorical and she concluded with some irritation, "This is getting ridiculous." John White shrank from her again, figuring he had best start over from scratch.

"They're waiting for three stars." Douglas Stern surprised Marilyn. He was a quiet boy. Now she added studious to it. "They can't leave until they've seen three stars."

"Go look, Douglas." Gena was obliging.

"I'm not at all sure what he's talking about," Quint said with his grimace, "but I'll go look with him." Forgetting herself, Gena followed them halfway down the hall.

"It's a scream," Gwen Pelt informed her husband. Helga, caught in mid-sentence, looked over for the first time. "This man does not have good timing," she announced.

"You know him? You know him?" Gwen was squealing.

Leonard looked at her gravely, as if she were his patient and not his wife. He sought to understand the cause of her intense excitement. "What's it to you, Gwen?" he asked rather sharply.

Helga gave him a disapproving look. "This young man came to Gena's on Rosh Hashanah. Now here he is and it's Yom Kippur. Poor schnook."

Smarting, Gwen turned her back on Leonard. "But who is he? Is he a salesman or what?"

"I think you could say so." Helga smiled grimly. "Jesus loves you."

"Honestly, they have just been all over this neighborhood. In fact, I heard one of them was picked up for questioning."

"Picked up for questioning? Are we on television? Please, Gwen!" Leonard hated a well-worn phrase in someone else's mouth. This had begun to limit his practice.

"Picked up. Who was picked up?" His son David was wandering in the vicinity and deigned to inquire.

Marilyn, who had a reputation for being everywhere at once, beamed a smile at Leonard to be held in trust for his son, for Marilyn believed that the stratagems of a hostess were largely wasted on those guests yet sweating through their minority. Such apparently was her hostly grace that Leonard Pelt reached out instantly to lay a dry fiduciary hand on his son's shoulder. "One of these 'Jesus Loves You' people," Marilyn answered, planting herself between Helga and Leonard. Their conversation, she considered, had run on far too long already. Mix and mingle, mix and mingle, that was her motto.

"They had to let him go though." Gwen felt it was really her story. "He was clean."

"Maybe he took a shower here while he was at it." Leonard mocked the mother to the son as the latter set out again to wander.

"Very funny, Lenny." Gwen gave him a thin smile. He hated being called Lenny. "You didn't think it was funny when they hit our house." The pain of that insult to their own salmon-color stronghold rarely left her. "Imagine how Marilyn and Bruce feel."

"Hit our house," Leonard repeated and walked away shaking his head in disbelief.

As satisfied as if the credit for his withdrawal had been her own, Marilyn surveyed the room. She had long since begun to cite what she called an "invisible wand" at work at her parties; it was to this phenomenon rather than to any talent of her own that she credited her reputation as a hostess. This becoming modesty, so uncharacteristic of her, she deemed to be the only appropriate posture in the face of that most profound of mysteries, the successful party. Yet she worked tirelessly. Mix and mingle, mix and mingle; she was on her way again. With a sigh of relief Helga sat down in one of the chairs surrounding the felt-topped games table. She had been on her feet too long.

"It broke my heart, Mrs. Grossman. The burglary." Gwen Pelt, undeterred by the double defection of husband and closest friend, pursued her own line of thought. "It really did when they took David's Bar Mitzvah cuff links. His grandma gave them to him. She's gone now too. My mother." There was a choppy urgency to this generational saga that a longer tale might have lacked.

Helga looked up, surprised. She searched her memory for a wisp of a recollection, a story of a cuff link found to meet and match this recital of cuff links lost, but in vain. She brought the heel of her hand to her forehead in a vigorous gesture of disgust. "Am I senile already?" she said aloud, impatient with herself. But Gwen, misunderstanding, scurried for cover, eyes blinking rapidly, sending an SOS. "Such things have great sentimental value," Helga added quickly to settle her. "I have very little, of course."

Gwen, who felt she already knew as much as she wanted of Helga's past, made her excuses and left the older woman to sit at the green felt table and reflect with grim emphasis on the ways in which life was or was not a game.

"Are you the one the cops picked up?" Leonard Pelt heard his son ask as he approached. He admired the kid, glad he had never encouraged reticence or taught him manners. That kind of boy would make his way in the world, Leonard thought. There was no stopping him. Insofar as Leonard was right, at least with regard to the latter judgment, he was a credit to his profession.

"It was a mistake," John White said serenely. "They cleared it up in about fifteen minutes." He snorted indulgently, making little of it. "The cops were real nice. They gave me a ride back and everything."

"They gave him a ride back and everything." At sixteen, Dave Pelt's sarcasm tended to have a hit-or-miss quality. "I don't suppose it could have anything to do with the color of your skin, could it?"

John White looked at him in surprise and then turned the other cheek. Billy took up for him. "Or what about his name?" Billy matched the boy's sarcasm. "Maybe they did it on account of his name. White." He spat it out.

Leonard put a hand on his son's shoulder. He felt inclined to be objective. "I don't think you can deny David's point," he said with quiet authority. His son shrugged and gave him a sour smile.

"Sorry fellas," Nathan broke in, at his heartiest, "I can't take this on an empty stomach."

"Don't tell me you're fasting, Uncle Nathan," Bruce called, overhearing.

"Fasting?" John White's head was spinning.

"Just being diplomatic, Brucie. I can't take it on a full stomach either."

"Am I the only one then?" Bruce studied his guests, head cocked, as if to sniff out the members of a secret society among them.

"No, I am," said Leonard Pelt.

"I, too," said Helga.

"I am too," said Douglas.

His mother stared at him. "What! He's joking." She appealed to the others. "He didn't have a Bar Mitzvah, but now he's fasting."

Jewish, Quint thought, bending toward her without discernible purpose. Good! The years in Bonn had unaccountably predisposed him to that people. He had known from the start it was a mistake to have Ilse come back with him. Of course, now she was claiming she had come for her own reasons. The bitch. She was pretending to have used him. Quint nearly laughed out loud.

"What's going on?" John White asked his brother at the first opportunity. They were standing together in front of a large modern work, all metallic red and orange and the deep, lively blue of midnight.

"Beats me." That was the old Billy talking, John noted with relief. "I'm not much for modern art." Billy sat down hard on a stylish wooden chair backed against the blue wall. The chair was hand built of an exotic wood and to a proportion undreamt of by the craftsmen of a more contemplative day.

"No," John said. "I mean these people fasting." He stared at the few square inches of canvas directly in front of him, keeping his voice low.

"It's a Jewish holiday." Billy shifted in the chair.

John looked down, grinning. "You know what Dad would say." For the first time he felt brotherly.

Billy leapt out of the chair, his face flushed. "I don't know and I don't want to know."

"Same old Bill, huh. Well, so much for the family reunion."

Nathan came bouncing across the room with a just-opened bottle of wine. He filled Billy's glass and took a sip from it. "Sam would have eaten this up," he said, gesturing with the bottle to indicate the party at large. "My brother loved being a brother, a father, a husband, whatever. He may not have liked me very much, but Sam loved being a brother."

"Well, I guess I ought to be going." John White looked across the room fearfully.

"No, you can't do that," Nathan said, jovial, interposing himself. "Marilyn's had another place set; it looks like a great spread."

"What're we having?" the brothers asked in unison, one suddenly hungry, the other a chef.

Mitzi entered, all apologies and without Jake. But in their haste to greet her and finally begin dinner, no inquiries were made as they swept her back down the hall and into the dining room. Jake stood all smiles in front of the buffet.

"What took you so long?" he asked, picking up one of Marilyn's austere black-rimmed plates.

"Look who's here," Bruce called out, taking the edge off Jake's joke.

"'Why it's good old reliable Nathan, Nathan, Nathan Nathan Detroit,'" Nathan sang as he and Jake danced toward each other, two whirling, blushing Russians on a binge.

"'Hello there, you with the stars in your eyes,'" Jake sang after their embrace, alluding to his uncle's home in the Hollywood Hills.

"'My boy Bill he'll be tall and as tough as a tree,'" Nathan sang in turn pointing to Billy.

"'Getting to know you, getting to know all about you.'" Jake put out his hand.

"'Getting to like you, getting to hope you like me,'" Billy replied in his light tenor.

Jake turned to greet his sister-in-law. "'This is a real nice clambake, we're mighty glad we came.'"

"Jake, please! Everybody's starving. Here, take a plate, Alvin, and you too . . ."—she paused, her mind a blank—". . . Billy's brother." She took a moment to give John White a dazzling smile.

Bruce, his plate already heaped high, sat down at one of the two tables they had set up. "Great to have Uncle Nathan here," he called to Jake.

"'Gonna take a sentimental journey to renew old memories,'" Jake sang from the sideboard where he was filling a liqueur glass with cognac. He handed it to Nathan and poured another for himself.

They toasted each other, singing "'L'chayim, L'chayim to life,'" and this time Helga and Gwen Pelt joined in.

"Enough already." Marilyn took each man by the arm and turned them toward the buffet. "Jake, Nathan, you're in everybody's way."

"Wait a minute." Jake put out a hand to stop John White as he passed. "If you can't beat 'em, join 'em, is that it?" Jake laughed, looking around the room, used to discovering things for himself.

It took a moment for John to make the connection. Stiffnecked; why couldn't he spot them? As if sensing his brother's sudden vulnerability Billy came and stood by his side. His plate was an exercise in moderation.

"There's no simple explanation, Jacob." Nathan plucked an

olive from Billy's plate, creating an uneasy tension among the olives left behind. "The door opened and there he was." He popped the olive between pursed pink lips.

"'Strange, dear, but true, dear,'" Jake sang.

"Move! I mean it." Marilyn was getting annoyed.

The buffet was crowded with platters of roast beef and turkey, a glass plate for the smoked salmon, baskets of bagels and rye bread, bowls filled with herring in cream, whitefish salad, potato salad and cole slaw, a relish tray and a cheese board. Jake jollied Marilyn along as she made up a plate for herself. In spite of her earlier cries of hunger, Marilyn believed that it was inappropriate for a hostess to eat, except as she must set an example for her guests. To appear to enjoy the food at one's own party struck her as unseemly, declassé, as if to imply one ate any less well on an ordinary day. Jake served himself some herring in cream and then from the sideboard coffee cake and a cup of strong coffee, fearlessly balancing the former plate atop the cup and saucer to keep the coffee hot. Marilyn watched him like a hawk, Mitzi held her breath; the dining-room rug was white. He studied the two round tables—one empty chair remaining at each—and sat down between Helga and Uncle Nathan at the "children's table." Nathan pushed a crystal bowl filled with whipped cream toward him and Jake spooned a mound of cream onto his coffee, sighing deeply, happily. This was the way to break a fast.

John White, having retreated to the powder room to smoke an illicit cigarette and consider his options in the face of Jake's implied challenge, felt calmer in the silence of the small silver-papered room. Pressed into a corner with one foot up on the toilet cover he flicked his ashes into the sink as neatly as he could. Best let the matter drop, he considered, stay away from the guy, lunch up and then get out. He blushed to think his presence in this home had been thus misinterpreted. The man's mockery had left him speechless, and this was happening too often as he made his way up and down these suburban streets. Perhaps he had gone out on his own too soon, before he had his part down pat, before he had all the answers. But self-doubt only discouraged him. And he was to remain unaware that he had gone out on his own not only without all the answers, but even before he had asked any of the questions. He held his cigarette under the faucet and dropped it into the mirrored wastebasket.

He vowed to work harder at his witnessing, to put a little more pizazz into his pitch. Hadn't he watched Big John at work, the master, seen the warmth in his eyes, the twinkle, and simultaneously been chilled by the cold wind of the End of Days? "Just let your faith well up," that had been Big John's advice, the sum and substance of it, and he, Little John, had been disappointed. It wasn't very much to go on. What would Big John make of this mocking challenge, this suggestion that Bible-believing, evangelical Christianity was just not up to the job: "If you can't beat 'em, join 'em"?

He pictured it: Big John in his black suit, the vest stretched across his manly paunch, stopping dead in his tracks to give the guy a pity-filled smile. "My friend," he would say, pointing at him with the Bible he always carried and giving it a friendly shake, "I'm going to get down on my knees here and now. That's right, here in front of all these folks. I'm gonna get down on my knees and pray for you. I'm a Christian, my friend, and Jesus tells us, 'Pray for them which despitefully use you and persecute you.'" By this time of course the guy would either take off, tail between his legs, or start talking a mile a minute and before you knew it Big John had him all signed up. He could do it anywhere; Little John smiled, remembering the gas station.

You have a ways to go, my friend, he told himself in the mirror, firming up his resolve. He looked at himself carefully and with some surprise. His unassuming lifeguard's features benefited from the flattering lighting Marilyn had had installed and he left the room heartened, as she had intended.

When he returned to the dining room the babble of sound hit him, nearly barricaded him in the wide doorway. He had noted

99

it from the first—these people were noisy. He saw with dismay that the chairs at his brother's table were all occupied and someone, he wondered who, had put together a plate of food for him and set it down next to the woman he had rescued at the delicatessen. Ignored by his dinner companions, he sat down and studied his plate. What had looked from a distance to be a plate of sliced ham on the candle-lit buffet appeared on closer inspection to be something quite different. He poked his fork at it, bobbed his head, and sniffed silently; it was fish.

"Look, I'm a newsman, a journalist," Alvin Quint, sitting on the other side of Gena, told Leonard Pelt. "You can't blame it on me. We don't make the stories up, you know, we just report them."

Leonard applied cream cheese to half a bagel. "I do blame it on you."

"Well—" Quint started to back off. "I guess there's enough blame to go around." He reached for the mayonnaise.

"I'm a psychologist, Alvin." The threat in Leonard's tone was ironical. "You can take it from me—some people deserve more blame than others."

Quint stared in disbelief. What did this rude man want of him? "I'm not sure what you mean."

Leonard Pelt added smoked salmon and a slice of raw onion to his bagel. "I can't help you there, Alvin. But I will venture this observation."

Quint tried to look interested. Bruce was up pouring the wine. No help there. He caught Gena's eye and served up a wink and a smile, more for his own sake than for hers. Nevertheless, she reached over and touched him lightly, briefly, on the leather patch at his elbow.

Leonard ate his bagel. "It's all very well for you to claim that you bring your viewers the world." He paused to indicate he meant the opposite. "Of course, you have no shame; a sense of shame is entirely absent."

"Shame," Quint echoed, taken aback, getting angry.

Leonard pressed on. "You banalize, you bastardize, you mislead . . ."

"Mislead!" Quint interrupted. "You're out of line there, Doctor. Ours is a heavy responsibility, but I believe we meet it responsibly."

"Really." Leonard raised his heavy eyebrows for effect. "Then tell me . . ." He paused for a sip of wine, letting Quint squirm. "How does a Nobel Prize winner feel when the announcement of the award is made?"

Quint drew back, suspicious; a piece of turkey breast quivered on his fork.

"Why, he's surprised, pleased, perhaps even gratified." Leonard Pelt answered his own question kindly, calmly. "And how does a mother feel when she learns her son has been shot by a policeman? Or an eight-year-old feel to have won a spelling bee? How does a young widow feel? How does a steelworker feel . . ."—he sneered the word—". . . after two years of unemployment? How does a mass murderer feel on his way to the chair?" Leonard's voice had risen with each question and the other conversations in the room had gradually stopped. All eyes were on him. Quint himself was staring, waiting tensely for the point to be made. So Leonard took the time to push his chair back from the table and carry his plate purposefully to the buffet. With his back to them he delivered the coup de grace, icy and precise. "How does an athlete feel, Alvin, before the big game?"

"I've never worked the sports desk and I never will." It was a matter of pride with Quint.

Leonard turned quickly. "He feels great. For Christ's sake, don't you even know that? He feels . . ."—he drew the word out and underlined it by slashing a mustard-coated knife through the air—". . . great."

Marilyn now approached the buffet and spoke calmly. "I want everyone to follow Leonard's example. There's lots here and more in the kitchen." She looked around the room for a catalyst. "Uncle Nathan, what about you?" Nathan obliged her, in spite of a dirty look from Billy, and the other guests followed, filling their plates with a little more of this or that or perhaps something else for which there had earlier been no room.

Jake had been quiet, sitting back, allowing Uncle Nathan and Billy to entertain Helga and the children with stories of the people they knew on the Coast. Among their acquaintances they counted several well-known cartoon voices, as well as one-half an intergalactic villain—a space giant, a hot property: "Wagnerian," a critic had recently called him. Jake listened as a reluctant Douglas Stern obliged his grandmother with a plot summary.

"You know," Jake broke in after Sandy Geller, who had also seen the movie over several times, corrected the younger boy on an arcane point, "that is actually what's happening. Except it's not life in the sense of blood and guts that's being drawn out . . ."

"Sucked," David Pelt amended.

"Sucked out," Jake agreed, "and replaced with an alien fluid, a diminished substance." The boys stared at him blankly. "Content is sucked out and form remains behind. And everybody conspires to believe that everything is just as it was. Isn't that what the Earthlings do?" He looked to Douglas for confirmation.

Uncle Nathan finished off his wine. "Is that what you're brooding about these days? Christ, you should hear them out at Santa Anita—it's all about the good old days: this good old colt, that good old jock. But I don't buy it. Things are different, but they're better too."

"Eat a tomato this winter."

"Jakey, I live in Southern California," Nathan reminded him. "Tomato, schlomato, we're very big on fruits." Bruce, who was pouring Billy a cognac, stole a look at Jake but received no gratification.

"Jakey?" Sara Geller echoed in wonder.

"There should be another name for this new tomato-type item; at least we should call it something else."

"I call it cardboard," Bruce said purely for the sake of his hostship.

Jake went on. "Otherwise these kids, for instance, will eat the tomato-type item and think that it's a tomato; they will believe they are eating a tomato; they will even feel like they are eating a tomato. The form has remained behind, round and red, but the substance is diminished, i.e., cardboard, and is in turn diminishing, i.e., it diminishes them not to know the taste of a real tomato."

"Billy," Nathan said, tapping his friend's shoulder, "I want you to meet the real Jacob Geller."

"'You say tomato and I say tomahto,'" Billy sang, unable to resist; but the conversation rolled over him.

Douglas was interested. "What about a paper plate? Could you do it for a paper plate? It's not a regular plate." He touched the tines of his fork to the porcelain. "Could you say it's a plate-type item?"

"It doesn't work as well for a paper plate because a paper plate is a plate made out of paper. It has an integrity of its own, a use of its own. On the other hand, your grandmother would probably argue that a plate is somewhat diminished by being made out of paper." Jake turned to Helga.

"I'm listening. I'm trying to learn something." Helga felt that modesty became her, brought her past to bear.

David Pelt spoke loudly from across the table. "I've got one for you. America is a democratic-type country." He leaned toward Jake.

"I think that's true enough," Jake said, on a roll, "but it doesn't really fit the paradigm. Although there have been from time to time attempts to drain the substance, I think that historically it is more true to say that we have tried to infuse the form. Don't you think so?"

David Pelt did not know the word "paradigm"; his chagrin turned him inward, caused him to lose track of what Jake was saying. Nevertheless, the matter-of-fact tone of Jake's words discouraged the four-flusher in him. "I don't really get what you mean," he said, his eyes on the table. This conversation might have continued, perhaps even moved forward, had not an urgent matter of geography arisen at the other table.

Marilyn, mortified that Quint and Pelt had come to words, decided to ride herd on further conversation. Travel, she thought, and steered the table talk smoothly through Bruce's account of a dinner check in Tokyo, then past the joke Mitzi heard on a Jerusalem bus, and on to Quint's impressions of the Berlin Wall. But when, secure at last, she rose to pass the petit fours, Gwen Pelt threatened to make all her work go for naught.

"Does anybody know what that lake at Tiberias is called? I was just thinking of a fish we had on that little terrace, Leonard."

"Lake Tiberias," Leonard answered, stunning her momentarily.

"No, the lake, I mean." Her small face gone slack with self-doubt, Gwen now addressed herself across the table to John White. "Have you been . . ."—she paused for a fraction of a second—". . . to the Holy Land?"

John White had not been paying attention. He was trying to listen in as Billy, behind him, told one of the boys about a meal he had prepared at the home of an L.A. Laker, a basketball prodigy, a gourmet. The kitchen had been customized: the counters, sink, stovetop, garbage can, everything raised six inches. It was slow going; all Billy's moves were off. Finally, he recounted, at the end of the evening he had scored. Swish, into the disposal from fifteen feet. Sandy Geller laughed.

"As you know," John White began, "we support the State of Israel."

"She meant have you ever visited it," Gena informed him politely.

"I was supposed to go one time, but I didn't. It's a special tour they take you on to see where certain things actually happened; like for instance John 6:18 was on the Holy Land Tour."

"Kinneret, isn't it, Jake?" Mitzi asked suddenly, turning in her chair toward the other table. "Lake Kinneret. It's the one where Jesus walked on the water."

John White blinked. "You're talking about the Sea of Galilee." He racked his brain for the reference. "It's called the Sea of Galilee and the Sea of Tiberias."

"You see, Gwen," Leonard arched an eyebrow at her, "Tiberias." He tilted his chair back on two legs, stretching, in charge. "Bruce, get an atlas out here will you, and put them out of their misery."

As he left the room Bruce again tried, unsuccessfully, to catch his brother's eye. He hurried across the foyer and into the den, checking his reflection in the entry mirror. Blond and strapping, he thought; good physical specimen, he thought; healthy-looking bastard, he thought, picking a cigar from the rosewood humidor on his desk. His fair skin was ruddy from the cognac and, though he looked perpetually well-fed, his corpulence was strictly of the macho variety. The fair-haired brother; almost, but not quite, a golden boy; taking in the luxury and the gadgetry, Bruce thought, not for the first time, that it was good to be blond in America.

He prepared the cigar slowly, rolling the end between puckered lips before lighting it, taking his time as one sometimes does when the outcome is secure. Yet this small moment of triumph was not to be. The atlas was gone again. He checked and double-checked but the atlas was missing. Bruce tore from the room leaving his cigar, so lately a beacon of brightest hope, to extinguish itself in an onyx grave. Reentering the dining room he found that the interest in geography had spread among the guests at large and half a dozen itineraries as well as several perennial tinderboxes and one genuine hot spot had been raised for discussion. With travel talk at a fever pitch, his entrance had gone unheeded by all but his son who now felt a heavy fatherly hand on his shoulder and, scowling, followed Bruce from the room.

The atlas had been loaned out, Sandy disclosed, to a friend. "You don't know him," he parried.

"I'm going to know him," Bruce threatened. "Who is it?"

"What difference does it make?"

"I want the atlas back here."

"All right, it'll be back here."

The reprimand continued in this vein, give and take, until they were both weary of it. "Just be sure and get it back on the shelf," Bruce concluded, and Sandy made a mental note for purposes of his own that the atlas could no longer be considered the least-likely-to-be-looked-at book in the house. Confronted by the magnitude which repetition conferred, Bruce felt once more the unease, the downright spooky feeling, about this odd conjunction between his son, incurious in the extreme, and the distinguished reference work. By eliminating the impossible, and here he was an unwitting disciple of the great Holmes himself, Bruce sensed he would discover that "whatever remains, however improbable, must be the truth."

He was determined to investigate at once. Instead, the father experienced an inconvenient explosion of love for his son; when it came to Sandy, his temperament lacked that hardnosed staying power a good investigator needs. Damn, he's a cool customer, Bruce thought, as the boy shuffled from the room. I'd like to shake him just once. He pictured himself taking his son by his yet bony shoulders and giving him a good, rough shake. Damn it, he would say, why can't you act like I love you?

Bruce returned to the dining room to confess once more to the lack of an atlas only to find that the party had broken up. The sliding-glass doors to the terrace stood open and his guests were congregating outside in the mild evening air. He stepped out and saw Jake in the middle of the yard in the light of the full moon standing with the Stern boy and his daughter Sara. He went to them. Jake was holding a hammer and a crudely sharpened stake.

"What's going on?" Bruce called, feeling left out.

"We're starting a sukkah," his daughter answered casually.

"Actually you're supposed to do this before dinner." Jake gave Douglas the hammer and bent over to press the stake into the giving earth. "Right after Yom Kippur you drive in a stake to start your sukkah."

"But we don't build a sukkah," Bruce said, looking on as Douglas gave the stake a few taps.

"The idea is to start building immediately because you shouldn't put off the chance to perform a commandment." Jake straightened up, smiling, his face flushed.

"But we don't build a sukkah," Bruce reiterated as Marilyn and Gwen joined him.

"I know. But the idea here is to show that you enjoy the holy days so much that as soon as one is over, you begin to plan for another. I like that, don't you? It's in the Psalms: 'they go from strength to strength.'"

"'They go from strength to strength,'" Douglas Stern echoed. He had remained, squatting, out of the way, sensing the tension above him.

"Jake, you need help. I'm serious." Marilyn was exasperated. "What is the point of all this?"

"'They go from strength to strength' is interpreted to mean from festival to festival. That's nice, isn't it?"

Marilyn sighed. "I'm chilly. I think we should all go in." She called to Sara, who had moved off to the sea wall and was staring out at the expanse of moonlit water.

Jake took off his suitcoat and put it around his sister-in-law's shoulders. "It's interesting," he said as they started in, "that same verse, 'they go from strength to strength,' is also taken to mean from study house to prayer house."

"Thank God," Marilyn said firmly, "the kids have no idea what you're talking about. They don't need this mishegaas, Jake, they really don't."

6

WEDNESDAY

Crammed like the Geese of Strasbourg

Alvin Quint had not telephoned in the ten days which had passed since their evening together at the Gellers', and Gena watched her television with grave attention morning and evening for a clue to his silence. But Quint appeared on the screen unaltered, constant, seemingly untouched by their encounter. She admired this in spite of herself. How strong he was, how assured, how in charge. She had already forgotten the Quint who had sought refuge from Leonard Pelt's dinner table assault behind the wall of her infatuation. She had quelled his embarrassment for him, soothed his anger, made him ready to address Marilyn's Berlin Wall gambit with his usual thoughtless fluency and trademark grimace. Surely she deserved points for that.

Though Gena was accustomed to having the television on in some part of the house for most of the day, her relationship with the set began to alter as the days went by and Quint did not call. She began to forget what she knew of him; he had been endearingly candid over breakfast at the Pancake House,

109

wooing her with glancing insights into his off-screen life. Now these hard-won, picked-over, cherished facts were beginning to erode inside her, were slowly being replaced by the exigencies of the medium. The poor shreds of reality with which Quint had managed to clothe himself seemed to dissolve in the wash of electromagnetic waves.

The return of the younger doctor from Spain was bruited about, his reappearance explicated in the literature as a function of protracted contract negotiations. Gena immersed herself in the details, marveling, speculating, fretting. The wounded vanity of his co-star and her threatened walkout led Gena to suspect that she might soon be dispatched by a careless anesthesiologist. The writers, however, went her one better. They thought and they thought and they thought and finally they sent her off to Spain. This creative decision caused quite a stir and was much talked about wherever people with nothing else in common came together.

Meanwhile, Gena struggled to retain whatever of her own vividness she could. From time to time, without quite knowing why, she would tear herself away from the set, away from the vibrant shadow figures who, Helga once said, had overthrown the gods. This was not it, of course. Loyal to a fault, however, Gena always showed up for those tantalizing, hopeful, introductory words from Mary Alice Mustard: "Good Morning! It's 8:25 and we're here to bring you your world."

On the morning of the eleventh day of his silence Gena was more aware than usual of the murmur of animated friendly voices right there in the bedroom with her. A fragment of music, pink and bold, accompanied them, bridging the gap as if for an appearance of angels. Gena sat down at her vanity, bidding them a silent welcome. Pat, a young professional, nearly a stewardess in her trim blue outfit, welcomed her in turn and introduced the other women who sat, apparent agents of free will, willy-nilly on the floor, chair, or sofa around her. One of these women was an expert, had written a book, would be called on for statistics and study results. Gena waited anxiously for the topic of the day to be announced. Pat, exuding the peculiar glamour of her careerism, toyed for just a veristic instant with her coffee mug before giving out the subject as "Is There Life after Divorce?"

The Expert's features, severe under a gray pageboy cut, softened at the mention of her book, for so coincidentally was it titled, while the women chuckled, looked morose, or nudged each other slyly according to the state of their affairs.

That musical fragment again, blending so artfully with the female sounds, smoothed Gena's way to the kitchen where she put on the kettle for instant coffee. She took down her own coffee mug—"Mom" it was inscribed noncommittally—and waited for the water to boil. There was no need for impatience or anxiety as her new acquaintances could, and instants later did, join her in the kitchen. It was solely for her own comfort that she preferred they all gather in the bedroom, for that and for the verisimilitude that the larger screen provided. Nevertheless, she sat with her coffee at the white Formica table, eager to share. And without further ado, a sweet-faced young woman went right to the heart of the matter. Dating was hard, she said.

"For you, Nancy?" Pat joshed. "Oh, I can't believe that."

"If it's hard for you," an older woman challenged, "how do you think it is for us?"

"My research does show that dating is hard," the Expert offered. "In fact, there is one fascinating study which did find that for some women dating is very hard."

The Older Woman, her face suddenly filling Gena's screen, nodded her agreement. She wore a scarf at her throat. Gena, hearing the faint strains of the familiar fragment, hurried to her bathroom. When minutes later she entered the bedroom it was to hear Pat's feisty reductio. "What it comes down to, doesn't it, is do you call him or do you wait for him to call you?" Gena listened ever more closely.

"I'd like to share an experience I had," a dark-haired woman of Gena's age said quietly. The others settled themselves;

there was electricity in the air. "I met this man that I really liked and he seemed to like me too, but then all of a sudden he didn't call. I was kind of upset because I really liked him. One morning I had the show on and I heard some advice and that same day, his name is Tom, he came by and now we're, I guess you could call it going together." She smiled and nodded as several of the women applauded while others cooed their delight.

"Isn't that just great!" Pat spoke for them all.

"These are wonderful insights Donna has given us," the Expert said, warm and encouraging, "but my studies show that nearly half of all divorced women under the age of forty are still relying on their own feelings and experience." Frowning, she looked around the room and several of the women were unable to meet her glance. The music rose forcefully to cover their discomfiture.

Gena decided to take a long bath. She allowed the tub to fill while two minority women exchanged snippets of autobiography. Time was running out. Pat expressed her gratitude to their expert, Dr. Zwick. Dr. Zwick finished with a flourish.

"How many of you ladies believe in post-divorce pre-marital sex?" Gena, naked now, peered in from the bathroom to get the results. An indeterminate number of hands were shyly raised.

"One hand only, please," Pat interjected to general laughter.

"Well, believe it or not," Dr. Zwick said, and paused portentously, "fully seventeen percent of the twice-divorced American women we interviewed got this question wrong." She shook her head intelligently, her gray pageboy bobbing.

"Thanks to all of you. See you tomorrow," Pat called over the swelling music, the gasps, and the chatter. In the tub Gena rested, her head against an inflated rubber cushion, her eyes closed.

Several programs later, she was dressed and putting the finishing touches on her face. It was nearly noon. She had attired and anointed herself with particular care and determination because somehow the thought had been engendered within her that something unforeseen would happen, something that required she look her best. When the doorbell rang she was excited but not really surprised. Notwithstanding, it was surprise which quickly gained the upper hand as she recognized her ex-husband, his back to her, looking out over the untended lawn. It had been, as noted earlier, a tiring marriage and just the sight of him now was enough to deprive her of the beneficial effects of a lazy morning and a long bath. There had been no keeping up with Stanley Stern. The sparks he threw off as he made his way to the top, instead of illuminating a path in his wake for Gena, set fire to his bridges, and after twelve years they finally burned down behind him. Set against a multitude of serious character flaws were his good looks and his energy.

Gena addressed his broad shoulders. "Why didn't you at least come when Douglas is home?"

"For exactly the reason that I didn't want to come when Douglas is home. What's with the lawn?" He turned around. "The neighbors will be up in arms."

"I stopped the gardener. It was too much. And the gutters are clogged too."

"Good old Benny, King of Lawn Care." There was perhaps more warmth, a more specific nostalgia, in Stanley's interest in Benny DiMaria, father of many sons and founder of a suburban-lawn-care empire, than in anything else concerning their life together. "What did he say?"

"You know I've never been able to understand him; and now he's got all these little Asian men working for him." Gena stepped back and Stanley stood with her in the hallway, seeming to fill it, legs apart, arms folded, a general getting the body count. "None of the boys are working for him now so . . ."

"It figures. Is Douglas still tight with the little kid? He's a tough little kid." Jimmy DiMaria was Stanley's kind of boy. His own son, though well-coordinated and ardent, had refused to toughen up.

113

Gena saw the opening. "You could ask him yourself if you would ever talk to him."

"I didn't come to discuss Douglas. I came to tell you I'm going to do something nice for you. I've made up my mind; I've just come from the marina. I'm going to sell the *Shooting Star*." He looked down benignly. "Now you can rehire Benny."

"Why?" This was the boat Stanley had bought with his first big killing. Gena struggled to interpret his decision.

Stanley shrugged genially and threw up his hands as if the course of action he had determined on was of so little consequence that he could barely recall his own rationale. "Either I never get out here," he sighed, "or if I do, it's the price of gas or some damn thing. Besides, what I need now is exercise." The truth was, a rumor had recently surfaced on the Street, the tip of the iceberg, as only Stanley knew. He had an inkling that he might be required to clean house soon. Like everything in Stanley's life, the *Shooting Star* would have its role to play. The doorbell chimes, hardly muffled by Stanley's worsted-clad bulk, were very present in the entry and Gena, her mind on the money, jumped.

"Well, what do you think?" He made a move toward the door. "Don't say I never did anything nice for you." There was just a hint of menace on his swarthy face, and the cutting remark she had in mind—an allusion to his having used their boat as if it were a cheap motel—went unspoken.

Gena had no clear idea that it was in fact she who owned the *Shooting Star*, nor did her ex-husband remind her of this tax-related technicality. "I don't understand it," she said with that worried, defeated look he had come to blame for breaking up their marriage.

"Never look a gift horse in the mouth." Stanley swung the door open and was amazed to face, although it meant tilting up slightly, a face he recognized. It did not occur to him to seek a reaction from Gena, or he would have seen that beleaguered housewife for an instant flushed and vital. By the time the two men rolled over her, Quint looming, Stanley booming, pressing her back into the hallway, the telephone was ringing, and Helga was the one to puzzle over the triumph and relief in her daughter's voice. Her visitors assumed positions side by side in front of the television set on the kitchen counter. But Quint did Stanley one better; having previously effected an electronic entry, he stood as well, with microphone in hand, on a crowded city street. Stanley turned up the volume and they heard Quint say, "Today at Four: Child Pornography. Watch for it. We bring you your world."

Gena, on the telephone, studied the two men. Stanley's power was evident. She saw it in his heavy thighs and broad back, in his expertly barbered neck. Aware that there was nothing physical about Stanley's work, she still could not escape the conviction that he beat lesser men into submission on a daily basis. Quint's physical presence, in contrast, was clearly of the on-camera variety. Here in her kitchen he appeared adrift, slightly ill-at-ease, gangling. Pending intimacy, Gena placed her faith in his powers as advertised. She longed to have him to herself. Meanwhile, her mother talked on. Once again, Helga would have to ride the bus if she wished to attend her class at Croton Community College. And this, she made her daughter uncomfortably aware, she wished above all things to do. Gena dealt with her guilt quickly, getting her coat and moving the men outside as soon as she finished the call. Conversation among the three had been patchy at best and did not revive in the brisk autumn air. As they stood at the curb between Stanley's little Mercedes and Quint's slick BMW, its hood still warm to the touch, logic and the will of God were with Stanley's leaving.

But Stanley took his time about it. He could make no sense of the newsman's visit, and this troubled him, for he had reason to fear the attention of the media. As far as his ex-wife was concerned, he wished her no ill; yet it could not be said that he wished her well either. Certainly, with regard to her remarrying, he trusted that this would be a long time coming. For at this juncture, vulnerable for the first time to the excesses of his capitalist heart, even the financial arrangements of their divorce were welcome to him as a reminder of his high-flying youth.

—◆—

Mitzi Geller's speculation notwithstanding, her tenant Mrs. Sloane enjoyed a good meal. Congenitally thin, widely travelled, wined and dined at all the best places, Mrs. Sloane had developed a lifelong craving for simple hearty food. Much to her satisfaction there existed not more than one long block from her own doorstep a straightforward establishment whose dedication (since 1931) matched her craving. She often lunched there among the local businessmen, small-time club women, and fellow forks. Usually alone, today she was accompanied by Jacob Geller as she took her place in the line which daily formed against the wall opposite the bar. As they had never lunched together before, Jake had been surprised to receive her invitation. The note contained a casual allusion to her "escapade," but no further material for conjecture. It had been written with a fountain pen and her script was, except for one blot below the signature, steady, bold, and extremely legible. Jake had thought of this as he guided her up the steps into the restaurant. So firm an expression of intent from so frail an elbow. A fine hand always cheered him up.

Once seated at a table by the front window, Mrs. Sloane seemed to feel that she was coming directly to the point.

"I love a cause," she began gregariously, offering Jake a piece of garlic bread from the red plastic basket. "Always have. From childhood I felt the appeal of a cause, of a dedication to something outside oneself. And it didn't seem to matter very much what it was all about; I was simply drawn to nobility, selflessness, passion. My first husband, as you know, was RAF, shot down, killed. Not compassion, mind you, but passion!" She tapped the exotic brooch she wore over her heart. "I suppose you'll say it's little wonder that Iris is a Sister and Geoffrey," she lowered her voice, "in the PRC."

Chewing on the garlic bread, Jake assigned to it such

116

folkloric properties as were sometimes associated with the pungent cloves themselves, hoping perhaps to enhance his capacity for the speedy identification of acronyms. Life being what it is, and a tavern a tavern, this effort resulted instead in an aggravated thirst. A waiter approached the table. He was a lithe, dark young fellow, dashing in spite of the dish towel he wore as an apron. His smile was big and flashy, a showgirl's smile. Mrs. Sloane saw fit to embellish their order with a few lines of English music-hall doggerel and the waiter, who aspired to the stage, attended her with new respect.

"Did you notice his smile?" Mrs. Sloane asked. "It is a rather extreme smile, but, I believe, absolutely genuine."

"I think you're right." Jake was taken aback. He had arrived at the conclusion that their stairway dialogues had been only apparently desultory; had she noticed this as well?

"Yet each went away for the right reason." Mrs. Sloane took up the thread of her story. "I was a passionate mother—dedicated, selfless, advanced. If I went a bit overboard, perhaps they, on the other hand, lacked the natural touch, as it were. In any event, they grew up quite one-sided." She sounded cheerful. "This was not what I wished, but better by far than what I feared. My children are not selfish, mindless, or bestial. Iris will be coming soon for a visit. I admire her very much." Mrs. Sloane raised her wine glass as if in a toast to that absent child.

Jake found this piece of analytic autobiography interesting enough, yet he had long since come to believe that causes were not the answer.

"There was a time when causes were of some help in keeping the idea of good alive," he said more calmly than he felt.

"Exactly. That's it exactly." Mrs. Sloane looked him in the eye.

Jake took a deep breath; here was the heart of the matter. "We are crammed, like the geese of Strasbourg," he said sharply and Mrs. Sloane gulped at her wine. "An unrelenting regimen of death and destruction, minor tragedy, profound evil, degredation, exploitation and terror—just off the top of

117

my head. The horror," he summarized, "and the junk, don't forget the junk; the junk pulls its own weight. All this has finally managed to drive out, to squeeze out . . ."—he pulled at the word, clenching his fist—". . . the great good man was once capable of imagining." He let his fist drop onto the table.

Mrs. Sloane gave him a sweet, pitying smile.

"I must caution you straight away that our work does not admit of hopelessness." She struggled to keep the conversation on her own track. "Accusations of futility are allowed to surface from time to time. But hopelessness is out. We facilitate, we enable, we gift, we grant, we fund, donate, and assist." Jake felt she was about to wag an admonitory finger at him, but instead she insisted simply, "We know there is still much good that needs to be done. We know that at least."

"Yes, of course. Good can be done, must be done."

"All right then," Mrs. Sloane said with spirit, putting out a small mottled hand for him to clasp. Her late husband's watch turned on her narrow wrist. "It has often occurred to me that you might like to be of some use to me and to my causes." She ended on an interrogatory note to shade the statement as an offer. "In so thinking, I have also taken into consideration that you might come to share my fondness for the food and the ambiance here at the Lynford Tavern." The waiter set down their luncheon plates as if to provide testimony for the case she was making.

Jake saw that she had misunderstood his polite assent. This was not at all what he had anticipated, this job offer, though the reference to their gustatory affinity was very like her. It's fine for you, he thought. But that is not what I meant at all. That is not it, at all. He let her down easy, asking to be allowed to lunch with her now and then in any case.

Her smile was rueful but it hid something harder than rue. "So you won't join me in the doing of good works!" She turned her fork round and round into the mound of spaghetti on her plate. "The work would suit you. The clerical business, the clipping, sorting, filing, typing, record-keeping is all done in the city. Once a week someone brings me my load. We could make the determinations together . . ."—she paused significantly—"over lunch. Mrs. Geller can hire a superintendent for the building." The spaghetti had been wound to unmanageable proportions; Mrs. Sloane was forced to pry her fork free and begin again.

"No, I like the work." Jake thought suddenly of his gypsy. That day on the beach he had had the impression that the gypsy too liked his work, liked to see the marks his rake made on the sand, liked to cart off the refuse, liked his independence. So why not Jacob Geller with his trash barrels, his ladder, his mop and pail? Sam Geller would have had an answer ready, made a joke perhaps to get his point across.

Jake conjured up his father, fresh from the office, coming upon him in the furnace room, Jake with his big janitor's mitts on. "Well," Sam would say jovially, "I was talking to Herman Marks today who tells me his son is getting to be a big shot, a macher, a big giver; he gets an honor from the UJA." Here Sam would put a hand on Jake's shoulder—his ring, Jake had it now in a small chamois pouch with a few shekels and an ancient tie clip. "Mine too, Herman, I say, mine too." Sam would begin to laugh. "United Janitor's Association." Many men had a store of well-circulated jokes for every occasion, but, as his son appreciated, Sam Geller made his up as he went along.

A "luftmensch" his father had called him; but in fact Jake had always had a job while Sam Geller was alive. He had worked as a bookstore clerk, a bookmobile driver, a cataloguer in a rare-book store, a bookbinder's assistant. Except psychologically, Jake had never been a burden to his father. So Sam must have had, as Marilyn suspected, something else in mind. Or perhaps it was just that Sam Geller was a forward-looking, future-oriented sort of man; perhaps he even had a presentiment that he would die in mid-flight, a heart-attack victim, returning with his second wife from a Hawaiian honeymoon. If so, it might account for his being so driven, so energetic, so emotional, and so overweight. And if that much were known to him, could he not also have known that Jake and Mitzi would use the money he left them to buy the building, that Jake would set up a card table in a corner of the stockroom, that he would never become a professional man?

To Mrs. Sloane Jake said, "Think of this. In an office building in New York City there is a man whose job consists solely in replacing burnt-out light bulbs. He does nothing else. He is always busy at work changing one light bulb or another." This information did not elicit a response from Mrs. Sloane. Her agenda was her own.

"May I speak frankly?" In the sudden clench of fortitude on her old face Jake saw something which had gone unexpressed. "It was on your holiday," she apologized for her timing; but that was not what she meant. "Never happened before; rather frightening." She took refuge in her British lip. "Officer Di-Maria was helpful." The waiter, hovering in the vicinity, seemed to start at the mention of that name. He might very well have swelled at this encomium had he not felt himself unappreciated by the brother in question. "I was embarrassed, of course." She pulled a small handkerchief from the sleeve of her plum-color jersey sheath and held it to her mouth for some moments. "Whatever it was began to lift ever so slowly, tantalizingly, when we got back to the building. Then, of course, at the apartment door, it came very clear. Autumn, you know." Here she alluded to the existence of her summer and winter homes, and smiled at him as if to suggest that her "escapade" too was merely a bit of eccentricity.

She could not have wished for a listener more attentive, more thoughtful, than Jake, and she seemed to require no comfort other than this. In fact, she might even have preferred a companion just slightly less interested, less thoughtful, but it was too late for that now. Mrs. Sloane talked on. Stories of the past were the core of her material and she told them well; yet, as her pace increased so did the tendency to punctuate for effect at the expense of meaning. The lunch hour was winding down, the restaurant nearly empty, the bar beginning to fill up again. When she had finished her second glass of wine she did not interrupt herself to order another but simply raised the glass above her head and waved it back and forth calling for attention. Joey DiMaria, lurking in the skimpy shadows of an empty coat rack, was grateful for the opportunity to approach. Misinterpreting her emphatic waving, however, he arrived displaying their check on a small black tray. Jake took full advantage of his intervention. Exuding policy and respect, he threw himself into the flood of words and held firm. Mrs. Sloane took hold of his outstretched hand; he reminded her he was always on the premises, that he was available should she ever need him, and this slowed her down a bit. He told her they would have lunch again soon, and then she stopped all at once, relieved and well-gratified.

And Joey DiMaria, over-tipped, saw them now in yet another light; he thought about the importance of gesture, of timing.

———◆———

Croton was a new community college. Its site had something of the appeal of a wind-swept landing strip of no strategic consequence. The several temporary buildings, Quonset huts from another age, had been pressed into national service once more, this time in the name of education. A building fund had been established; it's inaugural project, a state-of-the-art student center, verged on completion. The grim concrete facade aimed to dignify the extracurricular. In the Snack 'n' Wine Bar the indoor-outdoor carpet had been laid; the place was already a going concern. Half the light fixtures, however, were without bulbs so that the cavernous underground chamber was barely lit and had a sad, proletarian, down-at-the-heels look. Helga Grossman didn't like the place; but it was not a feeling she cared to confess to her companion. She was glad of the chance to be in the company of a fellow student, so she tried to put her surroundings out of her mind—once she had been very good at that.

Like the boys, Helga had first been drawn to M. L.

121

Johnson's voice. She found the contrast between its velvet blur and the ramrod precision of his speech in class both compelling and appealing. Even when there was anger, there was nothing of the tight-throated ranting of a fully-developed demagogue about him. Nevertheless, she had never really looked at him until today when he seemed to materialize at her side, to separate himself from the mass of mostly minority students, and invite her for a glass of wine. She suspected he thought it a European gesture. Now she saw that he was a nice-looking boy too, graceful but commanding. His eyes were capable upon small provocation of a hard, fiery intensity; Helga associated this look of his with a glass-blowing demonstration she had seen once, not with the craftsman but with the glass and the fire.

That he had a lively mind was clear to her from their classes, but now she learned that he exercised it in a circumscribed and eccentric manner. Sailing, for instance; he was uncommonly interested in the sea, in navigation, even in knots. During the summer just past he had worked at the Lynford Yacht Club, the first of his race to do the chores usually reserved for white boys home from prep school. He made himself useful to the members; and then little by little he made himself known to them, presumed with unfailing politeness and moderated enthusiasm to express his interest in "the water." The members liked him, liked the cut of his jib, liked his ambition, and, most of all, liked themselves for liking him. He began to crew on his day off. He learned the ropes. Then he learned the charts and, finally, the maintenance of motor yachts. It had been a productive summer, he told Helga.

It occurred to Helga that she had forgotten to remove her glasses after class. She took them off and put them into a flimsy felt case, handstitched, a gift from Douglas. Czechoslovakia, she said by way of explaining a part of her inattention, was landlocked. She herself did not like the sea; her son-in-law, ex-son-in-law, had a boat and his insistence that a day out on the water would do Helga "a world of good" had been a sore spot in their relationship. The sun at its zenith in a summer sky, pounding, put her out of sorts. Too bright, she told M. L., too strong, too pitiless, too much. And then it turned out that she could tell him after all that she didn't like being underground either, for that matter, that her skin shriveled. M. L. looked at her closely, studied her for a moment, but she had no sense, as she always had with Stanley, that he was prying for a weakness. She sensed his detachment from the intimacy he was himself creating, and found herself at ease, reassured by the former and flattered by the latter.

"O.K., you don't like being out on the water on a sunny day, O.K., you don't like being in this big cave, O.K., I understand that." He squinted at her. "I believe I can guess where you do like to be. You like to set in a big comfortable chair with your feet up and smoke a cigarette and keep the lamp down real low." He leaned back and crossed his arms in front of his chest, satisfied that he still had the touch. It was on this uneasy fulcrum, the point between public and private, that M. L. most liked to establish himself. It was a powerful position. He liked this lady. From the first he had noticed her, identified her height, her proud bearing, her foreign accent with a close-faced old actress, the faithful family retainer or the malevolent nurse: foreign policy Hollywood-style.

"You're very warm," Helga replied to his surprise.

M. L. rubbed at his arms, laughing. "I was just thinking it was kind of cool down here."

"Don't you know this game? The nearer you come to the mark, the warmer you are, the farther astray you go, the colder you are. You don't know it?" Helga was feeling lighthearted, very nearly frivolous. She wondered if this is how she might have felt as a student. "So! You guessed quite well, but you left out something very important—wherever I am, I like to talk to interesting people." She smiled at him.

"That's the way it is with me." M. L. returned the compliment, adroit, sincere. He offered to get her another cup of tea. Helga went to the bank of telephones in the corridor. Early in the semester as it was, the ochre walls were already covered over with notices; telephone numbers and microscopic advice were scribbled wherever the smooth grouting between the concrete blocks remained visible. There was still no answer at Gena's home. What did Quint want with her, Helga wondered irritably.

M. L. returned determined to ask Helga straight out a question the answer to which might enhance considerably her interest in his eyes. After politics, to which his study of navigation was tied, Jewish people were the other object of his preoccupation. Early he had got the impression that they were different from other white people, different even when they weren't being Jewish. Mama claimed it was just his imagination, perhaps unaware that from boyhood on when M. L. wasn't developing his charm he was enlarging his powers of observation. By now he had added to that a vocabulary.

"During the war we were hidden in a cellar for some time." Helga seemed to anticipate him. "I think that is why I don't like to be underground, somewhere without windows. There we were caught. Turned in. Betrayed." She took a bite of the chalk-dry Danish pastry, working her way toward the dollop of prune in the center.

"Jews and black folks have a lot in common in a lot of ways."

Helga tensed, pulling back. "Minority groups." She was noncommittal, barely polite.

"I knew a lot of Jewish people when I was growing up," M. L. assured her, certain now that he had gotten it right. She was a Jew. Though why this sudden certainty he could not say. Her wariness, he guessed, the mounting tension.

Helga drank her tea with greater concentration. What was the boy getting at? "You have the advantage of me, then, because I never saw, never even saw, a black person before we were liberated. Can you imagine? Some American soldiers. When I came to this country it was very strange for me at first." She looked around the room at her fellow students. "Of course now . . ."

124

M. L. followed her gaze, pausing as if to savor his own sense of belonging. "I can see what you mean," he said, laughing easily.

"It was always planned that I should go to university, but then the Nazis came . . ." Helga shrugged her shoulders, following along in her own track. "So better late than never. I listen; I try to learn something. I am taking only one course. And you are full-time?"

M. L. dismissed the description; his student status was the least of it. "I'm with STWP."

Helga checked her watch. "I am afraid I do not know that. I am here so little."

"Students for Third World Peoples."

"Oh it's politics. I am too old for politics." She pulled on the gray woolen jacket which did not quite match her gray woolen skirt, and thanked him for the tea. But M. L., ascertaining their common destination, insisted she drive with him instead of taking the bus, and they climbed up into the light together. He led the way through a construction site, past a steel-drum band at practice, and into the only other permanent structure on campus, an indoor parking garage. He seated her with some ceremony in his green Oldsmobile and closed the door gently. M. L. was no car enthusiast; he did not customize, he did not tinker, he did not drag. It was simply that this car was M. L.'s car and whatever was of M. L. was invested with fascination and meaning for M. L. Watching him pause to inspect what might have been a spot of rust but was not, Helga fished on the floor for the tail of the seatbelt and came up instead with a cuff link, a shiny gold cuff link. Instinctively she twisted away from the driver's side and shielded her find with her body. She had just time to read the engraving before M. L. settled himself finally, shook out his keys, and started the car. April 31. Suddenly Helga remembered quite clearly Jake's foolishness about the date. If this was not the cuff link he had found then it must certainly be its fellow; and then she thought all at once of

Gwen Pelt, and of Gwen Pelt's mother, and of the Bar Mitzvah cuff links. Politics. Was this what he meant by politics?

"What does your group do, the Third World group?"

"We have speakers, set up culture events, we have a radio show of Third World music, for instance, which I do. I host." He raised a self-deprecating eyebrow. "Music of the black diaspora. We're trying to get study groups going but it's hard."

Helga stared at him. "The black diaspora?"

Oblivious, grinning, M. L. kept his eyes on the road. "I told you we had a lot in common."

"But this I cannot accept." She was bewildered and angry. The cuff link pressed into her closed fist. "Black diaspora. What is that? Diaspora cannot be for everyone. You must call things by a name of your own."

"Hey, wait a minute now." He glanced at her sidelong, surprised by her tone. "If the shoe fits, wear it. As my auntie used to say."

As she considered the idea it only became more offensive to her, and they rode on in a spreading silence. In their class he and the others had already appropriated genocide, turned it into an everyday matter, but she had been able to dismiss that. What did they know? Even the Indian, even the dull-eyed, ponytailed Native American, had no idea, no right. Black diaspora. Then, in a shift attributable to nothing but her own scrupulosity, Helga softened. How sad that phrase, she felt suddenly, how pathetic. Her anger began to ebb. Next semester she would take the course in Black History, she decided. She would listen, try to learn something. It was the least she could do. This turnabout was characteristic. Where most people held fast to the worst in themselves when their minds confronted complexity, Helga's better nature tended to assert itself, to press for a hearing. Nevertheless, she could not swallow it, the black diaspora. Such chutzpah!

"The Jews weren't slaves, is that what you mean?" M. L. took her silence, even more than her words, as displeasure. As she had said, she liked to talk. "But that's the point," he said emphatically to obscure the fact that he was shifting ground. "Black folks had to start from nowhere, with no names, no nothing. At least you all were rich." Something public had crept into M. L.'s voice.

Helga sighed, her head was spinning; the transition had escaped her and she blamed herself. After all, a year of college was as nothing. She took her shoulder bag onto her lap. It was a large, many-pocketed, multi-flapped leather purse, especially ill-suited to the task at hand. "In the towns I have lived there have been many poor Jews."

"But they weren't slaves." M. L. twisted toward her as if to follow up a telling point. "They were probably . . ." But here his imagination failed him and he looked away again. As to whether Helga was more knowledgeable about the Plantation South or M. L. more familiar with rural pre-war Czechoslovakia, it was a toss-up.

Slowly and carefully Helga lifted a flap and unzipped a small outside pocket. Working awkwardly, her eyes on the road ahead, she concentrated on keeping the movements in her lap to a minimum. "No; not slaves," she said evenly and let the cuff link drop in. "We were swept up, carted off, and disposed of as less than slaves. We were nothing, so easily did they make us disappear. Money isn't everything." Her voice was dull now. She lowered the purse to the floor again.

"Slavery is genocide," M. L. asserted blandly in response. One of these formulations was more true than the other.

"It is too difficult, Mr. Johnson." Using his name for the first time, she could not bring herself to call him M. L. Not only was this intimacy unacceptable, but the name itself was strange for her: M. L. She kept wanting to call him Emil. Perhaps when they knew each other better. Weary, she looked out the window to see how far they had come. Never had a man driven a car so slowly.

M. L. for his part cherished each moment in transit; this was M. L., the man himself, making his regal way from here to there. You can't rush a good thing, M. L. would often say, quoting his auntie. When the Oldsmobile finally crawled to a stop in front of the toy shop, Helga could hardly have been more enervated had they just completed the last lap at the Indianapolis Speedway. With nothing resolved, their good-byes might have been perfunctory; but it was like Helga to take the time to thank him, to offer him her hand, to want him to feel, as she still could, the impress of the cuff link. Then, in her haste to finally leave the car, she gave her shoulder bag an impatient yank and dragged it out carelessly behind her. The shiny gold cuff link, which had dropped not where she had intended but instead had hidden itself in a crevice behind a wayward leather flap, was now dislodged. Bug-eyed, M. L. had it under his hand in a flash.

Where the hell and what the hell, he thought, knowing. Somebody has a hole in his pocket. But what was one cuff link more or less? Even a set wasn't worth the row out. There was so much stashed on board—good stuff probably, real gold, ice too, enough to buy into some little revolution somewhere. Get in on the ground floor, make a mark, help the brothers get started. Look out Baby Doc, look out you little sucker. Exhilarated, M. L. opened the car window and somewhere on Main Street, he didn't look to see just where, let the cuff link drop from the green Olds, and heard a score of tiny island nations preparing for his welcome.

7

SATURDAY

No Image, No Adage, No Charm

When Helga awoke from her Saturday afternoon nap, she sensed from the stillness in the air that she had not much time to prepare for her guests. However, as the preparations were few, she remained on her bed, the down comforter pulled to her chin, her eyes closed. She was aware of a weight on her chest, the giant textbook whose short sentences and copious illustrations had sent her straight to sleep. There was a lesser weight on the bridge of her nose and she drew her arm reluctantly from under the quilt to remove her glasses. Let the book stay, she thought, to impress a European heart. The sleeve of her robe fell back exposing the small blue numerals. "What's that?" Douglas had asked years before. What indeed! It occurred to Helga, putting the best face on it, that it was perhaps fitting that her education, terminated under the auspices of the worst intentions, should be begun anew with this simple text, these good intentions. But, in truth, she had expected something more.

Intentions. What were Quint's intentions, Helga wondered.

He had been seeing something of Gena, perhaps even saw something in her; yet the relationship had not progressed, had remained tentative, very nearly unstable as far as Helga could judge. He seemed to want to keep Gena off balance, unsure of herself and, more especially, of him. They never parted but he avoided acknowledging the possibility of their ever seeing each other again; and Gena, afraid to spoil a good thing, did not inquire. There followed those painful hours, then days, waiting for the telephone to ring. Thus was her daughter reduced, a divorcée yet, and a mother too. But in the end he always did call. Helga found the waiting unpleasant; it made Gena short-tempered, whiny. And when Helga telephoned, with disappointment then a factor, Gena was aggressive and rude as well.

Helga's small bedroom, like her living room, was spartan in concept while cluttered in effect, containing beside the bed, a night table and similarly styled dresser (black with orange knobs) and an old television set on a metal stand. The plain-faced clock on the dresser, though its flesh-tone housing was cracked and its electric cord frayed, was compelled by its essence to display the correct time, and Helga, knowing this, pushed back the quilt and yawned. She dressed quickly in gray slacks and sweater, applied lotion to her hands, and then began her preparations in the living room. Emil Johnson was right, she noted, about her predilection for the low-wattage light bulb; even with all three standing lamps aglow, vibrating on their spindly brass stalks, the light in the room was dim and gloomy. This, she decided, would encourage confidence and thought. It occurred to her that Quint, expected soon, was too full of one and too empty of the other.

Gena had phoned to say they had plans, they were invited to a Halloween party; they would leave Douglas with her for the night. Helga felt it was proper to invite them to stop for a cup of coffee. She would serve a coffee cake from the supermarket. It couldn't be helped. For Douglas she bought Halloween candy. In the kitchen she set the kettle on the flame, got down the instant coffee, selected a few tea bags, and filled the sugar bowl with the white cubes she reserved for guests. She had decided to invite Mitzi and Jake, to make more of a party of it, and Jake would come. Mitzi, leaving the store in the charge of a working mother, was in New Jersey recruiting for the National Association of Small and Independent Businesswomen. It's an NASIB Same-Gender Entrepreneurship Workshop, she had announced to Helga proudly, but also carefully.

The burnt-orange cloth already covered the table. Now Helga attempted to smooth out the wrinkles, pressing her palms against the no-wrinkle fabric, stretching it this way and that across the tabletop. In addition, she noticed for the first time a yellowish stain near the center of the cloth. Here she placed a white porcelain bowl containing three apples. She set up the table as a buffet because informality would be important. She wanted Quint and Gena to feel as comfortable as possible; she intended to keep a close watch, perhaps discover something of their intentions. The kettle was already whistling. Bending, she lit a cigarette at the flame and then shut off the gas. That instant of extinction, that instant when the flame was denied its life, that tiny gasp—Helga never failed to register it, to think "snuffed out." She completed her preparations by emptying the small triangular candies, striped orange, yellow, and white, into a free-form ceramic dish the color of mud, a work from Douglas's early period. Now all was in readiness. Helga sat down on the couch and drew on her cigarette with deliberation and pleasure, noting without a trace of impatience that Gena was late.

When she and Quint did arrive, Douglas lagging, they were in costume. Unprepared, Helga saw fit to bar the door for a shocked instant, but Gena pushed in, anxious to be there and gone. The sombrero she wore was heavy with fruit, a cluster of greenish bananas resting between brim and crown. For the rest, she had put on a multicolor striped serape over a black leotard and the pair of old black heels that had always spoken to her of flamenco dancing. Helga stepped back to see them as a couple for the first time. Quint's legs were bare. He wore lederhosen

131

and a short, piped, loden jacket. On his head was the Tyrolean hat with its little feather that he often wore on live-remotes and on his feet sturdy, barely scuffed walking shoes. He carried an alpenstock. Helga hardly knew what to say. Douglas, eyes averted, kissed her cheek, sleepwalking into the bedroom. She heard the television crackle and ignite. Gena covered the little telephone stand with her sombrero and led them deep into the living room proper while Quint told Helga how good it was to see her again.

Still adjusting, Helga had an idea. "I didn't think of it before, but perhaps you would like a schnapps, Mr. Quint?"

"You can call him Alvin, Mother." Gena sat down on the couch, arranging her serape.

"A German brandy," Helga encouraged. "It goes well with your costume." She gave him a frank once-over. Those Bavarian shorts were meant for sun-dried, elfin men whose scarred knees were the only indication that their legs were not all thigh. A tall, pale man in lederhosen, with skinny legs besides—it did not bode well. He must be either a self-confident fool or an eccentric without vanity; Helga would soon find out. She bent down awkwardly to open a low teak cabinet. One side held stacks of cancelled checks, used manila envelopes, a jumble of loose snapshots, and several partially burnt candles; on the other, three liquor bottles were on display. "Here, I have Kümmel too and a Scotch."

Quint settled for the Scotch and Helga went for ice. What a strange, dreary place, he thought, looking around.

"She likes it here," Gena said in a low voice, unsettling him.

"Nice and homey." Quint sat down in the Naugahyde easy chair, pretending he was at home here. In fact, he felt distinctly out of place. This declassé clutter was no setting for him; he needed to know where he was.

"It's not homey to me!" Gena set him straight, looking at her watch for emphasis.

Helga carried in an immense tray on which the short ice-filled glass and the bottle of Scotch formed a medieval landscape of sorts. She set it down on the coffee table at the corner nearest Quint who leapt at it sending his alpenstock banging to the floor.

"Gena does not approve of the apartment, Mr. Quint." There was a hint of challenge in her voice but it went unaddressed. "May I offer you a piece of cake, Mr. Quint?"

"You can call him Alvin, Mother." Gena got up. She had done her best to prepare Quint for Helga's odd blend of formality and casual hectoring by implying that he would have to feel his way with her. No problem, Quint had assured her; but Gena could already sense his discomfort. Stanley had managed Helga well, wowed her with his intensity, and then either ignored her or bulldozed her as the situation required. Yes, that was one thing she had seen in Stanley.

"She says I can, but you know—" Helga looked at Quint and suddenly, she smiled. "The problem is I really can't."

"Try harder." Thus Gena from the kitchen. The kettle was whistling.

"You have had this experience in Europe, I'm sure," Helga continued. "It is a much slower process to be on a first-name basis there."

"Yes," Quint said, although the girls he had known all called him Alvin. "It's such an old culture. On the other hand," he said, suddenly remembering, "I did find the people warm. It's something of a paradox then . . ." He chuckled. "They are a formal people and yet a friendly people." He settled back with his drink.

"Who?"

"Huh?"

"Which people did you mean?" This time she disguised the challenge and Quint was none the wiser.

"I was thinking of Europeans; but the Germans, of course, are the ones I know best. I got to know a few of them personally." He forced himself to set his drink down; it was too early and he was drinking too quickly, but Mrs. Grossman, with her hawk nose and direct gaze, was making him nervous. She

133

wanted too much. And then, too, a long night lay ahead. As if on cue, Gena entered with the kettle and began to make coffee. She had been putting him off, Quint acknowledged. But tonight was the night, he felt it, she would succumb to his charms tonight.

"I knew a few of them too," Helga said dryly, settling in, but Quint was distracted.

———◆———

Downstairs, at his table in the storeroom, Jake was copying an item into his notebook: "Dear Friend, In the ten seconds it took you to open and begin to read this letter, three children died from the effects of malnutrition somewhere in the world." There was no possibility that the coffee and cake he would be served at Helga's apartment could still be made available to a starving child somewhere in the world; nevertheless, his heart was heavy. He stopped at his own apartment to wash up, cheered as always by the prospect of a fresh start. Drying his hands, Jake was caused to recall what had been written on the subject: "We must be careful to have our hands thoroughly dried, and we should not dry them with our shirts, because it is harmful to the memory." He stopped and rubbed both palms deliberately against his shirtfront, but he did not forget the dying children. Sighing, he put on a fresh shirt.

Standing at Helga's door, however, it struck him suddenly and perversely that he was after all unable to remember something, or, rather, anything; he could come up with nothing: no idea, precept, or law, no image, no adage, no charm, nothing to set against the horror and the junk. The loss was as palpable to him as the cool brass of the doorknob. His was not a party mood.

As it was, Helga's little party was going nowhere. Gena had left Quint to parry and thrust with Helga on the flimsy pretext that they should get to know one another. But Quint had tired early and the silences grew. Helga studied her daughter, Gena didn't take her worried eyes off Quint, and Quint sat goggle-eyed between them. Strange, Helga thought, on television no one had a more focused, more steady stare; yet here in the living room his eyes were all over the place. She did not hesitate to assign this a negative value.

Finally Gena could take it no longer. "You shouldn't be using sugar, Mother," she counseled. "Don't you have any of the substitute?"

While Helga, glad of the change, stepped into the kitchen to look, Quint poured a little more Scotch into his glass and checked the time. Gena watched him, trying to make up her mind. As if he knew what she was thinking, Quint gave a low, insinuating whistle. "Sexy lady," he said, leering at her legs.

Then Helga returned with some wrinkled packets on a glass saucer, a selection of brands lifted over time from several local restaurants. A lively discussion of brand loyalty and comparative merit made the minutes that Jake delayed his arrival pass more pleasantly than any that had gone before; and so Gena and Quint were less delighted to see Jake than they would have been had he not paused at Helga's door to contemplate a modern predicament. No doubt it said something about Jake's state of mind that he was able to take in stride a serape-clad woman essaying a tentative fandango under the appreciative eye of a stick-wielding Switzer; for so had he first glimpsed Gena and Quint in a private moment as Helga opened the door.

"'I'm Chiquita Banana and I'm here to say . . .'" Jake started to sing the jingle but Gena broke in.

"I could die. Those bananas are Dole; I couldn't find Chiquitas."

Quint blinked. "You've got to be kidding." He gave her a grim, piercing look, a stickler when it came to form.

"We're going to a costume party at Todd Casper's," Gena announced, eager to tell Jake. "You know, Channel 8 Weather Watch."

"I was just thinking," Jake began pleasantly, as if in response, "that the mind of any given person is not meant to have to encounter all that is possible in this world, in its infinite, various, and vicious actuality." He paused but it was apparent that neither Chiquita nor the Cheese was anxious to express a similar concern. In fact, the modest delight, call it relief, which this couple had experienced at Jake's entry, vanished entirely. Even Helga, setting Jake's coffee and cake down in front of him, was surprised. Jake turned to Quint, who was suddenly filled with dread. "It's something I've been wanting to talk to you about anyway. You set up such encounters on a daily basis."

"I'm not following you, Jake." Quint sucked a tiny sip of Scotch in through his teeth.

"For instance, hundreds of thousands of stunned, starving refugees of war or of famine, just beyond the border of here or there, in this or that camp—should your viewer eat less himself? Should he harden his heart? Should he study irrigation or aeroponics? Should he give money? What is it? What do you want from him?"

"I'm at sea, Jake, I really am." Quint spoke as if from a height, looking at the others for a sign. It occurred to him that he was witnessing a minor breakdown, and curiosity replaced the dread. Nevertheless, he lifted his alpenstock and balanced it across his bare knees, just in case.

Jake answered his own question with the dead calm that precedes revelation. "You want him to watch the news show on your channel. It's as simple as that."

"Of course he does. Why shouldn't he?" Gena leapt to Quint's defense. What did her mother see in Jake Geller? He was so terribly urgent. What did he mean, barging in, ranting and raving that way? She approved of the attitude Quint was taking, Olympian, but she hoped he would come down hard when the time came.

"Let me take you up on the refugee issue, Jake," Quint offered smoothly. "Those pictures need to pack a wallop, they have to make you feel something. Our audience is used to seeing some pretty gross stuff on the tube, war movies, horror flicks, even cop shows. That's our competition; that's the standard we have to meet. The real stuff we use has to look that good at the very least. We deal with the boredom factor all the time." It suddenly occurred to Quint that Jake may have heard these very words from his brother Bruce, as Quint had taken the liberty of quoting that executive without attribution. He hurried on, "But good television aside, don't we have a responsibility to show it like it is?" Quint played his trump card. "What about the corpses at Auschwitz or wherever? What about those living skeletons in striped pajamas? What about all those shoes? People don't know it unless they see it. That's the bottom line today; knowledge is power."

Gena breathed a sigh of relief. Of course, that was it. She glanced at her mother out of the corner of her eye ready to accept some credit for the good impression Quint was making. Helga was stirring her coffee vigorously and without attention while the saucer filled rapidly with the overflow. But the object of her rapt gaze, her daughter noticed with disappointment, was not Quint but Jake. However, as there was concern rather than pleasure on Helga's face, Gena was encouraged to believe that she was at last seeing him for the fool he was. That, at least, was something.

"You're out of touch, Alvin. Television is power." Jake got up and threaded his way toward the door. He gave the picture of Kafka an exasperated look that cited Quint's use of the now standard rhetorical device: the Argument-Rendered-Unassailable-through-Holocaust-Association. Kafka seemed weary today; just forget it, he advised. Jake retraced his steps. "Show me the results of a public-opinion poll, or show me a mortar firing endlessly, or a prime minister climbing into a car. Show me as you must." He bent for a sip of coffee. "But don't pretend that I won't come away with more knowledge about the so-called properties of my breakfast cereal!"

"If I understand you right, Jake, you're having problems with the technology." Quint was the soul of reasonability. "Pictures is what it's about. Talk to Bruce." So, belatedly, he made amends. "It's about visuals, it's about graphics; it's about im-

137

ages." He tapped Gena on the knee with his alpenstock. "And he says I'm out of touch." He allowed himself a sip of Scotch.

Jake was pacing. "A picture is a picture."

"But what about what Alvin said about the corpses?" Plaintive, Gena asked Jake's back. "You know that expression a picture is worth a thousand words; you believe that, don't you?"

Jake stopped at her sombrero and pinched each of the bananas in turn. "It depends on what you mean."

"But that's such an old saying, Jake!" Gena objected.

Quint, suspecting a trap, leaned forward. "Are you saying a picture isn't worth a thousand words? You've got to be kidding." Forgetting himself, he finished off his drink. "I think you're being too tough on the medium, Jake. There's a lot of quality out there, a lot of creativity, and a lot of responsibility in the way we're handling the medium. When I say we, I mean news, I mean sports, I mean entertainment. We've got our bad eggs, but what profession doesn't?"

"I'll tell you one thing," Gena put in, disgusted, "television is here to stay."

"O.K., O.K. I'm not crazy enough to argue that one." Gena and Quint exchanged a look. "All I know is that it's hard for a person to be brought the world on a daily basis the way you bring it to him, without the comfort of knowing something else too."

"Oh, oh, you've lost me again." Quint chuckled indulgently. "Of course, there's a great deal of news we just don't get to, don't have the time to. If that's what you mean."

"No. I mean something grand and lofty, something noble and radiant."

"That's hardly my line, Jake." Quint folded his arms across his chest. "I believe we handle our responsibility responsibly, but there are limits." He could be firm now.

"Television is television," Gena echoed pointedly, bringing the conversation to a close.

"What about the cuff link?" Abruptly changing course, Jake turned to Helga. "Any luck?"

"None whatsoever." Helga had to clear her throat; silence did not agree with her. "I turned the pocketbook inside out and nothing."

Safe for the moment, Gena carried her cup and saucer into the kitchen, setting the stage for their departure. Glancing back, she half expected Quint to follow her, but he did not. Uncurious, uninvolved, he seemed to her to be increasing in stature while Jake and Helga conversed. I don't sweat the small stuff, he liked to say to cover his pronounced lack of interest in anything that did not concern him personally. He lifted one long leg across his knee and fussed with the cuff of the gray wool sock. Gena liked his legs; in comparison with Stanley's they were matchsticks.

She considered going into the bedroom to roust Douglas but decided quickly against it. He needs his own space, she thought conveniently, just like I need mine. Besides, she felt his disapproval. When she saw his little face go cold and impassive at the sight of Quint, she wanted to smack him. After all, Stanley was no prize as a father, and Douglas knew it too. So what was the big deal! Exactly. She would coax him out.

"Aren't you supposed to knock?" Douglas was relentless. He kept his eyes on the television screen.

"I'm sorry, sweetie," Gena said, apologizing too for the break-up of the family. "I want you to come into the living room now. You'll never get to know Alvin by watching television."

"Why not? He's on television, isn't he?"

"Oh don't be so smart. Put on your shoes." Gena waited for him, anxious meanwhile about Quint, a Christian between the lions. Yet he had acquitted himself so well; she must learn to have more confidence. Men didn't like the worried look, or so Stanley had said.

Minutes later Gena was settling her sombrero. What's the point, she said to herself bitterly, watching Douglas; he's not even trying. The others were trying, but the conversation was slow going. Then, just when Quint's threat of companionship

139

had left Douglas truly speechless, the downstairs buzzer began to buzz. Helga buzzed back. It was Mrs. Sloane came the reply, in search of the super. She made her slow way up the stairs as they waited in suspense, entered begging their pardons, wearing a striped turban, black silk hostess pajamas, and ballet slippers. Her face powder was very white. Catching sight of her, Quint poured himself another drink. Gena did no more than raise her wristwatch to eye level and clear her throat, but she had not yet learned which little gestures would catch Quint's attention. This saddened her as it allowed her to glimpse the magnitude of the job ahead. Douglas was just part of the problem.

"I see," Mrs. Sloane said, dipping her hand into the candy corn, "that today I am in no way remarkable for my attire."

"We're invited to a Halloween party," Gena said crisply. She introduced Quint, adding, "It's Todd Casper's party. The weatherman?"

"I see. How lovely." Mrs. Sloane gave Quint a vague look, effectively drawing the line. "I went down for the mail and it seems I've locked myself out. I haven't either key in my pocket." Though in fact the Chinese pajama had been designed and crafted without any pockets at all, Mrs. Sloane continued unembarrassed. "Of course, I thought I had them both."

"Mmmmmmmmmmhhhmmmm," a chastened Quint murmured sympathetically.

"It's terrible to be old." Mrs. Sloane paused, looking straight at Douglas as if the mere fact of his youth were enough to prove her point. The boy blushed, feeling that something private, perhaps even obscene, had just come to light. His grandmother was the last person to complain about her condition in life.

"Ah, Jake," Mrs. Sloane went on, "there is a letter from Iris in the mail. They've fixed a date for her trip, the sisters have agreed to it." Here was the merest hint that she did not look altogether kindly on a life under orders; yet satisfaction played the larger part.

"How many daughters do you have?" Quint inquired unexpectedly. For the first time during the visit he felt the opportunity existed for some pure socializing, and he did not intend to let it pass.

"Just this one." She took the seat Jake offered and allowed Helga to prepare a cup of tea for her. "She's in the Caribbean."

"Lucky her." Gena balanced the heavy sombrero on her knee. Impatient to be gone, it seemed to her that the bananas were ripening under her very eyes. Jake went out to get the landlord's key ring and Douglas accompanied him on no pretext at all. "Douglas!" his mother called weakly.

"Mary Alice Mustard had quite a scare down there last year. It's not exactly the tourist paradise it once was. The natives are restless, I'm afraid." Quint shot Mrs. Sloane his patented newsman's grimace, as if to validate the story.

"I should hope so!" she replied energetically. "I suspect that that is some of Iris's doing."

"Hhhhhmmmmmmmmmm," Quint lied, playing for time.

Helga set down the tea. "Mrs. Sloane's daughter is a nun, Mr. Quint." She served up a slice of the coffee cake, noting morosely that her other guests had left theirs largely untouched. Now she would be eating it herself for days because she could not stand to see it go to waste. "The sisters, you see," she added to show him just where he had gone wrong. Quint did not bring out the best in her, she could see that. Certainly Stanley was no prince, but on the other hand, very little got away from him. Helga decided she had better be on her guard. To begin with she brushed a sprinkling of crumbs from the front of her sweater.

"A nun! How interesting!" Gena willingly took up the cudgels while Quint caught his breath and drank deeply of the Scotch. Clearly it was not his day. And yet he nurtured great hopes for the evening. He would buy the newspaper before they turned in, check their horoscopes. "You always forget about them," Gena continued with determination. "I mean in this day and age. I never see them any more. Sometimes you used to see them in a stationwagon or out on the playground."

141

Quint looked at her in surprise, rolling the rim of his glass against his narrow upper lip. He had not seen her in quite this light before, had never heard her refer to a reality beyond home or screen. The effect on her was vivifying, he observed, but also short-lived. She now addressed him directly. "Did you see the program where they had on the priests and nuns who got married? Some of them were attractive and really put together." There was wonder in Gena's voice at the mystery of it all. "They said now they're all very happy."

Quint had an answer for her. "Changing life-styles are having a profound impact." Leaning forward, he tried his alpenstock for support but the wooden floor was unyielding and the stick skidded to one side. He hung on at some risk to the remnant of his dignity and righted himself, wondering whether the drink was beginning to tell. He felt it imperative now to drive his point home—for his own sake as well as for theirs. "Let's back up for just a minute—" His voice commanded their attention. "You have to consider certain facts and features if you really want to get the picture." He frowned. "I'm thinking, of course, of the Jonestown massacre, of Juan Valdez, of reggae music. I'm thinking of Castro, of the cocaine connection, of the boat people, and the cliff-divers. Death-defying," he inserted parenthetically. "It's an exciting, colorful, and complex part of the world."

"I worry about Iris." Mrs. Sloane tried the cake and set it aside without compunction. "With all that's going on."

Once again Gena put on her sombrero. "Well," she said, getting up satisfied. Quint had certainly anticipated those last words of Mrs. Sloane's. She loved to see him display himself, demonstrate his grasp of the "facts and features" as he called them. Yes! Seeing it through his eyes, it was indeed an exciting and colorful world. And he had a grip on it, she thought, rejoicing. "We should go," she told Helga without rancor. When Jake and Douglas returned moments later this decision was implemented without further ado.

Mrs. Sloane stayed to chat, but she stayed only as long as an

142

intrusion such as her own would justify and no longer. Punctilious though she was, she cherished every minute of it. Quint reminded her, she said, of a young actor from the provinces she had once known. For almost three weeks during the blitz he had played the role of doctor to perfection, performed several minor surgical procedures, and earned the gratitude of a beleaguered hospital staff. This in turn reminded her of something else, but she did not wish to press her luck. Jake accompanied her up the stairs to unlock her apartment, but declined her invitation to enter, pleading pressing landlord business.

◆

In the distance the windows of the large dining room at the yacht club were golden with light as M. L. Johnson made his way down the dark private road to the marina. He wore his wool cap and carried a knapsack on his back. As he walked carefully along the slatted walkways out to the farthest point on the maze of wooden docks, he was aware that the unseasonably mild weather was not likely to hold much longer. The marina was deserted except for the guard up in the dockmaster's house. He had a guard dog in there with him; but with his charge so curtailed by the season he had given up his regular patrols, and now only the nervy sound of children's laughter could call him forth to investigate and perhaps accept a friendly joint. Inside, a television, tape player, ice maker, and vending machine all in working order saw to his comfort. And if this was not a sufficient guarantee of safety, M. L. was perfectly prepared to spend some time shooting the breeze with the guard. After all, M. L. was no stranger to the marina.

But, in the event, M. L. found the dinghy he wanted tied where he had left it behind the boat crane. Out of sight of the dockmaster's house, he cast off and began to row silently and efficiently toward a cluster of boats, all that remained of the summer fleet. He maneuvered his craft into their midst and then made it fast on the Sound side of the *Shooting Star*. He had made the trip often enough to feel sure of his moves and he clambered aboard her in thoughtless haste, even humming

under his breath, and was down in the cozy stateroom before
he knew it. All this he did by feel, by habit, as the night was
moonless and it was very dark on the water. He reached out to
make sure that the tiny curtains were tightly shut, and then
opened his knapsack and got out the special flashlight he had
ordered through the mail. The light did not diffuse but shone
forth in a single bold beam. M. L. gaped at what he saw; he
was hot and cold in an instant; his heart pounded. Someone
had been there. The bed was a tangled mess. Two pillows. He
whirled, but saw immediately that his fortress was undisturbed.
The captain's chest, a brass-bound antique, was still piled high
with his own creative miscellany of Stern family junk. It struck
M. L. that a man with sex on his mind was not likely to be
observant with regard to his surroundings. Nevertheless, he felt
constrained to dismantle this outworks; within, in the bright
beam of light, he saw the glitter and the flash, and this second
wave of relief was the more sweet for being the more certain.
Satisfied, he looked further. In the galley he found an empty
champagne bottle, a plastic container from a gourmet shop, and
crumbs on the cutting board. Your daddy's rich and your
momma's good lookin'. Stanley Stern on the make, M. L.
guessed correctly. For thus had that born-again bachelor spent
the night before his impromptu visit to Gena. His companion, a
lightly freckled lady banker, lured by the romance of the sea,
had to grab an early train back to the city. Stanley had come to
prefer a working woman.

M. L. resecured the stash and drew a can of soda from his
backpack. He had thought to hang the other cans overboard to
maintain their chill, but best to play it safe and drink warm
soda, he decided in the face of his fright. He pulled the chintz
spread up over the bed and sat down, blessing with ironic emphasis the circumstance that had decided him to spend the
night on the water. He put his thoughts in order. First of all he
would have to pump Dougie Stern. Not that the boy knew
much when it came to his father, M. L. acknowledged, but this
assignation might signal an escalation, a shift in momentum,

perhaps even a decision taken on the fate of the *Shooting Star*. M. L. would have to know. Suddenly he saw that the man had left something else of himself behind. Under the built-in dressing table was a stained cardboard file. Now M. L. was caused to reflect that a man planning his future was far more observant than one enjoying his present. He was there in a trice, down on his hands and knees for a look. He pulled out a few papers at random: business letters, bank statements, account statements of other kinds, lists of letter combinations, columns of figures, nothing he need concern himself with, M. L. felt; simply the detritus of your average capitalist, the file would find a watery grave once he hit the open sea.

In the dark again, enjoying his cola, he began to relax and his thoughts returned to Douglas Stern. He felt sorry for that edgy little white kid who took his parents' divorce so much to heart. M. L.'s grandmother had been both mother and father to him; as she liked to say, she loved him like a mother and beat him like his daddy should have. He called her Mama and she called him her baby, and neither of them thought anything more of it. That was the way from the very beginning; Mama was all he needed; she told him that and he believed her. But when it came time to start school Mama's simple assurance was put to the test as geography determined that M. L. should become a credit to his race. The only black boy in the grade, he rose to that challenge with an appetite and flair which had gone unsuspected by his grandmother and the others who stayed with them as lodgers or relations. Clever, confident, and cute as a button, M. L. Johnson was a perfect token. Hardly a day went by that he wasn't invited to play after school at one house or another, which suited Mama who did day work until six and liked him occupied. Out of this he acquired over the years a warm jacket each winter and a taste for dinner-table conversation.

He was taken along to baseball and football games, to the golf range and the tennis courts, to the theater and the movies, and once even for a week of skiing half a continent away. It

145

was, of course, thought that M. L. envied his friends the advantages of greater wealth, but on the whole this was not the case. He had from an early age found another, less material, focus for his fascination: himself. And increasingly he grew preoccupied with this matter of his identity, his persona, the extraordinariness of simply who he was. By comparison, all else paled.

Nor did he envy his friends their families. He had been too much the intimate observer not to believe rather in the enviability of his own situation. So, involved, strengthened, amused in his singularity, made self-reliant and self-knowing by his circumstances, M. L. could claim a happy childhood. Now he came and went as he pleased; Mama was satisfied she had done her job and done it well. She was proud of him and trusted him to do right. M. L. stretched out on the bed. Don't push that one too far, he thought, smiling.

He pulled the knapsack up beside him and, reaching in at random, came up with his Spanish textbook. For the next half-hour, with the flashlight balanced on his shoulder, M. L. applied himself to Spanish vocabulary and grammar. This knowledge, he was convinced, would be invaluable, for he expected to anchor in some remote anonymous bay where the Indians or the natives or the urban masses were not likely to speak English. "Hermanos," he said softly, conjuring up his first speaking engagement.

It had come as no particular surprise to M. L. that he might have some facility for speech-making, something quite apart from his gift for glib, inventive conversation. In the beginning, when he had first taken their fancy and the boys were actually listening to what he said, M. L. would simply allow emotion to carry him. At that time he was always surprised and grateful when the sense of the thing would finally follow along. Gradually, when the boys had come to know his shtick, when his rhetoric was old hat, when they were unmoved by the appeals to their better natures, he began to understand that it was the voice; the voice had them hooked. That voice, of course, was not M. L.'s own voice, which was light and smooth, which was modest, reined in, and schooled.

He began to experiment on the boys, trying this trick and that pose until he felt he had prepared himself for a suitably meteoric appearance in the firmament of campus politics. And, briefly, the stage was his. As his ambition grew and a larger plan crystalized, however, he seemed to understand that some fidelity to himself was at the core of his strength; and this became the more vital the more he needed to appropriate bits of himself to promote accessibility—that is, to let himself appear to be known. He saw that it was time to eschew the inauthentic—the preacher, the teacher, the stand-up comic—in favor of the Cool he was most comfortable with. But would they get it in his sun-dazed Kingdom? Would they buy Cool, admire its icy heights, its control, its vaguely malevolent, surgical charm? Did it translate?

The proper study of M. L. Johnson was M. L. Johnson. He exchanged the textbook for a small spiral notebook and entered this thought: "in tropics climate hot: Cool = cool?" The little book was chock-full of such bits of speculative thought, commentary, quotations, good advice, lessons learned, and slogans of his own devising. For example, the afternoon with Helga had yielded: "'Diaspora n. 1. The scattering of the Jews to countries outside Palestine after the Babylonian captivity. 2. The body of Jews living in such countries. 3. Such countries collectively: the return of the Jews from the Diaspora. 4. (1.c.) Any religious group living as a minority among people of the prevailing religion.' Comes from Greek word. Black Jews?" Below this and at promptings obscure to himself he had written "Zorro," and below that "Cero." M. L. leafed through the book lovingly, seeing himself, hearing himself, on every page. Even the blank pages at the back gave him back something of himself: his future unknown, his promise unbounded, his inchoate destiny.

There was more he had planned to do that evening; but the book on celestial navigation and the charts he had acquired remained in the knapsack. He opened a final soda, looking forward to his first good night's sleep in a week. In a surprise move, Mama had taken in a baby—her greatgranddaughter, M. L. figured—and the infant had wailed its heart out the better part of every night. "You're too old to get another baby dumped on you," he told Mama, sorry for her, but in truth sorrier for himself. If once she had been all he needed, now she was all he had; and, in the way the mind has, M. L.'s hurt seemed to make his leaving more a matter of her forsaking him. The baby would soon enough discover that Mama was all she needed, he thought, not without bitterness; and even in his island exile he did not expect he would find another such home.

M. L. dreamt of the sea that night, a pleasant, nonsensical dream in which Miss Watson's Jim set out to challenge Mrs. Hyerdahl's Thor to a raft race; while beyond the waves a cabin cruiser with Lynford burgee sought shelter in a mysterious harbor, and was welcomed by one of the Ten Lost Tribes: black Jews.

8

SUNDAY

Lifelines Frayed

M. L. awoke as he had purposed, before dawn. Well rested, luxuriating in the silence and the solitude, he ate the peanut butter and jelly sandwich he had packed and put together his things. The sky was still very nearly dark when he climbed up onto the deck. The boats had shifted in the night and he had a clear view of the village beach now off to one side. This meant, he realized, stunned, that the two figures on the breakwater might see him with equal clarity. He ducked and then dove below deck, shivering.

But Jake Geller and young Doug Stern, waiting for the sunrise, hugging themselves in the morning chill, noticed nothing. They had come to the beach by bicycle, Douglas, slight for his years, balanced on the crossbar. The ride had seemed to make Jake drunk, and the boy met his childish gaiety with sleepy silence. The return to an activity of one's childhood may prompt a response that youth itself, suffering no comparable deprivation, does not recognize as its own. No doubt, too, Jake was better at it once, more certain at the wheel, smoother on the brakes, stronger on the pedals; and so Douglas would have been spared the stuttering, and the feeble, wobbling arcs as they addressed each corner.

Catching the sunrise had been Douglas's idea. Often on summer Sundays he had been used to awaken in his sleeping bag and climb quietly up onto the deck of the *Shooting Star* to watch the sun come up, warm in the cocoon and secure in the inevitability, as Gena and Stanley slept on below. But he had found in Jake a too-willing companion, one ready to concretize an idle fancy just as the fancier himself begins to back off. This was not an endearing quality.

Douglas's second thoughts revolved around the worry that he might see something more than the sunrise, might see, in fact, his father. Gena had let that slip, the use to which Stanley was putting the boat. It sickened her, she had told Douglas at the time when she was telling him things. It sickened Douglas too, and so now, standing on the breakwater, he kept his eyes averted, looking everywhere at once, except at the *Shooting Star*.

Jake, too, had a lot on his mind. First of all, he had no son. This thought did not rankle, but Douglas's company sometimes put his mind on that track, and he was prompted to review the particulars of his childless state. Having several years before thought he discerned the Hand of his Creator therein, Jake had accepted the disposition with a steadiness in which the foreknowledge of occasional regret mingled with present relief. For her part, Mitzi was more matter-of-fact, more comfortable, more modern. As her insistence on being up-to-date had made of her a voracious reader of magazines designed for women who insisted on being up-to-date, she was gratified to recognize herself in the literature. And as her own maternal impulse was largely satisfied by her marriage—a possibility made much of in one issue of *Today's Woman*—she too had for several years been content. As the women in her Wednesday Women's Group, mothers all, could not help but acknowledge, Mitzi was "a very together person."

150

Jake's thoughts blundered on, trying another tack. Tradition suggested a priority for the honor and duty a man owed his father: "His father brought him into this world, but his teacher who instructs him in wisdom brings him thereby into the world to come." Given that he neither had a teacher nor was a teacher, Jake had yet found an obscure comfort in this writing. But Sam Geller, presumed to be at peace, decided just then, as he had so often in life, to make his needs known to his son. All constituted of dew in the gray dawn, he was unwittingly literary in his attempt to save his son for secularity. "Remember me," was all he said before evaporating in the warming air. Jake sighed. Substance is substance, he thought, scanning the horizon. And glory, glory.

"'Oh, the road to Mandalay, where the flyin'-fishes play, An' the dawn comes up like thunder outer China 'crost the Bay!'"

Douglas started, for Jake had quoted these lines in a loud, rough, dramatic voice which was at odds with his own slowly developing mood. Gradually, the recollected comfort of milky sleep had receded and he had gotten caught up in the mystery of the diurnal arc and the romance of the early hour. "What's that?" he asked, barely polite.

"Poetry. Do you know some?"

"Not particularly." Douglas tried to convey the impression that he was more a scientist than a humanist by keeping his eyes glued to the horizon.

"'The dawn comes up like thunder.' Do you like that?"

"I guess so. . . . Hey—" Douglas motioned. "Here it comes." He pulled off the hood of his sweatshirt, threw back his head, opened his mouth wide, and took a bite of the morning air. "Hey," he said again.

This animal vitality touched Jake. He faced the sun, unprepared, indeed shocked, to receive a perverse reminder: here today, gone tomorrow. It was impossible that this thought should not bring tears to his eyes; a cliché truly felt may move a man like nothing else.

That had been the hardest part, the disappearance of Sam

151

Geller, here today, gone tomorrow. Suddenly the man was no-where to be found, nowhere in this world, not hiding, simply no longer in existence; he had vanished completely. But not without a trace. He had a son. Two yet. Jake shifted his feet, seeking comfort. Somewhere in the back of his mind he heard the solid, satisfying, hopeful sound of two billiard balls coming together. Thus did he put Life and Death in perspective and boost his spirits besides.

"I just remembered a poem I know." Douglas's eyes strayed to the *Shooting Star*, but he saw no sign of life there. "My Dad taught me. Red sky at night, sailor's delight. Red sky in the morning, sailor's warning." He spoke the words dully, du-tifully, as if reciting a bit of magic formula or an ancient ancestral prayer which the present had rendered incomprehen-sible.

It was fully daylight now and Jake felt his earlier exhilaration return. "Here's what one of the commentators said," he began enthusiastically. "When God created the world, God saw that 'it would not be fitting for light and darkness to function simul-taneously.' What about that? Do you like that?" The boy was noncommittal and Jake swallowed his disappointment. "Raise up many disciples"; so it had been written.

Douglas came right back, however, sensing that something had gone sour. "You remind me of my mother in one way. We'll be somewhere, at a restaurant, and when I ask for a hot dog, she'll go 'Hot dogs, Armour hot dogs.' You know? Or you'll be in the car and she'll say, 'Toyota, we are driven.' She just does that all the time."

"I see."

"Well," Douglas said, at a loss.

Jake led the way in off the breakwater. As they approached the bicycle resting in the sun against the bathhouse wall, he stopped so abruptly that Douglas, his mind elsewhere, walked straight into him.

"Those are commercials!" Jake began indignantly, wheeling, and Douglas gave him a wary look. Jake, he had noticed, often

152

delivered a simple sentence as if it were filled with meaning; and so now, hungry for breakfast, Douglas began a halfhearted exegesis.

A door creaked close at hand. Jake jumped at the sound while Douglas gaped at the sight. A figure emerged from the dark of the bathhouse, though that verb dignifies him, for what the man did was hop; zipped as he was into a green sleeping bag, he hopped out the door and hopped down the path toward them. He was significantly unshaven and his white T-shirt was grimy. He did not look well rested.

"What happened to you?" Jake asked, amazed.

"I got fired," John White said, starting to step out of the sleeping bag before he remembered his skivvies and clutched the plaid lining to his loins. "Not really fired but what they call it, reassigned. The prayer hot line. But I said, uh, uh, no way, the hell with that shit! They didn't even give me a chance. I was really getting good too; but Big John couldn't care less. Well, fuck him!"

Jake had never heard him so voluble, yet he could have wished the man's faith to have stood him in better stead. "I'm sorry," he said and actually shuddered, glimpsing for an instant that sunshine sailor's lifelines frayed, unraveling, snipped.

"Then on account of that," the other continued, "I got kicked out of the house." He imputed to his former mentor an effete, mincing voice, "'I don't like your language.' Well fuck him," Little John said again for good measure. Now his problem was, he was frank to add, that he was without funds, without friends. Big John had in his fury ripped the gold pin from his lapel, depriving him of a potential pawn. "The bastard," John White concluded, his anger no less for the plating.

Jake had by now determined to offer hospitality. He caught Douglas's eye as a formal courtesy. The boy stood a little apart, rolling the bike back and forth, his trigger finger itchy on the silver bell, looking for a way out. He had taken no especial notice of John White at their first meeting and the man's current condition did nothing to engage his interest. That seedy, down-and-out look which, were Douglas several years older, might intrigue him and so spark a career in politics or country music, did not yet take his fancy. But he did look up when he heard John White take the name of his Lord in vain.

"Jesus Christ, what is that?" White turned tail, hopping for the bath house. On the other side of the beach, perhaps fifty feet away, Jake's gypsy rose from behind a boulder and motioned for his youngest brother to follow suit. Vinny DiMaria was bored with waiting. His brother Victor had told him to keep an eye on the black guy, and last night Vinny had shadowed him down to the marina. Show up real early in the morning, Vic had instructed: and he had, and he had seen what he came for. He and Victor had put one and one together alright. No doubt about it, the jewelry had to be on board. He lifted the binoculars over his head and passed them to his brother who remained crouching behind him.

"Vic said to stay out of sight," Jimmy DiMaria cavilled, though uninformed as to the true purpose of the dawn outing. As the youngest of many brothers he had found attention to detail the surest way of earning their esteem. "Besides, that kid is Doug. He knows us." But it was too late for discretion.

"Big deal," Vinny said. "We could be here forever because that guy with curly hair loves to talk. Anyway, I'm taking Ma to Mass. And besides, who was the one to spot the dinghy? I know what I'm doing."

Jimmy put the binoculars away carefully. They were on loan from George and George treated everything he owned very well. George DiMaria, Assistant D. A., good-looking, able to cut a guy down to size with a few well-chosen words. Someday I'm going to be his campaign manager, Jimmy thought, coming out of hiding.

"Hey," Douglas called, and arranged for a ride home with his friend in order to broaden the horizon on his morning. The constraint and community he had felt in Jake's company began to drop away and the immediate prospect of having things his own way, living free, unfettered, unformed, unchecked, charged his skinny body with a paralyzing energy which dazed him, which dulled his taste but excited his appetite. And freedom would be all the sweeter for being inaugurated with a genuine, country-fresh, fast-food breakfast.

"Victor don't know everything," Vincent muttered to his brother in farewell, handing him five dollars beneath the Golden Arches.

"Hey," Jimmy responded, taking Vinny to mean "Don't have to know"; but here he was selling his brother short. Vinny was just as capable as the next fellow of slipping and meaning two things at once.

It was not until Jake saw the truck pull away that he recognized his gypsy. It was a side of the man that Jake had never contemplated—this interest in natural things, this brotherly love. He reminded himself, as he joined his guest at the bathhouse door, of the dangers of ill-tempered, ill-considered judgments. Perhaps John White, dressed now and carrying his suitcase in one hand and his sleeping roll in the other, would surprise him as well. His appearance presently, however, did not inspire confidence. They set off, Jake pushing the bicycle and listening attentively while John White recounted, with palpable nostalgia, his triumphs and defeats as they crossed the territory he had made his own.

On board the *Shooting Star*, M. L., finally risking another ascent, watched their departure. He wiggled his shoulders loose and shook the tension out of his hands. Below decks he had felt a veritable Pip among the gravestones with the convict Magwitch on the prowl. He smiled now, rid of his sickening fear. That was a good old movie, M. L. thought, warmed by the sun, climbing down into the dinghy.

◆

Few things could have surprised Jake more than how well Mitzi and John White got along from the very start. Mitzi, who was usually so adamant about having her Sundays to herself because she had "a lot of catching up to do," insisted on going out for the bagels while the erstwhile evangelist showered and

155

Jake searched for the sweatsuit Bruce had loaned him the month before. Although he shopped at the supermarket regularly, Jake had failed to notice that the covers of the magazines there were no longer devoted to the issue of Pregnancy Past Forty. There was something new, and reports of its appearance reached the magazine racks before the phenomenon itself came to anyone's attention: Older Women and Younger Men was the bold conjunction.

Now, Mitzi Geller was not a woman to be unduly influenced by hype and fluff, yet it was important to her to keep up with the times. Although she and Jake had no life-style per se, she was acutely conscious of changing life-styles and enjoyed charting her inner life according to the trends. In spite of the fact that Mitzi's credentials were limited to her Career and her First Wednesday Women's Group, she nonetheless made the impression of a modern woman in extremis. Indeed, she held forth from the very core of the Group, maintaining her sway there by virtue of a complete though covert command of the popular literature. She was able to pass off, without shame, every current sentiment, emotion, dogma, and complaint as if it were her own. She appeared such a seething cauldron of contemporaneity that the other women sometimes worried about her; but just when it seemed that it might all be too much, perhaps at the very moment when the drama began to wear thin, Mitzi would suggest they break for coffee, causing them to feel once again that she really was "a very together person."

For John White's part, he was on the rebound. "The prayer hot line," he would say intermittently, disbelievingly, as he ate the scrambled eggs Jake had cooked. "Damn!" He brought his fist down on the dining-room table, glancing automatically at Mitzi who, however, poured the coffee without a rebuke. He already felt at home in this happy little family. He was stunned by the intensity of their interest, especially the woman. Short, well-rounded, lively—his type, he knew at that moment, although heretofore he had always been drawn to its opposite. She was full of questions.

156

"What it is, is twenty-four hours any time of the day or night they're there to take your prayer request. The deal is they'll pray for you by name; so it's not just any old prayer, but they actually say your own name in it."

"That gives it a personal touch," Mitzi acknowledged, smiling. Her teeth were very regular and this impressed him, having grown up as he had among the snaggle-toothed, gap-toothed, and just plain unflossed.

"I probably wouldn't have minded that much if they would've gave me one of the night shifts, but no. They line me up for that first shift in the morning. Uh, uh, I told Big John, no way." He shook his head vigorously and Jake thought of amber waves of grain. "I mean, I'm not going up against 'Good Morning America.' Forget it. You know who calls. Someone who doesn't have a TV set. I can tell. It's pathetic. At night you get the good stuff; at seven A.M. all they want is a prayer to get them through the day." He held his coffee cup out toward Mitzi for a refill.

"'In a real dark night of the soul it is always three o'clock in the morning,'" Jake admonished, but Mitzi jumped in with a practical observation.

"You know, John," she said thoughtfully, "I think you did the right thing. It sounds like it would get awfully depressing."

"Damn right!" He was exuberant. "I just didn't know that until more recently." He followed Mitzi into the kitchen. "I'll do the dishes," he told her happily, pushing back the sleeves of Bruce's gray sweatshirt. "I grew up washing dishes you know, because my mother died. Bill cooked and I did the dishes."

"And now he's a chef," Mitzi said, delighted with the rightness of this world, and oblivious, as John White could not be, to the implied comparison.

"I'm not in too good shape right now," he admitted, nodding slowly, as if enumerating his defects, "but something will probably turn up."

Mitzi, who had been admiring his sturdy sailor's body, nevertheless did not controvert his premise, saying instead, "Of course it will, especially since you have such a good attitude."

John was amazed by the warmth in her voice. Unaware that the emotion had been summoned simply to unify his situation with her purpose, he felt better already. "The Lord works in mysterious ways, you know. Coincidence is some of it. The whole thing was I wanted to get into the music field and this was what Big John was heading for, the ministry where you got singers on the show, cut your records, and have all your facilities right there on the premises. See I was born-again anyway at the time, so I figured it would work out O.K. serving-the-Lord-wise." He looked sadly into the murky dishwater, considering a life lost. Mitzi saw him in a new light then. Where Jake had simply seen a man cut adrift, Mitzi had a glimmering of what it was he needed. As a businesswoman, she responded to need.

That afternoon, speaking in fits and starts during the Sunday football game, John White retailed the meager highlights of his life for Mitzi whose lively features were untiring in their efforts to mime her undivided attention. But John was having the time of his life. Nothing had prepared him for this, raised as he had been with a heavy hand and educated with a light one. Used to the customized confessions and homogenized homilies that Big John passed off as conversation, he had found no one with whom he could talk like this: her warmth, her interest, her undemanding hospitality, and, the capper, her knowledge of football. He expressed his gratitude shyly though in no uncertain terms as they watched a mountain lion leap onto the hood of a shiny new car.

And, true, Mitzi was a football fan. She appreciated the game especially when, early in the week, she would schmooze with a salesman or look over some plans with her carpenter. Then both of these men would briefly feel about her very much as John White did and this suited Mitzi's purposes very well. So, regardless of the rhetorical heights to which John drove himself, her interest in the game took a definite, if subtle, precedence. In any case, Mitzi was not much for confessions, heart-to-hearts, or even simple gossip. "Give me the short version," she often urged. She made an exception, of course, for the First Wednesday Group where her patience with speculation and self-indulgent meandering was legendary.

When all was said and done, however, Mitzi had seen and heard enough to decide to develop John White as her very own Younger Man. She was pleased that it had been so easy, had disrupted her highly organized life so little, had even, if one discounted the boredom, been quite pleasant in the consummation. And the women would surely be stunned by her revelation, she thought happily, the more so as she had always been such a staunch defender of monogamy. But this was no conventional fling; Mitzi would be, as always, on the cutting edge. And when it came to the details of intimacy, which several of them always had to know, she would simply substitute Jake, and they would be none the wiser. It was irresistible, better even than when, courtesy of an unintentional tip from that same Jake, she had told them the story of Lysistrata. "Draw your own conclusions," she had said. The talk had been frank, the laughter vicious, in all a succès fou. Contemplating all this put Mitzi into an excellent mood and she redoubled her efforts to make her guest feel welcome. John White was quite dazed by his good fortune.

———◆———

Meanwhile, downstairs, Jake, a baseball fan when it came to that, was facing an unpleasant reality. He paced the darkened aisles of the stockroom for some minutes before returning to hover over his latest notebook entry. He read again: "Great is hospitality; greater even than early attendance at the House of Study." What weight that lent his simple act! Yet did it not at the same time seem to take him to task; half-assed, it accused sternly, and Jake understood that the stakes had just been raised. There was no good pretending; early or late, he did not attend a House of Study. This card table, his precious library, his consuming passion itself, none of it, phosphorescent in its secularity, counted.

159

Oh Jake, honestly, who cares! It was his sister-in-law's voice. Marilyn, the High Priestess of the Here and Now, sometimes came to him at moments like this. There will always be people who are hospitable and some who aren't, she continued, and believe me, some of them I wouldn't be caught dead in their house! Jake nodded. He was thinking about hospitality: genial hospitality, a hospitality suite, the Jewish hospitality of his own mother. He supposed that he had gotten it from her. "That's all well and good," he said aloud, tapping his pen on the scarred table cover, "but it does not reverberate."

Reverberation, it should be noted, was not generally considered a suitable or even comprehensible characterization in this context. In addition, it was commonly held that things were not as bad as all that. After all, men and women were thought of as men and women, entire vocabularies were believed to be intact, and matters of life and death were addressed on a daily basis. Nevertheless, Jake pouted, man's deepest yearnings were being systematically mined and trivialized, hacked off at the root. Human nature itself, that grand and perdurable reduction, was being phased out in favor of something more visual. "Grrrrrr." He gritted his teeth.

If I were you—it was Marilyn's voice again—I'd be worried about what I was going to do with him, do I give him money or do I lend him, or what. Ah ha, Jake thought, his mood lifting in an instant. He sat down and opened one of the books piled to his right. It is written: "He who lends is greater than he who gives alms; and he who provides capital for a useful enterprise is greatest of all." But Marilyn was not impressed. And another thing, she continued, determined to put him in his place, you don't need to pat yourself on the back for being so hospitable; who do you think is upstairs right now doing the honors?

Jake looked at his watch and then switched off the reading light so quickly that he began at once to think that he had not in fact seen the time correctly. It was his good fortune, he knew, that Mitzi was very used to such a radically expanded minute, for it was for this measure of time that he had excused

160

himself. No doubt she had already made it good with their guest should Jake's absence have created any sense of lack, which, as we have seen, it had not. Above all else, he thought gratefully, he could depend on Mitzi.

Was it mere egotism on Jake's part to think that Mitzi loved him? No, it is not so unreasonable to believe that a woman might find a good heart, a high spirit, and even a penchant for worrying over nothing quite irresistibly appealing in this day and age. Sitting in the near dark, comforted by such thoughts, he let Marilyn have the last word: For God's sake, he imagined her reminder, return Bruce's sweatsuit, will you!

———◆———

That afternoon, however, as she entered Leonard Pelt's office, the sweatsuit was not on Marilyn's mind. Since she had said she wanted to consult him, Dr. Pelt felt the office was the proper place, although it was Sunday and she an acquaintance, and another practitioner might have gone another way. As it was, Gwen Pelt resented her exclusion; but in the long run, he knew, this could only raise him in her esteem. Marilyn had been surprised, then gratified that the meeting should take place in the office. It lent the situation a certain gravity which she had hoped would improve Bruce's attitude. Bruce, however, refused to accompany her.

Dr. Pelt's office had been tacked on to one end of his pink ranch-style house, its private entrance shrouded in greenery so that his patients could dash unobserved to and from their cars. Leonard bid her sit down in an ugly orange-and-green plaid chair and sat himself, perhaps a coffee-table's breadth away, in a large well-padded rocker. There was, of course, no coffee table. Marilyn looked around the small room with interest but found nothing to interest herself in. Gamely she fixed her eye on a straw wastebasket that stood empty in one corner under a Norman Rockwell print. Leonard reached up to switch on the standing lamp with the green shade and Marilyn turned her attention to him, wondering whether he would inspire her confidence, as the room did not, were she to actually come to consult him. She decided that he did at least look suitably professional in his curduroy jacket and turtleneck sweater, given that she did not quite consider therapy a profession.

"Well, Marilyn." Leonard sat back and waited for her to begin. She was, he noted, dressed for the city, and he assumed this was to make her appear more a stranger, more urban and anonymous and less a part of his own suburban circle.

"If I were a regular . . ."—she glanced again at the wastebasket, seeking the appropriate term—". . . customer, I guess, is that what you would say to me? Well, Marilyn." Censure and disbelief mingled in her tone.

"Yes." He gave her a sudden piercing look which meant nothing more than "Get on with it, I'm listening." Inexperienced as she was, however, Marilyn only frowned in discomfort and shifted her pocketbook around on her tweed lap. She had expected him to be curious about what had brought her there, and now to her chagrin it seemed as if he could not be less interested. Were it not for the fact that he never let up that steely look of his, she would have supposed him actually bored already. She tried to fool his eyes away, but this only made her feel foolish.

"Are you feeling uncomfortable, Marilyn?" Dr. Pelt asked gently.

"No, of course not. Why would I?" He had used a tone of voice she had never heard from him before, and it made her skin crawl.

"Being in an unfamiliar situation," he said more softly still, "finding our relationship so altered . . ." He let the possibilities multiply unspoken.

"Leonard, I would appreciate your treating me like a normal human being." She flung down the challenge, looking at him expectantly; but he said nothing. "Leonard, I am talking to you."

Dr. Pelt smiled faintly. "Yes, of course, Marilyn; and I am listening."

Marilyn opened her pocketbook and snapped it shut again.

"Don't you want to know why I'm here? Aren't you the least bit curious?"

"The important thing is that you know why you're here," Dr. Pelt said patiently.

Marilyn gave him a look in which anger and fear were unequally mixed. "Look," she said brusquely, "my time is just too valuable. I came to talk to you about Jake."

Dr. Pelt's face was devoid of any sign of recognition.

"Jake Geller. My brother-in-law."

"Mmmmmmmnnnnnnmn." Dr. Pelt was resolute.

Marilyn crossed her legs and then uncrossed her legs but she could not wait him out. "I hate to say it, but there's something wrong with him."

"I see. You feel there's something wrong with Jake. Yes. But what brings *you* here? You are the one who is here, after all." He smiled enigmatically. "I suppose you might feel badly about Jake."

"I do not feel badly about Jake." She laughed the idea to scorn. "I just feel it's my responsibility to point out there is something very wrong with him." It was enervating to meet Leonard's eyes; she dropped her gaze and saw for the first time that he was wearing slippers.

At that instant Dr. Pelt remembered that he had indeed forgotten to change into his shoes. Without lowering his eyes from her face, he called up an image of the brown, fleece-lined slippers. Well. Marilyn, in her burgundy leather boots, had the advantage of him there. He raised an eyebrow in acknowledgment. "Perhaps you'll tell me how that makes you feel." His voice seemed to Marilyn to be growing ever softer.

"For God's sake, Leonard, why do you think I called you? It's driving me crazy."

"All right, then." Dr. Pelt remained calm in the face of this revelation. "What exactly seems to be the problem?"

"He lives in a dream world. He never talks about normal things. It always has to be this or that. And the sad fact is, Leonard, believe me, no one cares. That's really what it comes

163

down to." She paused to see how he was taking it, when Leonard rose from his chair and tiptoed toward the door.

"Gwen," he boomed, "get away from there." He yanked the door open, but the waiting room was empty.

"It doesn't matter, Leonard," Marilyn comforted him, "she's heard it all already." And even before Leonard could resume his seat she was continuing eagerly. "He's in his own little world; he just goes on and on about all his little things and no one has the vaguest idea of what he thinks he's doing. Nothing's right, nothing's good enough for him. Oh no. He thinks he's so deep; he thinks he has the right to put down everything everyone else likes. I'm sick of it, I really am." And she did sound as if she had been sorely tried.

"I see." Dr. Pelt rocked back and forth several times. "Do you see Jake often?"

"Don't you understand what I am saying? I am telling you that this man is not normal, Leonard. He needs help."

Dr. Pelt rocked once more. "Tell me, how do you and Jake get along? Do you get along well?"

"Of course we do. I get along well with everybody. Besides, he's Bruce's brother." She leaned toward him. "But you're missing the point. Here he is, this cheerful little man, atrociously dressed, doing janitor's work, reading his little books and making his little notes, and he thinks he's so great. Cheerful, no less! He has more chutzpah!"

"And how about you? Do I sense. . . ?" This time he raised both eyebrows the better to draw her out.

"Leonard, I'm going to say this for the last time. The man is not of this world. Do you understand me?"

"Why don't you tell me a little more about that?" Dr. Pelt urged mildly. He had stopped rocking to relight his pipe.

Marilyn breathed deeply. "Oh, I love the smell of pipe tobacco," she said suddenly with girlish enthusiasm. "My father smoked a pipe and I used to love the smell of pipe tobacco." Then she tapped one purple-red nail on the gold clasp of her pocketbook as if to summon up again the more familiar perspective of her current self.

Dr. Pelt rocked and puffed and rocked and puffed in silence. Marilyn studied the Norman Rockwell print, unaware that she was drawing from it comfort, encouragement, and confirmation all at once. It may be seen from this that Dr. Pelt was not quite the man he seemed.

"My mother," Marilyn went on finally and in such a tone as to indicate that no parent and child could be less alike, "my mother used to say he was too good for this world—that's how she would explain him, his head in the clouds—but you know what I think, I think he wasn't good enough." She smiled grimly. "Well, back to Jake. What do you think? I think he needs professional help. I really do. Didn't you see him Yom Kippur at our house, out in the yard after dinner, with that stick of all things? It was too much, really! And I don't like the kids listening to him either."

She felt she was on solid ground here; everybody knew that Leonard Pelt had a blind spot when it came to his son. "It's hard enough growing up today without someone filling you up with ideas. And the trouble is the kids actually like him." She flared her nostrils at the folly of youth.

Dr. Pelt nodded. David had indeed been unusually charitable in characterizing Jake Geller. In fact, Leonard had already determined, on the basis of his high regard for his son, to include Jake at the first barbecue of the coming summer. As Gwen was no cook, they did not entertain beyond the season. And so the session went, give and take, hit and miss, with Marilyn struggling for satisfaction while the doctor held fast to the strategies of his calling. Finally he said, "I'm afraid we're going to have to stop for today, Marilyn." He leaned toward her, perversely gentle to deny the element of coercion.

"Stop," Marilyn echoed dumbly, seeing for the first time the miniature travel clock, half hidden by a packet of Kleenex, on the teak table at his side. "You don't mean," she began, gripping her pocketbook with both hands until her knuckles showed white against the burgundy leather.

Leonard interrupted her smoothly. "I think I'm beginning to have some idea of the problems you're having with your

165

brother-in-law." He had made something of a specialty of bringing these sessions to a close. In fact, he was intending to make this very delicate "art of closure," as he called it, the subject of a full-length article the moment he was invited to write one. "I think I know of someone who would suit you very well, but of course it's up to you. Aaaiiiiiieeeeeeoooo!" Dr. Pelt yelped as Marilyn with a great sense of purpose trod heavily on his slippered foot as she made for the door.

"As your wife's best friend, Leonard, I turn to you for advice—and this is what I get. You must be out of your mind. I have no idea what you're talking about . . ." She glared at him. "And neither does anyone in my family. But let me assure you . . ."—she threw back her shoulders—". . . if it is anything like our conversation this afternoon, I can only say I would much rather, believe me, much rather, listen to Jake."

And she was gone, leaving Leonard to massage his foot, a triumphant and very professional smile distorting his lean saturninity.

9

WEDNESDAY

Nowhere to Stand

The evening was young and John White, alone in the Gellers' apartment and left to his own devices, was determined to take his laundry down the street to the laundromat. He packed it all together with a carelessness that would come back to haunt him and made for his destination with a newly nonchalant, even worldly, gait, two shirt-sleeves dangling. He had not yet gone halfway when he stopped in front of the Lynford Tavern and, hitching up his bundle, understood for the first time that he hungered for the companionship of great athletes, the pyrotechnics of accomplished tapsters, and the badinage of the old sots of his father's circle. Inside, unattended by any merrymakers, he set his laundry on the floor and slid onto a bar stool. At the bartender's approach the words Old Crow suggested themselves to John White so forcefully that he had no choice but to make them known to that individual. He could give no reason for such a request. It was his father's drink; certainly he did not intend to drink it.

He had not seen much of Mitzi since Sunday, but he had in

those three days grown quite attached to his hostess, had unknowingly begun to look to her for his salvation. In the little time she was able to devote to him, Mitzi had begun to imbue him with a new sense of purpose, with a grand hope for the future. Although the apartment did not with grace accept the presence of a guest, John did his best. As soon as he heard Jake at the crack of dawn tiptoe past the foot of the convertible sofa and leave the apartment, he leapt up, performed his ablutions, dressed, and returned the bed to sofa form. Then he made the coffee, poured the juice, set the table, and so could sit down with an easy mind when the family of three assembled for breakfast. The meal was a largely silent affair, as Mitzi and Jake were in the habit of setting a piece of reading matter alongside their plates. John White, longing to belong, went to rummage among his possessions and came up with an advertising circular. This he read and considered from every point of view and angle in the time it took to consume two shredded-wheat biscuits before the milk got the best of them. Jake, by contrast, liked his cereal to turn to mush. What conversation did take place was likely to be disjunct and largely exclamatory in nature.

"My god!" Mitzi might say, sliding her magazine toward Jake.

"Oi!" he would respond after a cursory inspection.

"Whoa!" Thus John White, matching their tone but not always clear on content.

Several minutes later it would be Jake's turn. "Incredible!" he might exclaim.

"Wha—?" John White would begin to inquire, deciding to make a clean breast of it.

But Mitzi, halfway to the kitchen, would cut him off. "Too much!"

Then, talked out, they prepared to go their separate ways, but not before Mitzi had assigned to John White each day a single, honorable task. Monday she asked him to go by train to a neighboring suburb and report to her on the video arcade in the mall there. He had come through with flying colors, spending the better part of the day wandering around the mall, returning time and time again to study the makeup of the arcade and its patrons. Mitzi had advanced him some money on account, a portion of which he used to purchase a clipboard and pad to give himself the look of a professional pollster. This simple disguise seemed to have an electrifying effect on even the most casual bystanders, who found themselves entering the arcade simply for the sake of the interview. Unfortunately, the sophistication of John's survey technique was not such that it could take these ringers into account.

The following day Mitzi sent him into New York City to collect brochures, information, and figures; but as decisions had already been taken, this work was mainly character-building. In the dark as he was, however, John went at it hammer and tongs; and still had time left over to rendezvous with a certain young lady, a certified Christian, indeed she had been one of Big John's "special" Christians. This last had given John pause; yet his companion, who did not aspire to professional status, had seen fit to urge him on for old time's sake in spite of the fact that all her old time, as Little John knew only too well, had been spent with Big John. In the end however, it was for this reason alone that he had come to feel he should go with her.

That evening he had waited for Mitzi to come home from a meeting of the Zoning Board to make his report. Time dragged and he felt awkward walking in circles, doing nothing while Jake sat reading in an easy chair. "You've got something with video games, Jake." He finally broke the silence. "There's no limits to them. To me it's like anything else, but much bigger. Much bigger!"

Jake put his arm across the page to hold his place. He noted the urgency, the fervor, the pitch aborning. "Do you remember when Lennon said 'The Beatles are bigger than Jesus Christ'?"

John looked at him strangely. "But we're not saying that. Nothing like it."

Jake remarked the use of the plural form. It put him, he felt, in an awkward position. He felt the need to patronize; adopting a man-in-the-street pose, he feigned "more in sorrow than in anger." "As I told my wife, I'm just not being appealed to entertainment-wise, I guess." He and Mitzi had had words about it.

Certainly the subject deserved better, John White had thought, waiting for Jake to say more. After a moment of reverie Jake did speak again. "Entertainment-wise," he repeated petulantly, perversely. John pitied the man. No faith.

Had he been looking now for an excuse to celebrate, to extend his stay at the Tavern, John could have pointed to his new job. That morning Mitzi had taken him downstairs and into the storefront next to the toyshop to show him the video arcade in progress. Then, without turning a hair, she had informed him that he was no longer welcome, that this night would be his last at their apartment, that there was the matter of the money she had advanced. Let's just see if he's smart enough to ask me for a job, was Mitzi's thought, and, in short, he had been. Nevertheless, upon finishing his third highball and finding his fellow drinkers still determined against celebration, he left the bar without a qualm, continuing down the street, shirt-sleeves adangle from the bundle of his laundry. He had felt fine before entering the Tavern and he felt fine now, although the precise way in which he felt fine had apparently taken on a public face. At least we may judge this a possibility inasmuch as Officer DiMaria, on foot patrol across the street, stopped to watch his progress with an interested professional eye.

The laundromat was empty except for a young black man who was loading two washers from two carefully sorted piles of laundry. He looked up with a laugh as John White came in.

"Hi," said the Seabee, as friendly as ever, although the precise way in which he was as friendly as ever had perhaps altered. This, however, would be difficult to assess without speculating on the nature of racism in America.

M. L. Johnson pointed at the two washing machines. "One for white, one for colored," he said jovially.

170

John White giggled. "Listen to this. Oh shit." He began to laugh. "My name is White. John White." He shifted his bundle and extended his right hand. The two men shook hands and then, cutting back to a giggle, John traveled the room searching for a machine he liked. When he found it, it was located in the far corner of the laundromat, or perhaps that was why he found it. In any case, M. L. Johnson had no patience to indulge a tipsy fool; the day of his departure was nearly upon him, and mental preparation vied with physical for the time that remained.

Meanwhile, Officer DiMaria had walked the business district from one end to the other on the even numbered side of the street and started back on the odd, checking doors, keeping his eye peeled. He was passing the Lynford Tavern, his mind wandering to his brother Joey, a would-be actor in a family of serious men, when an unexpected unevenness in the sidewalk caused him to trip. He might have fallen headlong too had he not been an ambitious young policeman with fast, well-trained reflexes. Righting himself, he used his flashlight to illuminate the cause of his near-accident and found a narrow crevasse where the sidewalk slabs had cracked and heaved up and away from each other. Then he saw a glint of gold in the beam of his light and, squatting easily, reached in and retrieved a gold cuff link. He studied it closely back and front before rising to continue his patrol. April 31: his heart sang with that exotic blend of edgy excitement and flat certainty only a true anomaly can engender.

Although the rash of burglaries seemed to have ended with the break-in at the Geller house, the case had remained the subject of study and speculation on Johnny DiMaria's part. He had taken the trouble to keep himself well-informed, careful all the while not to step on any toes, and it had eventually occurred to him to wonder why, when the merchandise was showing up in all the usual places, none of the jewelry, not one piece that had been reported stolen, had ever surfaced. But now one had, and Officer DiMaria was jubilant. "April 31," he said aloud, "gotcha!" That bit of information about the grand-

171

mother getting the date wrong, why had it stuck in his mind? Good cop, he answered without hesitation. Thirty days has September, Granny. He turned automatically to check out the brightly lit interior of the laundromat; but before he actually saw John White, the image of a pair of shirt-sleeves dancing across the sidewalk popped into his policeman's mind. Good cop, he said again and entered the laundromat. Until that instant his joy had obscured the unlikelihood of any positive outcome whatsoever. Now he lifted his heavy hat and reset it securely, purposefully, ready for come-what-may.

"Excuse me, sir," he said to John White who was stretched out on his back across several folding chairs, an arm laid over his eyes, "did you by any chance lose something?"

"No." The subject exhibited neither surprise nor curiosity.

"Are you sure, sir? I happened to observe you on your way over here from the Tavern and a couple of those shirt-sleeves were dragging. You wanna check?" Officer DiMaria put one hand on top of the washing machine. If the gesture carried no threat, it was, nevertheless, meant to be an official gesture.

"No." The suspect appeared to have been drinking. His eyelids were heavy.

"Would you mind telling me your name, sir, and where you live, please."

The suspect groaned and muttered something unintelligible.

"I think he said 'John White,'" M. L. supplied helpfully. "It doesn't seem like he feels too good," he added with no apparent lack of sympathy. Nevertheless, schaden freude was the name of the game; it did M. L.'s heart good to see this white man hassled.

The name reverberated in the policeman's ear. This was the Jesus case they had picked up on the corner by the Gellers'. He called for a car and they took John White in to the Lynford police station to be questioned yet a second time. But to no avail, as Officer DiMaria was forced to acknowledge before his superiors. The mass of wet laundry which they had confiscated did not upon examination reveal a single French cuff. They had to let him go.

As it was the first Wednesday evening of the month, Mitzi was attempting to lay before her ladies the foundation for her fling and so was unable to accompany Jake and Helga, who had been invited up by Mrs. Sloane to meet her daughter Iris. Mrs. Sloane, all in green, received them at her winter home. She served coffee from a silver pot and a plate of chocolate truffles resting in pleated paper baskets. For Jake she provided a decanter of brandy, and for herself a glass of port which she saw fit to replenish with some frequency from a well-stocked sideboard.

Iris was a woman of about forty with an unlined, open face protected by heavy eyebrows and a hatchet of a nose. She wore a gray sweatshirt of the kind sold abroad as the genuine American article. The sweatshirt was lettered FUDGE; and, though a group of lesser conversationalists and thinkers might have resorted to such a topic more than once, the import of that FUDGE remained unexamined throughout the evening. In fact, a subject of substance arose almost immediately after the introductory pleasantries, when Mrs. Sloane bemoaned on her daughter's behalf the frequent lack of toilet tissue at her rural outpost.

"Well," Iris said easily, "we don't have very much of anything around there, so we get used to it after a while." She had a confident, hearty voice.

"Yes, in fact," Helga joined in, "one does get used to it. I know from experience. But one always remembers the other way, don't you?"

"Somehow, I suppose, but these comforts seem slight to me in comparison to the comfort I find in my work and my God."

Jake blinked at this simple, straightforward formulation. "Helga," he kept the impatience out of his voice, "it isn't the same thing at all."

"Oh yes," Mrs. Sloane put in eagerly, "I mentioned it to Iris. Of course I did." She gave Helga an understanding smile.

"It must be different," Helga responded with assumed mildness, "because the nothing we had could only corrupt us or

173

kill us." She pressed her lips together. "Now the interesting thing I think about when I help Mitzi at the store is that the opposite is the same, just as true. I see also there the corruption of having too much."

Rather than address this grim paradox, Mrs. Sloane chose to footnote Helga's employment picture for her daughter. "Maybe you can pick up a few trinkets to bring back to your children at the school," she added.

Iris popped a chocolate truffle into her mouth. "Mmmmmmm-mmmm!" she said after a long moment.

"They were always your favorites," her mother said with satisfaction.

Jake had been waiting patiently. "Here it is." He stood up. "We have everything and that obscures the fact that . . ."—he sat down again, rubbing his hands along his thighs—". . . at the same time we have nothing. Nowhere to stand. We don't know where we stand."

Helga started to object, but Iris overrode her. "I think that's it exactly, Jake. I know where I stand, I know on what I stand, and I know with whom I stand."

"And it's more than that," Jake said urgently.

"It is more than that," Iris agreed with alacrity.

"I do not take anything away from you," Helga addressed Iris, "because I am sure the world needs very much what you are doing. Yet other people name themselves Christians too. It was my pleasure," she noted grimly, "to have their acquaintance and not yours."

Jake started to object but Iris said, "They were not Christians according to my lights, Mrs. Grossman. I want you to know that."

Helga veered off accordingly. "What I want to say is that not everyone wants to go to a jungle. We must make something of life here in the horn of plenty."

Rather than correct Helga's geographical misconception, Iris removed another chocolate candy from the plate to her mouth. She sat back; having exhausted her own theological concerns, she hoped they could move on to the practical matters which were at the heart of her commitment to Christ.

"You have a context," Jake said to her, dashing her hopes.

Mrs. Sloane, pouring herself a bit more port, bridged a momentary silence. "Iris actually knows some of the PFLOC men," she told them, speaking the acronym as "flock." "She was telling me they are very friendly to her and the Father at the clinic."

"Politics as a context," Jake mused aloud. "A certain nobility, a certain splendor does attach to love of country, to the idea of nationhood, of the common good." He took a sip of brandy and began to sing "Allons, enfants de la patrie-e-e, le jour de gloire est arrivé." The melody brought tears to Mrs. Sloane's eyes. "But as a context, I don't know; too mixed, too vulnerable, too tainted, too dependent on men." He appeared to be addressing the crystal decanter.

"These are men of high ideals. That's the way I would say it." There was a finality to Iris's tone with which she aimed to choke off further talk of contexts.

Help came from an unexpected corner. "Jake, what is with this context business? This is life, we are the living, and we are living it."

Jake gave Helga a reproachful look. He poured another brandy into the snifter, seeking to focus his thoughts. "I see." He was sarcastic. "You prefer living a life . . ."—he edged those words in black crepe—". . . in which wit and will are turned and tuned to degrade, cheapen, undermine, and trivialize? What about that old 'ennobling relation,' that capacity to elevate, to exhibit truth and beauty and goodness? I am talking about a context," he sounded the *t* with scornful abandon causing the flame on Helga's cigarette lighter to quiver, "for man's highest and best feelings." Jake's cheeks were very red.

Iris reached for a chocolate truffle. "Perhaps what you're really saying is 'Man shall not live by bread alone.'"

"Or by chocolate truffles!" her mother joked.

A lesser woman might have been stung by the implied crit-

175

icism of this motherly remark, but Iris, secure in the justice of her deserts, ate on. In fact, she gave no indication of having so much as heard the words and simply continued with a very becoming placidity. "It strikes me, Jake, that you are searching."

"You're telling me," Helga interjected with a hint of sarcasm, feeling a little put out by what she saw as a developing tendency to tête-à-tête.

"Your brother was a searcher," Mrs. Sloane observed to Iris for no other reason than to assert the precedence of family. "I frankly did not encourage searching, did not bring you up to search. My feeling has always been that one who searches is likely to end up where he began. Though why I don't know. Of course, that was hardly the case with Geoffrey."

"China." Iris smiled. "Hardly." She nevertheless held with her mother on the question of searching. "I never saw the need. It was just as plain as the nose on my face. There was work to be done, the Lord's work."

"That's exactly how I felt," Mrs. Sloane assured them, "with the exception of course that I was something of an atheist at the time. However, as my husband used to say, that would be Iris's father, 'the color of your money is green.'"

Helga lit another cigarette. She could not find her way into this conversation and images of pariahdom assailed her.

"What you're talking about then," Jake said slowly, single-mindedly, "is another context for action, for doing good works, for noble causes." All three women looked at him aghast as if to say, Oh no, not that again!

"As I've told you, Jake," Mrs. Sloane instructed patiently, "I have always enjoyed a good cause." She sipped her port. "They have given my life some meaning."

"Yes, but why?" Jake was not one to be fobbed off by simple assertions of fact. Mrs. Sloane looked at Helga as if she might hold her responsible for this unseemly display of epistemological angst.

"Why?" Helga shrugged, responding as much to the one as

the other. "She enjoys doing a good deed; maybe it makes her feel good, is that a mystery?"

"No, that's psychology," Jake said morosely.

Mrs. Sloane decided suddenly she must step in and take things in hand. "Would you like to see some of the children?"

Appreciative, Iris raised herself up several inches and pulled a yellow envelope out from under her thigh. "They were starting to curl," she explained. "Some of these boys, Simon for example, are already with the PFLOC." Iris held out one of the snapshots.

"I wanted to ask already, before when you mentioned it," Helga said, accepting the picture. "These people are shepherds, then? So it cannot be a jungle where you are."

"Shepherds?" Iris looked at her blankly.

"You said flock," Helga accused her.

"Flock? Oh no, Mrs. Grossman." Iris blushed, abashed, "I meant the PFLOC, the Popular Front for the Liberation of Our Country." If Iris experienced even the slightest desire to laugh at this absurd misunderstanding, it was nowhere evident in her visage or demeanor. And yet the Father was always remarking on her fine sense of humor, and several of the local women regularly giggled at the simple jokes she made in their own language.

"Politics," Helga said angrily. "I'm too old for politics."

"Do you believe that old age has its prerogatives, Mrs. Grossman?" Mrs. Sloane called from the sideboard. Helga, who correctly believed herself to be at least ten years younger than her hostess, hesitated, considering the implications of the question. "I ask because it is nearly nine o'clock and I am afraid I must excuse myself to watch television."

"Oh I see, yes, certainly," Helga answered. With her own viewing habits so underdeveloped, she was flustered, out of her depth. "It's all right with me. I must think about doing my paper in any case."

In the face of the severe time constraint, Mrs. Sloane did not trouble with expressions of further hospitality or regret. "Jake, you'll stay and keep Iris company, won't you?" The presence of her daughter did much to bring to life the imperious manner of Mrs. Sloane's grande-dame period.

But Iris expressed the desire to broaden her horizons, and, as she was the guest of honor, the large color television set in the living room was activated without further ado. Nevertheless, Iris attempted to engage Jake with the remaining snapshots in the hope of disguising her complicity in the diversion at hand. "Look, this is the old Mission Church," she said, and Jake showed some interest in the church because, as has been noted, Jake did in fact have some interest in a great many things. Iris, however, used to a more discriminating audience, was unprepared for the variety and detail of his questioning, and their little conversation quickly foundered on this lack. With one well-practiced motion she helped herself to a chocolate truffle and resumed the posture that seemed to be habitual with her. It was as if she hadn't moved, never moved. One leg, bent as if for prayer, was pushed back underneath the chair, while the other was stretched straight in front of her, ready for action, the wide black skirt decorous. Thus did she appear the very essence of the modern nun.

"It's a bit silly," Mrs. Sloane said, her enthusiasm carrying no hint of apology, "but marvelously entertaining for all that."

"Entertainment . . ." Jake began; but Mrs. Sloane shushed him as the program began, and he was left to his own thoughts. He and Mitzi had recently had words on the subject of entertainment. When the storefront next door to the toy shop had fallen vacant, Mitzi had exercised her option on the lease. Jake, amazed by her ability to know what she wanted and to arrange to get it, told her, the evening before the renovations were to begin, that he admired that in her.

Tears had come to Mitzi's eyes. Then abruptly she broke the news: sports is out, video is in. "It's a natural outgrowth, Jake," she addressed his distress. "It's what kids want to be playing with now. It's the tip of the iceberg. Believe me."

He had surprised her by saying merely, "I follow your think-

178

ing, but there's no point in pretending sports are out just because you've decided to go with video. Sports are not out." And as Jake was no great fan, we may assume that this passionate denial was in fact a more general defense of the old-fashioned virtues.

Mitzi had objected feebly that she meant the sports store that had been under consideration. She came over to kneel by his chair and put her arm around him. "You don't have to feel bad, Jake. It's not what you think it is." She smoothed his hair, or would have smoothed it, had he hair that lent itself to smoothing. "It's only toys; it's harmless; it's just fun and games." She sold on. "You don't have to take it so seriously. It's entertainment!"

"Of course it is," he had replied sweetly. "It's all entertainment. In fact, the only thing right now that is not entertainment is entertainment itself." Mitzi left off massaging his temple. Jake leaned away from her for a better look. "Let me ask you a question: which is entertainment? A man juggling three oranges? An animated orange hawking for the juice people? Or the televised rape trial of an Orange County executive?"

"Jake!" Mitzi had been hurt. "Be serious."

On screen a man and woman were exchanging a few simple words, heartfelt on the wings of a portentous banality. A waiter appeared to interrupt their conversation which, pause by pause, had stretched to cover their mutual pleasure at seeing each other. It was then revealed that the waiter was just as pleased to see them as they were to see each other. And, of course, they, him. As that world shimmered on, the force of its wordless, spiritless density oppressed Jake, made him anxious, gave him the jitters. "What is this?" he asked finally, addressing a larger question.

"Shhhhhh!" answered Mrs. Sloane without taking her eyes from the screen.

"You know this show," Helga whispered accusingly.

Jake began to reply but Mrs. Sloane silenced him with a

look. The scene had shifted. Two characters met midway on an enormous staircase and exchanged a speaking glance. The man's glance spoke of lust and ambition, the woman's of distaste and fear. She uttered a single word in which refusal and supplication were mixed. "Please!" she said, hurrying by.

A visual medium certainly, and yet perhaps they went too far. The dialogue left one breathless at its suicidal tendencies, its apparent willingness to deny the human species a distinguishing gift.

"Ha," Mrs. Sloane laughed with delight. "She is a little minx, isn't she?"

"What makes you say that, Mother?" Iris evidenced the genuine wonder of the uninitiated at the ripened understanding of a master.

"Wait until the commercial," her mother ordered curtly, gratified nonetheless by her interest.

But when the time came, Helga had already positioned herself for immediate departure. "So," her hostess remarked without rising, "I see that you are not a fan, Mrs. Grossman. Don't you see the fun of it?"

"I am sorry not to." Helga backed slowly toward the door. "The people seem only to behave very stupidly."

Mrs. Sloane shuddered at this indelicacy. "But that's the fun of it, isn't it really? Besides, who behaves stupidly if not, for example, someone in Shakespeare!"

"My schooling," Helga began apologetically, but Jake cut her off, leaping over Iris's outstretched leg to land, crouching, at the side of Mrs. Sloane.

"What are you saying?" he questioned wildly.

Mrs. Sloane studied him without alarm. "It was an interview with the creators. They say they based the entire idea on something in Shakespeare." She reached for the television guide on the table, pausing to watch Iris help herself to the last remaining truffle. "King Coriolanus, I think it was," she said casually, as if this lineage were very nearly self-evident.

Jake returned to his glass and finished the brandy in a single gulp, causing Mrs. Sloane to shudder again. "What can this mean?" he wailed.

Helga had the door open. "What are you so excited about, Jake? It's only a silly show."

"You'll see," Jake said ominously and poured more brandy.

"Shush!" Mrs. Sloane commanded as Helga closed the door behind her and the program resumed.

But Jake had yet to be truly tested. A doorbell was sounding in a room the enormous size of which was brought into focus when a woman entered, attired for the very extremity of lounging, and walked its length. It was a long walk and she walked slowly. The bell rang ever more insistently and the tension grew.

"I imagine it must be Carleton at the door," Mrs. Sloane said with animation. After an interminable moment of suspense, the woman returned, alone so it seemed at first.

"I've agreed to see you . . ."—she paused to let the words sink in—". . . because I want my side of the story heard." She turned to the man who now suddenly stood framed in the archway behind her and smiled seductively.

Mrs. Sloane leaned toward the screen. "Who?" she worried aloud.

"What!" Jake shouted, lurching forward for a closer look.

A grimace contorted the man's lean face, an expression which surely did not know itself for what it was. He cleared his throat. "Well, then," he said with a distinctive cadence, "we do have something in common after all, don't we."

"It's Quint," Jake said frantically, squatting in front of the set. "It's Quint!"

"Jake!" Mrs. Sloane called out, suddenly a querulous old woman, "you're in my way. I can't see." As the two characters on the screen stretched the silence between them to imply menace, intimacy, compatibility of ambition, prerogatives of celebrity, first-amendment rights, and, of course, sex, the telephone in Mrs. Sloane's apartment began to ring. "Get it, Jake!" Mrs. Sloane's urgency had left her unmannerly.

But, immediately, the telephone stopped ringing. "Yes," the woman said, drawing out the word, as they moved slowly across the room toward the champagne, the caviar, the roaring blaze in the fireplace. Mrs. Sloane's telephone began to ring again. "Mr. Quint," the woman said, like the spider to the fly, and the ringing ceased.

"This is hardly the kind of fare a working journalist like me is used to." Quint gestured stiffly with one Nixonian arm.

"I suppose not. But a man like you . . ."—the lady of the house put her hand to his cheek—". . . a man like you could get used to it."

Quint appeared to flinch. Then, recovering himself, he raised his glass to her in a wordless toast, and the scene shifted to a hotel swimming pool in oil-rich Abu Dhabi. The telephone began to ring yet again.

———◆———

For the third time Gena set the telephone receiver down before her call could be answered at the other end. She was in fact relieved that the attention due her lover's lines had repeatedly kept her from reaching Helga. And relieved all over again that she had been able to turn down at the last minute the invitation she had earlier accepted to meet the nun. Now that the scene was finished, there was no longer any currency to her program note. Though Quint could not know it, there lurked behind the intensity of her own excitement the knowledge that Alvin's dramatic debut would do nothing to raise him in her mother's esteem. I should care, she thought.

"This is a highlight of my life, Alvin. I mean it." She glowed and he basked. "But I can't believe you didn't tell me. What if I had a heart attack!" And in fact she had experienced a great deal of pressure in the area of her heart when she first saw him standing there in the archway. As a treasured memory, their meeting at the Gold Cup Deli simply did not measure up. "This is even better than the news; I hope you realize that. Do you know what they call this show? They call it an unfolding saga!"

But Quint's concerns were technical. "I was wondering if I seemed enough like myself?" he asked with unaccustomed modesty. "There was some problem with my being myself, I guess."

He was genuinely thoughtful, for his short stint as an actor had caused him for the first time to think about who he was. It was one thing to play a newsman; this was Quint's bread and butter. It was quite another to play himself playing a newsman who was himself playing a newsman. And yet, if this debut was well received, what had begun as a network promotion might yet catapult him into the very empyrean, that bruisingly brilliant and contrastless firmament where such distinctions fell before the bright sword of celebrity. How this man longed to be merchandised, publicized, exploited, and sold! Quint stroked his chin to show her how thoughtful he was.

"I thought you were very natural, super natural," Gena reassured. "You were so real I couldn't believe it, I mean it, Alvin!" She closed her shining eyes at the memory and Quint took the opportunity to pass his hands over her breasts.

"Ha!" he said, "gotcha."

But Gena was not in the mood. She thirsted for the particulars. Was Diana as nice as she seemed? Was Carleton a fag, as she had heard? Was Francesca really dating Clinton? Was Shelby jealous of Madeleine, as had been reported? Did Arden have any children? So it went until Quint was feeling ill-used and vengeful and therefore not nearly as reluctant as he had been at the start to inform her that it was a one-shot deal.

Gena shook her head, little-girl-like, certain. "No, it can't be," she assured him calmly. "You'll be back. Madeleine has to get her side of the story out. She said so herself."

This attitude did not sit well with Quint. He turned his back on her and walked over to the large window. The view was of a busy Manhattan thoroughfare and of the nineteenth-floor apartments directly across the street from his own. I'm a New Yorker, he thought with satisfaction. Gena had moved to his side.

"I'm telling you that I was written out. It was a cameo, a stunt. That was it." Perhaps his irritation could be traced as much to this hard reality as to Gena's cozy, hearth-bound knowingness.

"Wait a minute, then." Gena grabbed his arm urgently. "I think that means Francesca will probably lose the baby." She was frowning, full of sudden knowledge. "The baby's father is the only son of the wealthy newspaper family; and Madeleine has been after him for years." She stopped on a dime, suddenly confronting a contradiction in sources. "But then again I heard he was supposed to be making a movie. . . ," she trailed off, puzzled, looking to Quint for an exclusive.

But Quint was anxious to have a moment to gather his thoughts, or mix himself a drink; he was not sure which. Gena's attention returned to the television. True, her eyes had strayed to the screen throughout her interrogation of Quint, but her usual intensity of commitment was lacking. Now she could already feel the resultant diminution of vitality; she missed that stimulated, engaged feeling the show always gave her. If you're going to do it, do it right, she told herself sternly; it's just like anything else. Gena thus bought into one of the great fallacies of the television era.

Nor was Quint, now occupying his tiny city kitchen, giving any consideration to the possibility that The Tube was sui generis. The thoughts he had retreated to gather proved recalcitrant, and, in an effort to solicit them, he went heavy on the Scotch. One sparerib remained in a spattered white carton; he chewed on it for several moments before it occurred to him that his restlessness, his vague dissatisfaction with the way the evening was going must inevitably be charged against Gena. He had a bone to pick with her. Quint pulled half his mouth into a smile. Although the show had been taped before he met her, he had become convinced that he had done it for her sake. Indeed, it seemed in retrospect that he had very nearly sacrificed his whole damn career for her. And now she was too simple, too selfish, to see the implications. He had reached a new

184

plateau. In a daring move he had cut his celebrity loose to compete in a free market; the sky was the limit now.

The telephone rang and he started from his reverie. It was Ilse calling in her review. "You ass!" she said fiercely. "Du! Idiot! Naar!" she finished him off in German.

"Bitch!" he replied. "Nazi bitch!" he amended, but she had already hung up the phone. Freshening his drink, he entered the den with a renewed appreciation for his current flame. She's a honey, he acknowledged, bringing to mind quickly all he meant to her; she's the one.

"I was just thinking . . ."—Gena gestured toward the screen where the nightly news was now playing—". . . the world seems better doesn't it? Don't you remember when they had all these items that no one had ever heard of on all the time? You would just wait and wait for something you could relate to." She took a macadamia nut from the jar on the rosewood table. "Quick, look, there's the one they keep talking about; he's something in the government. I guess that must be his chauffeur." She leaned toward the screen. "It isn't a limo though. The other one has a limo, I think." Gena invited speculation.

Quint loomed over her, smiling indulgently, but not to be deterred. "So what did you think of my dramatic debut?"

"I really loved it, I told you." Gena smiled back but her thoughts were elsewhere.

"How did it come across, me playing a television journalist? That was a nice touch, I thought."

"Alvin," Gena looked up from the leather couch, irritated now, "I was talking to you about the news. I don't know why I bother keeping up. You could care less."

Quint sneered. "I care the way a journalist cares."

"I guess I do it for Douglas's sake." Gena sighed dramatically. "He should know about current events. As a matter of fact," she turned momentarily gleeful, "you could try talking to Douglas about current events sometime. You're not making very much progress with him as it is."

"He doesn't like me," Quint objected—fairly—able to face

185

this ugly truth because Douglas was only a child. Children, he believed, could not appreciate his finer points, and he had long ago decided to father none of his own. Poor Quint had been sorely tried in recent years as all the women he knew—those hard-nosed, ambitious, career-oriented, high-style women he dated—one by one turned baby-crazy. Imagine his relief then the day Gena told him, with just the right touch of petulance, that she intended to start living for herself.

"Who was on the telephone before?" Gena asked out of the blue.

Quint pulled a blank face. "Wrong number."

"I bet you used to talk to Elsie about the news." Gena returned to the attack. "The Germans are very interested in the news I hear."

Quint pulled himself together. "All right," he sat down beside her on the couch, "we'll talk about the news." He had no intention of calling Gena's bluff. "You start."

Gena, suspicious of his quick capitulation, contemplated for an instant the advantage that phone call seemed to have given her before settling on the high road. She leaned back at her ease, more a presumptive tenant than a guest.

"Did you hear about that man today who was a bigamist and he was married to something like twenty-nine women at the same time?"

Quint did not show his relief. "And they all said he was a great husband, too." He gave her a lascivious grin before his professional self added, "Or anyway the wives they got to interview."

"Did you see the girl, the one who looked a lot like the one on that new show?"

Quint put his arm around her. "I liked the one with the big tits," he said jovially.

Gena smiled demurely and looked at her watch. "Alvin, I don't like to leave Douglas alone so late."

Quint took this, correctly, as a sort of invitation, thus establishing to both their satisfaction that though much remained to be resolved between them, there already existed a profound and intimate level of understanding.

But while their evening was destined to end in an explosion of harmony and passion, there was yet a tiny corner of Gena's mind that remained preoccupied with the news. A name slipped in and out of focus there, distracting her from the pleasure of the moment. In fact, she had been delayed tuning into the news broadcast by Quint's cat, Sylvester, with whom she was locked in a terrible territorial struggle; the cat had chosen the "top of the hour" to contest that very bit of couch Gena had so recently made her own, and she did not intend to let him have his way. Finally, however, flipping through the channels with the reckless speed of a much younger woman, it seemed to her that she had half heard something—a phrase, a name, she no longer knew what—that made her think it was Stanley, Stanley Stern, to whom the words applied. Guiltily and with some effort she worked to rid her mind of the insidious rhythm and sibilance of her ex-husband's name, only to find that faculty already engaged in an extensive review of all the hurt he had done her. The mind could do one thing and the body quite another, Gena noted, not for the first time.

———◆———

Mitzi's First Wednesday Women's Group was in disarray. Schism was the only word for it. Just over an hour before, indeed just as Mitzi was warming to the subject of Younger Men, one of the sisters, an elegantly coiffed mother of five, had demanded that the television set be turned on. The very leaves on the houseplants seemed to shiver in the general intake of breath. Cries of outrage followed, and accusations of revisionism.

Polly Finkle, the crack real-estate lady and longtime single parent, headed for the door. "I for one have better things to do with my time," she said, but she could not quite bring herself to leave.

"My God," wailed the recent divorcée, "can't we ever just have fun?"

The one who was taking ballet lessons stood up. "It's degrading for women. That's what I've read."

"Bullshit," muttered the cum laude graduate from Smith.

"Oh you're such an intellectual, aren't you!" the one with a loom in her basement snorted.

"Snob!" shouted the mother of five.

"Well, Leonard calls it dreck." Thus did Gwen Pelt, invited by a well-meaning friend, put a temporary stop to all manner of acrimony. The sisters stared at her as one; such an appeal to authority had long been unheard in those precincts. "But I like it anyway," Gwen said quickly, all appeasement, assertion, and innocence.

"So do I," said the one with the au pair in the apartment above her garage.

"I find it entertaining; what's so wrong with that?" the recent divorcée, teetering between self-pity and aggression, wanted to know.

"Women in a Group do not watch television." Mitzi was indignant. "If that's what you want, join a bridge club."

"Oh for God's sake, where's your sense of humor?" The one with all the step-children turned snide.

"Ladies." This month's hostess called them to order. "We're watching. It's my house and I just decided."

Mitzi led the rump out into the kitchen; but all the sisters knew that the First Wednesdays would never be the same again.

◆

While the Lynford police were harassing an innocent man, while M. L. Johnson was preparing clean clothes for his journey, while Mrs. Sloane was showing off her daughter, while Gena and Alvin were deepening their relationship, while the First Wednesday Women's Group was up for grabs, a daring nighttime raid on the cabin cruiser *Shooting Star* went off without a hitch. This according to its mastermind, a young Queens homeowner and part-time chauffeur. Victor DiMaria had, to his credit, been struck from the first by the absence of any piece of jewelry, typically so much a part of the suburban haul, in the lots consigned to his garage. This had set him to thinking. Then Vinny, unwitting, had provided the clue; they had guessed right the first time.

The boys he had sent knew their way around on the water. They had arrived in the country not long before, after spending weeks on a small boat making the dangerous crossing from a small island. "The right man for the right job," Victor had said to his wife, sharing only the general principle; they never discussed business.

"Stick to your own kind," was Candy's wifely advice.

Now that it was over, Victor could wax philosophical. "Immigrants, that's what we were too, you know." He pinned an elaborately worked brooch of gold and sapphires onto the lapel of Candy's robe, covering a cluster of bright red cherries printed there. "Just don't wear it around! Wear the stuff I got you down in Florida."

"Did you pick out an heirloom for the baby?" she wanted to know.

Later, as they got ready for bed, Victor, feeling good, saw fit to indicate that business was good. As if in confirmation, the telephone rang. "When it rains, it pours," he said, and Candy knew, without, of course, knowing, that her husband was gaining something of a reputation. In fact, Victor was beginning to diversify; he was a man with a lot of fingers in a lot of pies, with a sure touch, with a feel for putting the man and the job together. He returned to the bedroom clearly preoccupied, and Candy did not disturb him.

"Pa's a great guy, isn't he?" he said suddenly.

Candy, removing the pink-and-yellow-flowered bedspread, studied him closely. She was always on the lookout for these abrupt shifts and seeming non sequiturs: they enabled her to understand something of the currents, dangerous or benign, upon which their contented little bark was borne.

"Yeah." Victor grew nostalgic. "He was always telling us, don't be afraid to try something new. Christopher Columbus was like a hero to him. Every year he took us down to the parade." He had all of Candy's attention now. "On the phone before, it reminded me of that; you know, no harm in trying something new. The guy's got a sense of humor; light up the sky, Vic, he says."

"Is he related to us somehow?" Candy liked to think of herself as well-connected.

"Someplace he is." Victor, who was beginning to forge his own links, could afford to be casual about the place of a poorly placed second cousin, another man's messenger boy. "A lot of distance, you gotta put a lot of distance," Victor mused as the clothes dropped from his quarterback's body onto the white shag carpet. "I hadda laugh, you know, the same damn boat," he confided in a burst of well-being, "and Wall Street, for Christ's sake!"

They both knew at once that he had gone too far. "Do you know how handsome you are?" Candy lay down by his side, secure in the present, supremely confident of the future.

Yeah, Victor thought, galled momentarily by his heavy responsibility, by the harsh inequality predestined between the sexes, but where does that get me a torch? He brightened. Better still, blow it; he had the man for that job. He settled it in his own mind; let the boat blow. The Jews always left the dirty work, he noted. So much the better for me. The baby began to cry; and as Candy pushed away from him, he started to nod, having suddenly regained a sure sense of what was, after all, right with God's creation.

10

THURSDAY

The Media Sups

Bruce Geller, sweatsuit by Lothar, pedaled his exercycle, while at his side his son lounged on the black-and-white ponyskin couch. Together, suspicious and mostly silent, they watched the "Sunrise News" because newsroom and schoolroom required it of them. In Sandy's case, sprawled, blond head thrown back and eyes apparently shut, it seemed uncertain that he was watching at all. Bruce, who could not help but be aware of what this said about the state of the art, vowed silently to redouble his creative efforts. It was especially essential, he felt, to commandeer and enforce so laggard an attention as that of his wayward son. The competition was fierce. But Bruce did have this advantage: "ideas as such"—it was thus he phrased it to show that he held them, like old fish, at arm's length—ideas did not figure in his "creative" thinking. When I brainstorm, he would tell his colleagues, I do it without ideas. It was his contention that the viewing public was no longer able to respond to an "idea as such" with the kind of engagement and consumerist energy he deemed necessary. Instead of ideas Bruce toyed with what he called commodities: personalities, gestures, events were the most valuable of these. He was able to juggle and juxtapose them with undeniable and winning dexterity; and when, all unwitting, he could not do without an idea, it came to him in one of these guises, like Jacob who came as Esau.

Sandy's interest in the news—that is, in the condition and fate of his fellow man, always excepting those involved in professional sports or the recording industry—was virtually nonexistent. As far as he was concerned, the music of the day said all there was to say about the state of the world. In fact, rock 'n' roll was as close to politics as Sandy came. In this too, he was very like his father: attitude was all. The only trouble was, of course, that he should find most appealing that pose which would please his father least. Sandy liked the posture of silent menace, the expression of unbridled rage, the crude gesture of defiance, the threat of destruction. That's what he liked. Shocked and disheartened, Bruce was yet unable to recognize that he himself was most at home in this debased public space; nay, more than that, that he worked to create it, to define discourse, give currency to style, to rouse, and sell.

"I'm outta here," Sandy said from the door. In his torn T-shirt and parachutist trousers he looked like a young airman down behind enemy lines, wary and unyielding. Bruce had a sneaking admiration for this costume; as a boy he had been without a look of his own.

"Why so early?" Bruce was casual, still pedaling.

"Gotta meet someone." He ducked his head, shading evasion with modesty.

"Anyone I know?" Bruce asked with some bitterness.

"Yeah, you know these guys. I gotta go."

"How're things coming along?" It was unusual for Bruce to question thus in depth.

"Great! Right!" The boy reached through the T-shirt and scratched across his stomach. "Listen, I gotta go."

"Nice talking to you," Bruce sneered, succumbing at last. "I'm only your father, you know." The pain was localized in his thighs as his legs churned on the pedals.

"Shit, Dad." Sandy was off with a casual wave. "Take it easy."

Oh sure, Bruce thought, I'll do that. "Have a nice day!" he called after his son.

His dissatisfaction ran as deep as his love. At that age his own relationship with his father had not been so very different, yet it seemed to him he had hidden his feelings more successfully—mainly the impatience and the arrogance. Sam Geller could not possibly have felt the deprivation, the anxiety, the downright insecurity that ate at his own heart.

Bruce pedaled on, dogged in the face of these thoughts, his gaze wandering aimlessly over the lucite bookshelves, his interest gradually engaged by an entertainment reporter. "Investors," she told him primly, "were attracted by the idea of getting four dollars in tax deductions for every dollar they invested." Suddenly Bruce was truly attentive. Hadn't Stanley Stern approached him with a similar pitch? "Now these investors, many well known in the entertainment world, are wondering if they'll ever see any of that money again." She smiled, a small, weary newsman's smile, as if she were not herself a well-known figure in the entertainment world looking for a tax shelter. Bruce smiled too; he had been asked and he had been prudent. He continued to browse the sleek, shelved spines and contemplated the hours of his ease which they threatened so ineffectually. At the end of each shelf, house-proud, stood a shiny brass initial, a *B* or a *G*, Marilyn's idea for bookends.

The scene had meanwhile shifted to an empty village square, at once terribly familiar and terribly foreign, clearly tropical in its white crumble and its blaze. Soldiers darted in and out of doorways. The time for Caribbean travel is definitely over, Bruce thought. A nun had been murdered, possibly raped; Bruce's glance flicked at the screen and then away, finding there only rising dust and the man with the mike. "Christ," he said half aloud, "this is supposed to be television, isn't it?" He made a mental note before continuing with his cataloging. I bet I haven't bought more than one percent of these books, he figured proudly of his large library. Because he was in the news business, it was assumed that Bruce craved and devoured information of any kind; in fact, he was thought of as a voracious reader with a wide range of interests, and consequently an easy man to buy a book for. He was therefore a man to whom a book was given on the least occasion for which a gift of any kind was appropriate. Sometimes, to his chagrin, he was even given a book simply because the giver thought he might be interested. At such times Bruce was hard put to be gracious. Genuine interest had become less and less possible for him with the passage of years, until now interest itself was simply a function of some other consideration. This he gladly interpreted as an increasingly discriminating taste.

Raped nun, he muttered, for Bruce did have an eye for the news, for what would go, as his peers acknowledged. It occurred to him that this Island-Paradise-Threatened-by-Revolution, the name by which he knew it, was likely to come into increasing focus; it would be wise, he thought, to update himself, for so he called the process of informing himself on a subject for the first time. But this good intention came too late; seventeen stories of a hundred-story office building had been lopped off by a freakish gust of wind the night before and the news moved on. However, as the collapse of giant structures had become of late something of a commonplace, his own attention was again free to turn to bookish matters.

If the talk of the town was a candid autobiography which was the talk of the town because its candor exceeded the candor of the candid autobiography which had most recently been the talk of the town, Bruce was sure to receive more than his fair share of copies. Similarly, his shelves would soon bear the weight of any novel of more than five hundred pages with especial preference given to those covering thousands of years and daily menus for all levels of society. It went without saying that the memoirs of any and all Moscow correspondents were thought to be appreciated; and, of course, as an Exercyclist he received fitness books, as a Jew the Middle East was appropriate, and as a Provider, books on financial planning and stock-market strategies. In other words, they had him coming and going. There was hardly a book on the best-seller lists of the past ten years that Bruce had not owned. He dreaded most the books which remained on the list week after week until he seemed to own more copies than the local bookstores. On the other hand, the Gellers had not had to actually purchase a gift of any kind for many years. You couldn't go wrong with a book, Bruce assured Marilyn, the shoe now on the other foot.

He shuddered, however, upon hearing his host introduce the author of *Tot-Terrific: How TV Works for Your Child,* for if a book pertained to television it was certain to be his in a matter of days. Avoiding the author's eyes, Bruce gave himself up to his pedaling as his allotted time on the bike drew to an end; yet he could not help but be impressed by what this poised young woman had to say. The more television the average child watched, she had discovered, the more average she or he became. Bruce, who was endowed by nature with a very high degree and quality of averageness, the money-making kind, and who augmented this by a carefully applied veneer of the same material, felt inclined to applaud this outcome. The author began to develop her point.

"Because we in America value our individuals above all, what we are seeing now is a generation of individualists. I call these children Generic Individualists, by which I mean that they are all individualists in exactly the same way." She basked in the warmth of her achievement and Bruce found himself smiling back at her, buoyed in fact. He made a mental note. "For the TV Tot," the author surged on with a self-deprecating smile, "those solitary little thoughts, all the little fantasies, in fact the whole of his or her private mental life—all that's gone now." Bruce looked up to meet her polite Little-Miss eyes. "But I do want to make one thing absolutely clear." She smiled broadly now, bringing it all home, in control from start to finish. "These TV Tots still love their mommies and their daddies; they surely do."

"Well, it certainly sounds like a book every parent will want to read," her host concluded thoughtfully, and Bruce, climbing down from the exercycle, breathing hard, allowed his thoughts to return to Sandy. Once again he searched his library for the atlas of the world, and this time found it, balanced across the tops of half the volumes of the Family Encyclopedia. He glowed with innocent satisfaction. Reaching for the large, flat book, it occurred to him to research the identity of that Island-in-the-News, a name by which it was also known. Opening the atlas and taking in the Caribbean at a single glance, he ruled out any land mass larger than the head of a paradisiac pin. He tapped among the islands with a well-manicured fingertip, nearly a piece of coral, but made no real progress. As quickly as his intention had been formed, so suddenly was it replaced by visions of an island vacation, a destination for the pale and the flush.

Bruce was not, however, without his resources. He looked over the uniform, maroon, anti-decorator spines of the Family Encyclopedia and selected a likely volume. And he did find something; he found a one-hundred-dollar bill. Had there been a witness to his discovery, Bruce would have taken the time to behave so as to establish his own surprise, but as it was, he simply picked up each volume in turn and leafed methodically through the pages. If he found nothing, he returned the book with especial care to its place on the shelf, gingerly, as one might treat a saint among sinners. The others he set on his desk, leaving the booty to mark each offending entry. In the end he had found a tidy sum, mostly in small bills.

For months now Bruce had been possessed of the absolute conviction that something was wrong; he felt it in the air. As he passed his son on the stairs the silence around them inevitably grew lively, and the sense of foreboding had been especially strong on the landing where Marilyn had contrived a green-house effect in front of the large window. "Vibes," Bruce had been used to mutter with ironic emphasis, planting his foot on each stair with self-conscious precision. He mentioned the "vibes" to Marilyn and, in spite of her brave, perfunctory talk about "stages" and "phases," he could see that she was worried too. She had told him to look for the signs—traces of powder, wild spending, weight loss—but there was nothing beyond a Third-World surliness, a peripatetic atlas and the "vibes."

But now the hard part, the waiting, appeared to be over. Here, indeed, was the other shoe. They had hoped for "a phase," that figment which had seen them through so much—something extremely unpleasant certainly, but still neither unhealthful nor illegal. Well, clearly it was not to be. The money scared Bruce perhaps more even than a bag of white powder might have; it stank of superfluity and contempt. So while he was not surprised exactly, he was deeply shocked. His mind was numbed into apparent unthought; yet his intuition was running fast and deep. The sad truth sprang to Bruce's mind nearly formed, with appropriate vocabulary to boot: The robbery had been an inside job. This was Sandy's take. All the robberies. They were all in it together. Thus did he begin to clarify the suspicions which had lain upon his heart. "Damn, damn, damn, damn, damn," Bruce swore as he paced; and the original denial, royal speaker or no, could not have conveyed more heartache.

Bruce was aware that time was of the essence; nevertheless, comforted by the weight of his professional responsibility, he lingered for "The Early Scene: Local News and Weather." For a few minutes more, he was all business. Mary Alice Mustard, he noted with regret, was no team player. Not a mention of Quint's dramatic debut of the previous evening, no sly wink, no small joke, no casual sarcasm, nothing; and poor Quint, standing in the early morning drizzle outside the Plaza reporting on the arrival hours earlier of five albino musicians from the Caribbean, knew it and could not show his pain. Dumb broad, Bruce said, and made a mental note. Making mental notes, confronting tough situations, coming down hard, Bruce was at the peak of his form in spite of the shock and the early hour.

Leonard Pelt, on the other hand, was in the shower when Gwen announced Bruce's arrival less than half an hour later. While Bruce showed no sign of his extraordinary haste, Leonard was still slightly damp under his elderly brown terry robe, and Gwen was nearly eyeless without her makeup. The early morning exacerbating vulnerability as it does, Bruce decided to take the long way around. Making a joke of it, he requested that Leonard go and fetch his atlas, but Leonard, sniffing the air, only sat, staring at him, worried and uncomprehending. This nervous, awkward man, he thought, was a far cry from Marilyn's masterful consort. Bruce took another tack, asking Gwen for a cup of coffee, but this altered the stalemate in no way, for curiosity seemed to have immobilized his hostess as well.

"We have a problem, folks." Bruce tried to keep it light, but an unmanly giggle caught in his throat and his face flushed. "Could we go and take a look at Leonard's library, please?"

The Pelts trailed him meekly from the kitchen, hearts alert. To their surprise he bid them follow his example as he began to leaf through and shake out the collected works of Sigmund Freud. Then came the works of his followers, and the works of those who do not quite follow him, and the works of those who believe they follow him not at all, and volumes of biography, and collections of letters, and finally any other book in the vicinity of a certain bulk and color. As they worked, Bruce related how he had come upon the money; he speculated knowledgeably, bitterly, on its provenance. Leonard and Gwen disbelieved, pooh-poohed, protested, but they did not stop looking. It took both men to shake out the two thousand pages of the *Random House Dictionary*, but even here they came up dry, and now Leonard stopped shivering and began to perspire with relief. He asked Gwen to bring in some coffee.

"You and Marilyn have really had it," Gwen said sympathetically, setting down the tray on a rough mosaic-topped coffee table of Mediterranean hues. "First the burglary and now this on top of it." Trepidation had put a glint into her small eyes.

"Bruce is jumping to conclusions," Leonard warned her off with some severity. He crossed his long legs and rearranged the tails of the robe, nearly jumping at the touch of the wet, clammy terrycloth. "It would never occur to me to think that way. I'd think of selling dope first."

"Oh Leonard!" Gwen reproached, but this was the first thought that had come to her own mind.

"Burglarizing your parents' home. That has ugly implications." Leonard's voice had turned dreamy.

"Bruce isn't saying that," Gwen broke in frantically, although this was precisely what she understood Bruce to be saying.

"You haven't been listening again, Gwen." Leonard dismissed her. He took a Kleenex from his pocket and wiped his upper lip. "If I were you, Bruce, I wouldn't take this thing personally. Whatever it is, you can be certain there's more to it than meets the eye."

Bruce was sitting in Leonard's tweed-upholstered reading chair, his feet on the hassock, his gaze roaming restlessly back and forth across the room-width walnut shelving. It had given him something of a shock to hear Leonard speak aloud so casually the phrase he had not been able to face, but he gave no sign. Burglarizing your parents home. He had gulped his coffee in silence and burnt the inside of his mouth; but already his pain was relegated to the past. He rolled his tongue obsessively across the roof of his mouth, unable to identify a cause for his hurt. He was living in an eternal present, the empty coffee cup still in the air inches from his mouth. Suddenly his bloodshot eyes blinked rapidly and then held fast their gaze. He rose with deliberation and, crouching, selected a volume from the bottom shelf called *Gourmet Cookery for the Gourmet Cook*. Gwen, all set to remove her dainty cup from her guest's white-knuckled grip, stopped in startled amazement as her husband leapt to his feet with a snort. Hovering at Bruce's shoulder, Leonard's heart sank when he saw the title of the book Bruce held. His wife, as he knew too well, was no cook. Thus Leonard, no less than Bruce before him, intuited at once and accepted without thought the logic, if not the justice, of this hiding place. Unconscious of all but their hurt, however, neither man was truly able to appreciate that adolescent mix of ironic comment and attention to convention which marked, though it could not ennoble, the boys' conspiracy.

"Goddammit, Gwen!" Leonard said, and this may be considered a foreshadowing of late-night confrontations and endless recriminations to come. On her guard, but still innocent of his meaning, Gwen stayed put; she worried the elastic waistband on her cranberry-red jogging suit.

Now Bruce put down the coffee cup. He lifted the book high with an insolence born of his recent mortification and shook it vigorously. The money was there.

Leonard got dressed immediately and, leaving Gwen to her own cruel thoughts, the two men entered Bruce's Mercedes and sped to the home of Ben Finkle. There Polly, the crack real-estate lady and longtime single parent, was persuaded to witness the recovery of several hundred dollars from between the pages of a certain slim leather-bound volume containing the ecumenical wedding ceremony she and her husband-to-be had co-authored in the late sixties.

At the home of Jason Herz the drama was to be repeated once more. In spite of the challenge presented by an unusually large number of well-thumbed, loose-limbed paperbacks, these highly motivated men and women persisted and the money was eventually located in an ancient thesaurus which rested, humbled and jacketless, within a straw basket filled with old newspapers and kindling. It was clear at once to all of them that young Jason was lacking in some of the sophistication and maturity the other boys had shown.

"Yeah," Hank Herz sighed with a sidelong glance at his wife, "he's got some growing up to do."

"They all do, Lord knows," Polly Finkle added quickly, mostly to convince herself that her tall, cynical son was only a boy at heart.

"Boys will be boys; but Christ, I don't know." Bruce's heart was heavy. "What do you think, Pelt? You're the shrink."

But Leonard was unable to think. The best he could do was to say again, nodding his head to suggest an added measure of consideration, "It has some ugly implications."

The others looked at the money in Bruce's hand and shuddered. They did not look at each other, nor did they look at themselves. Suddenly embarrassed, suddenly dumb, they were relieved to hear Bruce suggest that they disperse to take thought before taking action. This suggestion, this confirmation that they were indeed a unit, gave them the strength to depart from each other for the present—which had been, since they came together, their dearest wish. Perhaps only Bruce was at all sorry to be on his own, for he still had Marilyn to face.

That suburban matron, already suited-up for tennis, met him at the front door with a volley of accusations touching on his sanity and provoked by his hasty and unexplained departure earlier. What she demanded was nothing less than complete enlightenment.

Bruce took up a position under the skylight, the hothouse Lear. "Marilyn," he began gently, "we have a problem."

Marilyn snipped that she certainly hoped so seeing that she would let nothing less interfere with her daily tennis game. Her husband, seized by the desire to punish her for so unmotherly an attitude, dispensed his news then without further preamble, down and dirty.

"I knew something was wrong; a mother knows." Marilyn's voice, always persistent and assured, did not falter, nor did she give ground. "You see, I knew it. I sensed something. I told Jake!" Her eyes were very bright and the look she gave Bruce was that of an ambitious, half-crazed featherweight. "But I'm not jumping to conclusions, sweetie. There are lots of explanations, and I think I know one. The black man, for instance, what about him? Do you think of him? No, you think of your own white son." She gave him a hard hot stare as if she could drill a hole and drop in the seed of her suspicion.

"What black man?" Bruce was relieved that he had after all spared Marilyn a tongue-lashing; it sounded like she might be on to something.

"I saw him with Sandy. I told Jake."

"What is Jake, your rabbi for Christ's sake?" Bruce stalked into the den. He took off his suit coat and pulled at the back of his shirt where it had been soaked a darker blue. Earlier, an automaton at the closet, it had not occurred to him that he would not go to work today; now he was puzzled by his attire, as he had been at the idea of getting dressed in a dark business suit for his father's funeral. "Being an obnoxious smartass is one thing, but he's my goddamn son for Christ's sake."

"It's growing up, sweetie. It's hard to grow up these days." Marilyn sat down on the sofa where her son had lounged only hours before. This appeared to have the effect of enhancing not only her understanding but her confidence too. "I mean you're just surrounded by kooks and criminals. You can forget the schools. Do you have any idea how low test scores are now?"

"That kid is going to a goddam kibbutz and I'm not kidding. I told Jake."

Marilyn looked up at him sharply. "There's no point in exaggerating, Bruce. The worst I can imagine is he gave the man a key. I mean he didn't do it of his own free will; he probably had to, for some reason."

"For what reason?" Bruce's eyes were bulging. "For what goddamn reason does my son let a man come in and rob me blind?"

"He's on drugs," Marilyn replied with the simplicity of a Quaker. "The black man is his connection."

Bruce's light complexion broke out in angry splotches and there was fear in him. His voice had grown hoarse in an instant. "Oh, I see," he said, mustering sarcasm, "my son is on dope; my son has a, a . . ."

"Connection," Marilyn supplied.

"A goddamn connection, but I don't know about it, right? What the hell is going on here?" Bruce cleared the tears out of his throat.

Marilyn walked over to him and put both hands on his arm. Although somewhere in the core of her being she had been almost as deeply shocked as Bruce, this hurt she was able to set aside in favor of an opportunity for self-realization, empowerment. Here was a challenge worthy of her wild determination and mother-love, her selfishness and her strong hand.

"Bruce, sweetie, it could be worse. You have no idea of what

202

some of these kids are into. Have you ever looked at David Pelt's eyes?"

Bruce had not.

"What are we going to do?" he wondered aloud, although at that very moment he had a dawning awareness that all might still be well. But when Marilyn did not answer immediately, she allowed the contrary certainty to reassert itself. "This has ugly implications, Marilyn. And that's a shrink's opinion."

Marilyn dug her nails into his arm, hard. "I don't want you to ever say that, Bruce. Don't even think it." She began to push him in the direction of the door. "You should have some breakfast now and I should call Gwen; she must be out of her mind."

Bruce pulled away from her.

"Look at this kid, would you?" He picked up a leather-framed photograph of Sandy, an eight-year-old in a tie and blazer, posed by a professional. "What a great kid he was!" It struck Bruce as unfair and confusing, the apparent incoherence of his son's development. He shook the portrait hard but, as it had been expensively mounted, he was unable to take any solace there. Marilyn took the picture from him, studying it for just the instant it took to bring tears to her eyes, before replacing it on the table where it ruled over photos of lesser size and consequence. Memories of happier days attended the pair into the kitchen.

As Marilyn had overseen and charted her son's development, she had always been ready to declare a stage a stage and a phase a phase, even if this meant spinning out such a construct on the spur of the moment. In fact, she showed a real flair for ingenious, even audacious, labeling, and one should not minimize the part her talent played in assuring both of them an overall sense of satisfaction with their lot. Although Bruce was, from time to time, vaguely uneasy with her bold yet subtle manipulation of unsympathetic reality, he was on the whole content to see an average boy.

God had given Marilyn a nimble mind, and she had used it to advantage to juggle after-school activities, plan large dinner parties, and organize foreign-travel itineraries; but here was her first real challenge since she had engineered the successful campaign to bring Sunday School hours into conformity with court times at the local country clubs. She felt a stirring within herself, a strength and a brutal dedication which were part field marshal and part lioness. She reviewed her troops: Bruce, suffering from his wound, fearing a Gellerian ghost, would not be good for much. But Leonard Pelt was in a helping profession, Gwen was a good listener, Polly Finkle was a fast talker, Hank Herz was a lawyer, and his wife was a passable doubles partner. Marilyn was encouraged.

She looked at Bruce where he sat caved in on the high stool, mourning, staring at the unfinished bowl of cereal his son had left on the counter, and her heart went out to him. She began to massage his shoulders and knead the muscles at the base of his neck as she considered what must be done. She was thinking very clearly. Bruce deserved a great deal of credit, she realized, for his control at the instant of discovery. In an unusual moment of empathy Marilyn intuited the tight-lipped grimness, the twitching muscles, the burning eyes which must have enforced this discipline on him. The volumes could easily be replaced, money intact, so that a discovery of their discovery did not catch them unawares before their own plan of action was in place. Such a plan might simply be a way out of the mess, an acceptable misinterpretation, a face-saver all the way around.

In a sudden move, Bruce's arm darted forward and brought a spoonful of Sandy's milk-muddied cereal to his parched mouth. He swallowed and began to gag. Marilyn addressed herself once more to his back, pounding hard now to meet the current crisis.

"Drug treatment facility," she whispered comfortingly behind Bruce's ear, "Southern military academy, prestigious prep school, summer job."

Rejecting her ministrations, Bruce stumbled from the kitchen, coughing, arms flailing. The soft, light-gray carpeting was so soothing at a time like this, Marilyn thought as she followed it up the stairs, down the hallway, and into their bedroom, monitoring her husband. On Bruce's night table lay a thick book, a present from Sandy, which had been selected, Bruce was sure, from among the brand-new books which lined the shelves downstairs.

"Oh goddamn it!" Bruce said between clenched teeth, and hurled the big book across the room. Marilyn, who played a very sharp game at net, sprang into action; leaping, stretching, she nudged shut the high wall cabinet that housed the television, and the heavy book fell to the floor, defused. Bruce sat down on the bed; tugging convulsively at the flowered sheets, he began to cry. It amounted in all truth to two rather harsh sobs followed by some deep ragged breathing, but it was as heartfelt as any mother's endless wailing. Marilyn sat by his side and took his hand. She did not begrudge Bruce his tears, nor did she envy him, nor was she at all impatient with him. Still, she herself had moved quickly, unconsciously, beyond tears to a hot-eyed denial of loss. Selfhood and motherhood both intact, Marilyn would brook no diminishment.

A short time later, her thoughts fixed on what she always called "My Concern As a Parent," when she meant her son, Marilyn left the house. The Lynford Four, as Leonard Pelt would soon dub them, the Lynford Five, as Marilyn would have it, had found a defender.

◆

By mid-morning John White was ensconced at the lesser of the two local motels. Tucked as it was between a wholesale rug outlet and a low, frequently untenanted office building, this forthrightly cheerless hostel was pleased to welcome an overnight guest. John did not take the time to appreciate fully the details of decor and convenience to which the management had given such scant thought, if in fact a red-faced widower with one lung and a three-pack-a-day habit living in Florida could be dignified with such a title. Instead, he hurried straight back to the side of his new employer, there to be nurtured and commanded as she would. For John's was a history of thralldom: first, the thrall of a mightly father, then of an adventurous

Commander-in-Chief; then demobbed to become a thrall to the devil's music, the evil weed, the boob tube; and finally born again as Big John's eager minion, he now came to offer his devotion to his Lady of Small Business. Here was a résumé indeed for the expanding service economy.

Insofar as hitchhiking can be construed as hurrying, John White was at the toy store in no time at all. Yet he soon had reason to regret his rush: Mitzi wanted none of his homage; worse yet, the old lady was there with her fish eye and her grousing.

"What happened with him?" that close-lipped lady-in-waiting muttered to her mistress. "What happened with his so-called friend?" She gave the onetime kitchen-table missionary a look which spoke plainly of her intransigence, and he smiled in the teeth of her pride.

"It's me again," he said as friendly as you please, perhaps thinking dimly that the way to the mistress might well be through her lady-in-waiting.

But all Helga said was "Ah!" which exclamation may just as well have been related to the pleasure she felt in seating herself and lighting a cigarette.

There was, however, something in that heartfelt "Ah!" that John White took personally. "There's more than one way to serve the Lord," he told her defensively, although he had decided that his own days toiling in that vineyard were over for good.

"Perhaps it's for the best," Helga suggested with a blandness that barely concealed the indifference with which she viewed his prospects.

"That's what I was thinking." He gave her a surprised look. "We live in a land of opportunity as far as I'm concerned." Helga could not appreciate the truly remarkable nature of this platitude in John White's mouth, for here was a man who personally knew nothing of opportunity. A man, then, we may conclude, of consummate faith.

"I am curious, Mr. White." Helga glared up at him through

the smoke. "I listen, I try to learn something . . . What happened with you?"

"Well ma'am, the Lord works in mysterious ways." He shifted his weight from one foot to the other and then back again. "I don't believe phone work, which they say that's a God-given talent, is my kind of work. I just feel the Lord is leading me on to other Christian service." He was pleased with his presentation.

"Christian service," Helga repeated for the benefit of Mitzi who had been out in the shop with a customer. The undercurrent in her echo, which John White could not hear for her accent, can be attributed to the fact that Mitzi did in fact require a kind of Christian service.

His Lady of Small Business knew just what she wanted; she wanted a front: a clean-cut, clean-living Christian man to manage her video arcade, someone to turn away the wrath of the conservatives, of the educators, of the families of foreign diplomats, someone to blind them with blandness, to quell their fears. It was a very specific assignment she had in mind, and as such not due to begin until the moment Mitzi deemed most propitious. Then she would spring him on them, the old fogeys, the chauvinists. So John White spent his morning between the toy store and the arcade abuilding; he lounged, he loafed, he loitered, and generally carried on as if he were an even Younger Man. All of this Mitzi noted for future reference, for color. Finally, in desperation, his Lady sent him out on a Fool's errand. Glad to be free of his pathetic attempts to balance his optimism and his despair, the two women quickly put him from their minds. Similarly, those who, enjoying an early lunch, saw him enter the Lynford Tavern at noon and make there a stand of some duration, paid him no mind. Only Joey DiMaria, a dance student in that large family of brothers and so no stranger to loneliness, bothered to give him a friendly smile. And John White, confused and unhappy in his freedom, was grateful.

At the motel, the television set which he had activated by

207

the unthinking insertion of whatever coins he had, continued to brighten the grim little room long after his departure. Because he had neglected, in his haste and his devotion, to pull shut the door, as time passed the set had drawn to itself not only the solitary kerchiefed maid, but an alcoholic salesman and a despondent, recently deserted father of three from a nearby town. And each was comforted according to his need. Such negligence, such disregard for security, would be roundly censured at the other, the greater of the two local spas; but here, poolless, cheerless, it was in fact rather smiled upon by the day manager, a horse-toothed young Midwesterner who was writing his own miniseries and was an assiduous collector of "moments," an inveterate hall monitor. Aspiring to the business himself, he was certain, then, to cock an ear just outside John White's door when he heard, among other things, the breath of scandal: ". . . leading figures in the entertainment world are listed as creditors as a fledgling financial empire crumbles," a male voice reported. "Called a genius by some, and a crook by others . . . ," a female voice broke in, but then the set went dead.

Sitting in Mitzi's crowded little office, Helga began, hesitantly, delicately, with an apology.

"Forgive me if it is not my business, but you know how I care for Jacob." She lit a cigarette, pausing to allow Mitzi to forestall her, but Mitzi only nodded and began to unwrap her sandwich. "He seems to me so very," Helga sighed, "how should I say it . . ." She discarded one by one the words that came to mind. "So, so, discombobulated, and by such small things." She gave Mitzi a questioning look.

It was Mitzi's turn to sigh. Even Helga then, even Helga did not understand. True, Jake's condition had become aggravated, yet this could only be a sign, Mitzi felt, that he was finally on the verge of a breakthrough. The store was very quiet and the new autumn heating smelled of winter.

"Did something happen with the nun?" Mitzi asked. "That didn't sound like such a great idea to me anyway—Jake and a nun."

Helga tried to pinpoint her concern. "It was more the television. He got upset with that silly program. But really upset! I could see it in his face." Helga sipped her tea from a sky-blue mug, a work of Douglas's Middle Period. Because the mug lacked a handle—a characteristic of his output from that time—the tea was, of necessity, drunk tepid, which, O Homo Faber, was the way Helga liked it.

"Oh that." Mitzi dismissed it. What Helga called "upset," she saw as righteous, perhaps even prophetic, indignation. High-flying, quasi-rabbinical, a dreamer, an intellectual, Jake was getting ready, she was sure, to pull out all his bookmarks, empty his files, repair with tape lifesavers his loose-leaves, and reveal in his very own words an understanding that would shake the world. In short, Mitzi believed that her husband was writing a book.

"He was still ranting when I got home. Apparently, Alvin Quint made a guest appearance."

"What! Quint came to Mrs. Sloane?" Helga's puzzlement was deep.

Mitzi laughed, shaking a pickle spear in Helga's direction. "No, no, on TV, on the show."

"Quint??!!" Helga stood up as if stuck with a pin.

"Playing a newsman," Mitzi elaborated without irony.

"This man goes too far, Mitzi."

Helga sat down heavily, took a large bite from her pastrami sandwich, and chewed slowly, censoring. "He has no idea." She hesitated. "I find it remarkable," she went on, again leaving something unsaid; but nevertheless, she saw fit to conclude, "I'm sorry to have to say it." Her dark eyes glistened and the depths of her unspoken reservations might readily have been deciphered there.

"I think that's Jake's problem too," Mitzi thought she could safely say.

"Yes, but Jake does not have a daughter who would marry him." Helga feared Quint. Outliving the war, though only in a manner of speaking, she had, through intuition and observation, evolved the position that all was not right with the world.

As she herself had come through uprooted, unhinged, and but crudely rejoined and patched, why then should she not believe the world to have been radically transformed, flipped, fundamentally altered? Quint, whom she saw as spineless and indolent, pretentious and superficial, was a man for such a world; a man who wanted to be taken in, who could be broken down, who was comfortable with the half-true and the half-clean, who could flourish in the thin, merciless air of the studio.

Who, she wondered, was Gena that she could love such a man? And who, she continued bravely, am I that I should love such a daughter who could love such a man? Mother-love, Helga thought with grim satisfaction, and vowed eternal vigilance against the Quints of the world.

"What was your own impression of him?" she asked casually.

Mitzi, whose thoughts had remained behind with Jake, said the first kind thing that came to mind. "He's tall, isn't he!" But sensing at once the pitfall here, she sought to take the sting out. "But then, I'm such a runt everyone is tall."

"Yes, he is quite tall." Helga, disappointed with this response, decided to make something of it. "But apparently it's no help."

Mitzi looked baffled and in a moment she would grow impatient. For the first time her mind turned to the continued absence of her little vicar.

"Quint is no basketball player, my grandson says. At least that would have been something for Douglas. He is an American boy after all." Though Helga was immune to the charms of the game, she was genuinely sorry that Douglas should be deprived of this birthright. To underline her empathy, she crumpled a square of white delicatessen paper and scored in the wastebasket behind Mitzi's desk. "Ah ha!"

"When you say American boy I can't help but think of John White." Mitzi leapt at the opportunity to return to her own concerns. "What do you think of him, by the way?"

"Ach, don't ask!" Helga lifted her book from the pink cloth, touched it to her forehead, and set it down again. "What can I say about a goy without a nose who comes on Rosh Hashanah

210

to convert me? He is another one who does not know what is what."

"My God, Helga, don't be so rough on the guy. He's harmless, honestly."

"I am sorry if I do not agree with you, Mitzi." Helga inhaled deeply and then the smoke issued from her nostrils in a rush. "His interests are sudden and shallow. He needs a strong hand."

"You may be right," Mitzi said cheerfully. "After all, how long does it take to walk up the street to the bookstore?" She had sent him out to buy a book for Bruce. "But right now he is from heaven. They may not trust a woman, it's an issue, I'm telling you, but what are they going to say to him!"

Mitzi began to miss the flash of his evangelical motley, the jangle of his bells. She stood up and started to rewrap the remaining half of her ham-and-cheese sandwich.

"I hope you were not offended." Helga thoughtfully returned the conversation to its starting point.

"Of course not." Mitzi was gracious. "Meanwhile, pity me. You can imagine how well Jake likes the idea of an arcade." She smiled wistfully as if there were another man somewhere in her past whom she had rejected but who would almost certainly approve of a video arcade.

Helga smiled and shook her head. A long-ignored cigarette ash fell into her lap and in trying to lift the gray column of ash from the gray skirt she managed to leave a bit of yellow mustard behind. To Mitzi's surprise, Helga's smile only grew.

◆

Jake sprayed the glass of the inner door with a well-advertised and odoriferous liquid and wiped it dry with paper toweling, pushing the paper down the bevelled edges of the glass and into each corner. He took pride in his work. Still, his view of it was neither sentimental nor strictly political: he did not buy the romance of the blue collar, he did not believe in the wholesomeness or in the curative power of manual labor, he rejected simplicity for its own sake. What Jake was drawn to was the freedom, the finitude, the known standards permitting

211

satisfying judgments, the ameliorative potential of his work. True, the improvements were always temporary, especially in winter, but such positive and pleasurable effect was capable of being repeated at will. And Jake's will was in no way impaired, all surmise to the contrary notwithstanding.

The black-and-white tiled stairway was newly washed. In addition, he had changed a light bulb and tightened a rattling doorknob. Now, propping the inner door open with his anodized bucket, he began to mop the little vestibule, staying out of his own way. Here we may see quite clearly one appealing aspect of this work: in no endeavor of the mind had Jake yet been able to stay out of his own way. He flung the large string mop about with vigor, a veritable Astaire. Meanwhile, his thoughts ran before him.

It was indeed thought itself—rumination, speculation, a brown study plain and simple—that kept Jake lighthearted. Rant and rave, grouse and grumble as he might, his mind floated freely through time and space, buoying him up. What his brother viewed as Jake's frivolous and indiscriminate interest was in fact rather more like a friendly compulsion, a deeply felt need to accumulate the details, to understand what was not apparent, to communicate with the core. This was no easy task. Nevertheless, this intent, or rather the consciousness of this intent, fostered the flame of the spirit and made for a merry soul.

So Jake had this going for him: he was, as his sister-in-law had said disdainfully, a cheerful person. "Receive all men with a cheerful countenance" and the rewards were not, Jake noted, limited to this world. When a certain rabbi, standing in a crowded marketplace, questioned the prophet Elijah about who among that throng was destined to enjoy a share in the World-to-Come, Elijah, after a time, pointed out two men. The rabbi approached and asked them what they did. "We are cheerful persons," they replied; "when we see a man who is downcast we cheer him up; also when we see two people quarreling with each other, we endeavor to make peace between them."

But take away the rabbi, thought Jake, take away the marketplace, take away the prophet, take away the World-to-Come, and what are you left with? A good game of squash, perhaps, and a taste for seafood; the vague hope that such minor manifestations of one's humanity might stand for the whole.

"Hey!" Mark Cone, in satin bowling jacket and beaded sweatband, broke into Jake's meditation with great determination, blowing through the door and up the stairs. At the landing he paused and checked his clipboard. "I'm looking for the nun," he called back down to Jake.

Out the door Jake saw to his surprise the red, white, and blue mobile unit from the television station. "None here," he replied cheerfully, set to be obstructionist.

"The nun, the nun." Mark Cone was impatient. "Quick."

Quint and his cameraman burst through the street door. "Top floor," Quint shouted, and the ferret was off. Quint greeted Jake cordially but did not slacken his pace. "Contacts, that's where it's at," he crowed. Yet this allusion to Helga's coffee klatch the previous Saturday did not satisfy Jake's curiosity. "Lead with it." Quint was panting as he approached the landing. "Top story!"

"Story," Jake echoed encouragingly; though breathing heavily himself, he refused to yield position to Quint's burly cameraman.

"All the elements." Suddenly Quint stopped dead, groaning, pressing both fists into his left side just above the belt of his black leather coat. "Stitch! Stitch!" he cursed.

"Yeah, boss." The big-bellied cameraman passed Quint up with this snide reference to the newsman knew not what.

Jake, who had stood aside, insofar as it is possible on a small landing to stand aside, now voiced his concern. "What happened?"

"Nun dead," Quint said, gritting his teeth, starting up again. "Real trouper." This last might very well have been said in praise of the dead sister, but wasn't. Jake had gone cold at the news. He walked the remaining stairs slowly, muddled and anxious, until the sight of Mrs. Sloane, all smiles in the doorway, prompted more far-reaching speculation.

Mrs. Sloane treated all men without regard to their rank. For this or another reason she gave no sign of having met Alvin Quint on the earlier occasion or of ever having seen him on television; in fact, she was prepared to dispense with pleasantries altogether in order to claim her place in the sun. Nevertheless, she did seem to take a particular fancy to the prole of a cameraman, sweating in his fleece-lined gray denim jacket, panning the room in search of a nun. Or perhaps it was just that she wanted him on her side. In any case, she went out of her way to include him in the series of delicate negotiations that followed. Quint had to fight tooth and nail to get his way.

In the end Mrs. Sloane was placed at her imposing oak sideboard in such a way as to shield the half-empty crystal decanters from view. She had chosen a simple black dress for the occasion and pulled on a multi-colored turban to cover her thinning hair and at the same time establish her rights to an exotic past. A lesser Dinesen, she liked to think, having met the writer at a luncheon at the St. Regis in the late fifties. At the time, of course, Mrs. Sloane had been much more apt to think of herself as a lesser Luce, but she had had from her youth a talent for storing up her impressions, and had developed an excellent nose for just which ones would come in handy.

Quint removed his massive coat. He was handed a microphone and with it outstretched he approached Mrs. Sloane. "Was Sister Bryn a close friend of your daughter's?" he probed gently, doing his research.

Mrs. Sloane addressed the sleeping camera. "No, I don't think so. Poor girl. According to the television, she had just arrived."

"I suppose your daughter's thankful to be away at a time like this. What are her feelings, can you tell us?" Quint's gaze wandered around the room.

"She's packing. She's terribly distressed to be away just now, as you can imagine." Mrs. Sloane tried to keep her tone neutral; after all, she had lived her own life, hadn't she?

"And how do you feel about that, Mrs. Sloane?" Quint signaled his cameraman, who activated the camera for the first time. "How do you feel as a mother?"

"I have always enjoyed a good cause," she said with a quick look at Jake. Quint followed her gaze, hungry for an out. "But on the other hand, none of us is growing any younger, are we?" Here she made the mistake of pausing to take thought.

"Thank you for talking with us, Mrs. Sloane." Quint hurried now toward Iris who hesitated in the doorway where the camera had found and pinned her helpless with an armful of undergarments. Behind her, Mark Cone rolled his eyes, allowed his tongue to lag and his head to loll, and drew a finger across his throat. But Quint, though wincing inwardly at the sight of his stern, hawk-nosed subject, had learned not to trust these pantomimes; Mark Cone had set him up more than once.

"Can you tell us how it feels, Sister, to be here visiting your mother at a time when another nun, a good friend of yours, has been brutally murdered and raped?" Quint felt very high, very acute, very powerful.

Iris looked him in the eye.

"We warned the Embassy," she said evenly. "They knew about the harassment . . ."

Quint broke in mournfully, "We understand that Sister Bryn's family—" he began.

Iris did not break stride. ". . . and intimidation. We work with the people and the government does not like that." She allowed Quint to see that she had made her point.

"We understand that she was very close to her brother, who, incidentally, we are told, is not a sighted individual." Quint had no intention of playing her game.

"The fact is," said Iris, placid and helpful, "Sister Bryn was aware of the danger. It is the work we do."

"I see." Quint decided to throw in the towel. "Well, thank you very much." He took no trouble to hide his disdain, but before he could turn away Iris put her hand on his arm. A nun touched me, a little voice inside him said, a nun touched me.

"I suggest you talk to them at the Embassy, Mr. Quint. That's your story there."

Mrs. Sloane cleared her throat, apparently prepared to take issue with her daughter's approach. "This is the local news," she informed Iris, as she favored the bear of a cameraman with a conspiratorial smile.

"Thank you ladies." Quint was magnanimous in defeat, but only Mrs. Sloane was granted the trademark grimace. "See you on the news." He would leave Mark Cone behind to attend to administrative matters; perhaps he had misjudged him.

"Well, how'd you like it?" He drew Jake to one side.

Jake had listened to Iris with a sinking heart. Unprepared, the best he could do now was to mutter, "'But that was in another country, and besides the wench is dead.'"

Quint was suspicious. "All the elements, like I said." He handed his microphone to his minion, hefted his coat, and stepped into the hall motioning Jake before him. "But would you believe that dopey broad! These days most people give you what you want; but this one—no way was she going to give it to me." He lowered his voice. "This business is an ethnic ghetto, remember that; but I deserve a break too sometimes."

Jake was surprised. "She seemed to be hinting that there are some political implications to this murder," he ventured.

"Brutal rape and murder," Quint amended automatically. "In a way, I deserve it," he continued fretfully as they went down the stairs. "I had a chance to go interview the brother, but no, like a schmuck . . ."—he tried to suppress a self-conscious smile—". . . I said I'd take the nun."

"Yeah, boss." The cameraman bellied by, insinuating for all he was worth his agreement with Quint's self-judgment.

Jake decided to change the subject. "It's easier to get an interview when you have a script," he joked, bringing together a number of loose threads.

"Yeah," the sometime actor assented indifferently; he was barely listening.

Jake forced Uncle Nathan's cartoon of a laugh, thinking to do

216

them both some good, but the sound of it in the empty, tiled stairwell made him cringe instead.

"Jake, I'm down; I am really down," the journalist revealed, his head nodding slowly as it did during an interview to indicate full attention.

Jake tried once more. "I saw you on television last night," he said, thinking perhaps his companion had missed his little joke, but the newsman would not be consoled.

But then, as Jake, ready to give up, bent to pick up his pail, Quint grabbed his arm. "Hold on a second," he said with sudden animation, "let's analyze this objectively. Alvin Quint is not on some godforsaken shit-hole of an island looking like a wimp in his little safari suit, and trying to make believe that all that Third-World crap is news. Some of the guys get off on that kind of thing. Macho man. But that, my friend, is not where it's at. This is a new age. Like they say, 'There's a new day dawning in America.'"

"Where Third-World crap is not news, you mean?" Jake queried uncertainly.

"You got it!" Quint sulked no longer. Mark Cone came down the stairs in noisy cowboy boots and plowed the air between them, incurious to the point of insult. "But listen, why single out those jokers?" Quint was on a roll. "It's all crap, my friend, you name it: NATO, the Federal Reserve Bank, the space shuttle, labor negotiations, the Politburo, the Highway Department—what is all that but crap?"

"And so consequently not news either, right?" Jake was following closely now.

"Right! But, in a story like this one here," he went on, nodding toward the stairway, "where you've got the elements, we can get down to work, really do a job, make a difference, get the viewers going, no politics, just people-to-people, get their emotions involved."

Jake heaved a great sigh, but, nonetheless, he had to be gratified to see Quint thus revived. He hoisted his mop and settled his other paraphernalia into the caddy. When he opened the door to the cellar, a thick cloud of silence rose to challenge the puny human silence that had grown between them.

"'That girls were raped,'" Jake recited helplessly to an attentive Quint, "'that two boys knife a third, were axioms to him, who's never heard of any world where promises were kept, or one could weep because another wept.'"

"That reminds me of something my very first boss used to tell us." A horn honked outside but Quint did not miss a beat. "Pluck and tug, he would say, tug and pluck."

"Plug and tuck?" Jake gave the words an inadvertently janitorial twist.

"Heartstrings." Quint chuckled apologetically. "He was an old-timer. We've come a long way since then; now we're primarily into responsibility, the First Amendment, what have you." He shifted his heavy coat from the crook of one arm to the other and shook that ill-used limb vigorously to encourage circulation. "You can say what you want about your Edward R. Murrows and so forth, but that was kid stuff. It's a heavy burden, a heavy burden I mean, and there's no way we're going to take it lightly. Believe me, when you realize it's the people's right to know, you better get your ass in gear." Quint spoke with some fervor, but the small vestibule nevertheless seemed adequate to the task of containing such fine and public sentiments.

Jake, listening to Quint's words, saw more clearly than ever that they referred him to an entirely new, yet obviously widely accepted reality.

"You're talking about a different world," he began weakly.

"That's what I was telling you." Quint was unduly enthusiastic, as if he were encouraging a doltish student.

Jake pulled out all the stops. "You're changing the nature of reality. You realize that, don't you?"

"That's what they pay us for, I've gotta believe. Anyways, I can't take all the credit; they've got some fantastic commercials out right now."

"The commercial break," Jake said pleasantly, "a roadside

chapel where the confused and the terrorized can take refuge, regain their perspective and composure, safe at last . . ."

"You're crazy, you know," Quint interrupted; things had been going along so well, he thought. Outside, a car horn sounded. "They're waiting for me." He held out his hand and Jake clasped it. It had been difficult at first to take Jake seriously, dressed as he was for janitorial work, but now Quint said, "We can thank the Women's Libbers for this, you know, being up front with each other, two guys talking about their feelings." Apparently moved, he hurried from the building. Nevertheless, they were not waiting for him; the mobile unit was nowhere in sight, Mark Cone had once again played him for a fool.

Quint was right about one thing, however. The brother of the dead nun turned out to be a horticulturist. That evening when Quint again hit Iris right between the eyes with his no-nonsense question, the picture shuddered for a split second before Iris answered simply that "Sister Bryn was aware of the danger." And even as she spoke the scene was shifting to a flower-filled greenhouse on Long Island. A blind man approached the camera and bent to pick a vivid blossom. The zoom-shot showed his fingers clumsy enough to certify his condition, yet not so clumsy as to lose precious time.

"She loved flowers just like I do," the man said, straightening. "When we were kids she would describe them to me, you know, because I'm not a sighted individual."

"We're told that you two were very close," a silky female voice remarked. "Can you tell us how you feel now that this has happened."

The man, who could not face a camera he could not see, now turned in the direction of the questioner. This did not make for good television. The cameraman attempted to change his position and knocked over three clay pots, causing the blind man to about-face yet again. When he spoke there was, however, nothing of discomposure in his voice.

"I always kind of felt she was like a flower herself; and now I guess the good Lord plucked her for his own bouquet." It was possible that he had started to weep behind his dark glasses. The camera held on him.

———◆———

"Flipper, Flipper," Gena urged, mixing the tuna and mayonnaise in a green plastic bowl. It was this bowl that was at the heart of her kitchen. There sounded a round of wild electronic chirping as the sweetest computer any set designer would ever conceive revealed that it was indeed "Flipper" for which the contestant had so vainly sucked in her doll-cheeks and furrowed her pretty brow. No such histrionics for Gena; she knew this stuff cold.

"Those dolphins are amazing!" their host tipped them. "Sometime if you get the chance you oughta take a look at them." This was no idle vacation advice; the man knew what he was talking about. In a show-business career which now spanned eleven years, he had, until quite recently, been employed first at Sea World and then Marineland, paying his dues, as he liked to imagine. "That Flipper, I'll tell ya."

The audience applauded this sentiment, Gena warmed to the warmth of the moment, and their host, as tan as ever he could have been while feeding the dolphins under a summer sky, approached the next contestant.

"Now we're ready to test your knowledge, Carl." Carl, a young black man wearing a yellow shirt under a striped crewneck sweater, leaned forward attentively. Gena studied him and felt reassured. She imagined that in certain parts of the country—Carl was from Michigan, for example—there were many blacks who dressed like this. It was, she thought, a good image.

"We hear a lot about religious conflicts in the Middle East these days, Carl. One religion there has over one hundred million followers in the area. Which one is it?"

"That would be Jewish, wouldn't it?" Carl answered promptly.

"I'm sorry, Carl," chirped the sweetest computer this side of set heaven, civil to the end. The audience gasped; Carl had until now been letter perfect.

"The Jews are certainly an important religion in the area," his host hurried to assure Carl, "but the correct answer, as our friend here shows us," he made a mock bow in the direction of that flashing, chirping worthy, "is Moslem. Moslem."

Carl grinned, a good sport, but later he would complain to the producer claiming that he had understood his host to say "One hundred million dollars," not "one hundred million followers." It was a long shot but he had nothing to lose. As his luck would have it, however, the producer, a Jew by some name other than his own, was quick to turn a deaf ear to his grievance.

Gena's own interest in demographics was slight. When it came to very large numbers of people, only the number six million was specifically familiar to her. Yet she did have the general sense that there was a substantial population of Arabs in the world "what with the deserts and oil and what have you," and on this shaky synonymy she based her own answer. A winner, she covered the green bowl with its plastic lid and put it in the refrigerator.

Hurrying into Douglas's room she emptied the clothes hamper, pulled the sheets, patterned in homage to a cereal box, off the bed, and rushed down the stairs to the basement. A shriveled sponge mop, grown gray in her service, followed her down; and she fled from its impudence. The low-ceilinged room with its unconvincing wood paneling and Israeli travel posters did not make a pleasant impression on her. The colorful plaid carpeting was only fitfully visible beneath exiled furniture, discarded small appliances, toys never used and overused. A small racing car crunched under foot as she threaded the needle into the laundry room. Here too all was a gloomy jumble. The empty detergent boxes were stacked high, a monument to her industry and her dashed expectations. Higher still was a short clothes line weighed down under layers of apparel all shrunk beyond wearing, or faded, or half-dyed, without warning or excuse. Gena stuffed the washer full, adding a variety of powders and liquids in what she hoped was a powerful combination. She had received from her mother no instruction in the fine points of laundering; nor did she know how to iron.

There had been a time when it was important to her to have the clothes look clean after they had been washed. Intuitively, however, and little by little, she had given this up as a priority, contenting herself with the mere supposition that the clothing could not help but be positively affected by the laundering action, the legendary power of water and soap. And, although Gena could not know this, the time was long past when clothing would in fact come clean at all. Things might have gone easier with her had she only understood that the more insistently the state-of-the-art reality proclaimed the whiteness of its laundry, the less clean, less bright, less white the clothing in her own home was likely to be. As it was, Lady Macbeth herself could not have been more troubled and defeated by a stubborn spot than this innocent and insecure homemaker. Gena always left the laundry room knowing something more of helplessness.

"Now it's time to test your knowledge, Donna," her host said to a large-nosed, long-haired housewife cum Tag-Sale-Consultant. "Way back in 1982, Donna, there were several very successful motion pictures. Only one of these, of course, was the biggest grossing film of that year."

Gena heard the sound of a door opening. Someone had used a key to enter the front door. In the instant it took for the extreme of dread to screw her into immobility, Stanley Stern burst into the kitchen. Gena screamed when she saw him. His apology was perfunctory, to the point: he had kept a key for himself, just in case. If Stanley was attempting here to play upon some ancient hope for reconciliation, this was not lost on Gena. She stared at him in wonder as he opened the refrigerator and took out the bowl of tuna fish. His well-tailored suit was wrinkled and his face dark with weariness, but he spoke with his usual ease, his customary command.

"I left something here," he said as if he were a friend of the family, or, better still, a paying guest. "I'll just be a minute." He put the bowl on the table in front of her and started down the hall. "Make me a sandwich, will you."

"What is it, Stanley?" She got up weakly and followed him down the stairs to the basement. "I thought I saw something on TV."

"It's all a mistake. Don't worry about it. They're jumping to conclusions." He squeezed around the corner of the model railroad and opened a low door to which a portion of papier-mâché mountain landscape had been affixed. "Wait here, please," Stanley said politely and stooped to enter the crawl space, pulling his capacious leather briefcase in behind him.

The toy-train world, dust lying like snow on the rooftops, its cheerful citizenry enmired in cobwebs, had known better days.

"What is it, Stanley, what did you do?" Gena attempted to focus her interest. "Why did famous people give you money?"

"Look, I have a couple of problems right now." Stanley duck-walked toward the light, securing the briefcase with two new bungee cords for good measure. "Nothing I can't handle; it'll just take some guts to get over the rough spots, but it's nothing I can't handle." He shut the door and a bit of mountainous terrain fell to the carpet. Coming back around the table, he wet a finger and wiped clear the round compact-mirror, a small lake in the park at the edge of town. Mirror Lake, Douglas had named it, he recalled. "Remember how Helga always talked about being prepared for the worst?" He gave Gena a wink and the briefcase a tug. "Well, here I am—a Jew-boy on the run."

"Stanley. Bankruptcy. What is it? What did you do?" It was unlikely that even the most upright of men could have answered this question to Gena's satisfaction, her associations with such terms as tax shelter and government security being, as they were, perversely restricted to ideas of hearth and home, a safe haven.

"Forget it." Stanley was brusque.

"But what about us? What are we supposed to do?"

"I said don't worry. If you'll just let me out of here, I can get this mess straightened out." Even Stanley himself did not quite believe this. Of course, tax shelter scams were a dime a dozen, he thought modestly. But he had other problems. He had made the wrong friends and introduced them to the right people. He was in over his head.

Gena, one arm hooked around the punching bag for support, was blocking his way. "Stanley, I asked you something."

"Gena, get out of my way." A presage; the slightest bit of panic tightened his voice. "I mean it. I've got a lot to do."

"Tell me how Douglas and I are going to live. And I don't just mean live." This was the old pre-divorce Gena, a battler, champion of the little woman, with just enough of a whine in her voice to force her opponent into a series of small concessions.

But Stanley pushed against her, forcing her back as he bulled his way into the open, his free arm around her waist to keep her from falling, so that it was more as if he were dancing with her than anything else. Gena took the opportunity to note the ways in which his body against her felt different than Quint's.

"You sound very desperate, Stanley." She was not without pity as he brushed by her and rushed up the stairs. "What should I say to your son?"

"We build quality," a male voice asserted confidently as she regained the kitchen, breathing hard. Stanley, the briefcase at his feet, was bent over at the sink, his eyes level with the windowsill.

"Fucking media," he said. "Look natural." There was a car parked across the street and the red, white, and blue mobile unit was just a nose short of the driveway.

"Come home to the honest scent of . . . ," a proud, well-satisfied voice invited as a taxicab pulled up and Gena saw Quint step out in his black leather trenchcoat. This is the image she would have had of him on assignment at Checkpoint Charlie, had that Berlin landmark been known to her: the swirling coattails, the sense of purpose, the leaden sky. The newsman looked toward the house with a practiced eye and

Gena backed off quickly. But a moment later she was at the window once more. A black and silver van had arrived—the I-Probe, she told Stanley in an excited whisper. Then it dawned on her and the color rushed to her face.

"I am the ex-wife," she said quietly and with a degree of awe; "I'm the ex-wife, Stanley. They want me." Her voice rose. "I'm going out there, Stanley."

"No you're not. And please shut up a minute." His stare forced her away from the window.

"That good old-fashioned taste of home cooking," twin voices contended in unison as Stanley lowered himself wearily to the floor. He sat there on the beige tiles like a huge baby, his back straight, his legs splayed, snapping the cords against the leather satchel, thinking. Gena could almost love him again, reduced like this. "Here's what you'll do," he ordered finally, and the spell was broken. He outlined his plan for her and she giggled, nervous to find herself, if only briefly, so much a part of Stanley's life again.

"They call that child abuse, Marian," a gruff, frantic voice charged as Gena followed him down the hall toward the bedroom.

"When I had that breezeway built I knew what I was doing," Stanley said companionably as he applied a well-advertised balm to his tired eyes.

Gena, stunned to see him there at the bathroom mirror, caught off guard, said only, "See America as it was meant to be seen." The comfort of this large, familiar promise which had sprung so readily to her mind provided a measure of ease. "This reminds me of when Roy would come over to visit Carla after the divorce," she offered, applying a fresh layer of lipstick with a steady hand. But Stanley hadn't seen the show in several years. The doorbell rang. Face washed, reddened eyes cleared, Stanley walked out onto the front steps to meet Quint and the others who had gathered.

Gena looked out the kitchen window: the coast was clear.

"But that would be murder, wouldn't it, Doctor, pulling the plug?"

225

Gena stopped halfway out the door leading to the breezeway. My God, she thought, that would be murder. With the toe of her burgundy boot she gave Stanley's briefcase a nudge and it tumbled down the few steps and came to rest, as Stanley had predicted, in the doorway to the garage. Stepping casually over the briefcase, Gena could from the cover of the garage lift it unseen into the car and then put it under a piece of bathroom carpeting on the floor in the back. Leaving the key in the ignition, she dashed back up the breezeway steps, across the kitchen, down the stairs into the basement, and into the laundry room. Stanley should have told me not to wear these boots, she thought, dragging the mass of wet laundry out of the washer, wadding it into the dryer. She set the machine and started it; outside, where the dryer vented into the greenery at the front of the house, Stanley saw the white billows forming in the cool air—the high sign—and began to wind things up.

"Today," the latest on the daily roster of hosts was saying from the middle of the latest of daily living rooms, "we stalk a murderer, a criminal so cool and cunning that he has escaped detection in state after state. . . ." Gena tilted the kitchen blind so that she might see but not be seen. "It's a horrifying story," her host continued, seating himself in a brown-tweed easy chair, "and one that began just over two years ago when the police found the nude body of young . . ." Gena glanced at the nude body. "Nearby the police found her bloodstained panties." Gena glanced at the bloodstained panties. "The popular high-school senior had been brutally raped and her throat partially severed. Miraculously, a thin gold chain remained around her neck, a poignant reminder of her upcoming marriage." Oh my God, Gena thought, glancing at the bruised neck, the thin, gold chain, that really is a miracle. She looked out the window again and saw Stanley saunter across the lawn toward the garage as easy as an old pro on a familiar course. The media, having supped, retired to the bonhomie of the street. Quint, Gena noted, was talking with great animation to a young man with a pointed chin and an insolent eye. Only the cameraman followed Stanley's movements now. These simple shots of a man-in-trouble on the move, walking—to a car, to a courthouse, to a helicopter—were, of course, at the heart of a news-gathering operation. Such images, at once self-evident and compelling, were the envy of series writers everywhere.

Gena heard the garage door open and the car motor turn over. Weary now from her fright, from his charisma, and from the sheer daring of their act, Gena wondered what had prompted her to come to Stanley's aid. Certainly he did not deserve such an accomplice. What had gotten into her? He's the father of my child, she answered herself primly.

"It's hard to feel safe anywhere these days, Gloria," her host said, his tone balanced between relish and resignation. Let me analyze this, Gena commanded. She began again from the beginning. He's the father of my child, for one thing.

"You're so right, Roger; and that's especially true if you're a woman." Gena closed her eyes. It occurred to her that it was hard to be a woman alone. That's another thing. And then too there was Roy and Carla; the episode showing the ceremony in which they remarried led the ratings that week, Gena recalled.

"A truly terrifying story, Gloria. Thank you." Roger's face assumed a transitional expression, the grimness modulating as he spoke until a cozy smile full of anticipation had taken a firm hold. Only then did he pick up the book from the table at his side. "Coming up next, the author of *Tot-Terrific—What TV Can Do for Your Child.*"

Ever followed by these sights and sounds so familiar to her, Gena brought the bowl of tuna to the counter and made herself a tuna-fish sandwich. Pressed, she would have denied watching or listening at all, would have insisted that she remained untouched by any of it, that she had never once been persuaded to buy this or that product, that she had, in short, a mind of her own. Of course, it was no longer possible to have a mind of one's own; but of this Gena was unaware. Americans, by definition, had minds of their own. And, without question, this was how it felt when one stood agog in the aisle of a supermarket, or switched the channel selector on the television set, or read the magazine guaranteed to "give you a mind of your own."

Nevertheless, it is also true that in an era of time-sharing and task-sharing, American minds were being shared with an astonishing generosity. Sole possession of a mind by a personal and circumscribed reality was a thing of the past; today it was all the average American mind could do to accommodate, to compromise, to tidy up after itself. Its claims were shouted down, private reality squeezed out, bumped, co-opted, reconstituted.

Gena picked up the envelope Stanley had left on the counter for Douglas and held it over the steaming spout of the teakettle; in his haste Stanley had not made the seal secure. Inside were two tickets to a professional soccer game. The note said: "Have fun. Love Dad." Gena blushed; what a horrible, miserable, awful person you are Stanley, she said aloud. I pray you get into real trouble. This prayer was an indication that newsmen, try as they might, were not always able to convey to their viewers an adequate idea of what went on in the world. Perhaps Douglas would consent to letting Quint take him to the game, Gena hoped without much hope as she pocketed the tickets. In any case, it could do no harm to have Quint present the invitation as his own. Often just such an activity could cement a relationship between a young boy and his step-father-to-be, Gena had heard.

11

FRIDAY

Life Plans

I t was shortly before seven the following morning, the weather strangely mild for the first days of November, when Jake went to take his bicycle from the garage. Where was the air's proverbial nip, he wondered, humming of the gypsy in his soul. The summer just past had been cool on the whole, and rainy too; but now an Indian summer seemed to be stretching straight through the fall. "Oh what a day," Jake half-sang in the style of Jerome, "oh what a day!"

Two rolls of pink insulation and a pile of wallboard lay in the empty half of the two-car garage. These materials awaited their joyous, if hardly skillful, incorporation in a do-it-yourself-room-of-one's-own; on a sawhorse close by lay the do-it-yourself book. A brand-new space heater stood amid its packing, and in the corner where the cement had been swept clean a small oriental rug lay, defended only by an old-fashioned lamp. These were the lonely precursors of the bourgeois comforts which would come to colonize this barren waste. Jake's secret wish was for a used refrigerator; that on-again-off-again hum was all he needed of civilization and of company.

The building of this room Mitzi took as a sign; and it was not so much that Mitzi's confidence in Jake was misplaced, as that she had simply gotten her timing wrong: there was no book in the offing. Accumulation and study would remain at the heart of the enterprise for some time to come. Files were being created rather than emptied, bookmarks multiplied. Cartons of books, yet unread, lined the back wall.

Exerting himself greatly, showing a denim rump to several of the great authors of yesteryear, Jake worked at pumping the bicycle tires. Right out of the blue—lapis lazuli, of course—a poet took the opportunity to remind him that "all things fall and are built again and those that build them again are gay." Jake sensed that these words were profoundly hopeful, were certainly apt and deserving of his consideration; and yet his mind fixed on Uncle Nathan instead, so deeply had a newer meaning come to color that short straight word. Had Sam Geller ever sought out his brother, as Bruce was now seeking out Jake, for a consultation? No meeting of this kind had become a part of family legend. Could there have wanted an occasion for such a summit? Jake doubted it. On the telephone the night before, Bruce had been tight and mysterious, urgent and yet unable to give anything away.

What could account for Bruce's feeling himself more in need of advice than his father had? In this respect, at least, Bruce was a New Man. When Jake opened the door to the Gold Cup Deli, Bruce, dressed for the office, was pretending to read the *Times*, cup of coffee and a bagel already before him. Had Bruce observed his brother's entrance, the white-globed bicycle helmet under his arm, his hair damp and matted, he might have been less sanguine about their meeting. He had selected the rear booth for privacy; moving to the back he had been able, with a negligent glance, to check out his fellow patrons. He dismissed them as an undistinguished working class crowd, as likely to influence his fate as to join his fraternity.

The Greek manned the cash register. The music of his homeland, playing through earphones clamped to his narrow head, caused the exquisite mix of pain and pleasure that presently marked his face. Dolores, luxuriating in his temporary abstraction, moved as smartly as ever to get Jake's order, but had more pleasure in it.

"When's the last time I had a Denver omelet," Bruce wondered wearily.

"Have one now." His brother was warm. "You look on the gray side."

"You'd look gray too," Bruce spoke sharply, his vanity pricked. He must seek out common ground, he had decided earlier, in order to engage Jake's interest and sympathy. "There's a book out, I've got three or four copies, I think, about tragedy striking. Have you seen it?" He looked away from Jake to the perfect fried egg pictured behind the counter.

Jake stopped breathing, his body rigid with fear. Cancer. A mid-air collision. A chicken bone.

"What are you saying?" he asked, his voice a croak.

Bruce gave him a reproachful look as if to say, Can't you go along with me just this once? "It's that book about tragedy striking," he said again as calmly as he could. "Haven't you seen it?"

When Jake merely and uncharacteristically shook his head, Bruce had no choice but to take the plunge. He started at the beginning. It had been a difficult birth, he reminded Jake. He skimmed over Sandy's early years: "What a great kid he was," he instructed his brother repeatedly. As his story wound its fearful way toward the brink of adolescence, Bruce could find no transition to the point of his tale. He tried one tack and then another until finally unable to stand the suspense he blurted out the ugly facts of the discovery, the uglier suspicions of guilt.

"That dummy son of mine and his goddamn little pals decided to rob their own goddamn parents." He paused as his gruff, casual tone did not prevent the tears from filling his eyes.

Jake, who could not admit to being relieved, fumbled for the right approach. "You had an inkling," he began, thinking per-

231

haps to flatter their perspicacity. "Marilyn mentioned her concern as a parent, and you've hinted around too."

Bruce was bitterly disappointed. This was hardly the reaction he had in mind. He wanted outrage, he wanted sympathy, he wanted reassurance.

"Goddammit! Jake. Of course I'll joke about the kid, bitch and moan and so on, but show me one father who won't. Obviously I don't know what Marilyn's been telling you . . ." He hurried on with this glib untruth thinking to compensate for Jake's lack of family feeling by gaining an outsider's point of view.

"She'd seen Sandy with someone, that's all. As I said, her concern as a parent. I told her she was on the wrong track."

Jake's delicacy infuriated his brother. "What the hell makes you so smart? At least she's got an explanation. Or do you have some other idea why my son has my house burglarized?"

Jake grimaced. "Sssshhhhhhh!" He made a patting motion with his outstretched arm to enforce the caution. "At first it feels like a kick in the teeth," he started slowly.

"Try 'ugly implications' on for size," Bruce sneered. "Try 'set-up,' try 'inside job,' try 'junkie.'"

But Jake went ahead with his own thought. "In the case of a stubborn and rebellious son, the Bible recommends stoning by the men of the city," he mused.

"Goddammit! Jake," Bruce cried out in frustration, "don't be funny."

"I'm trying to think." Jake buttered the pre-buttered toast. He had the sense that he was failing his brother once more.

"Then don't think. Do me a favor." Bruce took a deep breath. "I can only hope it does turn out to be dope. Then at least I can feel sorry for the kid; he was hung up, hopped up, strung out, wired, whatever. Because this is a cold-blooded thing, otherwise."

Jake tried to make a fresh start. "Boys who have everything decide to rob their parents. Why?"

Bruce closed his eyes and pressed his knuckles first against the water glass and then against his lids. "What's done is done. We've got to figure out what to do now. For me the kibbutz is the answer. In Israel they don't take shit like they do here."

"The only answer is that these boys do not have everything," Jake persevered. "They bite the hand that feeds them."

"You're right," Bruce said sarcastically. "Somehow I didn't think it was appropriate to hook my own son on drugs." He studied his bagel without appetite. "You're not much help, you know." He felt the need to make that much clear.

"All right then," said Jake, stung in turn, "what's your analysis?" He daubed at his buttered chin with a shred of paper napkin.

"You know what summer's like around here." There was a touch of the old authority in Bruce's voice now.

"'Jerusalem was destroyed only because the children did not attend school, and loitered in the streets,' a rabbi said." Jake felt compelled to offer this bit of corroboration.

"Exactly." Nevertheless, Bruce gave him a look designed to discourage frivolity and another interruption. "Here's a bunch of kids just hanging out, tired of shooting baskets, bored with the mall, no wheels, what have you. Maybe there's a black guy hanging around selling whatever it is; they're intrigued, you know how it is, and before they know it—" He snapped his fingers to indicate the likely ease and pace of their addiction. "Meanwhile I happen to know that that twerp Pelt is into this Third-World Communist bullshit in a big way. Have you by any chance ever looked into his eyes?"

Jake had not. He was taken aback by Bruce's casual application of this piece of right-wing demonology. Let it go, he counseled himself.

"I picture one of these asshole kids saying, Hey I got a great idea. Rip 'em off. They'll never know what hit 'em. They'll love us for it." Bruce laughed bitterly. Dolores, who was pouring him another cup of coffee, looked at him from the corner of her eye. What was this world coming to, she wondered, that so many should be so bitter so early in the morning? An American military attaché had been assassinated in Athens during the night, but she did not know this.

"I want him to learn a lesson," Bruce continued when they were alone once again, "but I don't think we need the cops for that. They weren't thinking in terms of committing a crime."

"On the other hand," Jake insisted, oblivious, "they had to know that they were committing a crime—ersatz politics and all." At this point he experienced an instant of doubt as to direction, and he might have done well to explore it in silence. "You have to consider the choice of the action—public and private at once—a public gesture filled with private content."

"What are you talking about, Jake?" Bruce broke in with a degree of brusqueness, making it clear that under no circumstances did he wish to find out.

Jake tried another tack. "Your feeling is that there's been some kind of turning upside down of the natural order. You . . ."

"He hit me where it hurts, I'll say that much for him," Bruce interrupted impatiently. "But be that as it may, let's get back to the kibbutz."

Oddly, Jake was unable to fulfill this simple request. He could not leave things alone; and, even in the passion of the moment, he was sorry for that. "There may come an instant of revulsion when a man's spirit says just let me get away from all this shit," he speculated.

"Shut up Jake!" Bruce was angry now. "I've had it. I'm over here really hurting and you start with that goddam crap."

"I thought you wanted to talk," said Jake, teetering between the naive and the perverse.

"I wanted to get some advice, some practical advice. Now, what about the goddam kibbutz?"

"I think it's a good idea."

"Then why can't you just say so?! O.K., that's settled. You agree with me. Good." He drank off his coffee with a touch of the old vitality and decision. "I'll have to tell Marilyn that her rabbi is on my side."

Jake took a sip of water, happy to have pleased his brother. "How is Marilyn?"

Bruce stretched. "You know Marilyn; when the going gets tough, the tough get going." He flicked at his blue-and-white striped shirt cuff to check his wristwatch. It was known to be the world's thinnest watch. "I want to make the eight-oh-five." Raising his arm above the booth he flashed his cuff for service.

The vigor those cuffs portended, Jake thought. "I'm sorry I couldn't help, Bruce." He was feeling his inadequacy deeply.

"I'm just glad to know you agree with me on this. I wanted to get your impressions; you know I value what you think about something like this." He stood up and looked around, blinking as if awakened from a deep sleep to the call to arms. "As Dad would say, what are brothers for!" He touched Jake on the shoulder and then the brothers shook hands warmly.

"'And He shall turn the heart of the fathers to the children, and the heart of the children to their fathers,'" Jake offered in parting. But, hopeful as this biblical prophecy was, it seemed certain that Bruce intended to take matters into his own hands. Even now he was moving at a fast clip, cash in hand, toward the mercurial Greek behind the cash register.

"Have a nice day," Dolores called after him, setting down another cup of tea for Jake. "Are you two gentlemen brothers by any chance, I hope you don't mind my asking." At Jake's ready admission of consanguinity her satisfaction was manifest but measured. "I thought so," she said firmly, and hurried off to settle the small wager she had made with the distracted, beetle-browed counterman.

"Whaddafuh!" he muttered, stabbing a muffin, for though he was Puerto Rican born and bred he had fallen under the civilizing spell of the increasingly morose and scatological Greek.

Jake now undertook to review the conversation, examining it step by step, painfully aware that he had failed Bruce at every opening. He was concerned and embarrassed; had he no fellow-feeling? Certainly he was shocked by the deed itself. It was spiteful and ugly. His stomach roiled with anger even now when he thought of how the boy had hurt Bruce. Marxist influence! Jake did not credit such a motive in Sandy's case. No, he thought with a heavy sigh, this pathetic act of terror had been launched by a shallow, over-stimulated, under-defended son against a father who, while trying to do his best, had nonetheless lacked the fortitude or the fancy to countervail, to intervene, to hold the line. Jake blushed; he shrank from the harshness of his thoughts. These were, no doubt, behind his inability to provide the tonic Bruce had so clearly required.

He leaned from the booth and confided in Ruta his desire for a sugar-glazed, nut-filled Danish pastry. She brought it to him quickly, with a pat of butter on the side, and a grim, watchful Greek in her wake. Jake was disappointed in himself; he had, he felt, let his brother down badly. Here, however, his understanding, which he thought to be broad and deep, was instead a captive of his own narrow preoccupations. Otherwise he might have understood that Bruce had in the end come away from their conversation well-satisfied: he had acted in the spirit of his father and gained the blessing of his brother. Now, already miles down the track, in a railroad car where the *Times* and the *Journal* swayed and held sway, Bruce was pumping a total stranger, a man with the courage to unfurl the *Jewish Monthly*, for his impressions of kibbutz life.

———◆———

Gena put off confronting Douglas until the last possible moment. No dope, however, her son had listened to the urgency of the vacuum cleaner, seen her rummage through their chaotic linen closet, noticed breakfast sausage in the refrigerator and the bottle of French wine on the counter. He had a premonition: Quint would spend the night; and this had prompted him to formulate a plan of his own.

If she wanted to go out with him she could, he had decided from the start; and if she wanted to stay overnight in the city that was O.K. too. But there was no way Quint was sleeping in their house. No way. When Gena had, the week before, tried to sound him out on the subject, she had gone the roundabout way, eschewing names and places; but Douglas had told her bluntly, "No way me and him are sleeping in the same house."

Gena, taken aback, could only assure him that "You won't even know he's here." This was the first response that came to her mind, but she could hardly have done worse had she paused to take thought. Gena's awkward hinting around, her unease, her obvious desire to keep his good opinion had made the last week difficult for Douglas. Finally he had unburdened himself to Jimmy DiMaria.

"It's creepy having a stranger sleep in your house," he had remarked apropos of nothing. The best his friend, from that house where brothers had always crowded out strangers, could do by way of empathy was to laugh the ghoulish laugh that was the envy of his playmates. "'Specially a creepy one,'"Jimmy had said, leaving Douglas to wonder whether he might not in fact have met Quint sometime.

Gena knocked on the bedroom door expecting the worst. Douglas was looking at a comic book. In a low voice he told her he wasn't feeling well.

"Sweetheart," she said, putting her hand to his forehead. It was cool and slightly damp to her touch. "And Alvin is coming tonight." She looked at him and then away. "I wanted you to have dinner with us." Her use of the past tense was the only indication of her relief.

"I said I don't feel well," Douglas reiterated calmly, still in the same small voice.

Gena, anticipating a major scene, was surprised to find him making it so easy for her. This affected her perversely. "Can't you make an effort, sweetheart? I know Alvin will appreciate it." But here she overstepped, and Douglas, smarting under her fib, flung himself down on the bed with a plaintive sigh. "All right, if you aren't feeling well . . ."—she flinched as her hand met the cool, damp doorknob—". . . I won't force you."

Stung by her willing capitulation, angry tears came to his eyes as soon as Gena closed the door. Then, for the first time in years, he cried, goading himself with bitter reflections, self-pity, and images of betrayal. With the exception of his tears, however, all had gone according to plan. While his mother luxuriated in her preparations, Douglas, under cover of her running bath, packed his school bag with what he would need to spend the night at sea. As he went purposefully about this business, the anger left him and was replaced by a numbing anticipation. But it was not like Douglas to be bold and adventuresome, and he knew it. All the more need then to nurse his grievances.

Quint himself would be arriving soon and that would help. There could be no greater stimulus to his courage than the sight of Quint, tall enough but without talent, showing off with a basketball in the backyard. It wasn't just that Stanley Stern had put up the basket; it was that Stanley Stern was his father. The newsman's false heartiness, his lack of modesty, his foolish, unmuscled body, were sufficient, even in recollection, to give Douglas a renewed sense of purpose. He put on his pajamas and lay down on the bed to wait. And his mind raced ahead to picture the shuttered windows of the last purely summer place in Lynford, the stripped log of a flag pole, the little boat still pulled up at the boathouse, and the dark, dark night. He wanted to steady himself, to make sure of his plan.

But his emotions would not cooperate; they were in a state of flux: dripping here as hope, raging there in a bitter flood, freezing elsewhere to icy fear. This was not the image of himself he wished to confront. He got out of bed, opened his door, and leapt up to catch hold of the smooth wooden rod which Stanley had set high within the doorway. He began to chin himself. In a little while the doorbell rang.

Several minutes later Gena was at his door with Quint looming behind her carrying the television set from the kitchen.

"Sorry to hear you're sick, Doug," Quint announced loudly, settling the television on the desk chair Gena had drawn toward the bed. "I wish your mother had told me." He coughed self-consciously. "That is death. Death. In this business."

"Oh Alvin," Gena nearly whined, "he just came down. Honestly." She plumped Douglas's pillow for more comfortable viewing and put her hand to his forehead. This time it was warm and dry. "It's nothing."

"Well," Alvin smiled down at her, "Mother knows best." Nevertheless, he kept his distance.

Gena turned on the television and flipped the channel selector forward and backward. "You might as well watch something," she said when Douglas did not respond. "It'll help pass the time."

Standing as she was, her eyes fixed on the screen, directly between him and the set, Douglas could notice only that his mother's black slacks were very tight.

Quint stood in the doorway, one arm casually crooked over the chinning bar. "Been keeping up with the news, Doug?"

"Sort of," the boy answered indifferently.

"What about the pandas? Did you follow that one?"

"It was on enough."

"What a great story!" Quint exclaimed, at the mercy of the implied criticism. "How about you, Gena? I betcha we get a nomination on it." He gave Douglas a man-to-man wink. "Better get my tux ready, eh!"

But Gena was not listening. On the screen an anxious mother, a divorcée, was attempting to broach a difficult subject with her teenage son. This struck Gena as most helpful and she listened closely; after all what solace could she expect to get from watching a character who was neither a divorcée nor a mother, who was not anxious, who made no attempt to broach a difficult subject? Gena liked her fiction so adulterated, so thinned out by fact, that only the names and faces needed to be changed to compromise the innocent.

"My mother gets involved," Douglas condescended.

Quint took a step into the room and picked up the first thing that came to hand, one of Douglas's dirty socks. This he flung at Gena, but she whirled instead toward Douglas, flushing. "How dare you," she whispered through clenched teeth.

"Hey, sweets. Over here. Alvin Quint." He spread his arms

and gave her his patented grimace. "I was talking to you. Live."

"I'm sorry, honey." She apologized to them both by addressing the air between bed and door. "I just love her looks, don't you?" Sighing, she moved reluctantly away from the television. "But he gives her such grief. What were you saying?"

"I was saying I could use a drink. I picked up some of that Deli Dip we like." This insignificant remark, delivered in the most pleasant manner imaginable, caused Douglas's skin to prickle and his body to heave up in protest. "Well," Quint said jovially, "get going, woman!"

But he stood so as to block the doorway, feinting this way and that, teasing Gena, detaining her. "What's keeping you here? Come on, get out in that kitchen and rattle those pots and pans." Gena was giggling, pushing at his chest with weak hands, finally shimmying as if to bribe her way past with the promise of her favors.

Douglas looked away at his schoolbag propped innocently in the corner. What does he need her for, he thought with unbecoming cynicism, he's already got an audience. Suddenly he jerked up, swinging his legs to the floor in a single motion, sniffing the air. "Mom," he called out urgently. Then, without further warning, the smoke alarm went off, its high, intense siren destroying a mood.

Later, when the air had cleared, and the doors and windows were closed again, and the blackened cheese puffs had been disposed of, Gena, who felt she had risked enough, returned the thawing steaks to the refrigerator and suggested they order Chinese. She did not know what had gone wrong, and Quint did not mention finding the grease-filled broiler foil at the rear of the oven. Instead, he countered with gallantry. They would go out. A change of scenery, he told her with a sly wink, would make their homecoming all the sweeter.

———◆———

Gena knew just the place to go. "It's where the Mafia goes," she told Quint, "everybody says, and it's right on the water."

She mentioned the Mafia because it was generally thought that such patronage was a kind of guarantee for authenticity and ambiance. With the confidence of a native she directed him through a succession of suburban neighborhoods, up a winding country lane and then down a back road, past homes of increasing modesty, past a sewage-treatment facility and a dog pound, to the restaurant, where the road, nearly gravel now, dead-ended.

The night was dark and still, the lights of the last few houses barely visible through the thin fog which seemed to sweep in as they stepped from the car. The air was surprisingly mild, but Quint shivered; all of a sudden and inexplicably he had experienced a moment of utter desolation. He put his arm around Gena and pulled her into his side, but the feeling lasted only the time it took to walk from the car in through the restaurant door. Here all was maternal and haphazardly nautical. Nets and buoys abounded. There were tropical fish in gloomy tanks, and seashells framed the mirror behind the bar. Small oil paintings featuring lighthouses and lobster boats lined the narrow hallway to the restrooms. These were for sale.

The dining room, all black plastic and white linen, was crowded, but if Quint had wanted to study its makeup in order to document once and for all the existence of organized crime in America, the impulse gave way when he spotted Bruce and Marilyn Geller at a table across the room.

"And there's that crank," he said to Gena, pointing out Leonard Pelt who, along with his wife Gwen, completed the Geller party.

"You know who else is here?" she responded, casing the joint, "Benny."

"Benny?" Quint asked, eyes wandering.

"Benny, the Lawn Care King. The gardener. Benny Di-Maria and the whole family. It must be someone's birthday." She studied the other patrons, table by table, only to come to the conclusion that after this brilliant beginning, they had come to the end of their acquaintances with the Gellers, the Pelts, and the DiMarias. This circumstance led inevitably to speculation and even downright fantasy. Two men who conversed over espresso at a nearby table commanded her particular attention. Soon Quint saw fit to change the subject.

"What's over there?" He was looking out the large window through the blackness to a yellow patch of light across the water.

"That's the dining room at the yacht club. Which reminds me; what are the Gellers doing here?" This question engaged Gena's interest until their drinks arrived.

At the Geller table, Gwen Pelt was speaking. "Gangsters come here," she informed the others. "Someone told me. That's why I thought we should try it tonight; it's supposed to be so good."

"You mean because our sons are gangsters," Bruce said roughly, irrationally. Marilyn kicked him under the table, but the greater pain obscured the lesser.

Gwen's hand twitched and rose to cover her eyes; her fork stood unaided in the mass of angel-hair pasta and she began to weep silently.

"Gwen." Leonard reached out and patted his wife on the head. "Bruce!" He turned with a dark look. "Speak for yourself."

"I say call a spade a spade and a shovel a fucking shovel."

"Bruce!" Marilyn reprimanded him. "Gwen and I are going to the ladies' room. When we come back let's try and be constructive, please!"

"I like a nice quiet place," Bruce said, but his sarcasm was feeble, uncompelling. He cast an irritated look over his shoulder at the noisy table of DiMarias in the corner. "This is all I need tonight."

"What did Tolstoy say? All happy families are alike?" Leonard, who considered his own small unit to be such a one, wondered in what way it might be comparable to the large brood whose raucous harmony was the object of Bruce's disdain. "Italians are big on family like Jews are; the whole syndrome, immigrants, pushcarts, blood is thicker than water, etc."

Bruce drank deeply of the wine. "Don't remind me. How do you think my father feels about all this?"

Leonard was so anxious to avoid for as long as possible the subject at hand that he jumped at the chance to discuss the nature of life after death. "Lucky for him he doesn't know."

"He knows," Bruce said glumly, "he knows."

"Wait!" Leonard put up his hand and rolled his eyes in an effort to recollect. "That was the punch line." He nodded slowly, savoring the joke. "Listen! A man dies and . . ."

"Is this the Johnny Carson show or what?" Bruce poured himself another glass of wine.

"Look, I'm not sitting shivah." Leonard was testy now. In the two days since the discovery he had worked hard to come up with an attitude, and, while satisfied with what he had developed, he was not at all anxious to present it publicly for the first time. "I don't think we should get into any of this until the ladies return." While he had, by and large, returned to his former self, Leonard continued to worry about whether his penchant for irony might not have been adversely affected by the initial shock. He began to hum under his breath with ostentatious nonchalance.

At the table in the corner the DiMarias raised their glasses.

"Here's to you, Mom," said George, the Assistant D.A., putting his arm around his mother's shoulders. "You made me what I am today."

Me, too, thought Joey, but he said nothing. Instead, he gave his mother his big showgirl smile when their eyes met, and she waved him a happy girlish wave.

"Hey Mom," Vinny called out.

"Happy birthday, Grandma," Candy teased.

"Look what the baby sent you," Victor added, holding up a small package.

"I made this thing in school, Mom." Jimmy poured a little wine into his Coca-Cola.

"Hey," Johnny said, grabbing his arm hard, "that's expensive stuff, my friend." He was not in a good mood tonight: the burglaries, he had been given to understand, were about to become non-crimes; and as if that were not enough, his wife had not wanted to attend her mother-in-law's birthday party. An argument had ensued and now she sat at his side, winding her golden hair around her finger, silent as a book.

"I'm celebrating something else, too." Mrs. DiMaria smiled and they all looked at her expectantly. "No one knows?"

"Vinny got a haircut," Victor guessed.

"Give this gentleman a year's supply of Rice-a-Roni the San Francisco treat. Now you're both beautiful," their mother told the twins.

"Does anyone notice anything about me?" Candy asked, scanning the circle of faces with innocent delight.

Joey, who sat on the other side of Victor, responded at once, "You've got a fabulous brooch on," and he stretched across for a better look.

"Isn't it fantastic! But you should see the one," she stopped suddenly and her mouth hung open for several seconds. "I mean, this is the one Vic got down in Florida. It's just so beautiful, you know, that," she tried to extenuate, but Victor cut her off without a glance.

"Yeah, I got this guy that hates to fly. He won't fly. He took me to some great stores down in that Little Havana. And some of them even speak English." Victor was expansive, at his ease.

"How much driving you doing lately, Vic?" his father asked.

"I got more than I can handle, I'll tell ya. I'm all over the place these days. Been going down to Atlantic City a lot too." He grinned at his brother, the cop. "Big tippers!"

"If they win, Vic," Johnny said grimly, "only if they win."

"Vic's a lucky kind of guy," Vinny put in. "We're born under that sign."

"Just don't let any of that luck rub off on me." George was smiling and he spoke casually, but Victor was certain he was trying to put some distance between them.

"I don't get it, George." Jimmy nudged him, trying to learn.

"Let me put it to you this way—we're Italian, aren't we,"

the Assistant District Attorney said cynically. "I mean, you've heard of Caesar's wife, right?"

But of course Jimmy DiMaria had not; and this could not help but further pique his interest in politics and raise his brother even higher in his estimation.

Across the room, Quint surprised Gena by asking her point-blank what Helga thought of him.

Gena scrambled. "She doesn't watch television very much. That's one of the problems I have with her. She doesn't know what the world is like today. She's on Douglas's case all the time about watching."

I'll go with the flow, Quint thought, swallowing the last of his martini. "I don't see him watching much," he said. "In fact, I was going to talk to you about that; he could be getting a lot more out of it, information-wise."

"That's just what I think. She doesn't realize how educational it is now. Why do you think these kids are so much smarter than we were? And then too," Gena went on passionately, of the opinion that it was possible in this day to have it both ways, "don't they deserve a little time off, a little pure entertainment, a little fun!" Her brand of rhetoric put its meager resources at the service of an awful personal neediness; simple sense, coherence, elegance, all fell before the frenzy of her self-justification. "Plus the fact . . ."—Gena put the crowning touch on her rhetorical edifice, climbing beyond logic and above paradox—". . . those shows just roll off his back; he's not even watching half the time. It doesn't have the slightest effect on him, believe me!" Thus she concluded what was surely a tour de force of television-age argumentation. She was buoyed up by her little tirade and even more by her companion's clearly sympathetic ear.

The waiter now brought Quint his baked clams. Gena took a deep-fried zucchini blossom from the basket on the table and made an attempt at identification before placing it carefully on the edge of her plate. She decided to ask the waiter's advice. That young man had impressed her with a crisp display of attention and a gondolier's sly grin. She wondered whether there wasn't some way to personalize their relationship.

Quint, who had been preparing a critique of the clams, did not know whom she was talking about. German cuisine doesn't do much with clams, he mused thoughtfully.

"He reminds me of the waiter at that place Madeleine and Carleton always eat at." Gena was wistful. "They know his name and he always says their names, too. It's an intimate place."

"Who?" Quint asked vaguely, polishing off the last of the clams.

"Honestly, Alvin." Gena was exasperated. "Madeleine, the one who said she would give you her story. Madeleine and Carleton."

"I thought we were talking about your mother and me," Quint said, egging her on.

She surprised him by turning serious again. "I should care," she said bitterly. "She acts like I don't want what's best for my own son. Her problem is that she has no idea what the world is like. What am I supposed to do— lock up the TV? How do you think he'd like me then?" Her eyes were blazing.

"You could do that," Quint said calmly, and here we may see the profound effect of one man's political oratory on the unconscious of a generation, "but it would be wrong!"

Gena was comforted by this vote of confidence; and Quint thought he could infer from all that had gone before that it would not be absolutely essential to his future happiness to win Helga's approval. The road ahead seemed suddenly free of obstructions, and he was momentarily giddy at the prospect of having the prize so near at hand. He gulped at his wine.

"I just remembered something." Gena brought to this introductory clause a calculated brightness. Then the waiter endeared himself to her still further by choosing this moment to create a diversion. "How would you like to take Douglas to a soccer game on Sunday?" she asked Quint casually as the young man served up the pasta.

Quint scowled at his plate until the mass of lasagna there seemed to quiver under his gaze. He had forgotten about Douglas.

At the Gellers' table, in the meantime, a great deal had been said, yet the subject which concerned them most had thus far barely been addressed. There was an empty bottle of red wine on the table and an empty bottle of white upside down in the silver bucket next to Bruce.

Leonard was finally ready to make his position clear. "As far as Gwen and I are concerned, we feel this is consistent with how we've brought David up. He's an unusual kid, artistic, sensitive, politically aware, with deep feelings of identification with the underdog. And I've encouraged that. I admire the kid for acting on his beliefs. If more of us did that, the world would be a better place." He gave his wife a perfunctory glance.

As Gwen had been largely silent until now, they were surprised to have her take him up on his invitation. "This wouldn't happen then," she said, blurring the issue, "if the world were a better place, like Leonard said."

"He's the shrink," Bruce said.

"How many times are you going to say that over and over?" Marilyn was impatient.

Bruce sipped at his cognac. He was imperturbable. "I've said it before and I'll say it again. You're the shrink." Bruce was feeling increasingly at peace with himself. "You're a shrink and I'm a Jew," he continued placidly. "In Israel they don't take shit like we do here. I talked to a guy on the train today."

Marilyn rolled her eyes. "First things first."

"Jake liked the kibbutz idea," Bruce said again. "Did I mention that?"

"Mmmmmmmmmmmm," his wife answered. She felt that Bruce's mellowness militated against her saying anything more to him. "Let's get the check." She turned to Leonard. "The officer we talked to, I told Gwen in the ladies' room, he's a captain or something, and we've known him over the years," she lowered her voice, "contributed and so on. He was very professional, but also very reasonable. Apparently this is by no means a rare kind of —" She paused, seeking an alternative for the word that came to mind.

"Occurrence," Leonard supplied nonchalantly. "Absolutely not. Hank Herz was saying just that. As a lawyer he's very familiar with it." Leonard sipped his amaretto.

"I'll say this much, it made me feel a lot better. Apparently what we can do since it's all in the family . . ." Marilyn gave Gwen a significant look.

"What about your famous black man?" Bruce interrupted morosely. He was beginning to slur his words just slightly.

"What black man is that?" Marilyn and the Pelts asked in unison.

Bruce frowned and nodded knowingly into his cognac. "Let me tell you what this guy on the train said about a kibbutz."

"What we can do is," Marilyn continued with a sidelong warning glance at her husband, "we can go over and explain our situation to the D.A.'s office; they may want the police to give the boys a little lecture, put a scare into them, what have you, but otherwise they'll let us handle it if that's what we want." She lifted her coffee cup but it was empty.

"Did he say a kibbutz would be O.K.?" Bruce wanted to know.

"I didn't ask him," Marilyn answered coldly. "Polly Finkle has met this George DiMaria. She knows some of the Democrats around and she says she's heard he's thinking of running for something." If there was a subtext to these last words, it would no doubt go unacknowledged, at least until a campaign committee of some sort was set up.

Bruce's mind had begun to review the events of his day, something it did without prompting in the last few minutes before sleep claimed him. Tonight, however, his thoughts were all a jumble. "TV news," he began ponderously, recalling his conversation on the train, "just doesn't cover the kitzibum . . . kibbitzum . . . kibbutzim . . ."

"Bruce, we're leaving. Get the check please." Marilyn had

grown so impatient with his maundering that she could hardly sit still.

Leonard signalled for the check. "As long as you bring it up, Bruce, it did occur to us that what we have here is some really excellent television material. When you stop to think, we have everything going for us. And Gwen got the idea of having Polly Finkle fall for the cop. It could be fascinating."

"At least it hasn't been done before as far as I know," Gwen Pelt put in, smiling for the first time all evening.

"I'm in television news," Bruce told them, his eyes now merely red slits.

Leonard was undeterred. "I'm talking about news, news and information. Here we have a pressing social issue, any way you slice it, and we're the ones in a unique position to provide the public with some much needed information."

"A docudrama, a docudrama." Gwen could barely contain herself.

Marilyn had stopped fidgeting. "I think it's exciting, Leonard. It's an important story." Her eyes narrowed as if she could already see from a great distance their story coming to life. "And," she said, drawing out the word for emphasis, "that takes us right out of the victim area and into the entertainment media area." She clicked her tongue against the roof of her mouth, savoring the possibilities for redemption. "You'll talk to someone, won't you, Bruce." She looked over at her husband; his head was propped up on his arm, his eyes were blinking slowly. The silly, drunken smile on his face caused Marilyn's skin to tighten, but inasmuch as they would need him if their project were to see the light of screen, she foreswore a wifely remark.

"Happy birthday to you, happy birthday to you," the waiters sang, making a beeline across the dining room for the DiMaria party. A large white cake with a pink rose and a circle of burning candles was set down in front of Maria DiMaria as the family and a number of high-spirited patrons nearby joined the waiters for the finale. Mrs. DiMaria drew back from the table,

249

her full square face beaming as she took a large breath. The family waited for what seemed like a long time as all the air which had so recently carried their good wishes and congratulations was sucked into Maria's round, operatic mouth. Finally she exhaled, and the candles went out without a flicker amid scattered applause.

Then BOOM! It was the dull, distant, but unmistakable sound of an explosion. There were shouts from the patrons seated nearest the windows. As if a burning ring of candles did not suffice to celebrate the birthday of this stellar matriarch, way out on the water, in what was probably the yacht club marina, a cabin cruiser had burst into flame. The tables emptied as the diners found places at the windows to watch. Suddenly, a new cry went up. Some of the men ran outside. A projectile of some sort had shot from the boat surrounded by a shower of sparks and fallen fast into the water. There was much speculation as to what this thing might be, but it did not occur to anyone, and especially not to Victor DiMaria, that it might be a human body. In the hallway outside the restrooms, Alvin Quint paced, a newshound at bay, while Officer DiMaria, imagination afire, was on the telephone to the station house.

———◆———

When the jet plane took off down the runway at La Guardia Airport nearly half an hour late, it was mostly filled with budget-minded travelers taking advantage of the pre-season prices in the Caribbean. For these goodnatured, upbeat vacationers, revolution itself meant only greater value for their tourist dollars. An Island-Paradise-Threatened-by-Revolution was nevertheless an island paradise. As the plane circled, banking over Long Island Sound, gaining altitude, one of the passengers was looking out his little window with especial interest. The gentleman had spent much of his life in these suburbs on the shore and now he did not know, he thought with a touch of self-pity, if he would ever visit these scenes of his early triumphs again. Are those the lights of the yacht club, Stanley Stern wondered, when, suddenly, thousands of feet below in the dark invisible water, something, which he alone of all the passengers knew to be a cabin cruiser named the *Shooting Star*, burst into flame. How does that make you feel, fella? he asked himself. The skin under his arms prickled. He felt relieved; sad, too, and excited, and something like a god. Stanley loved to make things happen. Staring down through the dark nothingness he knew that some would accuse him of over-kill; but he smiled at the very idea that over-kill could be thought anything other than pleasing to a man like himself. And all the more so when a man like himself had made the wrong friends. Better to be safe than sorry—it was the only way to fly. Stanley smiled again, appreciating his own little joke.

Now Stanley needed to talk. "Going down on vacation?" he asked the woman who sat beside him reading. Had his own life been less involving of late he might have wished for a less plain, less serene seatmate. This woman struck him with her absolute stillness; she was without a fidget or a tic or any sign of restless energy.

"No," she told him, putting a square of chocolate into her mouth with a smooth placid motion, "I'm going down to work." And it was indeed the former Iris Sloane catching the first available flight out since learning of her colleague's murder. "I'm a nun."

"You're a nun!" Stanley's mixture of surprise and delight was genuine. "I think we should all feel pretty safe with you on board, connection-wise." He barely resisted nudging her with his elbow, so full of good spirits was he.

Iris gave him a friendly smile. Did he intend to natter on through the whole flight, she wondered. She was anxious to read further in the Holy Father's poetry.

Freedom's just another word for nothing left to lose—the musical phrase once the anthem of bikers and bums rose to the lips of this die-hard Wall Streeter. A clean getaway, he mused, compared favorably with the Street's current drug of choice. Clearly, a friendly smile would not satisfy Stanley in his present state of mind. Talk was Stanley's stock in trade. It was talk alone really, his own and then the talk his talk generated, which had pulled in the millions and millions of dollars to those investment partnerships. "What does a nun do down there?" he asked his companion, sensing that the convent did not predispose one to elaborate conversational gambits.

Iris's reply was perfunctory. "We have a school and a clinic in the western part of the island. And a church, of course."

Stanley decided to up the ante. "That's the Communist stronghold, right? Where the rebels are concentrated?" His tone was noncommittal.

"It's the poorest part of the country. Very, very poor."

Stanley shifted in his seat to confront her. "Well," he said jovially, "if they've got the Russians behind them, I wouldn't hold my breath for that to change."

"Be that as it may," Iris said mildly, "the Church is the church of the poor."

"Well then!" Stanley said with mystifying emphasis, stretching his arms as if to say, here am I, take me in. The bankruptcy had been essential. Toward the end, he had awed even himself by just how much he was draining off. Hey fella, he reminded himself automatically, that money was compensation; I could point to assets of value, you know. Advances, for Christ's sake, what's the big deal! The lids came down over his eyes, paradoxically enlivening his heavy face with a touch of guile.

Iris gave him an odd look: she was uncertain how to interpret his open-armed gesture. There was something preconfessional, something needy in it, and she shrank from that possibility. She had learned the hard way not to squander her resources. On the other hand, the alternative seemed to be politics; she made a show of returning to her book.

And in fact, studying that hatchet of a nose, that smooth plane of a cheek, Stanley had, for a fleeting moment, entertained the idea of confessing to Iris right then and there. Best to lay the groundwork first, he figured by way of covering the bases as he willed that inconvenient impulse to pass.

"Don't take this personally!" he began energetically. "God

and Country are all right in their own way, but there's nothing to compare with money when you get right down to it. There's nothing that makes a man feel as good as socking away the big bucks, except, of course, spending them." And now he did nudge her. "Believe what I'm saying, I've been there, I know. The best of everything!" Stanley's heart began to pound behind his monogrammed shirt pocket as he conjured up all he had worked so hard to possess, all he must now leave behind. Paradoxically, this exercise of the soul only seemed to strengthen him. "Face it," he went on with renewed determination, "money runs things. That's what we go by. It's the scientific way; it's the fair way; it's the American way," he concluded proudly.

Iris barely looked at him to answer, hoping her discourtesy would finally drive him away. From this we may judge how slight was her aquaintance with the world. "As I say, the Church has a solidarity with the poor."

Stanley Stern was, however, made of sterner stuff. This unenchanting nun was not a patch on some of the tough nuts he had cracked in his time. He thought of the long list of names he had lured with promises of pie-in-the-sky tax deductions, of those among the well-known and well-born, prominent Wall Streeters with impeccable reputations, Hollywood big shots, brand-name artists, all of them throwing their money at him hand over fist. Stanley had some inkling of just how visceral it all was.

"Let me put it to you this way." He took up the cudgels again. "I've been rich and I've been poor, and believe me, as they say, rich is better." In his present circumstance, there was a poignancy to this formulation which he could not very well ignore. Eff-ing government, he cursed silently.

"The Church is concerned about materialism," Iris said, experiencing a degree of helplessness to which she was unused. She had vowed to make her break here, but he had caught her in mid-yawn; somehow he had shamed her into response. And Stanley Stern did have that trick down pat.

"I'll tell you frankly," he replied, taking pleasure in the agitation he had been able to create, "I don't believe there is such a thing. Materialism is the spirit of America. Americans are born free to have what they want, when they want it. We're the only country in the world where that is possible." He pressed his point, a man without an ironic bone in his body. "Otherwise, for instance, crime wouldn't be so high. As American citizens we're brought up to want . . . things." He cupped his hands out in front of him, fingers splayed, and shook them as if impatient for his due. "We're educated to want them, finally we're tempted to want them." He let his hands drop onto his heavy thighs to suggest the inevitability of it all. "And that's what keeps the flame of freedom burning bright. That's capitalism; that's democracy."

Iris yawned again, this time without undue delicacy. "That's an interesting philosophy," she said insincerely, for, as we know, her interest in such abstractions was extremely limited. "The Church wants to be close to people who suffer and are oppressed, and usually that's poor people more often than not. So that's my philosophy, if you can call it that."

Stanley once again stretched his arms open wide as if to say, here am I, take me in. Iris rubbed her eyes, only too well aware that the foregoing dialogue had done nothing to illuminate that puzzling gesture. "I think I'd best get some rest," she said, and in truth, but for no reason she could imagine, their conversation did seem to have taken a lot out of her. "I hope you enjoy your visit, Mr. . . ." and here Iris experienced a final moment of dread as it seemed likely that this silly bit of politesse would force further discourse. She faked a huge, face-distorting yawn before turning her head away, eyes squeezed shut more in trepidation than fatigue. She did not see, therefore, how her seatmate smiled, how he drew himself up, how he welcomed the opportunity.

"Russell," said silver-tongued Stanley Stern, for he had deemed it advisable, at least in the short run, to be thus known to the world. "Yes," he confirmed heartily, construing the words to his own liking, "it'll be great to get away."

He reached into his jacket to pat an envelope which rested there in the pocket against his heart. Let the nun sleep, what the hell, he thought; he had the name of someone who knew someone who knew Robert Vesco.

◆

Though both the former Iris Sloane and the Stanley Stern that was were to find what they were after on that Island Paradise which was their destination, there was another with a need as great and a spirit as strong who was to be denied a similar fulfillment in that place.

"This is the hero of the hour," Alvin Quint was saying into the camera. He was dazed, befuddled, just going through the motions. Possibly Gena herself did not even know yet; he had arranged for the Gellers to drive her home while he chased to the marina, losing his way only twice amid the welter of empty, unlit streets, to await the crew from the Late News. "This is the man whose courageous action saved a human life tonight. How does it feel, Mr. Johnson?"

"I feel fine now, man. I feel O.K. Yeah, I'm doing pretty good now." M. L. was pumped up, helplessly colloquial. "I feel kinda strange, a little weak maybe, but I feel good, you know." He paused to consider how he might best continue to do justice to the complexity of his feelings. "I feel high, but then too, I feel low in a way, you know. I feel bad about, about the kid. And I got a pain over here on my side." He hurried on wondering wildly whether he ought or ought not to know the boy's name. "It feels like maybe I pulled something."

"All right then," said Quint who had not heard a word of the above, so concerned was he with his newly rubber knees, "how did you feel when you saw that boat go up?"

"I didn't understand it at first," M. L. said truthfully, having just seen his life plan come to nothing before his very eyes. "I used to work at the marina over here," he told Quint, oblivious to that reporter's exclusive preference for an emotional reality, "and I got the idea, tonight being warm and all, to cruise around the place, you know, for old time's sake." All this had come to M. L. as a piece of whole cloth while he was struggling to get the body into the rowboat. He had shared a farewell joint with his youthful cohorts and was making his final run out to the *Shooting Star*. Then, Boom! He had very nearly lost an oar. Had that pathetic projectile not dropped into the water a yard from his dinghy, it is altogether possible that M. L. might have succumbed to a life-threatening depression. As it was, he pulled himself together, perhaps dimly aware from the moment of the splash itself that this could be the making of him.

I am nothing if not a pro, Quint thought, girding his loins. "Given your own expertise then, what do you feel might have happened to cause a potential tragedy like this one?"

M. L. switched hats smoothly, hero turned technician. "One possibility is that your gas vapors could have accumulated in your engine compartment," he said, his supple voice becoming graver still. "Any spark would set them off."

This was, of course, what might have happened; but the facts, should they ever come to light, would tell a very different story. However, buried as they are in the respective bosoms of a tax-shelter promoter on the run, a part-time chauffeur from Queens, and a bomb-for-hire, they are quite unlikely to do so.

"There you have at least one theory of what might have happened tonight, from the man responsible for saving a young Lynford boy's life." Quint took a shallow breath; the air was damp and threatened to stick in his throat. "This is Alvin Quint on the village beach in Lynford." The lights went out and a small crowd descended on M. L.

Much to his own surprise, Alvin Quint sat down in the dark on the damp sand and held his head in his hands, rolling the foam-muffed mike across his forehead to soothing effect. He looked across the water at the tiny colored lights which climbed the mast and prow of the old sailing vessel in front of the restaurant on the opposite shore. It was one thing to bring Gena her world, and quite another for Gena to bring him hers. The emptiness of the former promise contrasted favorably with the stark reality of the latter circumstance. He tried to think about what had happened that evening, but all he could come up with finally, standing up, attempting to shake off the thought and the damp at once, was the grim observation that he did not after all seem to have a way with children. Nevertheless, this circumscribed bit of analysis augured well for Quint's future in the television-news business. This penchant of his, this nose for the human-interest angle, was likely to preclude the development in him of that sinister jocularity which had hastened the end of many a promising career. Let others investigate and interpret, dissect and reveal, he was content to let the stories do the talking. The Late News crew, strangers to Quint, were now standing around waiting for him to pull himself together. They muttered among themselves about their luck and carved obscenities in the sand with sneaker-shod feet.

A short distance away another set of lights went on as another crew set up. The American people love a hero, an anonymous rubberneck told M. L. helpfully; and that bright, ambitious, highly flexible young man was instantly reconciled to seeing the brothers go forward to victory without him on that Island-Paradise-Threatened-by-Revolution. All right then! M. L. thought, hopes high, loving the light and the darkness equally. And, in fact, M. L. was soon in great demand. For example: a young Assistant District Attorney had decided to test the political waters. There was to be a Get-Acquainted-Cocktail-Party-Fund-Raiser at the home of Bruce and Marilyn Geller and Mr. George DiMaria would consider it an honor, M. L. was told, to have Mr. Johnson attend as an honored guest. The American people, the man explained, loved a hero. "I'm on my way, Mama!" M. L. exulted, oblivious to the cries of a baby somewhere in the house.

◆

At the hospital, Gena was hovering in the vicinity of the phone bank trying to muster the courage to telephone her mother. Alone and overwhelmed, intermittently weeping, Gena was ripe for terror, and terrified she was to see the camera-burdened figure, arms akimbo, backing down the long corridor toward her, just as if this were the way the man was

257

meant to walk. An instant later she recognized Quint taking his long-legged strides in the cameraman's wake. Who can describe what she felt then, and what she dreamed of in that moment? A budding comfort, the prospect of a safe harbor, an anchorman and provider. She ran to him and when she reached him it was as if she, another Alice, had passed through another kind of glass, and finally found a place in her world. As Quint held her, grimacing over her shoulder at the smirking cameraman, he had a split second to be grateful for the absence of Mark Cone before he found himself soothing Gena with an ease and familiarity which might have been a function of his celebrity, but, judging from the odd mixture of relief and strong emotion which threatened to sweep him away, was probably not. He deserves his share of happiness just as we all do, thought a passing nurse who had recognized his trademark grimace among the variety of frantic faces he was pulling in an effort to wave off his tenacious cameraman.

And Quint and Gena did enjoy a period of unclouded happiness from the day of their marriage, which took place soon after Douglas had been restored to perfect health, until a year or so later when Gena decided that she and Quint should have a child of their own after all. In due time, therefore, the Quints joined the ranks of those families which do nothing so well as form and come apart and form again in new combinations, until it seemed that there was no teenager in the land without an infant for a sibling. In this way did they parody those large families of yesteryear in which there was sometimes twelve or fifteen years between the oldest and youngest child. In the case of the modern version, of course, there was in this, as in so much else, no in-between. And Quint soon discovered, as it had been widely predicted he would, that his own child was different.

As for Douglas, he took less pleasure in this new family than the others. In fact, he felt betrayed and neglected; he pined for that less than a paragon-of-a-pa, Stanley; and though Gena did everything she could to make him feel part of his own family, this only fueled his sense of himself as an outsider. During this time he was able to become a very accomplished card counter and dreamt of playing for big money at the blackjack tables in Atlantic City.

◆

A paper of five pages had been assigned in the history class. After finishing a late dinner of chicken livers and onions, Helga remained at the dining table to take up her work. She was concerned; she had already written seven pages, and was still a long way from having had her say. Last year she had been reprimanded for the length of one of her papers and she was determined to do better this semester. It may be thought odd that Helga Grossman, who had turned herself so resolutely toward the future by resuming her education, should have chosen to study the past; but so it was. Perhaps odder still was her idea that while, as she so often said, she was too old for politics, she considered herself to be just barely old enough for history. This impulse toward what she called "the big picture" had become pronounced in her only recently. Up until now it had satisfied her to say merely, as she did so frequently to Gena, "I lived in history." But then one day it struck her, "Why should I not understand it as well?"

A familiarity with no less than the whole of Western civilization was what she was after. And who would try to deny her this inheritance? Her daughter for one. "It's not what you think," Gena had warned her, recalling her own college days. "Stanley always said you would be good at business; why not take that, and then, too, you could use the information at the store." Nor was the faculty at Croton Community College altogether sympathetic with her thirst for this brand of knowledge. "We cannot escape history," Helga had quoted Lincoln to them in order to remove any European onus from her quest. In reply she was told that "the process of restructuring the current curricula is ongoing and current plans include transforming the history major into something more contemporary."

"For example," her adviser had advised, "we have three

units called 'The Holocaust on Film and Tape.' That might be just the thing for you." When Helga did not respond the woman tapped her forefinger thoughtfully on the green-and-white computer printout. "Given your current life experience," she mused hopefully, "perhaps 'The Senior Citizen through the Ages' would fit in nicely?"

Helga had been sorely disappointed. Finally she settled on a course called "People in History—Personalities from Pericles to Presley." From the list of personalities the professor had provided, Helga had chosen to write her paper on the wives of Henry the Eighth. She comforted herself now with the idea that each wife must merit something more than a page and she therefore had some leeway with the length requirement. She checked over the guidelines the professor had made available, noting especially his injunction to "Edit! Edit! Edit!" Reading back over what she had written so far, Helga managed to cut out the one sentence concerning Pope Clement VII, and another containing a quotation from *The Merry Wives of Windsor*, which play she had read under the mistaken impression that these wives were those wives, and which she had included for the sole purpose of impressing the professor with her industry and initiative. Such ruthless editing cleared the air, indeed seemed to purify it, and Helga was able to outline the rest of her paper with a heightened, even impersonal sense of purpose, working right up until the moment that the ringing of the telephone in the quiet apartment returned her, startled, to herself.

Then she learned in a single, tentative, nearly endless sentence, of the explosion, the rescue, the prognosis, of Quint's support, of what modern medicine could do, and of her daughter's wish that she not come to the hospital until morning. Helga kept Gena on the telephone, questioning her closely, until a single coin no longer sufficed to defray her frantic curiosity; Gena was then quick to beg off claiming a lack of silver. Although Helga had pounced on the meager scraps of information she had pried loose from a frightened, distracted Gena, it

260

seemed that she had taken away from the call not the facts but rather the quiver; for now that she began to pace the crowded living room, chasing her fast-burning cigarette, she felt not fortified with information but confused and fearful. Passing and passing again the photograph of the other Franz, she sought comfort in the speaking penetration of his stare, but found none, as her gaze fell on the ashtray Douglas had made, on his crude wooden trivet, on the glasses case, on a framed snapshot next to the telephone: it was Douglas several years before at the helm of the *Shooting Star*. "Enough!" Helga said aloud, and left the apartment in her stocking feet.

Across the landing, she pressed her ear to the door of the Gellers' apartment and was relieved to hear the faint sound of music from within. Also, she thought she could discern by squinting and turning her head one way and another that there was light inside as well, but here the wish was mother to the thought. She gave the door a rhythmic series of raps and called out to further identify herself.

Jake and Mitzi lay in bed hand in hand, the expense of passion holding them unmuscled and unmindful; suddenly, however, certain matters relating to building management occurred to these model landlords, and Jake felt compelled to inquire, trousers at the ready, whether there was a problem. There was.

Helga apologized for her forwardness; it was not like her to make her life a part of anyone else's life. But she made an exception for Jake.

"Terrifying," said Mitzi. "But the important thing is he'll be O.K."

"O.K.," Helga repeated vaguely. "Thank God!"

"Grant a perfect healing to all our wounds," Jake thought, apparently convinced that the traditional formulation would be more effective than a heartfelt exclamation such as Helga's. For the short term, in any case, there was comfort at hand. They followed him into the kitchen. "Let's have some cocoa."

"Not for me," Helga and Mitzi said as one.

Jake made himself a cup of cocoa, measuring and pouring

with a precision born of anxiety, while the women discussed the impact of divorce on modern child-rearing, the cost of medical care, and the content of mother-daughter relationships.

"Is he in pain?" Jake asked, clenching his teeth.

"I think that he must be, but Gena said that he is resting comfortably, as they put it. She said he was very lucky, but I think he must be very frightened in the hospital just now. She could not get in touch with Stanley; she could not reach him. Stanley loved the boat," she explained with sardonic intent.

"What can we do, Helga?" Mitzi wanted to know. Her way was action. At times like this, when life presented itself straight forward, no frills, blemished, and a bitch, she was at her best. In this one may take her true measure, for it is one thing to keep up with the times, and quite another to do even a small kindness.

Helga did not know herself just what she wanted, except that at such a moment her lack of family was especially bitter to her. "I don't like to feel sorry for myself," she said aloud; nor did she like others to feel sorry for her.

"Did he go out to that boat with any frequency?" Jake asked as the memory of a yellow-slickered oarsman rowing out among the white motor yachts came suddenly to mind.

"It is possible, because he is very accomplished on the water. But this is what I do not like. His mother and his grandmother know nothing. They are blind fools."

"This was an accident, Helga." Mitzi gave Jake a meaningful look, as if to say don't make matters worse.

But Jake had moved on, his concern for Helga and the boy interrupted momentarily by the fantastic image of a fire burning on the water. Was it not more natural to believe that such a fire would go out, would not burn; indeed, had not a certain rabbi compared the solitary study of the Torah to an isolated fire— the words of the Torah will not be preserved, just as such a fire will not burn. And yet, Jake sensed, preservation was just what he was after; to arrive where he started and know the place for the first time. A place to stand. Then he was back.

"Things go on inside a boy," he began vaguely in response to Helga's last remark. But in the face of more pressing concerns there was no interest in his attempt to tackle the adolescent psyche. Things go on inside a man, he added silently, never more aware than at that moment that life did indeed go on.

"I do not like to go to the hospital if Gena does not wish it. She has Mr. Quint there; but I would like to know something, to have some information, to understand what the story is with Douglas." This, Helga had decided, was what she wanted.

"Well!" Mitzi, seeing Jake lost in thought, was determined to be as much the cheery hostess as was consonant with the circumstances. "Did you see whether there was something about it on TV?"

It had not occurred to Helga. She looked at her wristwatch; it was minutes past eleven. Ha! she thought, let us see; show us something, Mr. Quint. She had of late enjoyed using his name thus generically.

Mitzi turned on the television set. "Some folks in Lynford are calling it a miracle," the anchorman reported, "and yet it seems that a combination of the mild weather we've been having thanks to Glenn over there—" the meteorologist so named grinned broadly and cast his eyes heavenward as his colleague continued, "we'll be hearing from Glenn later of course—and the fact that the boy had apparently just come aboard, and, of course, the bravery of that young man we just heard Alvin interview, are the story here. Young Doug Stern had a very close call tonight, but apparently he's going to be O.K."

"O.K.," Helga echoed grimly, not at all as if this were a most positive outcome. In fact, Helga cringed before the inadequacy of these two letters to convey anything of substance about the condition of her beloved grandson. "O.K.," she said again.

Mitzi, misunderstanding, reached over to pat her hand. "What a relief! Oh!"

"We are often aware on this show," the anchor was announc-

263

ing solemnly, "of how life and death, news and reality mix and intermingle one with the other. We think you'll see just what we mean when we roll this extraordinary piece of tape. Watch it now; there's our man Al Quint in the corridor at Newtown Hospital. Now if you'll look closely you'll see young Doug Stern's mother, right there . . ."—he jabbed at the tape with his voice—". . . here she comes, watch it now, very distraught of course, right into Al's arms. What a moment for both of them, and for us."

"I don't find that acceptable on any level, do you?" Jake inquired mildly before flinging himself face down on the rug in front of the TV and pounding his fists into the floor.

"I understand you, Jake." Helga stood up.

"Sorry," Jake apologized, getting to his feet quickly, "but there are certain things a man must do."

"I just don't understand you, Jake!" Mitzi said tartly, but of course that was part of the appeal. "A grown-up man does not lie down and beat his fists on the floor. Whatever the reason."

"Do you want to know why I find that piece of tape . . ."—he spat out the phrase—". . . inimical to the spiritual well-being of every man, woman, and child in America?"

Mitzi and Helga, exchanging a glance, allowed simultaneously as how they would rather not. Helga was ready to leave.

"There's something abroad in the land," Jake began ominously. But the women were resolute, moving toward the door, filled with their own thoughts. Douglas was O.K., Helga tightened her lips, that was the main thing. Jake wouldn't fall asleep for hours now; Mitzi knew how his mind would churn. Jake, gracious in defeat, walked Helga across the landing to her door. She squeezed his arm gratefully in parting. Though she now knew her daughter's marriage to Alvin Quint was a foregone conclusion, Helga also realized that when, as she liked to say, push came to shove, the possibility of pounding her fists into some convenient surface could now be explored.

264

———◆———

The coin-operated television ran out of coins and the motel room benefited immediately from the complete absence of sound and illumination. John White lay on the bed, long since dressed for the out-of-doors, and considered the nature of coincidence, this evening's meditation occasioned by a story on the Late News. He seemed to recognize that brave young black man, but when he closed his eyes to imagine the circumstance of their meeting, what came to mind instead was the picture of a policeman pulling a yellowed mass of laundry from a washing machine, laundry in need of mending. He had been unable to confront the second inquisition with the serenity and sense of intact wholesomeness which he had brought to his first visit to the police station. He tried again to recall more of the scene itself, but his memory was spotty, appearing to select out images for their bizarre disjuncture, their power to make him fearful, rather than for how they might fit into a plausible, comforting whole. Now his desire to leave the little room intensified. Was it the tangle of wet clothes that made him imagine himself stripped in the extraordinary brightness of that laundromat, in its profound, unnerving emptiness? And yet, he thought sensibly, that space had been cluttered with chairs, littered with newspapers, full of machines.

He got up from the bed and walked to the door in the dark, eyes still closed, arms outstretched as if he were a sleepwalker. You're going to be doing your laundry there from time to time, he told himself gruffly, so you just better get used to that.

At the desk at the front entrance the night manager watched television with a notepad before him, for he, like his fellow manager, aspired to write for the medium. Some of his best ideas came to him while watching television, and this gave them the imprimatur of the tried, a significant advantage in the craft he aimed to make his own. "What about that," he called out to John White, "Lynford's on the news." He jerked his bullet head toward the television.

Nodding, smiling nervously, waving, John White started to

pass him by. Acquainted at an earlier late-night meeting with the little man's ambitions, John felt that he should for the sake of his soul avoid a relationship with him. After all, the man, harmless as he looked, aspired to be a purveyor of trash, an instrument of the devil, as Big John would put it. But, deprived as he was of Christian fellowship, Little John was tempted to stop for a chat; and stop he did.

"A hero," the night man said, "that's a big thing, right? What's a hero, right? I don't know, what do you think, you know." He spoke so fast and carelessly that John White had to strain to understand. "To me, everyone's got a hero every night, right . . ."—he jerked his head once more toward that alleged purveyor of heroes—". . . or you know as long as it's in the public eye, like they say. Who's yours?" he finished breathlessly.

John faced himself squarely. "You don't know the Reverend Big John," he began, suddenly aware of the pull the name alone still exerted on his non-humanist heart. "He's someone I look up to."

The other adjusted his black-rimmed glasses on his mottled face and gave John the once-over. "What do you mean, 'look up to'? Look up to? Because he's tall, you mean, Big John, or what?" There was panic in his voice; clearly he was out of his depth.

"He was my pastor," John White said in an effort to calm him.

The desk man looked at him without comprehension as his mind fell back before a stunning vision of this fad in heroes yet barely in the public consciousness. "Pastor," he said, smoothing the page of his notebook with a trembling hand. "O.K., tell me more."

But John, shaken by such intensity, such avidity, was unable to respond to this urgent request. Clearly this strange, fast-talking little man was from another world; there was an alien gleam in his eye, John noticed now for the first time, and his skin was rough and blotchy. It was even very likely, John thought, hurrying out the front door, that the little man was a Jew.

Not five minutes passed, just enough time for him to contemplate the grandeur of the heavens, the insignificance of man and the chances for hitching a ride, before a pickup truck stopped at the curb. Vincent DiMaria, still in his party clothes, was headed for the Lynford Tap, and this common destination made conversation easy. Conversational ease in turn dictated, once the tavern had been gained, that they seat themselves side by side at the bar and stand each other round upon round, and this in turn made them ripe for camaraderie. Their relationship matured by leaps and bounds as they dug ever deeper for common ground. Before long the Late Late News provided such a subject. Vinny had watched the fire from the front door of the restaurant in the company of several busboys and the coat-check girl; he was unaware—thanks to Vic's innate good sense—that he had any knowledge of the boat in question.

"See that black guy," John White said excitedly, pointing at the television which hung suspended in the corner at the end of the bar. "I think I met him, the one who saved the kid?"

"Black guy! No kidding!" Vinny took notice. Then it struck him. "Saved a kid! What do you mean, kid!"

"Did you ever notice," John began, oblivious to the focus of his companion's interest, "did you ever notice how they don't show you a black person's face on the news; I couldn't really make out his face; all they show you is just plain black."

"Let's see him." Vinny looked down toward the television screen: a hamburger was being adorned, adulated, and finally eaten. "I may know him." He was literally agog at the possibility and concluded with becoming honesty, "I don't get it, man."

"On a white person, see, they show you their eyes and nose and everything on their face. Did you ever notice that?"

"So you mean this guy rescued a kid from that boat or what?" Vinny's personal interest was quickly giving way before the dual appeal of heroism and adventure.

"Yeah. But listen, here's the point." John White was beginning to chafe under the other's apparent indifference to the philosophical implications. "It's like there's something right in front of you—but you can't see it."

"I don't know about that," a confused Vinny allowed, distracted, willing to be led. Then he caught a glimmer. "But sometimes it's the other way around. Something isn't right around you, but you feel like it is." He ran his fingers back over his hair, shivering as Samson must have done, surprised to find himself shorn.

"Yeah, that happened to me once." John White sighed. "I was in a gas station real late one night and this guy comes up to me and he starts witnessing to me and then he says will I accept the Lord Jesus as my personal savior. And I said yes, you know, and I felt great."

"I think I heard that story on the radio." Vinny spoke from the Catholic perspective, after a slight pause to indicate his general respect for the principle of religious pluralism. "Let me tell you what happened to me. I was in here one night, it was real late too . . ."—that it should be equally as late was a matter of macho for him—". . . and I got this great idea of trying every goddamn brand of beer they got in the cooler. It was great. I lined them up right over here on the bar and I'd just take sips, you know, sort of like a guy on a talent show playing the bottles or whatever. 'This Bud's for you,' I'd take a swig; 'It's Miller time . . .'" He began to tap his plastic lighter on the bar to establish a rhythmic ground. "'You never forget your first girl,' awww right!" He popped his fingers in time. "'Michelob Lite for the winner,' dutn-dut, dah-dutn-dut, 'Lowenbrau, here's to good friends . . .'" The tapping and popping and scatting reached a crescendo; and there was that faraway look in Vinny's eye which would have gladdened the heart of any myth-maker: indeed, visions had danced in Vinny's head that night.

"Jesus is your friend," John White broke in without thinking, by now several sheets to the wind. No words were ever sweeter to his own ears. "Jesus loves you."

"Hey," Vinny protested, but he said no more for fear of offending his companion. For, in truth, Vinny DiMaria needed a friend badly.

In any case, John White, beyond remonstrance, preached on. He had never sounded so good, he thought; he would make Big John eat crow yet! But sad to say, it was Little John who got into the crow, the Old Crow; and thus bit by bit and all unknowing did he become thrall to the whiskey which had held his father in thrall, thereby revealing the certain elegance that underlies even the most banal and unhappy of human equations.

And so in this way did these two bachelors pass the first of many nights out on the town together, the one ever in hope of winning a soul, the other of winning a friend.

12

TUESDAY

The Briar Patch of the Here and Now

U ncle Nathan was dead. Jake studied the satellite photos, the weather maps, and charts. In Los Angeles the temperature was in the seventies, the sun was shining, and Uncle Nathan was dead. He had been sitting on the back porch of his small but elegant hillside home wondering whether it was yet time to draw the thermal sheet across the swimming pool, when death stopped for him. Billy Blanc, whose recounting of this circumstance was mixed with wild tears and babbling, had gone inside for the plate of chicken-salad sandwiches. Returning, blinking away his low-grade vertigo, he thought at first his companion had nodded off; but no, Nathan was dead.

Jake proceeded with delicacy; accompanying the dead to the grave—it was, he knew, among those commandments the observance of which bore fruit in this life, while the principle, according to the rabbis, was laid away in the world to come. He broached the subject of airline schedules. Billy Blanc was gracious in his grief.

The following afternoon, the temperature in Los Angeles

was in the seventies, the sun was shining, and a film of airborne matter had already begun to sully the purity and obscure the sparkle of Nathan's cantilevered pool. The funeral had been well attended. Now Jake asked Billy Blanc to telephone the Jewish men of Nathan's acquaintance; Billy found five who could be pressed into service. Jake took to the streets. He drove down out of the canyons and into the valley; he walked the lush, always-sabbatical avenues, red-faced and perspiring, single-minded yet philosophical withal; and he found a recently fired studio executive, a Russian émigré cleaning out his taxi, an actor playing tennis, and a young comedy writer at a motel bar: Jake had his minyan.

With these nine men in place in Nathan's small but elegant living room, and Billy Blanc in the kitchen unwrapping the heavily promoted buffet dinner, Jake took up the prayer book he had packed and began to read the service. This was customary; the soul, it is told, gets pleasure and some sort of compensation as well from hearing the prayers recited in its own home. Jake read slowly and haltingly in the Holy Tongue making no attempt to follow what pertained to one occasion but not to another; in this way much was read that need not have been. The other men, bookless, stood like stones, bowed their heads, and gritted their teeth. Only one made a sound from time to time but it was impossible to know whether this was suppressed anguish or some long-forgotten fragment of Bar Mitzvah Hebrew. Jake read on, heedless of their stupor but not of the solace of their presence. When he was nearly finished he came upon the psalm to be recited in the house of a mourner during the week of mourning, and glanced over at Billy who, standing somewhat apart at the kitchen door, did seem to be taking comfort. He read this in English for the sake of the minyan, hoping even at that late date to give a shape to their silence.

Afterwards the men gathered around the antique chest which was Nathan's bar and drank a great deal of his liquor in a very short time. They were filled too, Jake saw, with good feelings for Nathan; even the four strangers warmed to the dead man as the others recalled his words and deeds, and their memories, though secondhand, were certain to be fond ones. These men spoke of Nathan with a measure of real esteem. Not bad, thought Jake. Uncle Nathan had gone his own way, and made his own way, and never made an issue of either. He had lived well and found much to please him in the world. Jake thought back to their last meeting at Marilyn's break-fast; that had been vintage Nathan—light on his feet, at ease, good-humored. Not bad, Jake thought again, but without much hope that he could benefit from this example of the light at heart. Billy Blanc, whey-faced but proud, passed a platter and they all ate bits of raw fish and seaweed.

At just that moment when it would have become possible for one to make good an escape without unseemly haste, Jake took up a position in their midst in front of the trompe l'oeil fireplace. More than usually handicapped in the making of small talk by the grip which American popular music had on his mind where his uncle was concerned, he had decided, of a sudden, cognac in hand, to unfold himself to this assembly.

"So, you work in television," he began innocently enough, turning to the one who was a scenic artist.

"Yes. Nathan and I go way back," the man answered politely. Beyond a dirty thumb he had very little of the artist about him.

"I see. The instrumentality that rules the public realm," Jake said cheerfully, "the one that attacks us as citizens and consumers, that undermines and unmans us."

The man gave Billy Blanc a sidelong glance. "Nathan and I played quite a bit of poker mainly."

"What instrument did he play?" the Russian broke in, reduced as he often was to trying to catch the sense of a thing.

Jake turned to him eagerly, feeling himself expand at this display of interest. "This power is so pervasive, so prideful, so indiscriminate that it draws to itself the smallest private weakness as easily as the most base inclination." Jake's skin prick-led.

The Russian frowned down at his new running shoes, at a loss. Several of the others began to make their way to the door, eyes carefully averted from Nathan's houndstooth fedora which hung on the brass coat rack. After all, having spent a life in show business, eccentricity, extremity, even gaucherie, had very little appeal for them.

"It drains the substance from the world," Jake continued, "it lives in the no-man's-land between truth and untruth . . ."

"No politics!" the Russian shouted suddenly and stomped off as if he were wearing clumsy black boots and not Adidas.

". . . between reason and unreason, between sense and non-sense; and from there it carries the battle to our finer nature."

"You must have been real close to your uncle, I guess," the actor commiserated while wrapping several small cookies into a cocktail napkin.

Billy Blanc stepped forward. "I want you to meet the real Jacob Geller. That's what Nathan would say, right Jake?" Billy refilled Jake's glass with the best cognac in the house.

"'Good old reliable Nathan, Nathan, Nathan, Nathan . . .'" Jake sang with a sad smile, and tears came to Billy's eyes. The few who remained shifted uncomfortably, first at the impropriety and then at the intensity.

The following day, with the sun shining and the temperature in the seventies, Jake took Nathan's car and drove out to Santa Anita. It was a sentimental journey and his heart was full of song. Standing down at the rail amid the multitude he wanted to take everything in—skittish ponies, flamboyant silks, the mechanics of the gate—anything with which to mark forever his memory of Nathan. Beyond the track palm trees lined the base of the purple mountains, like idols guarding all ascents. Jake, who believed in building on what went before, who bought into study, who longed for a praxis based in knowledge, maneuvered himself into position at the elbow of a sage. This ancient railbird wore a paper visor that shaded his face but left his smooth pink pate to roast in the sun; the tails of his loose white tunic of a shirt hung down over black trousers; his socks were white and his shoes were black; all in all the effect was sacral. A rather judicious man, Jake thought, a big winner who did not fritter away his winnings on the things of this world. The man labored over sheets of track data with the nub of a thick-leaded pencil, emitting small intermittent grunts and sipping absently from a cherry-topped highball. From time to time he flexed his long bony fingers, feeling the strain.

Casually and covertly but with growing boldness Jake did his best to follow this unwitting tout's every pencil scrawl and obscure notation; his neighbor remained oblivious to all of Jake's craning and stretching and even to the cup of beer which Jake managed eventually to overturn between them. Try as he might, however, Jake was unable to identify, understand, interpret, or otherwise make use of these symbols and marks. This did not, of course, prevent Jake from placing a bet on every race. There was the ethos of the place to be considered, not to mention the spirit of Uncle Nathan's memory. Finally and unexpectedly, before the last race of the day, the man took a breath so deep his tunic seemed to fill with air, and then drew a bold, unmistakable circle in his racing program. Thus it came about that Jake, after losing all day, placed a two-dollar bet on a long shot named Tickle-a-Lamb. The horse paid off at thirty-to-one.

The next day the temperature in Los Angeles was in the seventies, the sun was shining, and Jake departed for home. As the plane took off into the brilliant blue heaven it occurred to him to imagine Sam and Nathan Geller united and existing at last in that state of perfect fraternity which had ever been Sam Geller's highest good. Heaven, Jake thought, would not be bi-coastal. And this vision, he was surprised to find, had the effect of focusing his mind with uncommon sharpness on the briarpatch of the here-and-now . . .

Rant and rave, grouse and grumble, hector and harangue, to what end? Relentless as his outrage was, its expression, Jake knew, had little of the executive about it; rather it was puny, ineffective in the extreme. Still, these tirades and tantrums might serve, he believed, as a kind of provisional front—an impulse toward preservation and restoration in so far as the word may precede the deed. And there was the best kind of precedent for that. It was a stopgap solution: he took a stand, a little Dutch boy with one hell of a sore finger. In fact, had he not already begun to sense that something more far-reaching and potent was in the works! He must be content to allow it to reveal itself in its own good time. Toward this end he summoned up Rabbi Tarphon, that old "heap of nuts," the one who used to say: "It is not your duty to complete the work, but neither are you free to desist from it."

Well then, Jake thought, his spirit refreshed, press on regardless.